WILD PITCH

ALSO BY MIKE LUPICA

WILD

PITCH

MIKE
LUPICA

G. P. Putnam's Sons

New York

G. P. Putnam's Sons
Publishers Since 1838
a member of
Penguin Putnam Inc.
375 Hudson Street
New York, NY 10014

Library of Congress Cataloging-in-Publication Data

Lupica, Mike.
   Wild pitch / Mike Lupica.
      p.   cm.
   ISBN 0-399-14927-9
    1. Baseball players—Fiction.
    2. Fathers and sons—Fiction. I. Title.
PS3562.U59W55   2002   2002021952
813'.54—dc21

Printed in the United States of America
10 9 8 7 6 5 4 3 2 1

This book is printed on acid-free paper. ∞

BOOK DESIGN BY MEIGHAN CAVANAUGH

For my mother and father

I would like to thank the following people for their assistance as I was writing this book, and their generosity:

Kevin Shea, Director of Communications and Baseball Information for the Boston Red Sox, who gave me a backstage pass to Fenway Park and made winter afternoons feel like summer.

My editor, Neil Nyren, who is always a pro's pro, and somehow manages to keep his head when I am losing mine.

Bob Klapisch of *The Record,* who shared the Colonials of the Major-Metropolitan League and his summer nights at Vander Sande Field.

My friend William Goldman, who always stops writing when I ask him to drop everything and read.

Mr. M. Chew, who really does turn ART into art.

And finally my wife, Taylor. Just because.

AUTHOR'S NOTE:

Some old New York Mets discussed
in this book didn't actually exist.

But they should have.

WILD PITCH

THE KID was eleven or twelve, somewhere in there, big round glasses taking up about half his face, bangs all the way down to the glasses. Charlie thought the little bastard looked like Harry Potter from hell.

Little Sparky.

Probably the coolest kid in his class at SUV Country Day.

As soon as he opened his mouth, Charlie wanted to shoot him out of a cannon.

"You really used to be somebody, right, dude?" the kid said.

Dude.

Charlie looked at his watch. Ten minutes to five. That meant ten minutes left in the card show at the Meadowlands Hilton. He was already thinking about which one of his teammates from the '88 Mets wanted to walk out of the tacky ballroom with him and right into the bar on the other side of the lobby and have about nine thousand cocktails before the dinner they were supposed to attend in an upstairs ballroom later, part of the sweetheart deal—or so it seemed at the time, anyway—they'd all signed with the promoter. Meyer Somebody.

After finally meeting the guy the night before, a bridge troll in a pin-striped suit, Charlie thought his last name ought to be Lansky.

That'd been at the reunion party that some highrollers had been allowed to attend, to mingle with Charlie and some of the other colorful bad boys from the team who weren't either missing or still in rehab. How they'd managed to win a hundred games around the parties that year still shocked the shit out of Charlie, all this time later. So they'd had another party to discuss all that, which is why Charlie was so hung over now he felt like something that should have been stuffed and mounted in the Museum of Natural Dead Things.

In the old days, the line on Charlie Stoddard had been that he never missed two things, a start or a party. That's when he'd been Showtime Charlie Stoddard, because he was supposed to have been the only thing in sports faster than Magic Johnson's Showtime Lakers. When he'd won twenty the first time, on his way to what everybody was sure were going to be three hundred wins before he was through, a sportswriter from the *Daily News* had said to him one day, "You're on your way to Cooperstown, kid."

"Great," Charlie said to the guy. "They got girls there?"

He was always such a clever bastard.

He didn't feel clever now. Just tired. Tired of signing his name, tired of smiling, tired of bullshitting with these people who'd paid whatever they'd paid and waited patiently in the lines so that Charlie and everybody else at the tables would keep signing and smiling and bullshitting. Only now here was the little ball-buster with his autograph book and his blue Sharpie and his program and his blue shirt with the L.L. Bean logo on the pocket and his pressed khaki slacks, squinting at CHARLIE STODDARD on the nameplate facing him.

Charlie thought: I'd rather be behind in the count to Sammy Fucking Sosa.

"My dad says he remembers you and the rest of these guys," the kid said. "I wasn't born."

"Wish I hadn't been," Charlie said under his breath, turning his head as he did, toward where Kurt Taveras, the old Mets third baseman, had been sitting before he'd gone out for a cigarette about half an hour ago and never come back.

"What?" the kid said.

"Nothing."

"So, like, how big were you? In the old days."

Charlie said, "What?"

"Well, the program says you were 20–3 in 1988. So you must have been pretty good. And you were only twenty-five years old according to the program. But you were gone by the time I started following baseball. So I was sort of wondering what happened to you. You know, after."

Charlie had been sitting here all day between Taveras and Lenny Dykstra, signing what they put in front of him to sign, listening while the grownups in the line told them where they were sitting the night Dwight Gooden gave up that home run to Mike Scioscia of the Dodgers in Game 4 of the championship series, the night the Mets should have put the bastards away, and how sorry they were about what happened to Charlie later in the game, and what happened to the '88 Mets after that, not making it to the World Series after winning a hundred games, then the Mets not even making it back into the playoffs until the end of what Charlie had started to think of as the goddamn 20th century.

Jesus, they always wanted to tell you where they were when shit happened in sports.

Now Charlie wanted to be anywhere on the planct except here, at the end of the Meyer Lansky All-Star Card Show, with Little Sparky staring him down, acting like he wanted to bring him to school tomorrow for show-and-tell.

The kid said, "Were you better than Doc?"

Gooden.

"That year I was."

"That's what I mean. How come I've heard of him, but not you?"

"Most of those other guys kept going. Doc came back and pitched a no-hitter for the Yankees later. I got hurt in the last game I pitched in '88, Game Four of the League Championship Series, and I was never the same after that, because once you lose the arm, it's gone, goodbye, like Ralph Kiner used to say. And if I tell you any more than that, I'm going to have to charge you my speaking fee."

"Huh?"

"Nothing."

Charlie looked at his watch again. Five minutes to five.

"Were you better than Orel Hershiser? He won the Cy Young that year."

"You're *shitting* me? Was that in the papers?"

"You're not supposed to swear, dude, it's in the program."

Dude again.

"Sorry," Charlie said. "I lost my head."

"Were you?"

"Was I what?"

"Better than Hershiser."

"Nobody was in '88. You must have a *Baseball Encyclopedia,* right? Why don't you turn off PlayStation or Nintendo or whatever else Dad's got you hooked up with in the rec room and read it once in a while? Hershiser had one of the great years in the history of pitching. Broke the record for consecutive shutout innings, carried the Dodgers all year and then got better in the playoffs. If Gibson hadn't hit that home run on one leg in Game One, people'd remember Hershiser winning the World Series by himself. Yeah, he won the Cy Young. I finished second."

"You don't have to shout."

"Sorry, I thought I was a sportscaster for a second."

The kid tried to look tough now, like he was facing some other Little Sparky down on the playground back home in Yuppie-ville. "They said you were in a bad mood."

"Busted," Charlie said. "I am in a bad mood. You want to know the truth? I'm in a bad mood even when I'm in a good mood. Who blew my cover for you? That candy-ass Carter?"

The kid looked nervously down the row at the other Mets. "Actually, they all did."

Charlie grinned now. It was the grin he used to give to the girls behind the dugout when he'd come off after striking out the side. Maybe if he acted nice, he could get rid of the kid and get his hands on the cold beer he wanted even more right now than Rebecca from the front desk, who'd come by three times during the afternoon to see if he needed anything and to remind him, had she mentioned this before, that she got off at five, same time as the show ended, how funny was *that?*

"I might have something I want you to sign," Rebecca from the front desk had said the last time she'd stopped by the table.

"Listen," Charlie said now. "I'm just playing with you, kid. You want me to sign your book?"

"Sure."

The kid made a face, as if somebody were nagging on him to eat something green on the plate in front of him, and opened his autograph book and reluctantly slid it in front of Charlie. Charlie signed and pushed it back.

The kid looked at Charlie's scrawl, then back at him, eyes wide behind the big glasses.

"'Charlie (Big Dick) Stoddard'?" he said.

"I just wanted to make sure your momma remembered me," Charlie said.

He got up then and went to the bar.

At one in the morning he was sitting in a bar called The Last Good Year in Manhattan, 50th and Second, watching the Red Sox play the Angels from Anaheim, thanks to the joys of satellite television. He was with the owner of the place, Joe Healey, a crazed Yankee fan his whole life.

Healey was doing some math on one of his Yankee napkins, figuring out a way his team could still catch the Red Sox, who were ten games ahead in the American League East with maybe sixty games left in the regular season.

"If you were this organized with your love life," Charlie said, "maybe there wouldn't be quite as much of that messy overlap."

"I never could get that three-into-two-doesn't-go shit," he said.

Healey's old man, Big Jim, used to be a congressman from the Bronx, part of his district being the neighborhood where Yankee Stadium was located. Healey himself had made every Yankee home opener from the time he was five years old and the old man first sat him down there next to the Yankee dugout. He had even gone AWOL from Fort Dix once to keep the streak alive at sixteen, a story he told every time he got drunk enough, generally right before he wanted to sing show tunes and right after he had become forgetful about whether he was supposed to be meeting his horny real-estate agent here, or one of the coyote girls from *The Lion King*.

He looked like the young Jackie Gleason, curly black hair just now going to gray, big square ham face, nose that could sometimes get so red you thought it was battery-powered. He drank Canadian Club and ginger ale, which he still called his prom drink.

Bar owner was his official occupation, but his real career, Charlie knew from the old days, was fun. It was why the two of them had gotten along from the beginning, even if Healey considered Mets lower on the food chain than divorce lawyers.

"We made up fourteen games on those shitheels in '78, from about this same place in the schedule," Healey said.

Charlie noticed that Healey could somehow simultaneously make his squiggles on the napkin, watch the game, monitor the bar crowd out front, and keep checking the back door on the chance that Miss America was about to come walking in.

"No kidding," Charlie said. "I hadn't heard that."

"I'm telling you," Healey said, "they can't keep playing like this."

Meaning the Red Sox. He lit a Winston Ultra Light, his one concession to what he described as the alarmist bullshit about the tobacco industry that had finally worn his ass out after twenty years.

But the Red Sox were winning again on this night, 4–1 in the sixth, behind one of their kid pitchers, a lefthander named Tyler Haas, whose record, Charlie knew, was 12–2, with an earned run average so small it belonged on the bottom of an eye chart.

And Haas wasn't even the best of the Red Sox kid pitchers this season, Charlie thought.

Not even close.

Haas had this herky-jerky motion, a little like Sid Fernandez's when he and Charlie had been kids with the Mets, the body coming through first, and then, after what made you think somebody had hit a pause button, here came the left arm and the ball toward home plate, exploding on the hitters, a fastball that was only in the low nineties looking as if it were coming at them a hundred and ten.

And with all that, Charlie knew somebody better fix the kid's delivery, and fast, no matter how many wins he had, no matter how much of a dream season he was having, or someday his arm was going to blow up like an old Firestone exploding on the highway.

Once a pitcher, always a pitcher, even from the bar.

Haas put one on the inside corner now against the Angels' fat catcher, Almonte.

"It's their year," Charlie said, sipping his Scotch and reaching for Healey's cigarettes.

"My ass," Healey said. "They're the fucking Red Sox. It's never their year."

The back room, a shrine to the Yankees and to 1956, which Healey had declared was in fact the last good year, was mostly empty. Kurt Taveras, who'd matched Charlie drink for drink at Meyer Lansky's dinner, had dropped Charlie on his way to Elaine's, which was farther uptown and a place where he liked to drink with police commissioners, Hollywood producers, newspaper columnists hoping somebody else would pick up the check, anchormen hoping for the same thing, and all the do-me girls who showed up wearing no clothes at this time of night and said they were there for the fried calamari and highbrow conversation.

Usually, Charlie knew, they were just there trying to scope out who had the most dope.

Taveras said that next he wanted to stop over on Third, at a place called Montana, where some models he knew were throwing a combined fortieth birthday party for a couple of their friends from Ford.

In the backseat of the town car, Charlie said to Taveras, "You don't know any forty-year-old women."

Taveras, who still looked like a leading man and got laid as if he was still playing third for the Mets, laughed and said, "'Course not. I meant two twenty-year-olds."

Charlie said he might catch him later after he checked the bar at Healey's for any rogue personal trainers.

It was a few minutes later, Charlie alone at the table now, when it happened to Tyler Haas. Healey had said he'd be right back, he had to go console a soap-opera actress at the bar, her producers had followed through on their threat to kill her character in a car crash if she didn't lose ten pounds.

"Poor kid looks like she could use a Jenny Craig," Healey said.

"I know I'm going to regret this," Charlie said, "but what's a Jenny Craig?"

"A light Old Fashioned," Healey said. "Extra fruit."

The Angels had runners on first and second, Charlie couldn't tell from the little graphic in the corner of the screen how many were out. The batter was their designated hitter, Dennard Toussant, Jr. Charlie had seen the kid on television before and knew he had about as much knowledge of the strike zone as of Russian lit, but if you threw him a fastball anywhere near his wheelhouse, he'd hit it so hard you ducked on your couch.

Tyler had him 0–2, two straight breaking balls. Dennard Jr. just waved at both of them. Now Tyler Haas, young and probably half-stupid the way they all were when they were young and had the arm, the way Charlie had been when he'd had the arm, tried to get cute with what Charlie could tell from his arm angle had to be his hard-on pitch, a four-seamer. Screw trying to waste a pitch, he was coming right after Dennard Toussant, Jr.

Charlie knew he was trying to throw it up and in, especially after the way Dennard Jr. had been reaching.

He got it up, all right, but left it right over the middle of the goddamn plate.

Dennard Jr. hit the pitchers' nightmare shot.

The one right back up the middle.

As though the "B" on Tyler Haas's cap was for "bullseye."

The kid tried to duck out of the way at the last second but lost his balance, his cleats catching in the dirt at the bottom of the mound. Charlie knew the feeling the way he did his Social Security number. You got twisted up and twisted around, and for a moment, you didn't even know whether you were still facing the plate or not.

Now Tyler Haas's left hand flew up in the air, making it look as if he was trying to catch the ball, even though Charlie knew he wasn't, he was just trying to keep his stupid fucking balance.

The left hand was the one without a glove on it.

The kid's money hand.

"No," Charlie said in a loud voice, louder than he intended, in the back room of The Last Good Year.

It all happened in slow motion now, even though Charlie knew it was happening in real time, the ball deflecting off Tyler Haas's hand, changing direction, dribbling toward first base. They stayed in a wide shot so you could see it all, the Red Sox second baseman, Daggett, charging the ball, trying to make a barehand play of his own, because Dennard Toussant, Jr., whose nickname was Dump Truck for good reason, still hadn't made it to the bag.

Dennard Jr. beat the throw by a step.

The camera was close on Tyler Haas again, Haas still at the bottom of the mound, curled up in the fetal position as if he'd gotten hit in the balls, his glove next to him on the ground, rolling a little bit from side to side, his left hand tucked in close to his belly.

Shit, Charlie thought.

Shit, shit, shit.

The rest of the Red Sox infielders were standing behind Haas, along with the home-plate umpire. Then the trainer was there, and Ted Hartnett, Charlie's old Mets roommate, now the Red Sox manager. The camera went to the Red Sox dugout, showing the players in there up on the top step. They did a closeup on Tom MacKenzie, the twenty-year-old righthanded ace of the Red Sox staff, Haas's best friend on the team. Then there was a closeup of the kid, Charlie thinking of himself at that age, of course, wondering what would have been going through his head. If he would have been crying the way Tom MacKenzie was.

"Hey," Joe Healey said. "There's wonder boy."

Healey was standing next to the table with a pretty blonde woman who was holding a glass big enough for a root-beer float.

Charlie looked at Healey, then back up at the television. "Act happy about this and I'll have to kill you."

"Can I at least make an observation?"

"No," Charlie said.

The blonde said, "Did somebody get hurt?"

Charlie said, "The pitcher."

Healey threw a fist in the air and said, "The curse lives!"

The blonde giggled. "He's having cramps?"

Charlie gave her a look, and the smile disappeared from her face. She sipped her Jenny Craig and shut up.

"I love you," Charlie said to Healey, "but, Jesus, you're an asshole sometimes."

"Facts are facts," Healey said.

He was talking about what Yankee fans and Red Sox fans all called The Curse of the Bambino, the one about Babe Ruth, the one that said that bad shit had been happening to the Red Sox for nearly ninety years because of when their owner in the old days, a colorful guy named Harry Frazee, had sold Ruth to the Yankees. He had needed money to invest in *No, No Nanette* and had basically enabled the Yankees to invent the World Series, while the Red Sox had never won another one after 1918.

Bad shit like the kind that had just happened to Tyler Haas in Anaheim, up on his feet now, walking unsteadily off the field, hunched over, holding his left hand in his right.

Tom MacKenzie was the first to get to him once he crossed the third-base line.

"Fuck," Charlie said.

The blonde leaned against him and said, "Is that a question or an observation?"

Her name was Ellie Bauer, and she had been playing the cute, wholesome newspaper publisher on *One Life to Live* until, as she informed Charlie when the game was over, her character had tragically lost control of her car on that rainy night when she was trying to get to her ex-husband and tell him she still loved him despite the baby switch at the hospital all those years before.

"There's always the chance they can bring me back," she was saying now in her apartment on 52nd Street, just east of First, "either as a twin or with one of those cryogenics storylines like they used on *General Hospital* the season before last."

"So you might not be dead dead," Charlie said, trying to sound interested.

"The one who should be dead dead is that bitch head writer Carl," she said.

Ellie Bauer was, Charlie guessed, somewhere in her mid-thirties and didn't look at all fat to him now that they were out of the coal-mine lighting of the back room, just a real girl with curves from before the time when women had decided they had to look skinnier than the lead Ethiopian in the New York marathon. And despite an insensitivity about Tyler Haas's injury, which she had apologized for at The Last Good Year about the time her hand had first started doing bad-girl things to Charlie's upper thigh under the table, she had shown herself to be enough of a babe to stay with him drink for drink, smoke a few cigarettes, and laugh in just about all the right places.

Charlie also noted that Ellie Bauer seemed about as ready to go as a sailor back from extended submarine duty.

Those were the good parts.

The only bad part, as he didn't discover until they were walking the few blocks from The Last Good Year to her apartment, was this:

She was a Mets fan.

She was the kind of Mets fans who wanted to tell him all about it, as if she'd been waiting in line at the Meadowlands Hilton right behind Little Sparky. She was a Mets fan who had grown up in Little Neck in the '80s, and not only had she lived and died with the old Mets of that era, not only did she remember sitting in her father's box and watching Showtime Charlie Stoddard strike out the world when he was young, she'd had a crush on him all the way through St. Mary's of Manhasset.

She told him about that as they were crossing First Avenue.

Charlie had said, "Is there any chance you've held onto to any of your old school blazers and plaid skirts?"

"This is going to be a *great* night," Ellie Bauer said, and gave his arm a squeeze. "I'm feeling better about being dead already."

When they were inside the apartment, she poured two big-boy glasses of Hennessy without even asking if Charlie wanted one and said, "I cried when you hurt your arm."

"Me, too," he said. "Just not in front of the other soldiers."

"My girlfriends all thought Ronnie Darling and Kurt Taveras were the cutest," she said. "But you were the one."

"Wasn't I, though?" Charlie said.

"When you came out with your autobiography? After your rookie year? *Showtime Charlie?* I did a paper on it."

She was sitting in a big, roomy chair across from him. Charlie was on the couch. He patted it and said, "Why don't you come over here and we can play out what I think might be kind of a fun scene for you."

"What?"

"Career Day," Charlie said. "I'll be the visiting celebrity, you can be the lucky student showing me around."

Charlie had been waiting an hour for her to start acting drunk, but so far she seemed capable of outdrinking a frat house. Maybe it was all a tease, Charlie thought—it had happened before, even with actresses—and she just wanted to talk his socks off.

Charlie had always thought that you could talk about cold showers and fear of disease all you wanted; the most powerful weapon against sex ever invented was still conversation.

The anti-Viagra.

". . . you shouldn't have pitched in Game Four if your arm was already starting to hurt," she was saying.

"Three more outs from me and one more run and we were ahead three games to one and the thing was over," he said. "I always thought I could get three outs with my arm in a sling."

He had told this version so many times, he almost believed it himself now.

But then he'd always liked this version better than the truth.

"Besides," he said, "our bullpen was shot from that mess of a game we'd won the day before. And our manager—"

"—Davey—"

"—wanted to do everything possible so McDowell didn't have to face Gibson again, even if that ended up happening, anyway. It wasn't hard talking him into it."

"He still should have told you no."

"It wasn't his fault, it was mine," he said. He lit a cigarette, and from across the room she made a motion with two fingers like she wanted one, too. Charlie walked over and handed her the one he'd lit, and when he did, he leaned down and kissed her.

Ellie Bauer made one of those moan noises girl tennis players made when they leaned into their two-fisted backhands.

"You sure you want to keep replaying the 1988 National League Championship Series?" he said.

"I've waited a long time," she said, in a voice that seemed huskier all of a sudden, as if the smoke had done it. "Besides, all things come . . ."

"*Now* you're talking," Charlie said.

"It was sad what happened to you after that," she said. "Going from being the best pitcher in the world . . ."

Now it was like some scene she was playing, trying to make his great drama hers.

"It happened to a lot of other guys," he said. "Maybe it happened to that kid on the Red Sox tonight. So it happened to me."

"Does it still hurt? Talking about it, I mean?"

"Only like my shoulder used to hurt every day for the rest of what passed for the rest of my career."

The rest of his brilliant career: In New York. Philadelphia after the Mets finally had to give up on him. And Cleveland and Toronto and even the Montreal Fucking Expos. And the Syracuse Sky Chiefs and the St. Paul Saints of the Northern League, a team in that independent league that was like the Betty Ford Clinic of the minor leagues, a place where bust-out cases like Charlie and various recovering addicts and alcoholics went because they couldn't let go of the life. The Rochester Red Wings. The Orioles, at the very end.

Didn't you used to be somebody, Little Sparky had asked?

How big were you?

"You still miss it? Pitching, I mean?"

"It's fifteen years since Game Four against the Dodgers," he said. "And a long time since I pitched anywhere." He gave her the smile. "Nah, I don't miss it that much. Unless, of course, you count every fucking day."

Charlie set his glass down on the coffee table in front of him harder than he meant.

"Yeah," he said. "It still hurts."

He leaned back and closed his eyes, even though he was afraid he might fall asleep right here, thinking now about all the nights like this in the bar, not only Healey's bar but everybody else's from coast to coast. Thinking about all the girls like Ellie Bauer he'd known for an hour or two before it was either his place, or theirs.

All the four A.M.'s when he'd hung around long enough that his name could still get him laid, a way to convince himself that the name still meant something.

That it was something more than the third nameplate from the left at the card show.

The next thing he felt was Ellie the soap-opera actress working on his zipper.

"Where does it hurt?" she said.

Now Charlie was the one who made the tennis-girl sound.

"Welcome to Career Day at St. Mary's, Mr. Stoddard," she said. "I'll be your official hostess, Ellen Anne."

2

HE WOKE UP feeling as if Ellie Bauer had hit him in the back with what she said was her prize baseball possession, the Louisville Slugger signed by all the '88 Mets, including Charlie.

She had told him midway through the festivities that the firing from *One Life to Live,* which she pointed out wasn't technically a firing at all— that head bitch Carl had just convinced the producers not to renew her option—had been a physical wake-up call for her, that she was a lot more limber now thanks to her Lotte Berk Method classes and a general training regimen that had her in her best shape since she'd been a field-hockey player at St. Mary's.

"I mean," she said, "I wouldn't have *thought* about putting on thong underwear two months ago."

She had him pinned underneath her at the time, in what Charlie was pretty sure was an illegal move.

Charlie said, "I think our farmboy used this hold when he beat the fat Russian in the Sydney Olympics."

She told him to turn over, she'd be right back with more oil.

They'd finally fallen asleep around the time the sun was coming up over the smokestacks in Queens. Now Charlie was awake and trying to remember if he'd felt anything wrong before he passed out, or he'd done it while he was sleeping. Maybe he'd pulled something while he was trying to keep up with Ellie Bauer and was just too drunk by then to notice. All he knew for sure was that when he tried to turn toward Ellie's side of the bed, he felt as if someone had set fire to his lower back.

When Ellie heard him scream, she opened the bathroom door, all this steam coming out with her, her hair wet from her shower, wearing only a fluffy pink towel.

"Having a flashback, hon?" she said.

"My back," Charlie said.

"Can't right now, hon. I've got a callback for *All My Children* at ten. Besides, we ran out of the oil I like the best a couple of hours ago."

"I did something," he said.

His voice was somewhere between a whisper and a death rattle.

"Well, I think we both did," she said.

"Help," Charlie said.

She held up a finger, meaning one second, and when she came out of the bathroom, she was wearing a robe the color of the towel. She had a pill container that she said had Percocet in it, from when she'd had a little tummy work done a couple of months ago just to jump-start her make-over. Charlie said he didn't want any, just asked if she could help get him into a sitting position. Ellie Bauer asked if he thought it might be spasms, from when he'd lost his grip on the bedpost that time and ended up on the floor, sometimes the muscles contracted around the wounded area, at least that's what her trainer said. Charlie said he didn't know, he'd never had back spasms before.

Upper back or lower, Ellie asked.

Lower, Charlie said.

She wanted to know if sitting up was making him feel any better, and he said, fuck no.

She helped him lower himself back down, taking the pillow out from behind his head so he was stretched out flat.

"Can you move without pain?" Ellie said.

"No."

"You're absolutely sure?"

Charlie didn't like the tone of her voice.

"I'm sure."

Ellie Bauer started to take off her robe.

Charlie said, "Please, don't turn this into a hostage situation."

"I was going to do everything."

"That's what I was afraid of."

She shrugged and belted the robe, asking what he wanted her to do—instead of what she promised would only have been a very, very special form of CPR—and Charlie said that he just wanted to lie there for a second, and then maybe she could help him into the shower.

The hot water eventually helped him not just to get into a full, upright position, but to actually stay there without too much whimpering. When he came out of the bathroom, looking for some orange juice to wash down a handful of Advil, Ellie was already dressed for the day in a blue summer dress with flowers all over it and some kind of Southern-belle bonnet, white sandals that came halfway up her calves.

"You can let yourself out," she said, pecking him lightly on the cheek. "I'm sorry about your back. But it was fun."

"You don't know a good chiropractor, do you?" he said.

She reached into a big straw purse and pulled out a card.

"Forget chiropractors," she said. "This guy will get you feeling good as new, if he's got an opening, anyway. He's usually pretty booked."

Charlie took the card from her. Even that move gave him another little jolt. There was just one word written on it—"Chang"—and a phone number in the lower righthand corner.

"What is he?" Charlie said.

Ellie said, "A miracle worker with an attitude."

As soon as he got home, Charlie called the guy, who picked up the phone himself. "Chang," was all he said, then waited. Charlie told him his name and said Ellie had recommended him. When he was finished, Chang said Charlie was in luck, one of the Knicks had just cancelled, was there any chance he could come in at noon? Charlie told him he had a way of clearing his own schedule when he turned into the Hunchback of Notre Dame.

"Right," Chang said.

"What *do* you do, exactly?" Charlie said.

"You're making an appointment and you don't know?" Chang said. "Okay, you've blown my cover. I fix assholes. See you at noon. If you're late, I'll be at lunch," he said, and hung up.

Charlie had a sublet up on 66th and Second. It had belonged to an American flight attendant he'd been going with until she'd met the new Japanese outfielding sensation from the White Sox, Tora, on a charter from Toronto to Texas, and then had moved to Chicago with him two weeks later.

"It's a whole different sensibility with these little guys, what can I tell you?" she'd said. "A level of consciousness I didn't know existed. Plus, O'Hare's just as practical a hub for me as LaGuardia or DFW."

"Where'd you two do it on that first overnight, the back of the plane somewhere?"

"That is crude and bitter," the flight attendant, Brittany, had said.

"Humor me."

"Well, for one thing," she said, "he's really only about five-seven, no matter what the program says."

"So you did it in one of the bathrooms?"

"They're a lot roomier on those new 777's than you'd think."

Charlie had the apartment, a one-bedroom, through the end of the season, then Brittany said she'd have to make a decision about spending the winter with Tora back in Osaka. By then, Charlie knew he'd have to make a decision himself, about whether or not to stay on with the Mets or just support himself the way he had been for the past few years, at card shows like Meyer Lanksy's.

He'd been living in a condo in Jupiter, Florida, just north of Palm Beach, commuting to card shows from there, occasionally helping the Mets out with kid pitchers during spring training, just up the road in Port St. Lucie, and working some of the fantasy camps the Mets Alumni Association would put together, the ones where dentists and insurance agents got to dress up in real baseball uniforms and pretend they were real ballplayers for about five grand a week. Then the Mets had decided to put a New York–Penn League team in Brooklyn. Pete Monan, the Mets general manager, had asked Charlie if he wanted to spend at least some of his summer working with the kids up there, no heavy lifting, it would be a part-time job with full-time benefits. Charlie hadn't even asked what kind of benefits, he'd just seen it as a chance to live in New York for the first time since the Mets had let him go, and so he'd grabbed it. Monan had told him he'd only have to show up a couple of days a week when the Cyclones were in town, do a little face time over in Brooklyn, and give the fans as much of a thrill as the college boys on the pitching staff.

"We're thinking that down the line you might want to try broadcasting," Monan said. "The Metro Channel's doing some Cyclones games, maybe you could start out there."

Charlie said, "You sure you want somebody up there who actually knows what pitches guys are throwing, instead of making the whole thing up?"

Charlie Stoddard had last pitched in the big leagues five years before, that last gasp coming with the Orioles. It had been an interleague game against the Mets at Shea, Fourth of July weekend. The week before, the Orioles had put three starting pitchers on the disabled list. Charlie had been pitching for their Triple-A team in Rochester at the time, having just missed making the Orioles' twelve-man staff in spring training, in what he'd sworn was his absolute last comeback attempt. He was 6–2 down there, keeping his earned run average right around four runs a game, keeping the Triple-A ya-ya's off-balance with his off-speed stuff and general bullshit.

The Orioles had decided to call him up the day before the Mets series, give him an emergency start on Saturday. The New York media went crazy with the story, building it up as one more day in the sun for Showtime Charlie Stoddard, one more start for him at Shea Stadium, all these years after he'd owned the place.

The shoulder was completely shot by then, and the hardest he could throw his fastball was in the low 80s, which was not much better than one of those Little League kids lying about their age. All he wanted to do was not embarrass himself, though he knew that if he were really that goddamn worried about embarrassing himself, he would have retired long ago, that he hadn't ended up in Rochester because it was the one garden spot in baseball he'd missed. But the Mets weren't hitting at the time, and Charlie thought he could get through the batting order a couple of times, fool them for five innings or so, maybe even get pulled in the middle of an inning. That way, he could walk off with his head up, get one more ovation, tip his cap, adios, amigos.

If he could just do that, he promised himself he'd walk out the door at the end of the day and never come back, at least not as an active player. It wasn't Ted Williams hitting a home run in his last at-bat, it wasn't the goodbye he'd imagined for himself when he was young. It wasn't Michael Jordan's goodbye in the NBA Finals that time, even if Jordan had come back a few years later, another guy who couldn't give up the life, who had to be dragged off the stage.

But it was the best Charlie could do.

The Mets had runners in each of the first four innings, but somehow Charlie kept pitching out of jams and was still leading, 4–3, when the Mets came up in the bottom of the fifth.

Two on, two out, Alfonzo at the plate. Charlie got ahead of him 0–2 and then dinked around, afraid to come in on him, his nerves as shot as his arm by then. He went to 3–2, wasn't close with what was left of his fastball, walked the sonofabitch. Which meant bases loaded for Mike Piazza.

Charlie looked over to the Orioles manager, Mike Hargrove, who gave him a little fist like, go get him.

You go get him, Charlie wanted to say.

The catcher, a nice kid named Fordyce, came out to the mound.

"Shit," Charlie said. "I got him once with off-speed stuff away, I can do it again."

The kid grinned. "That's the way I want to remember you," he said. "Courage like this in the face of insurmountable odds, right to the end."

Piazza took a fastball for strike one, then Charlie threw him two more that weren't even close. Two balls, one strike. He threw him another fastball, and it would have been ball three except that Piazza chopped it foul outside third. It was here that Charlie tried to get him again with off-speed stuff away, a splitter.

He left it out over the plate, what Gabby Hartnett used to call a mattress pitch, because guys would just lay all over it.

Piazza hit it so hard and so high off the scoreboard in right-center that the back pages of both the *Daily News* and the *Post* the next day actually showed the dent underneath the sign for Fleet Bank.

The pricks ran the same back-page headline, too:

SORRY, CHARLIE

It was the last official pitch he'd thrown in the big leagues.

Now he was forty, and the kind of guy he used to make fun of when he was young and had the arm, all the old guys who tried to look happy carrying bags of balls and hitting fungos and timing pitchers' moves to first with a stopwatch even though they'd been stars once. Charlie, who'd been a bigger star than all of them, acting that way now: acting as if he'd actually bought into the idea that he was as much a roving ambassador for the Mets as a pitching coach.

Actually thinking about trying broadcasting, one more way of convincing himself he was still in the life.

"You know," Grace had said the last time they were together, "it really is time for a change of pace."

It was her sweet voice, like she was trying to help, only Charlie knew from past experience that it should have come with a Surgeon General's warning.

"What kind of change of pace?"

"An acting-your-age, growing-up-finally type change of pace is sort of what I had in mind."

"I've got a regular job," he said.

"You've got an *excuse* not to have a regular job," Grace said. "And an excuse to set up party headquarters in New York again." In the same sweet voice, she said, "By the way, who's this month's flavor of the month from the airline industry, Amber or Ember?"

"You know it's Brittany."

It was still Brittany then, she hadn't run off with Tora the midget centerfielder yet.

"Grow up, Charlie," she said. "It might be fun for you."

"You've been telling me the same thing for twenty years."

This was two weeks ago. They were sitting at a corner table at Café Boulud, across Madison Avenue from the Carlyle. The maître d' at Boulud was a French guy in zippy clothes who looked as if he wouldn't know Shea Stadium from the Statue of Liberty, and liked hugging a lot more than Charlie thought was normal, but it turned out he'd never gotten over the Mets of the middle '80s, even if New York was back to being a Yankee town now. So when Charlie and Grace showed up there, he treated them both like they were food critics from the *Times*.

Of course, Charlie knew that Grace didn't need any help from him getting the best table at any restaurant in town, not now that her show-piece cookbooks, the ones that told hysterical women on the go and overstressed moms how to entertain like champs and look like Grace doing it, were selling about a bazillion copies every time she wrote another one.

She'd started out simply enough after their divorce, by opening one of those designer shops in San Francisco where women could buy a hundred different kinds of cheeses, wine to go with them, the best bread, the best cookies, more kinds of pasta than they had in Italy; then slide into the elegant coffee shop in the back and have a latte while they discussed what pigs men were.

She was originally going to call it Amazing Grace, until Charlie had pointed out to her that there was a famous casino by that name in Vegas, run by a friend of his named Billy Grace, a semi-mobbed-up character who liked girls, athletes, and, from what Charlie had been able to pick up on occasional visits there, hard guys named Vinny. So she'd gone with Grace Under Pressure instead. And from the start, she'd been smart enough to gear everything she was selling to all modern women who felt like there just wasn't enough time to take care of everything in their lives that they needed to take care of, from jobs to husbands to boyfriends to kids to keeping their butts tight at the gym.

Within a year, the place took off like a rocket to the moon.

It wasn't just the food and the atmosphere, with cool jazz, Miles and Coltrane and Brubeck and Getz, on the sound system. It wasn't the word around town that Grace Under Pressure was the place to shop now; or to just sit around in the coffee shop that was Starbucks before Starbucks, Grace even ahead of the curve on coffee, or to just linger, at a time when people usually went through food stores as if someone were clocking them.

All that helped Grace Under Pressure take off—but not as much as Grace herself, even Charlie was smart enough to know that.

Because more than anything else, Grace Under Pressure was an idea. And the idea was *her*.

Grace never came right out and said it in some kind of mission statement or in the smart television commercials she eventually ran on local television, but she wanted women to think they could still feel cool and glamorous and in charge no matter how often they felt like everything was spinning out of control. And Grace was the living proof of that, walking through the store, standing behind the cash register sometimes, just as a way of letting everybody know that no job was too small for her, that this was her operation and her vision from the ground up. Her baby. And it never hurt that she was the best-looking woman in the room.

She'd always been the best-looking one in the room, all the way back to high school.

Her father had been in the restaurant business, in New York and Boston and finally in the Hamptons, a charming, handsome bad boy whom she'd adored, even after he'd divorced her mother. Grace hadn't just inherited his looks, she'd inherited his touch and his flair, a talent for people, whether they were customers or the help.

"He said he had to leave me something, and he didn't think I'd have much use for his black book," she'd once told Charlie.

After a couple of years, a friend had convinced her to try some kind of flashy cookbook, the kind you could keep either in the kitchen or on the coffee table. So she did. It was called *Grace Under Pressure: A Guide to Gracious Living and Good Eats.* The picture on the front had been of Grace in the store wearing a white turtleneck sweater and a short black skirt, her blonde hair backlit in a way that made it look like gold.

The book had eventually sold a million copies in hardcover, and Charlie had always wanted the publisher to find out how many of the buyers were guys—men who said they were buying it for the women in their lives but thought this might be the *Victoria's Secret Cookbook* because of how hot Grace looked on the cover, men who hoped there'd be pictures of her inside wearing some kind of teddy while she served up crab puffs.

Two years later, the second book had sold even bigger than the first, and Grace had sold the store in San Francisco to General Foods. Now she did a couple of holiday specials a year for NBC, hosted big-ticket weekend seminars all over the country for all the Grace wannabes, and showed up about once a month to dish with Katie Couric on *Today*. Her book schedule was one every two years, and in between, she'd do some kind of video.

When Charlie met up with her at Café Boulud, she was in town for *Today*. She'd cut her hair short for the summer, and it looked a little lighter to Charlie than the last time he'd seen her. Even as cool as she was, about almost everything, she guarded information about coloring her hair the way the CIA guarded mole lists. Her eyes were the same color as always, a shade Charlie'd always thought of as "Grace blue." She was forty, just like he was; they'd been in the same class at Lexington High since they'd been juniors. That was when she'd moved to town with her father; by then, her mother had decided she wanted to go live in England, somewhere near Cornwall, where she'd said she hoped to find some English guy who didn't think there'd been a law passed that it was all right to cheat on your wife.

Grace had told her mother that as much as she loved her, she was staying in America to finish high school, but to say hello to John Le Carré if she ran into him.

"He's a writer who lives over there," she'd explained to Charlie way back then, knowing things at sixteen that nobody else in the class did. "Not a sportswriter."

Charlie had fallen in love with her the first day. He'd already been the sports star of the high school by then and could have had any girl he wanted. He only wanted her. He still did, even though he was the one who'd blown their marriage sky-high after just three years. If you saw her walking toward you on the street, or just stared at her across Boulud, the way most of the guys in the place were now, you would swear she wasn't a day over thirty.

They had been divorced, Charlie hated to admit to himself, for almost half their lives now. She was the one who had come closer to remarrying, to a San Francisco neurologist, one Charlie always called Dr. Bob.

Dr. Bob had wandered into Grace Under Pressure one day, wanting to surprise his girlfriend with a gourmet dinner she was supposed to think he had prepared. Grace had picked out everything for the guy except the wine, and he'd been a goner before he had his Visa card out. Before long, he'd broken up with his girlfriend and was having a great big thing with Grace. The great big thing had lasted until Grace had discovered, almost three years later, that he was still seeing the original girlfriend on the side.

He'd tried to blame it on Grace, saying she was spending too much time trying to build Grace Under Pressure into an empire.

"Not nearly as much time as I'm going to," she'd told Dr. Bob.

She'd been single ever since, having the odd romance with a series of rich guys who kept getting better-looking and more boring, at least as far as Charlie was concerned, even though he had to admit he didn't think anybody was good enough for Grace. Himself included.

She never forgave Dr. Bob for cheating on her, any more than she'd forgiven Charlie, who'd found out the hard way that young and stupid was a more dangerous combination than gasoline and lit matches.

He still loved her and she knew it, because he told her often enough. He loved her despite all the years they'd been apart, all the Brittanies he'd put between them, and the way he knew he'd let both of them down. And occasionally, when she'd have enough wine, she'd let down her guard enough to let him know how much she still loved him, even though she'd point out right away that it might just be the three thousand miles she'd put between them doing the talking.

"You'd be good on television," she said in Boulud. "You know how many games I watch now, and I listen to some of these announcers, and there's clearly big money to be made with glib, charming, and shallow."

Charlie said, "I'm not shallow."

"No," she said, "you're not. You just want everybody to think you are. Somehow I think *you* think it keeps you young."

He said, "You look great."

"You like my hair this way? You don't think it makes me look like a butch Kournikova?"

"You make the real Kournikova look like a prizefighter. Is it a little lighter, by the way?"

"Don't worry about whether or not it's lighter."

Charlie said, "How's he doing, by the way?"

"If you are referring to our *son*," she said, "he is doing just fine, thank you."

"Tell him I said hi."

She wouldn't. The kid wanted nothing to do with him, so it wasn't even worth trying.

She stared at him, wine glass in both hands, a long look, the kind he always had trouble holding, mostly because he was always thinking about the same thing, coming around the table and kissing her like it was the first time out of the blocks for them, a hundred years ago, behind the football field in Lexington.

"You may not have noticed," he said, "but I'm getting to be a much nicer guy. More dependable. You don't think this is regular work, but it feels like it to me."

"You're sure it's not just some kind of massage therapy settling you down?"

"He'd like me more, is all I'm saying."

"I'll be sure to pass that along."

"Why don't you stick around for one more night?"

She waved at the maître d', who was all the way across the room showing off his new silk sports jacket to a table of models.

"You'd only try to make a move on me," Grace said.

"Is it wrong for a man to have these feelings for his wife?"

"A wife, yes," she said. "But rated ex."

"Perfect," Charlie said. "They're all x-rated thoughts, believe me."

"There's a bombshell."

"Yeah," he said, "yeah, yeah, yeah."

Grace smiled, eyes full of fun. "How can I be expected to top a snappy comeback like that?"

"So you're smarter than me. You were always smarter than me."

"Maybe you should've listened better when I was trying to explain the difference between the big-boy world and the jock world."

"I always listened."

"You said you did. But you didn't. You thought your arm was all you needed to be happy."

"I knew you were my best part," he said, knowing that it had come out sounding lame.

"Not until it was too late," she said.

She didn't say anything and neither did he. Charlie sipped some of his coffee. He never let himself get drunk in front of her, or even close. She was right, of course. He hadn't figured out she was the best part of him—and the only one able to cut through all of his bullshit and see the best in *him*—until it was too goddamn late, when he'd figured out you couldn't do anything you goddamn well pleased on account of being famous.

The funny thing, he knew now, was that it had all turned around from when they were young: It was Grace who was the star now, Grace who sometimes got asked to sign the autographs when they were out in a place like this, people acting as if a babe Martha Stewart had walked through the door. And the even funnier thing, not that it made Charlie's sides ache from laughter, was that he still thought there was something he could say to her, something he could do, so that it still didn't have to be too late.

"What if I really did grow up?" he said. "Really worked at something?"

"The way you should have worked at pitching?"

That again.

Always that.

"Goddamn it, Gracie, you know it wasn't my fault that my arm gave out on me the way it did. And you sure as hell know how hard I worked once it did."

"You worked on your own terms, even though you wanted everybody to know how much suffering you were doing. But you needed to change. That had to be part of the work. Only you wouldn't change. You were as stubborn about that as everything else."

Now he wanted a drink. Or just some air. He took a deep breath, not wanting to play this game tonight.

"But what if I did, Grace?"

"What?"

"Really changed."

She said, "What if you did?"

"You know," Charlie said, "became solid and upright like you thought old Dr. Bob was."

Grace grinned at him—there was something about the solemn way he always said "Dr. Bob"—and put her cheek in her hand. "Dr. Bob's problem, as you recall, was not being upright nearly often enough."

"Cheating on you is dumber than . . ."

"You?" Grace said.

"I didn't know any better," he said, knowing he sounded even lamer now. "I just thought I was doing what everybody else was doing, that it didn't count. You were *there*, Gracie. You know how fast everything happened right from the start, my rookie year . . ."

"It's as sad hearing that excuse now as it was then." She put a hand over her heart and said, "I swear, judge, it was baseball made me do it."

He said, "I know better now, is all I'm saying."

"Yeah," she said, "yeah, yeah, yeah. That's what my father used to tell my mother."

"You loved your father."

"Yeah," Grace said.

She insisted on paying the check. They walked a couple of blocks together down Madison, and then she said she wanted to walk the rest of the way to the Pierre herself. She had gotten tired of the Carlyle and didn't think the suites at the Lowell were roomy enough, and now she was at the Pierre.

She kissed him lightly on the cheek at the corner of 66th. She said she was taking the shuttle up to Boston, and then she'd call him when she got back to San Francisco.

When she got halfway up the next block, she turned around, as if it was a safe enough distance away.

"Can I ask one more question about Amber?"

He didn't even bother correcting her.

"Do I have a choice?" he said.

Grace said, "After you get past hair-care products, what the *hell* do you talk about?"

In the apartment now on 66th Street, two weeks later, the morning after his near-death experience with Ellie Bauer, his back killing him again as the Advil started to wear off already, he smiled, picturing Grace there under the streetlight on Madison, remembering how happy she still looked getting off a good line on him.

He looked at his watch, the cool Rolex Explorer she'd given him on their second anniversary, then went to take one more hot shower. When he was finished and dressed, he drank a Coke, smoked one more cigarette, and was ready to go see Mr. Chang, who sounded like another ball-buster.

But then, why should he be different than anybody else?

Chang's office, part of what looked like some sort of much bigger sports training complex, was on the second floor of the Millennium Hotel on West 44th, next to the old Henry Hudson Theater, around the corner from one of those ESPN theme-park restaurants where guys could keep watching the game even when they were in the men's room taking a piss.

Charlie had taken a cab downtown from 66th, another frustrated

Formula One driver at the wheel, the guy in the same kind of African knit cap Jim Brown started wearing when he gave up football to save the Bloods and the Crips.

They had only gone about five blocks when Charlie figured out that "Slow down" to Akeem apparently meant, "Try to cut off another bus and clip three more bike messengers."

By the time he got to the waiting room outside Chang's office, the fire in his back was raging out of control all over again.

When Chang came out, he said, "Fun night? Ellie still into using heavy equipment?"

He was a handsome sonofabitch who reminded Charlie of the martial arts actor he always thought of as Jet Ski. But Chang had clearly spent more than a little time at bodybuilding college. He wore a white golf shirt, black jeans, black Reebok trainers, had his black hair in one of those crewcuts with a high fade in front. No earrings, no tattoos, no facial hair. He was Chinese, no question about that, but not all the way; Charlie thought he was dark enough that he might have some Don Ho in him, too.

All in all, he looked as if he could bench-press a Vitamin Shoppe.

Chang shook Charlie's hand and pulled him up and out of the chair at the same time, causing the same kind of scream that had started his day at Ellie Bauer's instead of an alarm clock.

"Thanks," Charlie said.

"I can't fix you in the waiting room. Besides, you'll scare the other customers."

"Ellie mentioned you might have a bit of an attitude problem."

"I do," Chang said. "No attitude. Let's rock."

They went inside an office that was smaller than Charlie had expected, simpler, just one chair set up by itself in the middle of the room, a massage table against one of the walls, a desk, a filing cabinet, no tricky equipment. There were some framed certificates on the wall and a lot of photographs showing a much younger, even more bulked-up Chang in various Schwarzenegger poses, wearing some kind of small Speedo deal and looking fierce, showing off forearms with irrigation-map detail to them.

"So," Charlie said, "you were a competitive bodybuilder?"

Chang ignored him.

"Take off your shirt."

"I don't know if my name meant anything to you, by the way, but I used to pitch for the Mets . . ."

"You mentioned that on the phone. I'm trying not to show how impressed I am. You need help getting undressed there?"

"I think I can manage."

"Try managing before your hour's up."

"You think this could be some sort of spasm deal?" Charlie said when he had his shirt off.

Chang didn't answer, he was already behind him, running an open palm down the middle of Charlie's back, then back up.

"Or maybe it could be a tear, something like that?" Charlie said.

Chang stopped, came back around so he was facing Charlie. "Do me one favor?"

"Have I ever denied you anything?"

Charlie waited for a smile. Nothing. Just the same prison-yard stare.

"Shut up," Chang said.

Charlie shut up.

"This is going to hurt," Chang said.

He wasn't the life of the party, but he didn't lie.

Charlie said, "Can I ask a question?"

Chang had his hand on the back of Charlie's neck and was pushing down way too hard for what felt like the twentieth time.

"One."

"What you're doing, what's it called exactly?"

"Fixing your back is what it's called."

Chang went over to the filing cabinet now, opened a bottom drawer, got out a jar of cream, uncapped it, and began rubbing it roughly into Charlie's lower back, the bad place. It was like the deep-tissue massage some trainers had started using at the very end of his career, even in the minors, during the period when that kind of massage had become the new hot treatment. Only the way Chang did it made Charlie feel as if some of his internal organs were being kneaded like bread dough.

"Stand as straight as you can," Chang said.

Charlie did as he was told.

Now Chang took Charlie's left hand and pulled it slowly around until it was touching his right shoulder, telling him as he did so to bring his right arm underneath and around without twisting his upper body, as if he were trying to touch the palm of the right hand into the small of his back.

"Oh," Charlie said through clenched teeth, "*this* is where Ellie learned the pretzel thing."

"Let's go back to the shutting-up thing," Chang said, behind Charlie now, showing him where he wanted the right arm to be, by nearly pulling it out of its socket. "It was working for me."

Chang said, "We'll do this six times."

Charlie counted ten before they were through, the ones at the very end making him tremble with pain. When they finished, he could feel the sweat pouring off him. He hadn't moved from the center of the room and felt as if he'd done a full workout.

"You want to stop for a drink?" Chang said.

"How about a Dewar's and water."

Chang sighed. "*Do* you want something?"

"I'm good," Charlie said.

Chang looked at one of those big runners' watches. "Then let's keep going. Go over and lie down on the table. On your stomach."

Charlie did that, his face on a towel, just wanting to go to sleep.

"That scar behind your shoulder?"

Charlie said, "I blew it out when I was still a kid. With the Mets. Torn rotator cuff, labrium, the whole right side of the menu. I'd started a game the afternoon before, thrown a hundred and forty pitches. Then we went into extra innings and had a chance to go up three games to one, and I thought I could pitch an inning in relief. A hero deal all the way. I got talked into it, and talked myself into it, even though I knew I was too tired and too sore. We lost the game and the series and I lost my arm, even though they promised they'd make me as good as new."

"Who's they?"

"The Mets doctors."

"How'd that work out for you?"

Charlie tried to think of something smart to say, but couldn't, just because he never could, not about this. "It didn't."

"No shit, Sherlock." Chang had the cream out again and was rubbing behind the shoulder where there was the long scar, in the shape of a question mark.

"I thought we were fixing my back."

"This will help your back," he said, using two fingers to probe the area below Charlie's right shoulder, as if he were looking for something he'd lost in there. At the same time Charlie felt a little pop and heard a cap-pistol sound, Chang said, "There we go," actually sounding happy about something.

"There what is?"

"The mess they made."

"You can tell that with your fingers?"

"I can see it."

Chang pressed harder with his fingers. Charlie felt another pop, a little bigger than before, just not the pain that usually followed when the area behind his shoulder started to jangle like a pocketful of loose change.

"Scalpel jockeys," Chang said. "They've ruined more careers than dope and women combined."

"You're not a fan of sports medicine, I take it?"

"Do me a favor," Chang said, ignoring him. "Get your right shoulder underneath you and then stick your butt as far up in the air as you can."

"Okay," Charlie said, "but afterward you have to tell me that you love me."

Chang grabbed him around the waist with both hands then and arched his back, this time making Charlie Stoddard scream as if he were in labor.

"I love you," Chang said.

"**I** want to try one more thing," Chang said.

Charlie pointed out that he'd said one more thing about five more things ago.

"Stand up as straight as you can and lift your right arm like you're try-ing to touch the ceiling. Keep your left arm pointed straight at the floor."

When Charlie assumed the position, Chang stuck his thumb in Char-lie's armpit and started twisting. "Knock yourself out," Charlie said through clenched teeth. "I'm not screaming anymore, fuck you."

To keep himself from doing that, he took his left hand and pinched himself hard in the soft area right above his left hip. Later, he wouldn't be able to distinguish the mark he'd left from some of the vampire things Ellie Bauer had done to him.

Chang kept pressing with his right thumb, somehow even harder than before.

"Is there something in particular you're looking for? Something I could help out with, maybe point you in the right direction?"

Chang said, "You said rotator cuff, right? That basically ended your baseball career and turned you into a full-time comic?"

"Complete tear. Back in the days before they'd made some of the ad-vances they've made since then."

"Screw advances," Chang said, grabbing Charlie's arm as a way of telling him to keep it up there. "Screw them with a Phillips-head screw-driver. They did then what they do now: Cut first, ask questions later."

He was back behind Charlie's shoulder now, bracing himself, driving a closed fist into him.

"What . . . the . . . hell . . . are . . . you . . . *doing?*"

"Not doing," Chang said. "Undoing."

When it was finally over, Charlie noticed that he was able to get his shirt back on pain-free. Chang was explaining that what he'd done was a variation of active release techniques, or ART. He said if the people running sports teams would wake up, ART could completely revolutionize the treatment of muscle injuries in sports, not to mention cutting the number of sports-related surgeries in half. And that was probably a conservative estimate, he said.

"You know what most trainers on sports teams know? Ice."

Without being told to, his shirt not yet tucked into his jeans, Charlie reached down and touched his toes.

"Sonofabitch," he said. "You really fixed my back."

Chang looked up, bored, from where he was seated at his desk, filling out the insurance forms he said Charlie should submit to his employer. "Who is your employer, incidentally?"

"The Mets."

"You do have medical with them, right?"

Charlie was instinctively reaching for the pack of cigarettes in his jeans, but stopped when he pictured Chang coming out of the chair and across the office and making some kind of flying, open-field tackle as he tried to light up.

"I don't know," Charlie said.

"I figured. You're the type. Like the actors I train."

"What type is that?"

"The type that always had somebody doing everything for him."

Chang finished the form, folded it neatly, stuck it inside an envelope, handed it to Charlie, and told him to have a doctor from the Mets—"Whichever genius is on call today"—mail it back to him.

"I want to see you in a week," he said to Charlie.

"But I feel better now."

"Now. But you won't tomorrow, and the day after that, because of what I did to you. You'll want to come back, believe me, probably before next week. If you feel like you can't wait, call."

"Only if you promise to keep your thumbs to yourself."

"That just broke up some of the scar tissue in the fibers between your rotator cuff muscles. They're called the subscapulars."

"I knew that."

"That's the good news. The bad news is that there's a shitload more."

"Scar tissue."

"Sports doctors make scar tissue the way Warren Buffett makes money."

"But you did clear some out today. I felt it."

Chang went over to a corner of the office, underneath some of the Schwarzenegger photos, picked up a blue free weight.

"It's only ten pounds," he said, handing it to Charlie. "Pretend it's a baseball. Show me that motion of yours that used to dazzle the hitters."

Charlie said, "No."

"Do it."

"I can't," Charlie said. He knew he sounded like he was whining again and didn't care. "If I even try, it will make the shit you just fixed feel like it was nothing more than a stubbed toe."

Chang smiled for the first time. "No offense, but you sound like a titty baby."

"You don't understand," Charlie said, "The thing with my back, I knew it was temporary. My shoulder's been killing me for fifteen fucking years. You made it feel a little better. That's enough fun for today."

"I'll make you a deal. If you do what I want you to do, and your pitching motion hurts you the way it always has, today is on the house. And when you open that envelope, you'll find out how good a deal that is. Because I'm not cheap."

Charlie took the blue weight, holding it lightly in his right hand, then lifted both arms above his head like he was starting his windup, brought them down, made a short stride to the door to Chang's office, brought his right arm through, and then waited for the pain.

Which didn't come.

He felt some pull back there.

A little more popping.

That was it.

He said, "I could tell you it killed."

"We'd both know you were lying."

"It wasn't bad, actually."

"Couldn't be. Do it again, but bring your arm through like you mean it."

Charlie did, sure he'd feel something this time.

Only he didn't.

Now he smiled.

Chang said, "There's so much shit you don't know, because they won't tell you, or because they don't know. Or they won't change. You hurt yourself and then they cut on you, saying they've fixed the problem, only they haven't. But that's the shit you don't know. You think if you work hard and do all the exercises they give you, you'll get better. And before long you're doing the same unnatural thing with your arm— throwing a baseball—that all pitchers have done since the beginning of time. But every time you do, there's more swelling back there." He stopped and looked at Charlie. "You care about this?"

Charlie said, "At least you're not touching me in places I don't want to be touched."

"Swelling closes off oxygen," Chang said. "Oxygen that's supposed to be going to the injured muscle, and the muscles around it, and the tissue and fibers around them. It's called hypoxia."

"I knew that."

"Now," Chang said, "it's like the scar tissue is feeding on itself and spreading like a goddamn virus, sticking to the muscles. And they can't move."

"And you're fucked," Charlie said. "Big time."

"You never got better because you never had a chance to get better," Chang said. "You still had the same arm you had before, just not the proper flexibility, the kind of flexibility that made you different from the next guy, gave your ball the extra hops that great ones have. You'd pitched in one gear when you were healthy, and then after your surgery, you were stuck in a lower gear. You just didn't know it."

Chang crossed the room then, opened his door, looked out, and said he'd certainly love to chat more, but his one o'clock was here, so hit the road.

"You're telling me you can fix my shoulder?" Charlie said.

"Sure," Chang said. "Why not?"

CHARLIE NOW REFERRED to Chang's office as Chang's House
of Pain. Before his third visit, he was describing some of the things
Chang would do to him, and Healey said, "There's a girl in the Village I
used to go out with'll do them cheaper, but she's gonna wanna tie you
up at some point."

Charlie had just come back from a Cyclones game in Coney Island,
the last game before the team went off on a two-week road trip, longest
of the year for them, through upstate New York, Jamestown and Batavia
and Auburn. He and Healey were in the back room of The Last Good
Year, watching the Yankees play the Blue Jays, Healey as twitchy as ever
with the remote, going back and forth between that game and the Red
Sox playing the Orioles, seeing if he could manage to do that without

missing a pitch. Charlie noticed that he was wearing a navy tie with the Yankees logo all over it and had gone heavier than usual on the aftershave.

"You're dressed up."

"It's just a tie."

"A clean shirt is dressed up for you," Charlie said. "You also smell as if you've been dipped in Old Spice. You must have a date."

Healey brightened. "Want to know who with?"

Charlie said, "Sometimes you can have too much information."

Ellie Bauer had just called, asking if Charlie was around, and Healey told her that his old pal had either died or gone to Europe, he couldn't remember which.

"I can't remember the last time a broad scared you this way," Healey said, when he came back to the table.

His bar wasn't the only thing that was a shrine to the '50s, so was the way he talked. Like he was living *Guys and Dolls* instead of just singing it.

"I think back to her saying, 'Hey, this way might be kind of fun,' and I get the shakes all over again," Charlie said.

His appointment with Chang was at ten the next morning, which is why he was still nursing the one beer he'd started when he'd made it back from Brooklyn, which even at midnight, no traffic, was more challenging than changing planes in Chicago. The week before, he'd shown up at Chang's after a long night that had ended at Elaine's with Keith Hernandez, now doing some television work for the Mets. As soon as he was on the table the next morning, Chang had said, "I'm trying to work scar tissue out of you, Bar Boy, not a goddamn distillery."

"You're saying this voodoo shit is working, then," Healey said.

"I've even started running a little bit again."

"I'm happy for you," Healey said. He'd always thought being able to run long distances was about as useful a skill as being able to eat a lot of blueberry pies.

"Guy does the voodoo on the shoulder, then he has me get right up and do some range-of-motion deals, and for a few minutes, no shit, I feel like I've got somebody else's right arm."

Healey was half-listening now, the way he usually did when baseball was on. Now he pointed the remote at the set and realized both games were in commercial at the same time, which meant he could actually focus on the conversation for the next two and a half minutes. Charlie didn't know a lot about attention deficit disorder, just that it was the new designer affliction in pro sports, something your agent thought could get you over when they caught you with a gram in your pocket or your girlfriend had to get a restraining order.

Whatever it was, he was pretty sure Healey had it.

"You do any real throwing?" he said to Charlie now. "Like pitching-type throwing?"

"No. Why would I want to do any real throwing?"

"I was just asking."

"What does that mean, you were just asking? It sounded more like asking to me, like you were trying to make some kind of point."

"I was just wondering how Showtime Stoddard would feel if he tried to crank a few just for the hell of it."

On the television set, the Red Sox game, the camera was focused on Ted Hartnett, studying his lineup card. His old roommate, Gabby, on his way now to Manager of the Year in the American League. Ted (Gabby) Hartnett: who'd stayed a friend even though they both wanted Grace. Even after the fight they'd had the night before Game 4 in '88, all the shitty things they'd finally said to each other, about Grace and everything else. A backup catcher who could call a game better than anybody but couldn't hit for shit, not at any level he'd ever played, never more than .230 in his life.

Ted Hartnett knew how Charlie could crank it, when he still had the arm. He used to tell the writers that the only goddamn thing louder than the airplanes over Shea was the sound of Charlie's fastball in his mitt.

"Maybe when the Cyclones get back from upstate, end of next week, I'll grab one of the catchers early one day and just screw around a little bit. Just for the hell of it."

"When's the last time you threw really hard?" Healey said. "I mean, balls-on."

"Year of Our Lord nineteen hundred and eighty-eight," Charlie Stoddard said.

When they were finished the next day, Charlie asked Chang what his afternoon schedule was like. Chang checked his book and said he was free between two and four, there was a screenwriter he home-trained and then he'd planned to go for a long run in the Park.

Charlie said, "I've got a better idea."

He told Chang what he wanted to do, trying to make a joke of it, not that you got anywhere joking with Chang. As if it was no big deal.

"You're serious?"

"No," Charlie said. "*You're* serious. I'm a customer willing to pay you for two hours of your time that you didn't expect to get paid for today."

Charlie was sitting on the table, buttoning his shirt; Chang was in the middle of the office, looking bigger than he really was, as always, somehow seeming to hum like a generator even when he was completely still. He'd flipped his clothes today, black t-shirt, white jeans, white sneakers. "I did a little reading on you. On the Net? They all wrote you were crazy."

"Still," Charlie said, "after all these years."

He was waiting for Chang at one of the ballfields in the Park, all of them lined up one behind the other. Charlie had walked over from his apartment, carrying a faded denim bag from some giveaway day at Shea a hundred years ago. Now he sat in the back row of the bleachers on the first-base side of the field, thinking that there was nothing better-looking in this world—Grace being the exception, Grace as beautiful at forty as she was at twenty—than an empty field on a day like this, one of those summer days, not too hot or too sticky, in what Charlie liked to think of as the dream New York. He didn't even know who was in charge of maintaining these fields, the Parks Commissioner probably, or maybe some other commissioner just in charge of Central Park. Charlie vaguely remembered playing in a charity game once on one of these fields, the Mets of the mid-'80s against the Yankees of that same era, him and Keith and Darling and the boys against Mattingly and Winfield and the rest of them benefitting widows and orphans of firemen who'd gotten killed at the World Trade Center. He didn't remember the field being as nice as this one, though, the baselines white with new chalk, the grass green and freshly cut, home plate looking as clean as if somebody'd just bleached it. Jesus, he thought, rolling the new ball around in his hand, feeling the slickness of it, the way the seams always felt with a new one, Jesus *Christ*, just looking at a field like this on a day like this could make you feel fifteen again.

Or twenty-two?

He'd been 24—4 that year, and had had the best goddamn earned run average, 1.50, since Mr. Bob Gibson himself, and had struck out 310 batters and walked 42 and no-hit the Cardinals twice, the first time anybody had ever no-hit the same team twice in the same season.

He'd been twenty-two and had numbers like those and the world by the fucking balls. . . .

He didn't know Chang was there until he heard him climbing up through the six or seven rows of bleachers to where Charlie sat daydreaming. Chang had changed into a *Hearts in Atlantis* sweatshirt with the sleeves cut off that he said the screenwriter had given him, baggy running shorts, and running shoes the color of strawberries.

"I just want to tell you, going in, this was never my sport," Chang said.

"It was mine," Charlie said.

He reached into the Mets bag and pulled out his Louisville Slugger glove, mostly black, the web brown, TPX written down the middle finger and below the pocket inside, his last gamer, the one he'd used that last game at Shea against Piazza and the Mets, as soft as an old blanket. Then he handed Chang the old Rawlings catcher's mitt that had been Ted Hartnett's gamer when he'd been Charlie's personal catcher. Charlie had just felt more comfortable with Hartnett than with Gary Carter, had liked the game Hartnett called better, not that he'd had to do much more with Charlie in those days than hold down one finger, for fastball.

The Mets had been playing a series against the Dodgers in Los Angeles, halfway through a West Coast swing in August of 1990, when they'd finally released Charlie. He'd packed up his shit, hadn't waited around to talk to the reporters, spent the afternoon drinking at the Ginger Man in Beverly Hills, took the redeye home. He'd been living in the Gramercy Park Hotel in those days. He'd slept all day when he got to the apartment. When he'd gone out to buy some supplies late in the afternoon, there'd been a FedEx box waiting for him at the front desk.

Ted Hartnett's mitt was inside, a note taped to the pocket.

Rooms,
This baby's already had as good as it's ever gonna have.

Gabby

They'd called him Gabby for the same dumb clubhouse reasons ballplayers had always called bald guys Curly, because Ted Hartnett had always talked about as much as a goldfish.

"I'll try to be gentle," Charlie said now, motioning Chang toward home plate.

"Isn't that what I usually say to you?"

"No," Charlie said, "you don't."

Charlie went all the way to second base and started out soft-tossing the ball to Chang from there. He smiled when he saw Chang try to throw it back to him from where he stood, a few feet behind the plate. The guy was a superman, everything about the way he looked and moved and carried himself and even looked at you told you that, but he threw a baseball like some actor—or actress—tossing out the first pitch of the game. Charlie remembered watching a Mets game on television one time when Jerry Seinfeld had been throwing out the first pitch, back in the days when his show was the biggest thing on the air. The Mets were good again, and celebrity Mets fans like Seinfeld were showing up, watching their team, or what they said had always been their team, try to get back into the playoffs for the first time since everything had gone bad in '88.

Seinfeld had waited until the ovation for him had died down, waved to the crowd when it finally did so they'd cheeer a little more, mugged for the mini-cams positioned at the side of the mound, then delivered the ball the way a stroke victim would have.

"We need to work a little bit on your form before next time," Charlie said.

"Bite me," Chang said. "And there isn't going to be a next time."

"Another catcher who can't take a little bit of constructive criticism," Charlie said.

"Shut up and pitch."

"This isn't pitching," Charlie said. "This is what comes before pitching."

They threw this way for about ten minutes, and then Charlie came in behind the mound and threw easily from there for another ten minutes, wanting to make sure he was good and warm, that he was completely loose. Finally, he went to the mound and, without throwing the ball to Chang, went through an imaginary motion, stepping toward the plate a couple of times, seeing where his left foot landed, making sure the dirt wasn't loose, solid, not wanting to slip. He was wearing a pair of old Nike spikes with a blue swoosh and orange trim, the Mets colors; he'd found them in a pile of old spikes in one of his closets, one of the closets filled with what he called his Stuff. All the Stuff he could never bring himself to throw away, a lot of it in one of the huge travel trunks that Charlie Samuels, who was still the Mets equipment manager even now, had let him keep.

"Now I'm gonna pitch," Charlie said.

"I told you to pay attention or I'd knock you on your fucking ass," Charlie said.

"Paying attention."

"To the high school soccer girls, maybe. Not to me."

"Bullshit."

"You've got to be set now, even for strikes. Or if one sails on you, tips off the fingers of your glove, you'll get hit between what Ellie called those flashing dark eyes of yours."

"I'm supposed to worry because you're throwing so hard?" Chang said.

"Not yet," Charlie said.

Maybe not ever.

That's what he was here to find out.

He rubbed the ball, hard, out of habit, remembering how he hadn't been into spring training for two weeks, the spring training after the operation, and already he'd known he was never coming all the way back, no matter how hard he worked. He'd fucking known. He hadn't told anybody, of course, not the trainers, not the doctors, not Davey Johnson, the manager, not Ted Hartnett, certainly not any of the sportswriters who thought they were his buddies, who wanted him to think they cared.

He'd known, though, known they could hit him now as sure as he'd known before that no one could hit him, or catch up with him. The only other person who'd known that early was Grace, all the way from San Francisco, just by talking to him on the telephone. She'd always been able to do that, from the time they were kids, even if Grace had never really acted like a kid, not that Charlie had ever noticed.

From the beginning, she'd ask him a question about something, and no matter what kind of bullshit answer he'd give, she'd be able to pick up on some little change in his voice, and before long it was like one of those cop shows on television and Charlie'd be ready to confess to snatching the Lindbergh baby.

"You told me going in that you might not be the same."

"I was looking for sympathy."

"No, you weren't. You meant it."

"What's the old saying? Expect the worst and you won't be disappointed? I thought the worst was gonna be that I'd lost something off my fastball. I didn't know I was going to lose everything off it."

"You told me yourself that plenty of guys have come back from this same injury and this same surgery."

"Oh, I'll come back, Gracie. I've got nowhere else to go. But I'm just another guy now."

"You can't possibly know that already." Trying to be funny, she'd said, "You're still only fourteen years old, you've practically got your whole life ahead of you."

When he hadn't said anything, Grace had said, "All I'm trying to say is, you're still young."

"Not anymore," he'd said that night, what felt like a million years ago, and she'd said there was no way he could know for sure, and Charlie'd said he didn't know much in the world outside of baseball and bars and blondes, but he goddamn fucking well knew his right arm.

He still did.

"Can I ask what you're doing?" Chang said.

"Thinking."

"Not your strong suit. Show me what you got."

"You're sure you want to do that?"

Sounding to himself like the old Charlie for a second, the one with the arm, the clever bastard who used to tell people he could throw a fastball between the cars of the 9:30 Metroliner.

Chang said, "Bring it on, woman."

Charlie pitched out of the stretch now, just for fun, using the shorter kick he used when he had runners on base, not messing around with curves or cutters or splitters or even the screwball he used to throw sometimes—at about ninety—to lefthanded hitters. Just fastballs, strictly regulation. Even now, after throwing for more than half an hour, he was waiting to feel something behind his shoulder. Waiting for the Rice Krispie sounds from that shoulder—snap, crackle, pop—that David Cone said all pitchers eventually heard when they got old, or after they got cut.

The only thing Charlie felt now was good.

Very good.

He threw one now with a little more mustard on it than the rest. It made a different sound from the rest in Chang's mitt. Not as big as Charlie used to make, but big enough. Chang pulled his left hand out like there was a lit match inside, shook his fingers, said, "Hey, that one actually hurt."

Sounding surprised.

Charlie grinned. "No offense," he said, "but you sound like a titty baby."

He was still only throwing in the high eighties and knew it. No pitcher who knew his dick from a garden snake ever needed a radar gun to tell him how fast he was throwing a baseball, on the side, in the bullpen, on the mound. On those nights in the old days when Charlie'd hump it up past a hundred miles an hour, and they'd put the number up on the scoreboard to make the crowd hot, Charlie knew before Ted Hartnett even threw the ball back. He imagined it was the same way when Tiger Woods hit a drive on the screws, just absolutely nutted one past everybody. You couldn't describe it to somebody unless you could do it, feel your arm come through like a locomotive, see that hop on the ball the last couple of feet before home plate, like it was some kind of optical illusion, the ball rising or tailing or doing some goddamn thing. It was what Charlie thought of as his personal hops, the kind basketball players who could jump out of the gym were supposed to have.

You couldn't describe it any more than Jordan could have described what it was like to take off from the foul line when he was a kid, when he could run the length of the court and fly from the foul line all the way to the basket and throw another one down. You couldn't describe it or explain it any more than Barry Sanders could when he used to go one way with the ball, with all his momentum and weight and speed, and then he'd stop while the defense flew past him and, just like that, he was going the other way and the guys trying to tackle him were eating mud.

That's what it felt like when Charlie's arm was coming forward.

Charlie thought about that, and what Shea used to be like when he got those two strikes on a guy, two outs already in the inning and now two strikes, maybe he was trying to strike out the side, and they'd be on their feet everywhere, from the upper deck to the top step of the dugouts, and this'd be the kind of moment when other guys sometimes said they didn't want to look around, they couldn't think about what the place sounded like. Only Charlie always did. This was when he felt like the whole thing had turned into a rock concert instead of a baseball game. Like he was Mick, out front, in the band but out all alone, the one they'd all come to see, the whole place in the palm of his hand. Charlie'd milk it as long as he could, like he was taking a big hit of the whole night, and then he'd finally give his shoulders that little shake, and then the only thing he heard was the sound of his own breathing. He'd put the ball inside his glove and then start his motion and not even know himself how hard he was going to bring it this time.

In those days, he knew that no matter how hard the batter thought he was throwing, he still had more in his arm if he needed it, an extra gear only he knew about.

Even if he never had to use it very much, never felt as if he'd thrown that one fastball as hard as he could, the one that would have busted the sound barrier . . .

Chang looked at his watch. "You find out what you wanted to find out?"

"Who said I wanted to find out anything? We're just having a nice, pain-free game of catch. Maybe I'll take you for ice cream afterward."

"Let me put it another way: How much longer?"

"Only a few more. I promise. But I want you to get down into a crouch like a real catcher would and stick that old mitt out like it's a great big target. I'm gonna open this thing up a little bit."

He was sweating. He took off his Cyclones cap, the blue one with "BC" on the front, which used the same lettering as the old Brooklyn Dodgers "B." Another new thing trying to look old. He was wearing a ratty old Mets sweatshirt, long-sleeved, as if he still had an arm to keep warm. He wiped his forehead with the left sleeve, the way he used to on the mound when he wanted to buy a little time.

He said to Chang, "You're the one who's been feeling me up back there. You think it's all right if I open up?"

"Yes."

"You're sure?"

"For Chrissakes, have I ever lied to you?"

He went to the big windup now and let it go too early, almost like he was afraid to follow through, and threw the ball about five feet over Chang's head, like some wild kid who couldn't find home plate.

"Halley's Comet wasn't that high the last time," Chang said.

He retrieved the ball and threw it back. Charlie cleaned it off, rubbed it up again. Now he was smiling.

"What's so funny?" Chang said.

"Nothing. You ready?"

"Even I can catch them when they stop rolling."

The second fastball, right down Broadway, was the one Charlie had warned him about.

That was the one that knocked Chang on his ass.

"YOU'VE GOT TO let me write something about this," Rob Kendall said to Charlie.

It was a week after he'd thrown with Chang in Central Park, three days after he'd convinced him to do it again. The key was always how your arm felt the next day. Both times, it had felt fine, even before Chang worked on him.

"No."

"The game's on Tuesday night. I'll write it for Sunday's paper. You'll be safely back in the big city by then."

"Men," Charlie said. "Why can't you ever understand that no means no?"

"I made this happen for you. Shouldn't I get something in return?"

"I'm not doing this for publicity, I told you. I was just jacking around with the Cyclones the other day and my arm felt pretty good, and I decided, what the hell, it would be fun to go pitch a game where I could have some laughs and nobody'd bother me."

"That's it?"

"That's it. Remember that itch Jordan talked about when he came back with the Bullets?"

"Wizards."

"Whatever. I just want to scratch it for one night."

"What was that line from *A Chorus Line?* Singers gotta sing."

"I loved that show," Charlie said. "Remember that girl with the great ass, played Cassie in the big revival back in the '80s? I went out with her."

"You were always the lover of the arts, Charlie," Kendall said.

Rob Kendall had covered the Mets for the *Daily News* back in the 1980s. Now he was writing a syndicated column for a paper called *The Record*, whose circulation area covered most of north Jersey. He was also writing baseball books that showed he actually knew something about pitching, maybe because he had been a pitcher once, back at Columbia University; sometimes when it had been Columbia against Yale, it had been him against Darling.

In the old days, the Mets starters, Charlie and Gooden and Darling and Bobby Ojeda, would sit around all the time and bullshit about pitching with Kendall, at least if there were no radio idiots in the area wanting to stick a microphone in front of your face as if mining for plutonium and ask you how the old wing felt after last night's start. Kendall wanted you to show him how you gripped your fastball and the subtle change you made with your arm angle when it was a splitter instead of a slider, and sometimes just what it felt like getting a fastball in on the inside-half on a cold day in April and the batter stood there at home plate shaking his hands and wanting to cry because of the ball he'd just fouled off.

With Kendall, you didn't feel as if you were trying to communicate with the cab driver in the funny hat.

It also didn't hurt, not with the Mets team he was covering, overrun with bad boys, that he liked to match them beer for beer, stay up as late as the ones who didn't need any sleep at all, like Dykstra, and run around the National League chasing halter tops and big hair with a vengeance.

"By day, Woodward and Bernstein," Kendall used to say. "By night, just another horny Jersey kid looking to get his ashes hauled."

What Charlie liked more than anything was that Kendall used to cover the hell out of them without being another of the world's ball-busters. That's why Charlie and almost all of the other Mets—minus the few assholes on the team—used to share inside things with him that they wouldn't with any of the other guys on the beat.

Now all this time later, Kendall was using the same tone of voice he would put on Charlie when he wanted to know what had really happened in the clubhouse yesterday between Keith Hernandez and Lee Mazzilli after the two of them had gotten carried away again.

"There's no story here, trust me," Charlie said.

"Let me be the judge of that. Did I ever screw you in the past?"

"Shut up," Charlie said, "and give me the directions."

Charlie was following those directions now, over the George Washington Bridge to 80 West, driving the old BMW convertible he'd held on to more out of nostalgia —something else he couldn't bring himself to let go of, more of his Stuff—than anything else.

Kendall said the trip from the East Side of Manhattan was just over ten miles if he wanted to clock it, but Charlie had forgotten to set the trip odometer. So he'd just kept following Kendall's detailed directions, past Teaneck and Hackensack to Exit 62, which was also an entrance to the Garden State Parkway. He nearly missed the sign for Saddle Brook's local streets, which Kendall said would have put him on the Garden State heading south. From there, Charlie was sure he would have ended up in Atlantic City or Philadelphia or maybe Disney World before he was able to get off.

It was easy after the Saddle Brook exit. Right at the stop sign. Half a mile until the intersection. Quick right behind Coolidge Elementary School. Charlie parked next to the school, the parking lot filled with what looked like all young-guy cars, the same Mustangs and Camaros and IROCs he saw in the players' parking lot over at KeySpan Park, the ballpark in Coney Island where the Cyclones played.

Charlie had the same Mets bag with him he'd brought to the park the day he'd pitched to Chang; he had his spikes inside, glove, some cream Chang told him to rub into his arm right before he went out to start warming up, some of the old socks he used to wear so high when he was a kid, a pair of the oldtimey Mets pants with the stripes on the side so much thicker than they were now, a retro Mets warmup jacket he took with him wherever he went, that ugly blue of theirs with black leather sleeves. On the other side of the parking lot, he could see the Ridgefield Park Orioles—it had to be them, they'd copied the real Oriole uniform exactly, all the way up to the dopey little orange bird on the fronts of the caps—warming up on Vander Sande Field.

The players for the other team, the Colonials, Rob Kendall's team, were doing some light running in the outfield.

The first thing Charlie noticed, because pitchers always noticed, was that Vander Sande was deepest in right and right-center, but ridiculously shallow in left, less than 300 feet, Charlie was sure; he'd always been able to judge outfield distances better than a Scottish caddie at one of those Royal and Ancients.

It was five in the afternoon, an hour until the game between the Colonials and Orioles was going to start. Charlie could already see the rush-hour traffic crawl up and down the Garden State through some openings in the trees behind the outfield.

Welcome to Jersey, Charlie Stoddard thought.

Good seats still available.

Charlie was wondering how to get inside Coolidge Elementary to change when Kendall, already in uniform, came walking out a side door.

The Colonials jersey in his hand had to be the one Charlie was going to wear when he pitched against the Ridgefield Park Orioles.

"And you never thought you'd make it back to the big time," Kendall said.

"I owe it all to my personal savior and my teammates," Charlie said. "Whoever the hell my teammates are."

"Shit," Kendall said. "Before long the Red Sox will probably be calling you, the way they've suddenly got the incredible shrinking lead. Sixteen games over the hated Yankees a month ago. Eight now."

"Yeah, yeah, yeah," Charlie said. "After that, I'm going to play quarterback for the Giants."

Kendall was a wiry, good-looking guy, black curly hair, dark-skinned, Charlie seeming to recall he had some Portuguese in him, either on his mother's or his father's side; it was another thing that gave him the jump when he was covering the Mets, he could speak fluently to the Dominicans and Puerto Ricans without using a translator, using sign language, or shouting slowly at them in English the way the other sportswriters did.

"Thank you so much for bringing me to the Bergen County Bar League," Charlie said.

"I told you," Kendall said, "it's the Major-Metropolitan League, not a frigging bar league." He grinned. "Though we might be forced to have a few celebratory cold ones afterward at this bar I know over in Fort Lee."

Charlie grinned back at him. "They got girls there?"

"Yeah," Rob Kendall said, "and no dress code."

"You mean no clothes."

"Oh yeah," Kendall said.

Kendall turned the jersey around so Charlie could see the back, No. 32, same as he'd worn with the Mets. It was Magic Johnson's number with the Lakers. Most of Charlie's white friends growing up outside Boston in Lexington, Mass., had been Celtic fans, and Bird guys. Charlie, who'd been tall for a point guard, even when he was a sophomore, had always been a Magic guy, from the first time he'd seen him play at Michigan State, the year his team played Bird's in the college finals. That was before they'd made Charlie a pitcher in the spring of his sophomore year at Lexington High, and everybody had started to talk about just how much money there might be in his right arm.

Him wearing Magic's number was another reason they'd started calling him Showtime Charlie later on.

Kendall said, "Ed Bell's wife? Ed's the guy who runs the Colonials? She made this uni up special for you this afternoon."

"Who'd you tell I was coming? Besides Bell, I mean?"

"No one. I didn't talk in the old days, I don't talk now. Name, rank, cell-phone number, that's it."

"You're sure he won't turn around and call the papers?"

"Charlie," he said. "You know I love you, but it's not like Clemens came over and wanted Ed to give him the ball.

"Besides," Kendall said, "when it comes to baseball, I pretty much *am* the papers around here."

Charlie said, "I just don't want to look over and see a cameraman from ESPN wanting to turn me into some twenty-second comedy clip on *SportsCenter.*"

"Picking on the old man."

"Hey, there's poor old Charlie Stoddard, leading off our wacky Plays of the Week. Or month. Or year."

He took the uniform from Kendall. It seemed to be the right size. Charlie said, "Did you change inside? Or did you drive here in your uniform like we used to in American Legion ball?"

There was a tiny locker room, Kendall said, down the main hallway after you went in the door he'd just come out. He could leave his stuff in one of the lockers, wallet and watch and phone if he had one, somebody always locked all the doors right before the game started.

"You said the game started at six," Charlie said. "Is that a real time?"

"Real time," Kendall said. "That's provided we get all the television commercials out of the way, of course."

He gave Charlie a little shove toward the school.

"Now go get dressed, man. You're starting for the Saddle Brook Colonials tonight."

Charlie said it was his first start in five years, he was just trying to savor the moment, leave him alone.

Mostly, Kendall had told Charlie, the rosters in the Major-Metropolitan League were made up of kids who still had their heads full of dreams, even if the best prospects their age had signed pro contracts long ago. These were guys in college or just out of college still thinking they might catch some scout's eye, or get enough pub in *The Record*—which covered the league games and printed the standings and even published directions to places like Vander Sande Field—that they still might be able to move up to the next level in the area. That meant they could play Independent League ball for some team like the Newark Bears, who were being run by the old Yankees catcher Rick Cerone, or go with the Jersey Jackals, who played in the ballpark behind Yogi Berra's museum in Montclair.

Point being, Kendall told Charlie, that they weren't here to fuck around, they were serious about these games.

"Please don't tell me they're going to use aluminum bats," Charlie said. "I should have asked about the bats before I let you talk me into this."

He was dressed now, walking with Kendall toward the field.

"Right," Rob Kendall said. "It was me who called you, asking if you'd allow me to broker this deal with my team which you've always made fun of, get you a start, and, by the way, could I keep it as quiet as possible so nobody would come and make fun of you?"

"Just so we're clear," Charlie said. "You still haven't answered my question. Are they wood, as the Good Lord intended? Or assault weapons that make that ping sound before they come shooting up the middle at you?"

"Wood. Even though most of these guys, the young guys, played their whole college season using aluminum."

"Fuck 'em," Charlie said. "They're hitters."

"There's the old Charlie we all knew and loved."

"The old Charlie?" he said. "Or just an *old* Charlie?"

"I thought that's what we were here to find out," Rob Kendall said.

■   ■   ■

It turned out that Kendall, the oldest guy in the league at forty-two but still getting by on his off-speed stuff—"I couldn't throw hard even when I could throw hard," he said—had given up his start with the Colonials so Charlie could pitch.

"It's a far better thing I do," Kendall said, after introducing him to Ed Bell.

"Think of all the times I fixed you up with my discards in the old days," Charlie said.

"There's that, too," Kendall said.

Bell had called the rest of the Colonials over to the bench. Up close, Charlie saw, they were even bigger and younger than they'd looked from a distance.

"I'm sure you guys have all heard of Charlie Stoddard," Ed Bell said. He was about five-ten, a square box of a guy with long red hair brushed back, big hands. Big, soft hands, Charlie had noticed when Bell was fooling around on the field, sharing ground balls with the Orioles' shortstop while the Orioles took batting practice. They were the kind of infielder hands that somehow killed every bad bounce, the ball spending so little time in the glove before it was on its way to first base that you wondered if it had ever been there at all. Ed Bell had no range, Charlie could see that, too, he was probably one of those guys who'd put on twenty pounds since his glory days for the Seton Hall Pirates, for whom he said he'd been All–Big East three straight years.

But he sure could pick 'em.

"I mean," he said, "everybody's heard of Showtime Charlie, right?"

The first baseman, who'd introduced himself as Gus, said, "I forget, did you have more success with Ruth or Gehrig?"

"Cobb or Hornsby?" somebody behind him said.

"Shoeless Joe or the other scummy fixers in the movie?"

"Shit," Rob Kendall said, getting into the act, "he's not that old. But you should have seen what he could do to Mantle when Mickey was the one hung over."

"Go ahead, boys," Charlie said, "have your fun, I know I'm here on a special one-day pass. I can take it."

The smiling kid who was going to be catching him was named Ruben Escobar.

"I heard that before I was borned, was you taught Nolan Ryan to pitch sooooo fass," Ruben Escobar said.

Charlie said, "Hey, Chico, here's the signal I want you to use for my fassball."

Charlie gave him the finger, then laughed along with the rest of them.

Look at me, he thought, one of the boys again.

Already he knew how good it felt, even here, just off Exit 62, almost as old as his old friend Kendall, twice as old as anybody else in the game.

The third baseman came up to him, shook his hand. "Darrin Kosner," he said. "I just graduated from St. John's. I was in the picnic bleachers at Shea with the rest of our team the day Piazza hit that bomb off you in your last game."

Even here at Vander Sande Field, they wanted you to know where they were when shit happened.

"I think that sucker hit the scoreboard so hard it landed back at second base," Charlie said. "And on that happy note, I think I'll go warm up to face the hated Orioles."

Ruben Escobar ran back to the bench to get his chest protector and mask; he'd already put on his shin guards. Kendall told Charlie that Escobar had played a couple of years in the Mexican League and had only been in the United States six months. But everybody who'd seen him play so far thought he might have enough game to make it all the way to the big leagues, he was one of the guys who still had a chance, who wasn't kidding himself behind Coolidge Elementary.

"How old?" Charlie said.

"Well, no one's exactly sure."

"How old does he *say* he is?"

"Twenny," Kendall said, giving him a bean-dip accent. "Goin on twenny-wan."

"Wait, don't tell me," Charlie said. "The courthouse back in Cuernevaca, the one with his birth certificate inside, burned down."

Kendall said, "I hear you. I swear I was in Spanish history at Columbia with the guy."

When Escobar was in full gear, he and Charlie walked behind the bleachers on the third-base side, so the bleachers were between them and the field there; there was a pitcher's mound back there, which meant this was as much bullpen as the Colonials had when somebody needed to warm up.

Charlie was ready to go. He'd done the stretches Chang had told him to do in the locker room, some of them making him feel dumber than one of those cable exercise shows. Then he'd rubbed some of the cream, from the unmarked jar, into his upper arm and into the area behind his shoulder, even under his arm. As dumb as that made him feel.

But he didn't feel dumb now, feet together on the mound behind the bleachers, waiting for Escobar to stick his mitt out and give him a target.

Just excited.

One of the boys.

It took him a few minutes to get loose. Nothing unusual there. It had always been that way for him, out in the bullpen at Shea before a game, taking his time, waiting on his arm, waiting to know it was all right to turn it on. Waiting for what he always thought of as the *hot* to come over him. Always knowing it would come, some days or nights faster than others, because those were the days when he knew his arm was going to be hot forever, at twenty and thirty and even forty, the way it had still been hot for Clemens, still throwing in the high 90s when he'd been the exact same age Charlie Stoddard was now. It didn't matter how tired he was, how much he'd had to drink the night before, whether he had had three days' rest or four or five, if there was a day of rain in there somewhere. Didn't matter if at the time he got to the ballpark he was so hung over he couldn't remember the name of the girl whose apartment he'd just left; sometimes he'd have to identify them by street address if one of his teammates cross-examined him.

"Who was she?" somebody would say, and Charlie would say, "West Eighty-third, between Amsterdam and Columbus."

"What does she do?"

"Everything," Charlie would say.

Then he'd go out and pitch if it was his turn to pitch, and by the time the game started, it wouldn't matter that his head was still full of static or haze or some weird kind of white noise. He'd get loose finally and then that hot feeling would be running like a current up and down his right arm, and then he didn't feel like shit anymore, he just felt like this was the day he might strike everybody out.

When they finished, he wiped himself off with the towel he'd dropped next to the mound. Escobar, smiling the way he had since Charlie had started to throw hard the last couple of minutes, came up to him and stuck the ball in the pocket of Charlie's TPX Pro.

"Was this?" the kid said to him.

"What?"

The kid was serious now. "You know the way you throwin."

"I feel pretty good lately, what can I tell you?"

"These college boys here, they feel pretty good," Escobar said. "Got big motions, so they look pretty, too. You *pitch*."

It sounded like peach.

Charlie said, "Let's see what happens when they try to hit it. I've found it's a little different in life when somebody hits back."

Escobar reached down with his right hand and grabbed his crotch. "Them college boys gonna get some tonight," he said. "Right here."

"Well," Charlie said, "it's pretty to think so."

Escobar just looked at him.

"It's some line from a book, my ex-wife used it on me all the time," Charlie said.

"Here's you book tonight," Escobar said, clapping him on the back. "Fassballs up they ass."

Charlie said, "From you lips to God's ears."

HE WALKED TWO in the top of the first, strictly nerves, a momentary choke deal, pure and simple.

Charlie'd always hated it when media guys or fans talked about choking, mostly because they didn't have a clue. But it had always been part of the language of clubhouses and locker rooms. He remembered one time, in the old days, when he'd ended up drinking at P.J. Clarke's with Don Meredith, and finally it had been just the two of them at the table, talking about the only things that mattered late at night, at least according to Meredith, sports and pussy. And somehow they'd gotten around to the subject of choking, and what it really was.

You sat around the bar long enough, you always came to the hour when you got down to it.

"I'll tell you exactly what chokin' is, and was, and always has been," Meredith said. "It ain't nothin' more than a cold rush a shit to the heart."

Charlie felt it at the start now, even over here in Precious, New Jersey, pitching to college boys, just because it was the first time he'd pitched to anybody who was taking the whole thing seriously since Piazza.

So he threw eight balls out of the strike zone out of his first ten pitches, and then with runners on first and second, he gave up a bloop double down the rightfield line to Ridgefield Park's number-three hitter, a guy about six-five swinging one of those shiny new maple bats everybody'd started using since Barry Bonds had used maple to hit 73 home runs. Charlie was fine with the bats but thought that maybe Bonds's power surge at the end of his career might have had a little something to do with the fact that he'd showed up one year in San Francisco with a whole new body, looking like the black version of the Michelin Man.

The number-three hitter's name, Kendall had told Charlie, was Jason Carlino, and his father was the prick who'd coached the New York Knights but got fired because he wouldn't play that girl Dee Gerard they'd signed a few years ago, the point guard babe who'd lit up the NBA for a couple of months before going back to Europe someplace to run a bar.

"Throw him changeups in to start, and he'll be so out in front he'll either fall on his ass or pull them 900 feet foul," Kendall said. "Go away after that and he'll chase it so bad he'll end up looking like a drunk falling down a flight of stairs."

Charlie threw him junk inside, twice, like Kendall had said. Carlino, a righthanded hitter, pulled the first one toward the Parkway. Then he came with what felt like a perfect splitter, a foot off the plate, dying like a sick bird when it got there, but Carlino reached out and got the ball on the end of the cool maple bat and just dropped it behind Gus at first base. One of those cheap hits that Charlie'd always imagined had grease dripping off them. The Orioles' coach had started the runners for some goddamn reason, even with nobody out, so the hit scored two runs. Charlie struck out the next guy and then threw another nasty splitter that the number-five hitter pounded to Ed Bell at short, and Bell, with those soft hands, started the double play that ended the inning.

Charlie was saying shit, shit, shit to himself as he came off of the mound, thinking of the two walks that had started the inning, when he noticed that Jason Carlino had come up beside him and was walking with him toward the Colonials' bench.

Charlie noticed that Jason Carlino was holding a baseball.

"Mr. Stoddard?"

Charlie looked at the ball, then at him, somehow knowing it wasn't just any ball, it was the one with which he'd just pitched the first inning, after Carlino had lost that long foul ball into the woods.

The ball Jason Carlino'd hit for that greasy double.

"My name's Jason Carlino? I play first base for the Orioles?"

Up close, he was a pretty good-looking kid, even darker than Rob Kendall, with long sideburns.

Charlie said, "Jason, I don't know what the protocol is over here in the Future Baseball Stars of America League? But generally I like to get my arm warm after the inning and spend as little time as possible chillin'— is that how you boys say it?—with the other team."

He kept walking toward the Colonials' bench, hoping that would blow the kid off.

Carlino stayed with him.

"I know, I know," Carlino said. "I was just, well, I didn't know if you'd hang around after the game, or even 'til the end of the game, so I was wondering if you'd mind signing this ball for me? The one I got the hit off you?"

Charlie stopped now, took a deep breath, about to tell Jason Carlino what he wanted to do with the ball, and where, when Rob Kendall, who'd watched the whole thing, came walking over and casually handed him a ballpoint pen.

"Hey, Jason," Kendall said.

"Rob."

"C'mon," Kendall said. "Sign the kid's ball so you can go put your jacket on. I'll tell you how to pitch this asshole next time."

He grinned at Carlino, then gave Charlie a look that said, Sign.

Charlie signed.

"Wow," Carlino said. "Thanks."

"Gives you goosebumps, doesn't it?" Charlie said.

When they got back to the bench, Kendall said, "He's much bigger than you are. Much. And you've got to face him at least twice more. I just wanted to point that out before you said something hurtful."

"Sign the goddamn ball during the *game?*"

Kendall said, "He's just as excited as the rest of us about the great Charlie Stoddard joining our brotherhood."

"Eat me," Charlie said.

"I noticed from the peanut gallery you didn't throw any gas," Kendall said.

"Not yet."

"The two splitters were bitchy, though."

"Wait 'til I back them up with gas."

"Which you haven't thrown."

"Yet."

Ruben Escobar came over, sat next to Charlie, slapped him on the knee with his right hand, one of those catcher's hands that looked like somebody'd run it over with a truck, Escobar already having taken too many foul balls at whatever age he actually was.

"You okay with Ruben's pitches?"

Charlie knew he meant the pitches he'd called in the top of the first.

"I am loving your peaches," Charlie said.

Escobar said, "Maybe next inning I give you the finger." He put up his middle finger and said, "Like you said, for the fassball."

"If I shake it off, it isn't because I don't love you, it's because I'm still easing into this."

The catcher nodded. "No prolem. Ruben know you ain gonna pitch like a *maricon* all night."

"*Maricon?*" Charlie said. "That's not a good thing, right?"

"Fag thing," Ruben Escobar said.

Charlie walked the leadoff batter in the second, too, then got the next three guys, the bottom of the order, including the Orioles' pitcher, whose stuff Rob Kendall had described as matronly.

He finally opened up in the third, two outs, Jason Carlino up.

Charlie motioned for Ruben Escobar to come out to the mound.

Ruben took his time getting there and then said, "You mees me?"

"I want to go away, then away again. I don't care if he swings or not. I don't care if I go two-oh on him. Then let's have some fun."

"Fassball?"

"Up the ass."

Carlino was a good soldier, swinging and missing at the first pitch, fouling the second one back. Oh-two now instead of two-oh.

Charlie gave his shoulders a good shake. Like he used to. Felt the familiar grip of his four-seamer, *his* hard-on pitch, turning the ball slightly in the pocket of his glove to get it just right. A big-league hitter probably would've tried to think along with him here, wondering if he was putting a splitter grip on the ball or a fastball grip or what. Thinking Charlie was going to throw one even further out of the strike zone than the first two had been. But also having it in the back of his thick head that Charlie might come in on him, try to sneak a fastball right down the middle because *Charlie* was thinking he, the batter, wasn't going to chase shit and would be taking all the way.

Jason Carlino stepped out, because he thought Charlie was taking too much time.

Which Charlie was.

When the assholes were anxious, make them wait.

Carlino stepped back in. Charlie went into his windup, arms coming

up, then he was rocking back on his right heel and everything was starting to come together now, as he turned slightly toward third, left knee
coming up, not feeling like a pitcher now, even if he was doing all the familiar pitcher things, feeling more like a fighter gathering himself to
throw a big punch, loading up on his right leg now, arm coming forward, not thinking about arm angles or release points or any of it, even
though there should have been a shitload of rust on every bit of this,
every single move he was making, just locked in now on Ruben Escobar's glove, throwing a fastball that Jason Carlino didn't swing at until it
was in Ruben's glove, Carlino still holding his follow-through as Ruben
rolled the ball back toward the pitcher's mound and got out of his crouch
and jogged away from home plate.

Charlie was walking before Jason Carlino finished his swing.

From behind him, he heard Carlino say, "Jesus H. Christ."

Charlie got to the chalk line between third and home and stopped,
turned around.

"Hey," he said, like he'd forgotten something.

Now he turned, walked back to the mound now, picked up the ball,
held it up so Carlino could see it.

"You want me to sign this one, too, slugger?" Charlie shouted, loud
enough for the players on both teams to hear.

Jason Carlino just stared, like Mr. Chips had suddenly turned on him.

"I'm actually surprised anybody found it," Charlie said, "considering
how far I stuck it up your ass."

There was no getting around it, Grace had told him once.

If you're born round, she said, you don't die square.

He was careful after that, treating the rest of the game like it was his
first start in spring training, like it was the first week in March and he
was going to get four innings, tops, no matter how juiced he felt, how
good his arm felt. He wanted to go six tonight, but he told Rob Kendall
to make sure he stayed under a hundred.

"Pitches, or miles per hour?" Kendall said.

He threw a few more fastballs like the one he'd used to knock Jason Carlino's dick off; the rest of the time he fooled around with his stuff, like a kid with a new toy. Or an old one he'd found in the back of his closet along with the rest of the shit he thought he'd put away for good. Charlie even tried to see if he could throw a goddamn changeup, the goddamn pitch he knew could have kept him in the big leagues, but one he had about as much success mastering as that TiVo deal on your television, the one that said, in theory, anyway, that you could tape and watch only the shows you wanted to watch.

Only when Charlie would hit playback, thinking he was going to get the Yankees-Mariners game, he always ended up with Emeril the shrieking chef.

Somehow he'd never had the touch or the discipline or maybe the lack of ego to throw the change. Maybe he was just too stubborn, after having been able to blow everybody away when he had the arm. Most people he knew always voted for stubborn. Dick Pole, his pitching coach with the Indians, had told him once, and kept telling him, to look around at all the old guys who couldn't throw a fastball harder than eighty-five miles an hour to save their lives and won twenty games every year throwing changeups away. Charlie knew it was true. Tommy Glavine of the Braves had never had the arm like Charlie did and was still going, on his way to the Hall of Fame, not just because he was one of the toughest and smartest bastards who'd ever pitched, but because he could throw his change low and away to hitters, righthanded or lefthanded, he didn't give a rat's ass, he'd throw it anytime he wanted. He'd mix in his fastball occasionally, show the batter what passed for his hard stuff at least once an at-bat, then get him to look bad on another changeup and go sit down.

Charlie had tried, in the majors and minors and even one winter in Puerto Rico. But he gripped it too hard or threw it too easy, or too hard, and eventually he'd leave one up and out over the plate and get another case of whiplash watching the ball land in the upper deck. . . .

Just not tonight. The Orioles were so intent on setting themselves for the kind of in-your-face fastball he'd thrown to Jason Carlino that he had them off-balance the rest of the way. He walked a couple of guys in the fourth, trying to be too fine with the off-speed stuff, and gave up two hits in the fifth, one of them an infield job when he vapor-locked on a slow roller to Gus's right at first base, just out of the reach of the Colonials' second baseman, a crewcutted little guy who reminded Charlie of the young Pete Rose.

Charlie should have been over covering first; pitchers are always supposed to be there on anything hit to the right side that the first baseman moves on, you're supposed to be hauling ass from the jump, busting it over there like the batter coming out of the box. Only Charlie had just stood and watched the play, and by the time he woke up, remembering a move he used to make in his sleep because he'd always had to practice it about a thousand times in Florida, it was too late. This was the sixth, which he'd decided was his last inning for sure, especially after Rob Kendall had told him he was up to ninety-two pitches.

He struck out the next two guys, the runner still on first, and then it was Jason Carlino again. Charlie decided, what the hell, and started him off with the same fastball he'd thrown him in the third. Then another one, a little something off it. It was oh-two, again. Charlie could see how hard Carlino was gripping the bat now, looking for one rip. So he threw what passed for his Glavine change, a rotten cantaloupe that died a foot off the plate. Carlino was so far out in front, the maple bat flew out of his hands, scattering Rob Kendall and the three other guys sitting on the Colonials' bench.

"Incoming!" Charlie said.

He gave Jason Carlino one last, long look and walked to the bench, through for the night.

"You weren't very nice to young Jason," Rob Kendall said.

Charlie said, "This is still hardball, right?"

"Last time I checked."

"Tell him that's why he wears a fucking helmet."

It was later, over at the topless bar in Fort Lee called I'll Show You Mine, that he got down to it with Rob Kendall. The two of them were seated at a table as close to the huge, horseshoe-shaped stage as you could be without being part of one of production numbers that Kendall had described as smutty and tasteful at the same time.

"There's some very interesting storylines, you can tell already," he said.

The theme to the number just ending, as best as Charlie could tell, was Lesbian Speeding Ticket, featuring a lot more leg room than Charlie remembered in the backseat of a Firebird convertible.

They had only been there about half an hour, but Charlie was working on his third Scotch. When the waitress, dressed like a shirtless schoolmarm, set the drink down on the table, Kendall had said, "Wait a second, you told me your body was a temple now."

Charlie picked up the glass and said, "*Shalom.*"

He knew he didn't have to see Chang for another three days and didn't plan to pitch again for another week—even though he hadn't told Kendall yet that he planned to pitch again. He had also decided after the second set at I'll Show You Mine that he was about half in love with the featured dancer, a Julia Roberts reminds-me-of he wanted to take to the Sheraton down the street, the new one across from the big CNBC complex just off Route 46.

He'd already used Rob Kendall's cell phone to make sure they had rooms.

"Obviously, you're feeling lucky," Kendall said.

Charlie told him to look around, he didn't think luck was going to be as essential here as, say, at one of those new casinos owned by the descendants of Sitting Bull.

"I'm just celebrating my first win of any kind since 1997," he said. "Doesn't a guy have a right to celebrate something like that?"

They both knew the deal, anyway, without Charlie saying anything;

there had never been a triumph in Charlie Stoddard's pitching career that didn't demand a celebration.

Showtime Charlie Stoddard, who'd never missed a party or a start.

In I'll Show You Mine now, Rob Kendall said, "What's this all about, Charlie? Really? There's no way you just came over here for laughs."

"No," Charlie said, "I did not." He lit a cigarette and said to Kendall, "This is off the record, right?"

Kendall made a motion that tried to take in all the naked flesh in the place at once. "No, Charlie," he said. "It's a Barbara Walters special."

Julia Roberts was leaning over them now, long red hair in her eyes, smiling at Charlie, about to take off the kind of top gas-station attendants wear.

Technically, it wasn't a top, it was the whole outfit, there was no bottom.

Charlie motioned her closer and then stuck a hundred-dollar bill in the pocket under "Nick's Exxon."

"I'm coming back," he said to Rob Kendall.

TED HARTNETT SAT in his office at Fenway Park, which was a little bigger than the kind of prison cell you might get in Afghanistan or Turkey.

Hartnett liked the place fine. He was happy anywhere he had a door he could shut.

He had his pregame and postgame sessions with the media in here, just because there was no other logical place to do it at Fenway, which Hartnett always believed had been designed by hobbits. He had his coaches' meeting in here, usually about two in the afternoon. The rest of the time, both his players and his coaches knew the deal with him, and the deal, basically, was this:

Leave him the fuck alone.

Hartnett had been in baseball from the time he'd signed with the

Mets out of high school in Nashua, New Hampshire, and for more than twenty years he'd been part of one team or another from south Florida to Portland, Oregon. It meant he'd spent most of his waking hours with his teammates, in the clubhouse before the game, in the bullpen or the dugout, in the clubhouse after the game, in some bar later, just because there was some rule that had been passed in baseball that you were supposed to go straight to the bar once you left the ballpark. Being a professional athlete, he'd always thought, was a lot like joining the Army and never really getting out, signing a lifetime contract guaranteeing that the only time you were really alone was when you were in bed.

And, if you were a red-blooded, skirt-chasing American jock, you weren't even supposed to be alone then.

Charlie Stoddard, his old roommate, had always thought bringing a girl back to the room with him almost every night of his career, even when he still had Grace waiting for him back home in New York, was just part of the whole long baseball day, like stretching or batting practice or infield. But then Charlie had had a phobia about sleeping alone that Ted thought had been as strong as the one for people afraid of flying.

Ted Hartnett liked being alone.

He liked it best now that he was a manager, which was something he'd started planning for when he'd figured out, way early in the game, that as smart as he was, as great as he was defensively, in throwing and blocking the goddamn plate and calling a game, he was never going to hit enough to be a star, or even enough to be first-string for very long. He never broadcast the fact that he was in training to be a manager, but somehow people knew, just by the way he'd be locked into the game, even watching from the bullpen. *Especially* from the bullpen, where it never took long for the relief pitchers out there with him to know enough to keep their distance. Which was usually fine: Relief pitchers, especially the bottom-of-the-staff guys who worked middle relief, were all the same, they were just there to fuck around until the phone rang and the bullpen coach told one of them to grab a glove and start warming up. Until then, they just shot the shit, or tried to get phone numbers off the bad girls leaning over the railing. Or kept searching the outfield bleachers like surveillance cameras until one of them would say, Jesus H. Christ, will you look at the tits on that one? All the while, Ted Hartnett, backup catcher, or sometimes the backup to the backup, was in his own little world, thinking baseball thoughts, about the count or the situation in the game or who he'd have warming up if he were managing the game. Charlie used to joke with writers all the time about how little talking his buddy Gabby did. But if you could get inside his head during a game, Charlie said, there'd be such a racket you'd think it was some kids' playground at recess.

Nothing had changed now that he really was the manager. If you were a Red Sox coach or player or even clubhouse attendant, and you didn't know how to keep your mouth shut around him, you'd get the kind of look Eastwood used to give to punks in the *Dirty Harry* movies right before he showed them that his gun was a lot bigger than theirs and asked if they felt lucky today.

Sometimes he'd be in a real office on the road, in one of those new designer ballparks, where his office would look like a suite at the Four Seasons, outfitted with everything except a Jacuzzi and walk-in closet, watching some game beamed onto the oversized television screen by satellite. And they'd show one of the dugouts, and there would be the manager with his bench coach next to him, and the coach would be chattering away a mile a minute.

Hartnett would watch them and think: Another asshole who thinks he's a wife.

Wally Garner, his bench coach and best friend on the team—maybe his only friend—said you got along dandy with Ted Hartnett just as long as you got your ass to the ballpark on time and then understood that you talked to the manager only after he talked to you first.

Hartnett wasn't one of those modern-day managers or coaches who thought of themselves as guidance counselors. He didn't see ball games, no matter how insanely long they were, as group therapy, or as a chance to bond or to listen to somebody impress you with how much they thought they knew about baseball.

"You're by yourself even when you're with somebody," Garner said to him one time.

"Shit," Hartnett said. "I've blown my cover."

"Once the game is over, you've got no life," Garner said, because he could say things like this, whether Hartnett wanted to hear them or not, just because they'd known each other since they were playing against each other in Class-A ball.

"I'll have a life when I'm done with this life."

"See, that's the thing you don't seem to be able to understand, there's never gonna be no done with this," Garner said. He'd never been more than a utility infielder and had still managed to last thirteen years in the big leagues as a player. Now he was working as Hartnett's top sergeant, another smart guy off the bench in training to manage someday. "There's just gonna be baseball for you until finally nobody wants you no more, which isn't gonna be anytime soon, the way we're going. All you know is this. Fuck," Wally Garner said, "all you *are* is this."

"What, being married didn't count?"

"Not when you marry the first runner-up."

"What's that supposed to mean?"

"You know exactly what it means. You married the one who was the first runner-up in the Girl of Your Dreams contest. Yeah, that had a great chance of working out, I'm amazed you weren't married longer than Bob Hope." Garner shook his head, resigned. "You've been carrying around that torch longer than the fucking Olympic torch has been *lit*."

It was just one more conversation between the two of them that ended with Hartnett giving Wally Garner the look that they both knew meant, get out, he wanted to be alone. The way he was alone now, in the white-walled office with all the stupid red trim, Stan Getz playing softly on the pretty decent sound system they'd managed to set up for him in here, having the kind of pregame meeting he really liked best, the one with only him in it. Him and his scouting reports. Him with all his computer printouts showing how his guys did against the other team's starter. Him with lineup cards spread out on his desk, different ones on different-colored index cards, seeing which one looked right to him, like he was trying to put some kind of puzzle together.

Him with the stack of newspaper clips his p.r. man, Kevin Oslin, would leave every day before he got to Fenway, not just from the *Globe* and *Herald,* but all the internet stuff telling about what the other teams in the American League had done the night before. Oslin would leave the out-of-town stuff, even knowing that Hartnett already knew most of the details from Detroit and Cleveland and Anaheim and Oakland because he'd go home after the game, when he finally was ready to leave the office, win or lose, and then watch every highlight from every game until he fell asleep. The exceptions were when he decided to watch some of the tape of the game the Red Sox had just played, watch it from start to finish, until the sun came up, looking for some small thing he might have missed yesterday that might help him win today.

Or maybe he'd sit there in his apartment in Cambridge, a couple of blocks from the Harvard Coop, or the suite the Red Sox got for him on the road, drinking coffee, wondering what the hell he was going to do about a lead that had been officially cut in half, had shrunk from sixteeen to eight games now that Tyler Haas was gone for the season and Lew Gentry, his number-three starter, a lefthander whose arm had been rebuilt three times, was on his way to the disabled list. They were going to do the MRI on Gentry's arm this afternoon at Mass General, but Hartnett already knew Gentry had done something bad the night before against the Rangers, maybe something final, just by the way he'd dropped to his knees in front of the mound after that last pitch in the top of the sixth.

Hartnett was just waiting for the doctors to call and tell him that the pictures of Gentry's elbow looked like they had worms crawling across it.

They had been rolling at the start of July, god*damn* they were rolling, looking like they were going to have the kind of regular season Seattle had had a few years before, when the Mariners had ended up winning 116 games, even if they had ended up losing to the Yankees in the play-offs. Sixteen games ahead. Sixteen. A Red Sox team doing that. Maybe Hartnett should have known right then that something was going to happen, something bad, just the pull of history at work here like the pull of the moon on the tide.

And now, just like that, it was the 28th of July, which meant it had taken four weeks exactly for the Yankees to cut the lead in half. When he looked over at the big day-by-day schedule on his office wall, he did feel like he was in solitary, looking at two more years of hard time instead of two months, wondering how the hell he could hold off the Yankees with three starting pitchers and nobody in the bullpen he trusted behind them and kids in the minors greener than outfield grass.

He thought about what the lead over the Yankees had been and what it was now, and he could swear he could sometimes hear a clock ticking in here.

He heard a knock, and before he could say, "Come," Kevin Oslin's head appeared inside his door.

Hartnett said, "At least you knocked this time."

"The Jesuits taught us to be polite."

"I thought what you mostly learned to do at Boston College was drink."

Oslin said, "Got another cheery Bosox anniversary I thought I'd like to share with you."

Hartnett didn't even bother to look up. "Don't bother, I already know what it is."

"My ass."

"This was the last day in July of '78 when we were still fourteen games ahead of the Yankees, before the Yanks started the big comeback that ended with Bucky Fucking Dent's home run."

"Damn," Oslin said, "you're good."

"You forget I'm from New Hampshire," Hartnett said.

"Do not," he said. "Live free or die."

"I'm from around here, is what I mean," Ted Hartnett said. "I know all the gloomy shit by heart, same as you do." He looked over his reading glasses at Oslin. "Just on account of, you better if you sit in this office. You take this job, wherever you're from, and don't know all the Pearl Harbor days in the history of this franchise, you've got no chance, because everybody from Eastport to Block Island who's a Red Sox fan thinks you don't share their pain."

Oslin was a kid, still just twenty-five, three years out of BC. He'd hooked on with the Red Sox as an intern after he figured out, after only one year writing high schools at the *Globe*, that he wasn't ever going to be good enough to cover the Sox. He'd grown up a Sox fan in Marblehead, but he didn't treat it like the tragic fatal illness most of them did. He was the one who'd told Hartnett his all-time favorite Red Sox line: Baseball in Boston isn't a matter of life and death; it's much more serious than that.

He said, "You go through the clips yet?"

"No," he said. "I watched the end of the Yankee-Mariners game from Seattle when I got home. Fucking New York's down, two out in the ninth, and they still come back and win."

"There's a story I thought you might be interested in, I put it on top," Oslin said. "From a Jersey paper. *The Record*."

Hartnett cleared away his printouts and index cards, and there it was, right on top like Oslin had said, with this headline:

SHOWTIME AT YOGI'S PLACE:
CHARLIE STODDARD TO START FOR JACKALS

Hartnett adjusted his little round reading glasses and read enough of Rob Kendall's story to get a sense of it, the bare bones being that Charlie, who hadn't pitched in the big leagues in five years blah blah blah, was going to make this start for the Jersey Jackals, an independent team that played in the little ballpark behind Yogi Berra's museum over in Montclair, the proceeds from the game going to Yogi's favorite charity, the Boy Scouts of New Jersey blah blah blah.

"Cool, huh?" Oslin said.

"What's cool about it?"

"Your old rooms doing something like that for charity."

"I'm going to let you in on a little secret about my old rooms, and then I want you to beat it," Hartnett said. "He always thought Charity was just another lap dancer's name, like Faith or Hope."

He picked up the clip, put it back down, looked up and saw Oslin still standing there. "What part of 'beat it' didn't you understand?"

"You're curious about this, aren't you? You can admit it to me, I won't even tell Wally you showed some normal, human-type curiosity."

"I'm not curious."

"Sure you are," Oslin said, grinning at him. A kid who didn't faint dead away when he got Hartnett's famous glare. "Why don't you give him a call, find out what's going on?"

"No."

"I could wait and ask . . ."

"No."

Hartnett looked up him. "The door?"

"Closing it," Oslin said, "on my way out."

Ted Hartnett would find out about Charlie later. Maybe Grace would know, Charlie always said she knew everything, even though they both knew she didn't.

For now, he sat there in his office and thought about October of 1988, when it all changed for all of them. When he had told Charlie he could get three more outs when he should have known better than anybody that he couldn't.

There was a time of night when Grace knew it could only be Charlie calling, usually around eleven, San Francisco time, when he was finally back in the apartment after he had left The Last Good Year or Elaine's or one of those other places.

Or sometimes he hadn't been out at all, which meant he hadn't put himself in the line of fire for some model or flight attendant or dancer or aerobics instructor or actress or cheerleader; or some socialite who'd finally figured out a creative way to get into Charlie's tuxedo after her husband had spent the whole charity dinner talking to him about the old Mets.

"I was strong all night," he told Grace once, when she pressed him for details on where he'd really been until three in the morning. "Right up until I was weak."

"Spirit or flesh?" Grace said.

"Well, both," Charlie said.

Even when he didn't go out, he was up late, his explanation always the same, that his body was still on baseball time. And if he didn't have somebody to talk to, he would go find a bar someplace, no matter what hour it was, because there was always a bar open somewhere in New York and always somebody in there who wanted to buy him a drink.

Grace knew a lot of things about Charlie Stoddard, too many, that he didn't know about himself, and one was this:

It was as if his right arm, his pitching arm, had gotten shot off in a war.

All because he'd pitched one time when he shouldn't have.

That was a little dramatic, the part about his arm being shot off. She knew that, too. But there had always been something dramatic about him, all the way back to the day she'd met him in Mrs. Benedict's sociology class at Lexington High School. Like he was a kid playing the part of the star jock in a school play. Grace had always loved the boy in him, the fun, even after his definition of fun turned out to be way too broad for her.

Broad, she always thought, being the operative word.

She'd loved him even after he'd crossed the line, all those years before Grace Under Pressure became big when she wouldn't have anything to do with him while she had her hands full with another bad boy just like him. . . .

He was still handsome, even as tired as he looked to her sometimes when they were together, or as sad, even as he kept acting like nothing was wrong and it was still his job to be the life of the party. But it was more than looks that had drawn her to Charlie Stoddard in the first place, and he still could draw her to him when she'd occasionally drop her guard. It was more than the way they'd fit together in bed, even if people had always talked about how different the two of them were, as if for all his baseball talent and his fame even before he'd turned twenty, Grace had somehow married the pool guy.

What no one seemed to understand was how much Charlie had always made her laugh.

No guy since—no matter how much they had going for them, all the guys who thought their bank accounts were going to make her weak with desire—had ever made her laugh like he did.

She sat in the front of her house on Washington Street, in Presidio Heights, one of those San Francisco places that looked as small as a row house from the sidewalk and then seemed to go forever once you got inside, with high ceilings and long, spiral staircases and more rooms than you'd think was possible when you were coming in through the garage. That was Grace's house on Washington Street, across the street from the famous director and three doors down from the reclusive comedian, the interior looking like a spread for *Architectural Digest*, which it had been a couple of months before, Grace on the cover, reading in her sun room.

Grace on the cover of anything sold now, everybody knew that; she was the kind of sensation Charlie had been in baseball twenty years ago.

She sat in the sun room now, only the Tiffany lamp next to her lighting it, sipping a new Chardonnay from Napa she thought they should be stocking at Grace Under Pressure. Even though she'd sold the place, she still kept an office upstairs, and the new manager, Giselle, was up five times a day when Grace was there, asking for advice or just bouncing things off her, and it was all fine with Grace, she got bored up there sometimes, writing or going over the photographs or layouts for the new book. She wanted to go downstairs and just have her hands on things, the way she used to, be up to her elbows in the day-to-day energy of the place. Her place.

She'd never admit it, but sometimes she hoped Charlie would call.

Grace knew it could never work for them, oh God no, not ever again, he was never going to clean up his act entirely, it would have happened by now, especially after everything he'd been through. Somehow, Charlie kept running in place, kidding himself the way he always could, knowing how much it still hurt that he'd had it all taken away from him, but not fully understanding, even now, exactly how much.

You're the smart one, Gracie, he always told her.

Even about baseball, he said.

Yeah, yeah, yeah, Grace thought, hearing his voice in her head, yeah, she was smart enough to know that smart had nothing to do with why you loved somebody, why you kept loving the bad boy who always made you laugh.

The phone rang, at the Charlie hour, five past eleven, as if he'd been reading her mind.

Only this time it wasn't him.

"Did you know he's pitching again?"

No hello, or how are you, just get right into it.

No small talk with this one, ever.

The two men in her life, so much alike and so incredibly different.

"You mean in whatever-that-league-is over in New Jersey? He mentioned something about it the other day."

"That was just some kind of bullshit has-been league. This is an actual minor league team. The Jackals, they're called."

He told her how to look up the story Rob Kendall had written in his newspaper, and Grace said she'd call it up after they were off the phone.

"Why do you even care, T?" she said.

"I don't."

Then he said, "I'm just wondering what's going on, is all."

"I think all that's going on," Grace said, "is that he's bored and having a little fun until the next old-timers' game. Or until he can figure out a way to get his next round of applause."

"Then why make such a big thing of it in the press? You know how it goes. He does anything, and then pretty soon I have to answer questions about it. Like I'm supposed to care."

Grace said, "I'll talk to him in the morning. It's a little late in New York to call him now."

"Not for Showtime Charlie."

Grace acted as if she hadn't heard. "I fell asleep for a while. Did you guys win tonight?"

"Barely. Two-one. We're still not hitting for shit."

There was a silence, but she was used to that by now, it was as much as part of the conversation as anything else.

"You'll find out what's going on?"

"Tomorrow, I promise."

"I love you," he said.

"Me, too," Grace said.

7

"**CAN I ASK** you something?" Charlie said to Chang.

"Ask me this, why don't you?" Chang said, pulling Charlie's left arm behind him, hard, like a cop trying to restrain a perp. "Ask me why I gave up a date with the new Channel 11 Lotto girl to drive all the way over to Yogi Bear, New Jersey, to watch you give up, how many runs did you give up last night?"

"Seven," Charlie said. "And it's Yogi Berra, not Yogi Bear. Yogi Bear was the cartoon character. His trusty sidekick was Boo Boo, not some Chinese-American prick."

Chang pulled harder on his arm, making Charlie yelp.

"I thought it was eight runs," Chang said.

"Eight total," Charlie said, "seven earned. Six hits, six strikeouts, one home run, three walks. And I hit a guy, just because he irritated me one time by stepping out when I was ready to pitch."

Chang told Charlie to lean forward, then placed one hand on his left shoulder and grabbed his left wrist and gave another pull, clearly confusing Charlie with a slot machine.

Charlie said, "I know you couldn't tell it by the way I pitched last night, but I'm still right-handed."

"We'll get to that side in a minute," Chang said.

Then: "You haven't been doing your rotation exercises. And if you don't do them, and I mean religiously, you have no shot."

"I have, too, been doing them," Charlie said, trying to sound indignant, but knowing this was just one more time when he was caught.

"Don't lie to me. I've told you plenty of times already, if you're not going to take this seriously, I'll go find another has-been looking to better himself."

Chang took the death grip off his wrist. "I think has-been is a little impersonal," Charlie said.

"It's what you are," Chang said. "A celebrity has-been. I train a lot of actors like that, ones who haven't had a big part since Bush's father was president but still think every head in the room's supposed to turn when they walk in. Now I got you, whining about these card shows at the same time you're scared to death people are going to forget you." Charlie noticed that the only time he ever saw Chang sweat was when he got this worked up about something. "Go lay down," he said now.

"You ever notice you talk to me like I'm a dog?"

"I'm actually trying to get the dog out of you."

"Woof," Charlie said. "Woof."

He got on his stomach and then Chang was rubbing some cream into the area between his right shoulder and his neck, some version of Ben-Gay as hot as an iron.

"Does this stuff have a name? No shit, how come none of these jars ever have names on them?"

"Shut up and listen for a second," Chang said. "I'm going to put you out for a couple of minutes, I want to try something and it won't work the way I want when you're awake. You said your arm felt dead last night, right? The first time that happened since you started throwing for real?"

"Yeah," Charlie said. "It would happen the same way in spring training sometimes, after my first couple of starts, like halfway through March. It was like my arm was idling for a few days, then it would come back as good as ever." Charlie paused and said, "Back when I had the arm, I mean."

"Close your eyes."

Charlie did.

"Keep taking deep breaths."

He did that, too, then felt Chang putting two fingers in the same area where he'd just rubbed the nameless cream, pressing down hard on a muscle Charlie thought he actually knew the name of, Chang had mentioned it before. Ulnar? No, ulnar was in his arm somewhere.

He was still trying to come up with the name when the lights went out.

Chang was talking when Charlie woke up, as if he hadn't stopped while Charlie had been asleep. It happened that way with girls sometimes after sex, when they wanted to review the whole thing like it was some controversial play in a football game. Charlie would nod off, and when he'd wake up ,they'd still be going on wanting to know if the same rockets had gone off for him.

Only now what he said to Chang was, "What the fuck was *that*? That Vulcan death grip Spock used on *Star Trek*?"

Chang said, "It was just a little trick I learned out in Colorado one time, from a chiropractor who went straight with ART. Now sit up," he said, slapping Charlie on the ass.

"I thought you might be a Vulcan, the first day," Charlie said, still feeling groggy. "You just had a little work done on the ears, to make them look regulation."

"Your arm's fine now," Chang said, ignoring him. "But I want you to throw today, even though I know you said you never throw the day after a start, you wait for your next throw day."

"Hardly anybody does it that way. Maybe Clemens, but he's a freak."

Chang said, "Hardly anybody tries to come back after being out of baseball for an entire goddamn Presidential administration to pitch in the big leagues."

"Who said I thought I could pitch in the big leagues again?"

"You."

"Not to you."

"You didn't have to."

Charlie said, "I'm not gonna do shit pitching the way I did last night."

"I forgot," Chang said. "You were going to start throwing seriously again after five years of not doing that, and then a couple of weeks later you were going to shut out the Yankees at Yankee Stadium in front of fifty thousand people." He gave Charlie the asshole look he gave him a lot. "You really do live on the Planet Charlie, don't you?" Charlie started to say something, and then Chang said, "You want to quit? Quit."

"I didn't think it was all going to be easy, I'm not a total moron."

"You sure?"

"About which part? Me not thinking it was going to be easy or me not being a total moron?"

"The first part," Chang said.

Charlie smiled now. Caught again. "Maybe I did think it was gonna be easy," he said.

Sure he did. Who was he kidding here? Maybe he did? Of *course* he did. The game had been against Winnipeg. Yogi had even shown up to throw the first pitch, then sat with his wife, Carmen, both of them up there watching him from the back porch of the museum that served as Yogi's private luxury box when he felt like taking in a game.

Charlie repaid the honor from old Number 8 by going out there with nothing.

Less than nothing, really.

They'd packed the place, even had to build temporary bleachers for the extra media who'd showed up, all the New York papers and local television stations, plus ESPN and Fox Sports. Both the Yankees and Mets had the night off, so there was a news cycle in sports that Rob Kendall described as being slower than chess. And even though Charlie tried to joke about it afterward, act like it didn't matter—"You see Yogi up there? Shit, even *he* wanted to grab a bat"—he knew he was going to be the one who was the joke, that night on the eleven o'clock news and in the papers the next day, the way he had been all those times when he was at the end of the line, when it was like this every time he went out there. He felt like that little Korean who pitched for the Diamondbacks in the World Series a few years ago, the poor bastard they kept sending out there to serve up bottom-of-the-ninth home runs to the Yankees.

And he'd known while he was warming up. Sometimes you did, and there wasn't a thing you could do about it. This was one of those times. He was throwing on the side with the Jackals' catcher, Darren Preston— when did Darrens start taking over the world, Charlie wondered now that he was hanging around with young guys, them and Justins?—and they'd both known. Preston had played on this same field for Montclair State a few years ago and had knocked around the Tigers' system for a couple of years, he'd told Charlie, and now was back home, still holding on to his own dreams, like one of them still might turn out to be a winning lottery ticket.

After a few minutes on the side, Darren Preston had blown a bubble the size of his head and yelled, "You can go ahead and turn her loose, you want."

"She is loose," Charlie said.

"Then never mind," the kid said.

Then it was two runs for Winnipeg in the first, two in the third, on a home run that some huge black guy hit just inside the left-field foul pole, and finally three more in the fifth. His arm didn't hurt, he *was* loose, he just had no snap on the pitches, no life, no late movement. None of the above. He kept smiling, mugging a little for the press, shrugging his shoulders every time some guy who'd never get near the big leagues hit another rope, as if none of this was a big deal, but the whole time he was thinking that nights like this, exactly like this, the ones when he had nothing, were part of his DNA now.

The Jackals' manager was an old Yankee relief pitcher named Tommy Joyce, middle relief for them back in Charlie's time, trying to use the Jackals to hook on in the majors as a pitching coach. He came out to get Charlie after Charlie had somehow managed to strike out the first Winnipeg batter in the sixth.

"Whyn't you walk off and get a nice cheer from Yogi and the rest of the nice people who came out to see you?" Tommy said.

"You're just allowing me to surrender with dignity," Charlie said.

Joyce turned his head and spit some tobacco juice. "Fuck yeah."

Charlie handed him the ball, waved his cap, got his cheer, bowed from the waist when he passed the media section. Like he was still Showtime Charlie. Then he disappeared into the small dugout. Rob Kendall was waiting for him, Kendall in there to write the big inside story on Charlie's night with the Jersey Jackals.

"Jesus," Kendall said, trying to give him mock horror, "you pitched like me."

He talked to the media behind the first-base stands until he ran out of material about how much he'd sucked, went back into the dugout and thanked Tommy Joyce and the rest of the Jackals for the use of the room, drove straight to The Last Good Year and sat with Healey until it was just the two of them, a little after two in the morning. Finally he was back in his living room, looking straight down Second Avenue, smoking his first cigarette in a couple of weeks, nursing one last Scotch. He thought about calling Grace in California, he knew she'd still be up, but decided against it.

She liked getting his woe-is-me calls about as much as heavy-breather calls.

What was he going to tell her, anyway?

He couldn't pitch?

She already knew that.

"Hel*lo?*" he heard Chang saying now, snapping him out of it. "I *said,* sit up straight and look at me."

The snap in his voice now was like the first morning's, when he'd let Charlie know they were there to work and not fuck around.

Chang said, "I'm serious about what I said before. I'm not going to waste any more of my time with you if you're going to act like this kind of loser."

Charlie wondering now if Chang's mojo included reading minds.

"I'm here, aren't I?" he said.

"Yeah, you're here. Hung over. Counting the minutes 'til you can get outside on Forty-fourth and light a cigarette. Or maybe go someplace and start drinking, telling yourself there's some time zone where it's already happy hour. Telling yourself you're putting in the time, you're really working, but still going about things in the half-assed way I imagine you've done for the last fifteen years or so, or maybe your whole life. Because let me explain something to you: Smoking stiffens your joints. Drinking does the same thing. Even staying up half the night because you want to set the North American bimbo record messes you up if it cuts into the sleep you need. And *all* of that inhibits what we're trying to accomplish here."

It was amazing, Charlie thought, how so many of these sparkling insights sounded like Grace.

"Is that so?" was the best he could do.

"You bet your ass. You come in here feeling sorry for yourself, and even though you don't come right out and ask, I'm supposed to feel sorry for you, too. You had a bad game, and the sportswriters and TV people saw, and now it's nobody-knows-the-trouble-you've-seen all over again."

Charlie said, "You know something? I never have to get married again. I'll just have you bitch at me a couple of times a week, and the rest of the time I'll have fun."

"Let me ask you something, Charlie," Chang said. "How's fun been working out for you?"

He had no snappy answer to that. So he just took it. Why not?

From the time his arm had gone, nobody'd been better at taking shit than he was.

At least he was still good at something.

Maybe there was a book in it: *Taking Shit and Liking It,* by Charlie Stoddard.

"I can still pitch," he said to Chang. "People'll think I'm nuts when they see I'm really trying here. I don't care. People came out last night to watch, and then they went home thinking, Poor old Charlie, at least he raised a lot of money. Poor old Charlie, you should've seen him when he could pitch. And I don't give a shit. I just want to pitch again."

Then he told Chang about Dave Stieb of the Blue Jays, about the kind of arm Stieb had had when he was young, back in the '80s. How Stieb could throw one of the best curve balls anybody had ever seen, and then he'd hurt his arm and finally quit and was out of baseball for five years. And how Stieb's arm had started to feel so good, after all those years, that he'd come back for one more shot, when he was forty-one. Pitched in nineteen games for the Blue Jays in 1998, Charlie knew, because he'd looked it up in the *Baseball Encyclopedia* a couple of nights before, an earned run average of 4.83, fifty innings and twenty-seven strikeouts.

One win.

"You think it was worth it?" Chang said. "One lousy win, after going through all that."

"Not one win," Charlie said. "See, that's the thing. It was one more *time* for him. Which is what everybody wants. Michael Jordan. All those fat football coaches who can't quit. Everybody. Whether they admit it or not. Even the guys who go out on top, the ones who tell you they left the right way, it's all out of their system, the ones who never try to make a comeback, they're full of it. Jordan didn't need the money when he came back with the Wizards. He didn't need to be any more famous. The bastard couldn't live without being *Michael Jordan.* And the only way he could be the Jordan he wanted to be—get the old stroke, the old buzz—was by playing ball again. You think Joe Montana wanted to grow wine in the Napa Valley, or wherever the hell he was trying to grow wine, or play quarterback in the last two minutes of the Super Bowl? It's why he wouldn't fucking quit when the 49ers gave up on him. You think it'd been some lifelong dream of his to go play in Kansas City? He was another one who didn't let go until he finally got his brains scrambled like eggs once too often."

Charlie told Chang about Jim (Catfish) Hunter, dead now to Lou Gehrig's disease, how great Catfish had been with the old Oakland A's teams when they used to win the World Series all the time, but how *his* arm had been shot by 1978. He'd been with the Yankees then, and all the innings he'd pitched for the A's and the Yankees had caught up with him, and people had thought he might even retire before the season was over rather than pitch like some kind of bum. Before he did, though, he'd gone to see some physical therapist a friend had recommended, as a last resort—a guy like you, Charlie told Chang, maybe just ahead of his mojo time—and the guy had done some kind of manipulation thing with Catfish's arm, Charlie couldn't remember the exact details after all these years, some kind of deal where he'd worked the arm in the reverse way of a pitcher's motion.

And all of a sudden, the pain had gone away and the life had come back into Cat's arm, and he could pitch again.

When the Yankees had come back on the Red Sox that year, Catfish had pitched like a star. He hadn't been the ace of the staff, that was Ron Guidry, but all of a sudden Catfish couldn't lose, and the Yankees ended up winning their division and the pennant and the World Series.

Those couple of months were all he'd gotten, his arm was officially shot the next season, and this time he had retired before the season was over.

"He didn't care," Charlie said in Chang's office. "*Because he got those two months. The way Stieb got that one win. Cat even got the win in the last game of the '78 Series against the Dodgers.*"

"One more time," Chang said, not trying to be a wise guy, showing Charlie he got his meaning.

"I want that," Charlie said. "What Cat had."

"Then you've got to do what I tell you," Chang said. "I'm not talking about just doing the exercises. A whole crash program. That means the vitamins I want you to start taking, the cigarettes I want you to stop smoking, and maybe there's no law that says that you have to close the bars every night with your barfly friends."

"I can do that."

"I'm not sure you can. I told you the first day, I can fix your shoulder. I'm going to need some help with that hard head of yours."

"Ellie said you were a miracle worker."

"I'm not," Chang said. He was wearing biker shorts on this day, a green "Bridgehampton Library" t-shirt. Charlie also noticed he'd buzzed his hair in the last couple of days. "I'm just a guy who really is ahead of his mojo time." He actually allowed himself to smile. "When are you pitching again? In a game, I mean."

"I'm not sure . . ."

"No bullshit, okay? Starting right here, today."

"I sold out the park for the Jackals. They basically told me to come back anytime. I thought I'd take a few days off and then throw for a couple, and if I felt all right, maybe go back and give it one more shot next week."

"Play it out from there," Chang said. "Past next week. Where do you want to be next month? Provided you don't trip over your dick in the meantime."

"I want to pitch for the Red Sox," Charlie said.

"Why them?"

"I've got my reasons."

"You keep saying they need pitching the most."

Charlie said, "It's a little more complicated than that."

"When do you plan to pitch this big idea to them, so to speak?"

"Soon," Charlie said. "I'm not getting any younger, you know."

"Actually, maybe you are."

"You Chinese are so good with mysterious."

"Right," Chang said. "That, and extra starch."

CHARLIE GOT OUT to Yankee Stadium at noon, knowing Ted Hartnett would already be in the visitors' clubhouse at Yankee Stadium, getting ready for a game that wouldn't start until seven o'clock. The plan was to get to him early, then get the hell out of there, before all the craziness of a Yankees–Red Sox series started up later in the afternoon.

Charlie'd never pitched for either team, but everybody in baseball knew the Yankees against the Red Sox was one of those fierce rivalries that made sportswriters damp.

It was different with the players, most of whom just said what they thought the media wanted to hear when talking about the importance of any rivalry in sports, even this one. He'd laugh watching *SportsCenter,* watching these young guys who barely knew which of the two teams Joe

DiMaggio and Ted Williams had played for, talking about all the history between the teams, how there was nothing bigger in sports, no sir, than a big Yankees–Red Sox series, either here or up in Boston. But they all knew it was a rivalry only up in the stands, and by the first pitch tonight, the stands would be dumber than body piercing, all the drunks in their Red Sox t-shirts and Yankees t-shirts trying to out-shout each other about which team sucked more. By that time, Charlie planned to be back downtown, safely at his yoga class at the Reebok Sports Club.

Yoga.

It had been Chang's idea, of course.

"Think of yourself as Yoga Bear," he said.

"Berra."

"Whatever," he said. "The point is, I'm trying to make you smarter than the average Berra."

"Bear," Charlie said.

Charlie'd already been to three classes in the last week, taking one day off for a spinning class at Reebok, spinning being another thing Chang had gotten him into, this new deal where you tried to see how long it took you to have a massive coronary on a stationary bike. One day a week, he'd run around the reservoir in Central Park; he was up to three miles now without stopping. But he felt most like some kind of health-nut–New Age asshole doing yoga, the breathing things and the stretching things, only violating the cleansing spirit of the room by constantly imagining himself jumping into the whole pile of the sweating, Spandexed babes all around him in the mirrored room.

He hadn't had a drink since the day after his first start with the Jackals. Every morning, he would choke down a fistful of the vitamin pills Chang had given him. Every other day, he would drive over to Coney Island and throw on the side for half an hour with Kwamee Maryland, the Cyclones catcher.

Three times a week, including this morning, he was with Chang.

"When does boot camp end?" Charlie had said, before he left for the Stadium.

"Doesn't," Chang said.

"What if I do get a shot with the Sox?"

"Then we work even harder."

"The yoga babes say they can notice a change in my muscle tone already."

"Yeah," Chang said, "and I know which muscle."

It was two days now since he'd gone over to Jersey and pitched a second time for the Jackals, his appearance low-key this time, no announcement the day before, no alerts to the media, giving up three hits in seven innings, striking out nine, breaking so many bats that by the fourth inning, he'd felt as if he were going through the batting order with a power saw.

It'd braced him enough to make him come see Hartnett now that the Red Sox were in town, to call in everything he had.

"How are you going to play it?" was the last thing Chang had said to him in the office.

"I'm going to beg, that's how I'm going to play it," Charlie said. "No kidding, I've got a yoga position I think's gonna be perfect for it."

He went to bed early that night but had the same dream he'd been having for fifteen years.

The one where he was falling, and there was no one to catch him.

The cab dropped him off on the narrow cobblestone street between the players' parking lot and the Press entrance at Yankee Stadium, which is also where you entered if you were on your way to the clubhouses downstairs. The guard working the door, a stocky guy with dark hair and glasses, had a name tag that read GERALD. He recognized Charlie right away, pumping his hand vigorously, saying, "What're you doing here?"

Charlie was wearing a blue blazer, blue t-shirt, jeans, old Adidas Country running shoes, white leather with the three green stripes. Old school. Like him.

Or just old.

"Didn't you hear?" he said. "I'm making a comeback."

Gerald gave him a big laugh. "Seriously."

Charlie let it go. "I am actually here to see my old roommate, Mr. Ted Hartnett of the hated Red Sox," he said. "He's expecting me."

"He come in about an hour ago," Gerald said. "Maybe more, now I think about it. You know the way down to the visitors', right?"

"Down the stairs. Take a left. Blue line goes right, to the Yankees clubhouse. Red line for the bad guys."

"There you go," Gerald said. Then, almost like a reflex, Charlie thought, he said, "You look good, Charlie."

"That's what you say to the old-timers on Old-timers' Day," Charlie said.

The visitors' clubhouse was on the third-base side at Yankee Stadium. When Charlie walked in, all he could see was a couple of clubhouse kids, teenagers, watching some skateboard show on what had to be one of the ESPN channels. The room was as ratty as he remembered it, which was just fine; he hated all the new ballparks with their retractable roofs and shopping malls and sushi menus, all the other creature comforts that had nothing whatsoever to do with baseball.

It was just baseball at the Stadium, the way it had always been and was always supposed to be. Even a career wise-ass like Charlie Stoddard knew this whole place was the home office.

He hadn't been in this clubhouse in six years, at least, and still knew the layout like he did his own apartment.

He knew something else, too.

That being on the inside again, even on a day pass, was better than sex.

He walked around the corner to his left, to where he knew the manager's office was. Ted Hartnett was hunched over some computer printouts, a cup of coffee next to him, the start of the gallon of coffee he would drink before he left here at midnight or later. Hartnett's hair was a little grayer than the last time Charlie'd seen him. And the cute little granny reading glasses at the end of the nose were smaller than the ones

Charlie remembered him wearing. He was getting older, but he was still a handsome bastard, still reminded Charlie of an aging Paul Newman.

Hartnett's catcher hands still looked so messed up, it was as if somebody hadn't assembled them right.

"All right," Charlie said, his voice sounding so loud it startled even him, "we'll have one more drink, and then nine more after that, and then we are out of here."

If Harnett was startled, he didn't show it. But then he'd never shown you anything, his face never telling whether he was happy or sad or pissed off or totally shitfaced; whether he was looking at the world's greatest ass or ball three outside.

Charlie remembered Ted Hartnett being like that when he'd get his ass tossed out of a game from time to time, usually because some home-plate umpire had decided the strike zone was the size of a matchbook. He'd take it all game long and then Charlie would put one on the outside corner and the guy would call it a ball and somehow, in the course of a few seconds, without turning his head or even moving his lips that Charlie could see from the mound, his old roommate would call the ump blinder than Ray Charles and queerer than the head queer at the Halloween parade in Greenwich Village, and, if there was time before he was out of his crouch and on his way to the showers, throw in some especially good shit that Charlie could actually hear about what a whore the ump's mom must have been, all without ever changing his expression.

"What do you want?" Hartnett said now, not moving.

"You always were such a sentimental bastard," Charlie said.

"I could always lie and tell you I missed you."

"How 'bout I just come over there and give you a big hug."

"Don't take another step," Hartnett said, "I mean it." And actually smiled then, even if it was only with his eyes.

Charlie took the couch against the wall, to Hartnett's left, nearly sinking all the way to the floor. "I wanted to get here early so I didn't make a scene."

"Or maybe you didn't want to be seen," Hartnett said.

"I'm not here to talk about that."

Hartnett nodded toward the clubhouse. "It doesn't have to be this way, you know."

"I know that," Charlie said. "It's why I'm gonna take care of it soon." He waved his hand in front of him, like he was trying to get rid of smoke that wasn't there, the way he always did when he wanted to change the subject. "I promised Gracie."

"She was up in Boston," Hartnett said.

"She told me."

There was a bark of laughter from inside the clubhouse. Charlie poked his head around the corner and saw the clubhouse kids looking up at the television, where the fattest white woman Charlie had ever seen was standing over a black man just as fat, wagging a finger in his face. Underneath them on the screen, in big letters, was this message:

"Tyrone Caught Earlene in Bed with Her Home Trainer."

Charlie turned back around and explained that it was just Jenny Jones going down on Jerry Springer.

"So what's up?" Hartnett said.

"Honey," Charlie said, "somebody shrunk your lead."

"Yeah, but it's like I keep telling the guys, once we start watering it again, it'll grow."

"Isn't that what the girl from Channel Five used to tell guys on the team when they'd try to impress her with their winkies?"

"Libby Boucher," Hartnett said. "She'd stare at their dicks like she was curious and then hit them with the line: Water it, I'll bet anything it will grow. Did you go out with her?"

"Sure," Charlie said. "I mean, if you count being inside the backseat of a limo one time as going out." He got up, walked across to the other wall, poured himself a mug of coffee, just for something to do, came back and sat down. "You want to do more small talk," he said, "which I know is your favorite, or you want to know why I suddenly showed up here out of the blue?"

"Let's skip to the good parts," Hartnett said. "Like we always wanted to do with the dirty movies in the hotel."

"I need a favor," Charlie said.

Hartnett took off the little reading glasses, folded them up to the size of what looked like a half-dollar to Charlie, placed them on the desk. "You got it."

"I didn't say what it is yet."

"You still got it."

"Usually I'd accept," Charlie said. "But you probably need to hear me out."

Hartnett just looked at him.

Charlie said, "I think I might be able to help you out."

"You're here to help."

"With pitching."

"You brought a pitcher with you?" Another smile, really just a little crinkling around the eyes this time.

Charlie said, "Let me talk, okay? Without interrupting?"

"You talk, I listen," Hartnett said. "Just like the old days."

Charlie said, "We can skip all the preliminary shit, right? How you were always like a brother to me, even if it turned out we both were in love with Gracie? And how I know you've always been more serious about baseball than church, and so I wouldn't come here looking to screw around?"

Hartnett nodded.

Charlie got up then, shut the door, told him about Ellie Bauer and Chang and his back and his arm, throwing in the park and then on Rob Kendall's team, all the way to the way he'd pitched the night before for the Jackals, trying not to rush any of it, thinking to himself the whole time that in the old days, he could talk Ted Hartnett into almost anything, any hour of the day or night.

When he was done, he felt as if he needed to do one of his breathing exercises.

"Bottom line," Charlie said, "I think I got my arm back."

There was a silence between them. Charlie knew from the old days how comfortable Hartnett was with silence, how he was never in any rush to fill it. It was always Charlie who spoke first. He did that now, impatient to get on with it in this office that smelled like Lysol and cigarettes and coffee, get some kind of reaction out of him.

"No shit," he said. "I really do."

"You're serious," Hartnett said now.

Charlie said, "Didn't you tell me one time, real late at night, you could say any horse's ass thing to your friends without worrying how they were going to react? You did tell me that, right?"

"Right."

"You need pitching, right?"

"Like you always needed tank tops and tight jeans."

"I can pitch. Or at least I think I can."

"You mean for the Red Sox."

"Yeah."

"This season."

"Yeah."

Hartnett pushed the reading glasses around on his desk with his mashed fingers, making little circles. "You mention this to anybody else?"

"My trainer."

"He doesn't talk?"

"He makes you look chatty."

"Good."

Charlie sat there, waiting.

"'Cause if you only told him, then it's just the three of us who know that the inside of your brain has finally turned into the dog's breakfast."

They had gone around and around for the last fifteen minutes, Charlie saying it wasn't as crazy as it sounded, giving him Stieb and Catfish, Hartnett saying it wasn't crazy relative to *what,* pigs flying?

Hartnett watched him, fascinated, the old fire in Charlie's eyes, all the excitement he'd work up in the old days when he'd suddenly decide that there was this after-hours club in Chicago they had to go check out, or some strip club in Atlanta, or some card game down in Chinatown he'd heard about from Dykstra.

Live a little, Charlie Stoddard would tell him, and before Ted Hartnett knew it, they'd be in the cab.

Or be walking the horse they'd bought from the hansom cab guy into the lobby of the Warwick Hotel.

"I'm asking you to catch me for half an hour," Charlie said, back up off the couch, pacing in front of him now. "If you think I'm kidding myself, that I don't have the arm, I walk away saying sorry I wasted your time."

"If I even do that," Hartnett said, "I'm acting like I think it might be a possibility."

"We don't even need a mound. We could do it in the park like I did with Chang."

"Chang."

"My trainer."

"You don't need a trainer, you need a shrink."

"That's what he says."

"You're forty years old, Charlie."

"It's why I've got to know right now, not when I'm fifty, still chasing card-show money after my second hip replacement."

"And now you think, because you dazzled them over behind Yogi's museum, that even though it's been fifteen years since you scared anybody, you're going to come walking out of the cornfield like Shoeless Joe in the movies and help pitch me to the pennant?"

Charlie said, "Something like that. Yeah."

"And doing this, for the Boston Red Sox, isn't going to bother other members of your family?"

"Hell, if I can sell this to you, I can sell it to anybody. And besides, my family's my business."

"Fuck you, it's your business," Hartnett said, feeling some heat now in the back of his neck. "It's my goddamn business, too, and you know it."

"Let's not get ahead of ourselves. Right now, all I'm asking you for is a game of catch."

"On account of me having nothing else to do," Hartnett said. "On account of I'm going so good these days."

"Half an hour," Charlie said.

Smiling at him now. The way he used to when he was telling Hartnett that where they were going, it was great, there might even gonna be girls.

The bad-boy smile that always meant trouble for Ted Hartnett.

"Wait," Charlie said to him, "I'll make it easy for you."

Charlie disappeared out the door and came back in carrying an old Mets gym bag bleached out to the color of a hazy sky. He unzipped it, and as soon as he did, Ted Hartnett knew what was in there.

The catcher's mitt he'd FedExed Charlie the day the Mets had released him in Los Angeles.

Hartnett thought: The one time in my life I get sentimental, and all this time later it comes back to bite me in my fucking ass.

Charlie said, "I'm asking."

He was staring hard at Hartnett now. Not pleading. Just asking. Hartnett had always been aware of how unusual-looking Charlie Stoddard's eyes were. They were in this old First Avenue joint called T.J. Tucker once, in their favorite table at the front window, and he'd heard this fashion designer who was already halfway onto Charlie's lap at the time describe the eyes as "periwinkle blue." Hartnett just knew they were bright and seemed to get brighter the more you looked into them and he had looked into them enough, back when he sometimes didn't even need hand signals to call the pitches, when he could read Charlie's mind and Charlie could read his. All he needed was that eye contact, a small nod from him on the mound, let's go.

He made that kind of nod, and Charlie tossed him the glove. Hartnett slipped it on, knowing that was a mistake, because he knew how good it was going to feel, like he'd put his left hand on a cheerleader's sweater. Wondering if Charlie had been feeling the same way with a ball in his right hand, his fingers searching around to fit just the way he liked them on the seams.

"I'm just asking . . ."

"Is there some kind of echo in here? You said that already."

". . . for maybe an hour and a half out of your day, counting travel time."

Hartnett pounded his fist into the pocket, still as soft as a pillow, and heard Charlie say in a quiet voice, "You owe me."

Without looking up, Hartnett said, "That I do."

"You've told me you owe me since the night I got hurt."

"And the night after that," Hartnett said.

"Not that I would ever bring that into play."

"It wouldn't be like you, playing on somebody's friendship—or guilt—to get what you want."

Charlie said, "But if I was planning to call it in, what you owe me . . ."

"You'd do it now."

"Fuck, yes."

Hartnett said, "This ratty old thing I'm wearing always knew whether you had good stuff or just some slop you were trying to get by with."

"Now you're talking."

"That's all I'm doing here. Talking."

Charlie said, "But let's say it said I still had good stuff instead of slop."

Hartnett said, "If it ever got out I was thinking of signing you up, the whole world would think I was having some kind of meltdown. The next thing they'd want to know is when I was going to sign Gooden and Darling and the rest of the old Mets."

"But what if you really thought I could help you? What then?"

Hartnett said, "Is that door all the way closed?"

Charlie reached over from the couch. "Yeah."

Hartnett said, "Then I'd go right around my creepy little general manager and take it to my owner."

"Mr. Patrick Keenan himself."

"That's what he calls himself."

"What?"

"Himself," Hartnett said, trying to make it come out sounding Irish.

"I know about him," Charlie said. "Guy's got some style to him. All that circus show-biz stuff in his background. I was talking to some old Red Sox players at a signing a few months ago, and they said Keenan's the only baseball owner they know who still thinks the best reason to have his own team is because it helps get him laid."

"Your kind of guy."

"He'll love this idea."

Hartnett took the catcher's mitt off and set it on the desk. "When were you planning on doing this?"

"Tomorrow morning, I know you've got an afternoon game Thursday."

Hartnett reached into the middle drawer of his desk and took out a pack of Marlboros, and a box of matches, and lit one. "I'm only smoking again until my lead is back in double digits."

"You don't have to explain to me," Charlie said. "Frankly, I never could tell the difference between you smoking and you quitting anyway."

Hartnett smoked his cigarette and let it be quiet again in the office and finally said, "Meet me at Shea at eleven o'clock sharp." Then he told Charlie they were shooting some kind of commercial at the Stadium tomorrow morning and early into the afternoon, the cluhbouse kids had told him, he just wanted him to know in case some of the Red Sox wanted to take early batting practice. Then he told Charlie he was going to bring his catcher, Pooty Shaw, with him, because Pooty was just coming off the disabled list and needed the extra work and it would give them a cover story in case they needed it.

"What's his birth name?" Charlie asked.

"That's it," Hartnett said. "Pooty."

Charlie came over and shook his hand and told him he wouldn't be sorry, and then left. Hartnett sat there behind his desk, the mitt back on his left hand, thinking, Jesus, what if he *can* pitch?

Really thinking:

If that was true, what was the *good* news?

PATRICK KEENAN watched the two blondes set up headquarters at the far end of the bar, near the big window facing out on Second Avenue, both of them nearly six feet tall, both over-chested and under-dressed, one in a red dress and one in a blue dress, and actually heard his chair moving away from his power table at Elaine's—right-hand wall, last one before you took a right for the bathrooms—before he'd actually decided to go up there.

Keenan gave Elaine a peck on the cheek as he passed her on his way to the bar. She asked if he was leaving already, and he said, Lord no, dear, his dates had just arrived.

Elaine jerked her head around and saw Keenan pointing. "The two small forwards," he said.

She said, "They're too old for you, Patrick."

Keenan made a fake motion with his hands, like he was straightening his great head of white hair, straightened his tie, and said, "If they die, they die."

"Well, then," Elaine said then, bored-like, "quickly into the forecourt."

He knew his manager, Ted Hartnett, wouldn't be here for another hour at least, just because the Red Sox' game with the Yankees—Yankees 8, Red Sox 2, the lead now down to six games—had just ended.

Patrick Keenan would put on his mortician's face later when Hartnett showed up later, what could it possibly hurt to have some company for now?

"Ladies," he said to the blondes after he made his way through the crowd, somehow gliding into position without actually touching anybody, "my name is Keenan. That car you see through the window, the vulgar thing taking up about half the block, belongs to me. I own it, and the Boston Red Sox baseball team, and the only thing I like better than expensive champagne are naughty girls. Would you two naughty girls care to join me for a drink?"

They both giggled, and then the red dress said to the blue dress, "He's cute."

"And rich," the blue dress said. "You really are rich, right? Because a lot of old farts say they are and they're not."

"We hate that," her friend said.

"Cute *and* rich," he said. "Guilty on both counts, I'm afraid."

Red dress said, "We're with Delta."

Blue dress giggled again and said, "We love to fly."

"And it shows," Keenan said.

He extended both his arms in a courtly fashion and led them back toward his table. "Have either of you girls ever heard of Ernie Banks?" he said.

"I've heard of Fleet banks," the red dress said.

"I went out with a guy from Outer Banks once," the blue dress said. "In North Carolina? But the shitheel was married."

Red dress said, "It wasn't even his own RV, remember?"

"Well, Mr. Banks was a famous baseball player, and he had a very famous expression."

The blue dress said, "Play ball?"

Patrick Keenan made a discreet wave at his waiter.

"Close," he said. "What he said was, let's play two."

N o one was absolutely rock-solid certain how old Patrick Keenan really was, which suited him just fine, thank you.

His official biography in the Red Sox media guide and in all the *Who's Who* collections of shakers and movers had him at sixty-seven. And Keenan's position on that was that if it didn't bother anybody that he would have had to have been a teenager when he won all those medals in the Taebaek Mountains of North Korea, it sure as hell wasn't going to bother him. When some snot-nose reporter would press him, Keenan would give him the usual bullshit about how he'd just had to lie about his age to go off and fight for his country, and then tried to change it back a couple of times later in his life, just to set the record straight, but by then he'd lost his damn birth certificate, which meant that he wasn't even sure anymore just what year in the 1930s he'd been born, if you could believe it. And some of these dumb bastards actually did.

In conclusion, he'd say, at the end of his class in head-spinning math, he'd just decided to go with the age he'd given his Uncle Sam when he went off to Korea, that way no one thought he was still in his twenties when he started running Ringling Bros. Barnum & Bailey Circus later on.

Patrick Keenan was at a point when even he couldn't separate the truth from the colorful fiction of his life sometimes. He just knew he'd preferred the company of older people when he was younger, and younger people now that he was however old he really was, and so far that had worked out in a delightful fashion for him.

"Ah," he loved to say to the boys and girls in the bar, "if you didn't know how old you were, how old would you feel?"

And when some darling would ask him how old *he* felt, he'd say, "Three."

"Three years *old?*" the darling would say.

"A three-year-old thoroughbred," he would say. "At stud, of course."

His dear mother had told him when he was growing up in Philadelphia that he would need more than charm in this life to get by, and how charm would never pay the bills, he had to have a decent education and the credit she believed she'd racked up with the Catholic Church to back him up. But now, after a long life filled with wine and women and all the weepy Irish songs he would sing in even the best bars late at night, he knew Emma Keenan, out of the most heartbreakingly beautiful part of the west of Ireland, had been right about a lot of things, the Church included, but dead wrong about just how far charm could take you in this world.

Patrick Keenan believed he had become rich and famous on charm the way some of those mirthless boys from Silicon Valley had gotten filthy rich on little computer chips.

He was a bright boy, too, he knew that, and he'd never needed a mirror to tell him what a handsome devil he was, the ladies had always done a good enough job of that. He'd even made *People* magazine's list of the sexiest men alive recently, in there with the jocks and rock stars and hunks from the movies and the rest, and the writer of the piece had said he reminded her of the aging Cary Grant, after Grant's hair had gone white as baby powder.

And there had been a profile in *Vanity Fair* just the previous month that had begun with the Oscar party right here at Elaine's, the writer saying that when Patrick Keenan had walked into the room, all of the women had wanted him and about half the men.

When a friend of his asked him about that description, the two of them watching the game from Keenan's suite behind the high windows above home plate at Fenway Park, Keenan had just smiled and said, "Fuckin *ay.*"

He didn't think of it as a homo thing, the guys wanting to be with him, they just liked being in his company, drinking and laughing and saying fuck and talking about women and sports.

Fuckin ay, indeed.

He *had* run the circus when he was still a kid, and had parlayed that into a job as the number-two man over there at NBC, and had gone from there to the job of running Madison Square Garden and even putting some of his own money up to back a couple of hit Broadway shows. After that, he'd decided to try Hollywood for a while, thinking he might like to set out on his own as an independent producer, but finding himself, through luck and circumstance and the fact that the moguls out there fell for him, too, ending up running Paramount. He'd lasted a year there, managed to sidestep a couple of high-budget disasters—one the epic about the alien President and subsequent war of the worlds—that were green-lighted under his watch, and finally set out on his own, with the kind of production company they always give out like welfare to failed studio executives. And it was there that Patrick Keenan had had the outrageous good fortune to back a sitcom about a gruff, gay garage mechanic and his ditzy sexpot roommate, the one who everybody had thought was going to be the second coming of Marilyn Monroe. It was No. 1 for ABC for seven years running, and even though it had been off the air for three, it would be running in syndication, Patrick Keenan surmised, for as long as *The Honeymooners* had.

Keenan knew how much money the circus had lost when he was running it, even if he had gotten the goddamn thing more publicity than it had ever gotten before, and got it back into some of the best arenas in the country. He knew better than anyone that he had left the Garden floating in a Hudson River of red ink, even with the makeover he had given the place, and the way he had gotten New Yorkers back to thinking of the place as one of the main plazas of the city.

He knew about all the people, even the ones who said they were his friends, who'd always said that Himself had turned failing upward into an art form, as if he'd somehow figured out a way to reverse gravity.

Then came *Up Yours,* and Patrick Keenan had finally made the kind of score he'd always promised his mother he would make someday, and all of his critics could kiss his Galway arse.

"Patrick," his old assistant at Paramount, Barry Stanton, had told him, "your shit has finally come in."

He had been married twice, the second time to the ditzy blonde from *Up Yours.* He had dated most of the eligible and attractive women who had crossed his path for nearly half a century and had laughed even more than he'd planned after surviving Korea, and after *Up Yours* had broken all records when it was purchased for syndication, he'd even thought about retiring to the farm he'd bought near Ballinasloe. Then some old friends from Boston had told him the Red Sox might be in play again, because the group that had bought the team from the Thomas Yawkey estate a few years before had already grown tired of dealing with the preppy gangsters from the players' union and all the gangster Boston pols still trying to hold up the building of a new Fenway Park.

Somehow his group, with him as the front man, had beat out the boys from the cable-television empire and the boys from AOL Time Warner, and now, in more ways than one, this was his last adventure in what had been a life filled with adventure, Patrick Keenan promising Red Sox fans that he would spend any amount of money and do whatever was necessary to get the Sox their first World Series championship since 1918; make right everything that had gone wrong in baseball in Boston since Frazee had sold Babe Ruth to the Yankees.

Only now he'd owned the Red Sox for four years, and they'd only made the playoffs once in that time, and lost to the Yankees in the American League Championship Series in five games when they had. Now there was this collapse he was watching play out in front of his eyes, what looked like a dream season starting to go terribly wrong, one of his pitchers getting hurt every couple of days, the Yankees even roughing up his golden child, Tom MacKenzie, for six runs in the sixth inning, which is when Keenan had left George Steinbrenner's suite at the Stadium and told his driver, Booker Impala Washington—"Only thing my parents loved more than black history," he'd explained to Keenan about his name, "was that lime-green Chevy of theirs with them big-ass fins"—to point the car toward 88th Street and Second Avenue, which is where Elaine's was.

All of a sudden, even though the Sox were still ahead six games, it felt as if they were chasing the Yankees instead of the other way around, and Patrick Keenan, who kept acting as if he were laughing off the slump and the way his team's lead was disappearing, was running out of patience.

He didn't let on at Elaine's, though, in the new suit he'd picked up that afternoon at Paul Stuart, with the fresh rose in his lapel, with Morgan, the red dress, on one side of him and Meghan, the blue dress, on the other, waiting for Ted Hartnett to show up and tell him whatever it was that was so important that it couldn't wait until the morning.

Keenan was showing off his new palm-sized BlackBerry pocket computer to Morgan and Meghan—"I believe we might be able to order from Cartier *online!*" he told them—when he spotted Hartnett at the front door, trying to advance a few feet through the bar crowd, searching the front room with his eyes.

"Well, here's my skipper now," Keenan said, giving Hartnett a wave.

"Another cutie," Morgan said.

"He'd be perfect for you," Patrick Keenan said, shaking his head almost mournfully, "if his tastes didn't run the other way."

"He's queer?" Meghan said.

Keenan said, "Alas."

"Shit," Morgan said, "another good one bites the dust."

She and Meghan got up and said they were going to the ladies' room to powder their noses and they'd be back in a little while, depending on the traffic in there and if anybody wanted to share some good pills.

Ted Hartnett, as usual, was dressed like a preppie instead of an old catcher, in a blue blazer and khaki slacks and a blue open-necked shirt. He ordered a beer as Patrick Keenan poured himself a little more champagne.

"Tough one tonight," Keenan said.

"The kid's been carrying us," Hartnett said. "He was due for a bad one. And he might maybe have gotten out of that sixth if my backup catcher, Mr. Hadley, had managed to hold onto the pop foul that would have been the third goddamn out of the inning."

"Who pitches tomorrow?" Keenan said.

"I have no goddamn idea who pitches tomorrow," Hartnett said. "If Cantreras's elbow is still tender, I may have to call somebody up from Pawtucket. Or even Trenton."

Pawtucket was their Triple-A affiliate. Trenton was Double A.

"I haven't talked to Gary today," Keenan said, referring to Gary Goldberg, the team's general manager. "I keep reading all these hot rumors in the papers about all these pitchers he's supposed to be trading for, but when I ask him about it, he just goes off about dick-sucking, goat-humping sportswriters again."

Hartnett said, "He hates sportswriters more than he does Arafat."

Keenan asked him if he wanted a hundred-dollar plate of pasta and Hartnett said no, and after they talked about the game for a few minutes, Keenan starting to wonder where his two flight attendants had gone to, he said to his manager, "What's this all about?"

Hartnett, who never minced words, Keenan knew, got right into it, telling about his visit from Charlie, and how there probably wasn't anything to it, but Charlie *was* his friend and he owed him, and did Keenan have any problem with him going over to Shea in the morning and working him out?

He was more anxious than Keenan had ever seen him. Maybe it was because of all the history between him and Charlie Stoddard. Or maybe this free fall the Red Sox were in was starting to get to the manager the way it was getting to everybody else.

Patrick Keenan smiled and slapped the table and in a loud voice said, "Well, let's do it then!"

"Just like that?"

"Just like that," Keenan said. "In fact, I'll go with you."

"You don't think I'm as nuts as Charlie?"

"Of course I do! It's why I love it! Even the chance of it! We could sit here until last call and I could tell you about all the crazy plays I've made in my life." He leaned in, focusing in on Hartnett, the way he did when he was about to work a line of what they used to call blarney in the old days and now just thought of as bullshit. "Before you were born," Keenan said, "everybody thought it was nuts for me to think a couple of my highwire boys from the circus could walk a tightrope between the Plaza and the Sherry-Netherland. You don't take a chance once in a while, you don't know you're alive, son. What time do you want me to pick you up in front of the Hyatt?"

Hartnett drank the last of his beer and left. As he did, Patrick Keenan noticed Morgan and Meghan coming back toward the table now, looking much perkier than when they'd left.

"Where's the gay guy going?" Meghan said.

Patrick Keenan knew his reaction had made Hartnett feel better about taking this flyer with Charlie Stoddard. It's why he hadn't bothered telling him what had happened to the Flying Divac brothers that day when that big wind had put what seemed to Patrick like an insignificant ripple in their highwire just as the older brother, Cha Cha, was directly above Fifth Avenue.

10

THEY WERE ONLY about ten minutes into it when Pooty Shaw stepped out of the batter's box, adjusted his sunglasses, spit some tobacco juice, and said to Hartnett, "Y'all?"

Hartnett took off the catcher's mask he'd borrowed from the Mets equipment manager, adjusted the first chest protector he'd worn since he stopped playing, stood up. "Something wrong?" he said.

Pooty squinted out to where Charlie stood on the mound, waiting, and said, "How old you say Father Time is?"

"Forty," Hartnett said. "Just turned. Same as me."

"Bullshit," Pooty said, dragging the word out, as if it really had three or four syllables to it.

Hartnett had trouble understanding him sometimes, primarily because of a slight lisp, which made the last word sound more like "bull-thit."

Pooty said, "And y'all know I could be hittin' better than I am, goin' with the pitch, *drivin'* the damn ball, if I had my stroke back."

"Pooty," Hartnett said, wanting to laugh the way he always did when he said the man's name out loud, "I *told* you, I'm not here to evaluate you or your stroke. I know what you can do, which is be the best-hitting catcher in the league again, soon as you come off the DL tomorrow night."

"Just so we understand one another."

"We do."

"Get ourselves on the same page and whatnot."

Hartnett nodded toward Charlie. "He does look pretty good for an old man, doesn't he?"

"Thit," Shaw said, and spit again.

Charlie had always wanted to meet Pooty Shaw, just not under these circumstances, which had him feeling as if he were up on an empty stage doing one of those auditions for a Broadway show.

He'd gone to one once with an actress he was dating and saw her squinting out into the dark after she did her reading, and thought a proctologist would be more fun than putting yourself out there that way, naked, waiting for some voice in the dark to call out, "Thanks, we'll call you," which really meant, Get out.

Everybody knew Pooty had always been one of the toughest outs in the league, first for the Yankees and now for the Red Sox, a catcher who could work the count on you and hit for a high average and even had enough speed to steal bases. But that wasn't why he was as famous as he was around baseball.

Pooty Shaw was actually a minor legend in the sport because of the day in his Yankees career when his estranged wife, Vonette, who'd been following his girlfriend, Sun, finally caught up with her in the players' parking lot at Yankee Stadium. Vonette was driving Pooty's leased Lincoln Navigator. Sun was driving the sporty BMW 735IL Pooty had purchased for *her* in cash—not wanting a second lease payment to show up on his bank statements—when his All-Star Game bonuses had kicked in.

Most people were skeptical about some of the more colorful details of the incident, now known as the Pooty Shaw Grand Prix. But Charlie had an actual eyewitness, Joe Healey's cousin Seamus, who had been working that summer as a security guard at the Stadium.

According to Seamus, Sun entered the parking lot first that day, Seamus directing her to a spot in the far left-hand corner of the lot, nearest the northbound Major Deegan Expressway. Vonette showed up in the Navigator a few seconds later, and before Seamus could tell her that the woman almost directly in front of her in the blue Beamer had already identified *her*self as Mrs. Shaw, Vonette rolled down the window and said, "How 'bout I just follow Slut Girl?"

She'd gunned the engine then and rammed Sun's car the first time just as Sun was about to make the left turn that would have taken her to parking space No. 175.

At this point, Sun stuck her head out the window and saw who it was behind her.

"Don't blame me you got them rolls of fat on you and couldn't hold your man, Aunt Jemima!" Sun yelled.

Vonette backed up a few yards and proceeded to ram the BMW again.

Seamus said that what impressed him over the next few minutes was 1) what a game girl Sun was and 2) the Navigator's ability to corner as well as it did, a feature no one had ever mentioned in the television commercials.

There were six rows of cars in the players' parking lot, and Sun began making a series of hairpin turns around each row with Vonette in hot pursuit, both of them occasionally brushing other cars, one of which was the brand new Mercedes that the manager of the Yankees at the time, Earl Dobbins, had just picked up from his dealer in Old Greenwich that morning.

Seamus was on the street side of the fence now, and said he was frankly surprised, just considering the amount of damage Vonette had already done to the BMW, that Sun didn't try to make an escape through the entrance facing the ballpark. Finally, on what was her second or third lap around the lot, Seamus said he'd had lost count by then, Vonette trapped her behind the Channel 11 television truck, lined her up, and made the direct hit that completely caved in the passenger side.

"It was just another case of a good big car beating a good little car," Seamus said the night he told the story to Charlie and Healey at The Last Good Year.

Pooty was traded to the Red Sox the next week, despite a .342 batting average at the time, for a middle-relief pitcher and what were described as "future considerations."

"You still married to Mario Andretti?" Charlie had asked, when Hartnett introduced the two of them at home plate.

Pooty squinted at him.

"Messin' with me?" he said.

"No way," Charlie said.

"In answer to your personal question," he said, "Pooty Shaw is committed these days, least committed as he's capable, to a sweet little thing named Alqueen."

He took off a cap that said POOTY's on the front. Even on a suprisingly cool morning for the first week of August, Charlie noticed a light sheen of sweat on Pooty's bald head, looking like tiny bubbles on the smooth, mahogany-like finish.

"Think I faced you one time when I was a rookie," Pooty said to Charlie. "By then you was pretty much washed out."

"And blowed dry," Charlie said.

"Yo," Pooty said, and then started the process of putting on his bright red batting gloves, one for each hand, and then wide red wristbands just as bright.

In the middle of all that, Pooty stopped suddenly, closed his eyes, shook his head from side to side, and then produced what Charlie considered to be an amazing spray of tobacco juice.

"You okay?" Hartnett said to him.

"It's just you got me thinkin' on that bitch Vonette," he said. "When that happens, my sports psychologist says I'm supposed to have myself a quiet moment, clear all the ugly out my mind and replace it with something pretty."

"I think I read the same book," Charlie said.

He walked out to the mound and started off throwing easily. Pooty just reached out with half-hearted swings and poked the ball to all fields. Then Charlie started throwing for real, and a few minutes into it, he saw Pooty stepping out and saying something to Hartnett.

He knows, Charlie thought to himself.

He knows and I know.

And Ted Hartnett knows best of all, Charlie was sure of that.

Maybe white-haired Patrick Keenan, sitting behind home plate with a guy who looked like some kind of Samuel L. Jackson wannabe, knew, too. Usually fans, even the ones who owned the team, knew as much about pitching as those non-pitching fakes who announced the games. But if Keenan didn't know how hard Charlie was throwing, Harnett would fill him in afterward.

Because Hartnett *knew*.

About how hard Charlie was throwing. About the late break on all his pitches, especially the cut fastball he'd taught himself when he was teaching the pitch to the kids on the Cyclones, the one that broke the way a screwball did and jammed righthanded hitters like Shaw.

About the way he kept changing speeds and keeping Shaw off-balance and generally pissing him off.

By the time they were half an hour into it, Charlie taking short breaks to at least simulate the breaks he'd have between innings in game, it was like one long, fierce at-bat between him and Shaw, the kind you'd see in a big moment in a game, both of them into this all the way. Neither one of them fucking around or treating this like batting practice now. Shaw knew his manager was sitting right behind him, watching him take his hacks against this old man. Charlie only had to look to the other side of the screen to see Keenan and the black dude sitting next to him, leaning forward in their seats, watching this, knowing that if Hartnett wasn't taking this seriously, then Keenan wouldn't be sitting in Shea Stadium on a Wednesday morning.

Pooty Shaw started taking pitches even if they were close to the plate, the ones a guy would normally swing at during batting practice, not having the luxury of waiting around for your perfect pitch.

He started stepping out more often, adjusting his gloves, making Charlie wait the way he'd make a pitcher wait in a real game.

Which is exactly what this had turned into now, without anybody saying a word about it.

Charlie had watched as Shaw got more and more serious, checking the set of his hands, where his feet were in the box. Shaw didn't want to look bad or lose face, even if he was rusty, even with nobody in the stands watching, just because losing face in sports was like losing your deferred money.

Of course it isn't very serious for me, Charlie thought.

Just my whole life.

Sometimes Shaw would read him perfectly and get him for two or three line drives in a row. Then Charlie would come right back on him, Shaw having more and more trouble catching up with Charlie's fastball as he started to get a little tired, probably making the most swings he'd taken in one day since he nearly tore his hamstring muscle in Detroit six weeks ago.

Hartnett finally called out, "Okay, one real at-bat. Bases loaded, bottom of the ninth. Two out. Charlie's team up by a run. Like we're all of us just kids in the schoolyard."

Shaw smiled out at Charlie. "You want some a me?" he said.

Charlie said, "I'm going to beat you like that speed demon ex-wife of yours. What was her name again?"

Pooty Shaw spit again. Charlie wasn't sure he heard correctly, but thought Shaw then said his ex-wife's name ought to be Ann Thwacks.

Charlie went to a 2–2 count on him, all fastballs. He leaned in for the sign from Hartnett, who didn't give him a sign, just nodded, which meant one more fastball.

Charlie went into a full windup, making him concentrate on Hartnett's glove, the same one he'd brought to the Stadium yesterday, and not the twitchy windmill thing Shaw liked to do with his bat. Charlie brought his arm forward and heard himself grunting as if trying to put a little extra on the pitch and then delivered a slow curve that had Shaw so off-balance when he swung and missed that the bat came flying out of his hands and ended up at about the same spot behind first base where Bill Buckner had let Game 6 of the 1986 World Series go through his legs.

Shaw stared down there at his bat, then at Charlie, unsnapped his batting gloves, and spit out his whole wad of tobacco, his lisp apparently going right along with it.

"Pussy," Pooty Shaw said. But he was still smiling.

"Yeah," Charlie Stoddard said. "Ain't it thweet?"

Shaw said he would take a cab back to the city and see Ted Hartnett over at Yankee Stadium later. He also mentioned before he left that judging a man when he didn't have his eye back was worse than having to pay alimony and child support to a greedy damn bitch refused to remarry.

Patrick Keenan and the black guy with him walked through the rows of seats behind the first base dugout and let themselves down on the field through a little gate near the photographers' box. Hartnett introduced Charlie to Keenan and the black guy, who turned out to be Keenan's driver, Booker, then they all sat down in the Mets' dugout, Hartnett and Keenan and Booker on the bench, Charlie on the top step, his back to the infield, facing them.

He had put on his old Mets jacket, just to keep his arm warm. It also covered up a long-sleeved cotton shirt soaked with more sweat than a fat center at the free throw line.

The sweat, Charlie knew, was more from nerves than the seventy-five or so pitches he'd thrown to Pooty Shaw.

Patrick Keenan looked as if he'd just stepped out of some men's magazine, in his blue summer blazer, a button-down shirt Charlie thought was the color of ballpark mustard, light grey slacks, black loafers, no socks. He reminded Charlie of the actor who used to play pirates in those old movies, one of those swashbuckler guys, but he couldn't come up with the name.

Booker, whose full name was Booker Impala Washington—No shit, Charlie almost said to him, you've got a car parked in the middle of your name?—sat between Keenan and Ted Hartnett, looking cool and detached, his black t-shirt and slacks and rubber-soled black suede shoes going with the black Kangol cap he had turned around, small brim behind him, like the dudes always did nowadays.

"Well," Keenan said finally, "let me get the ball rolling by saying that was a rather impressive performance, Mr. Stoddard, even to the untrained eye. Apparently, you set your watch for the wrong year this morning."

Booker, who Charlie didn't think was even listening, said, "That last curveball you spun up Pooty's ass looked pretty damn *current* to me. Slip pitches like that done ran me right out the game."

"You played professionally?" Charlie said.

"Hit," Booker said. "Got as far as Triple A 'fore they started throwing me that kind of hook. I was one you hear about all the time? All I knew about good pitching in the end was I couldn't hit it for shit."

Charlie, who'd always gotten along with cool brothers like Booker, grinned at him and said, "Fuck hitters."

Ted Hartnett lit a cigarette, gave a small shrug to Charlie as he did. "I hate to break this up, but I've got to get over to the Bronx, which means we've all got to get down to business." He waited as an airplane came low over the ballpark on its way to LaGuardia—some things hadn't changed at Shea, it still sounded like a holding pattern—and then looked right at Charlie and said, "You looked good."

"I don't mean to press you," Charlie said, "but are you saying good because I had more than you thought I was gonna have, or good meaning I had legitimate stuff?"

"Good stuff."

Charlie started to say something else, but shut up the way he did with Chang before he made some smart-mouth remark that would make Chang hurt him.

"The question," Keenan said, "is where do we go from here?"

"First I need to talk about this with our fine general manager, Mr. Goldberg," Hartnett said, "and explain to him what's going on."

"Why don't I talk to him," Keenan said, "and explain what we want to do?" He smiled. "What *do* we want to do, incidentally?"

Hartnett shook his head, as if he couldn't believe what he was about to say. "We tell Gary that we want to sign Charlie to a minor-league contract and give him a start with Trenton."

Now, just talking to Keenan, he said, "You can put it on me, say Charlie's my old friend, say if he shows something over the rest of this season, he might get a chance to come to spring training *next* season with the Sox. Not a word about this season. Then he goes and pitches for the Thunder, and if he gets hammered a couple of times, then we all walk away from it, no harm, no foul."

Nobody said anything while another plane, sounding even closer than the one before, went overheard. Then Booker said, "What about the other?"

Charlie liked his attitude, the way he had of being in this and laid back from it, all at the same time. Whoever he was, he was a lot more than Patrick Keenan's driver.

"What other?" Ted Hartnett said.

"The other, meaning, what happens if he goes down there with all them fresh-faced Double-A boys and shoves it up them the way he did Pooty?"

"Then he moves up to Pawtucket," Hartnett said. "Triple A."

"And if the old man dazzles them there, what happens after that?"

a voice behind Charlie said. "A fucking parade from there up 95 to Fenway Park?"

The others, facing the field from the bench, could see who it was. Charlie didn't need to see, but turned around anyway to see Tom MacKenzie, twenty-year-old ace of the Red Sox pitching staff, standing on the steps near the bat rack, wearing a t-shirt that said something about a Dave Matthews Band tour, baggy carpenter's jeans about to drop off his skinny ass, a cap just like Booker's, turned around the same way, a small hoop earring in his left ear, one of those little blond hairballs under his chin. He was six-three, not even filled out yet, still looking like the skinny high school kid he'd been when the Red Sox had signed him, his striking blue eyes ignoring his owner and his manager and Booker Impala Washington and staring a hole right through Charlie Stoddard.

"What's the matter?" Tom MacKenzie said. "Cat got your tongue? I thought you were the guy who always had funny lines for all occasions?"

Behind Charlie, Hartnett said, "I don't think there's any need to get ahead of ourselves, Tom, this probably isn't going anywhere. You want to blame anybody for this, blame me, I wanted to see for myself."

Charlie watched the kid try to hold it all in, not come off like some kind of hothead he had a perfect right to be.

The kind of hothead, Charlie thought, he couldn't *help* being, if you added it all up.

"You think you're going to pitch for us, don't you?" Tom MacKenzie said. He made a snorting sound. "This really is, like, *epic*."

"Yeah," Charlie said. "I do."

The kid smiled, but they all knew he didn't mean it. "It's still all about you?" he said.

He paused now and said, "Isn't it, Dad?"

"T-Mac," Charlie said, "that's not the way it is, it's a lot more complicated than that. If you give me a chance to explain . . ."

"Here's what you do instead, dude," Tom said. "Why don't you head on back to the Old Pitchers Home, or wherever it was you came up with this cool plan of yours, and explain to somebody who cares how you're, like, *demented,* enough to think you got your fastball back." He seemed to brighten. "Tell you what," he said, "get drunk tonight and call Mom and explain it to her, she's about the last person left who doesn't see you for the asshole you really are."

He looked like he was going to say something else, must have decided against it, just said "Fucking epic" to himself, stuffed his hands in the pockets of his baggy jeans, walked up the dugout steps and toward the runway.

When he was directly behind home plate, he turned around and stared directly at Charlie.

"By the way," he said. "That hook you got Pooty with at the end? Don't take that shit out of town."

Now he left without looking back. Charlie started to get up and go after him, but Ted Hartnett put a big hand on his arm that felt like forceps.

"There's nothing for you right now," he said. "I'll talk to him later at the ballpark."

"Good luck," Charlie said. "He is a stubborn goddamn hardhead sonofa*bitch.*"

"Ya think?" Hartnett said. "I wonder where he gets that from?"

"It should be me talking to him, I'm gonna have to sooner or later."

Hartnett said, "Talking to each other hasn't exactly been a strong suit for either one of you."

"Ted," Patrick Keenan said. He stood up and smoothed out the wrinkles in his slacks, even if Charlie couldn't see anything he thought needed smoothing out. "Maybe we should both talk to him tomorrow, when he's had a chance to cool down a little."

It was Booker Impala Washington who spoke next.

"Man," Booker said, "I thought all that father-son shit in baseball was s'posed to make all you white boys get weepier than the family dog getting hisself run over."

GRACE COULDN'T REMEMBER exactly when it was that she decided she wasn't even going to let the boy use Charlie's last name.

It was one of those things that happened when you got older. You could remember how angry you were about something but couldn't remember for the life of you what had started it in the first place.

You remembered that Midge Porter from high school was a world-class bitch, for example, you just couldn't pinpoint why.

It was getting that way for her when she would try to sort out Charlie's indiscretions. She would try to put names and dates to them and finally give up because the whole process was more complicated and time-consuming than going through the channel guide for the satellite dish that Tom had given her so she could watch Red Sox games whenever she wanted.

"He's my son, too," Charlie had told Grace MacKenzie when she'd informed him of her decision. She was in San Francisco waiting for the divorce to be final, and he was still in New York, and their mutual old friends back there had been always more than eager, the big-haired wives of Mets players especially, to keep her up to date on how Charlie was trying to break all of his personal bests in bars and bimbettes.

"My son, too," Grace said, mimicking him. "Give me a break."

"You didn't used to hold grudges, Gracie."

"I'm going to make an exception just this one time."

"You can't stay mad at me forever."

Grace said, "Why don't we just go ahead and find out?"

This was one of the conversations she could still recite word-for-word, like it was the end of *Casablanca*.

"You're the one who left me, remember?" Charlie said that time. "Now my son has to be punished for that?"

"From now on, he's *my* son, okay? Maybe down the line he can carry around the baggage of people knowing he's yours, too. Just not now."

"Nobody made you move out to San Francisco," Charlie said.

"Actually," she said, "you did."

"All because of one last thing," he said.

"But it was the big one, Charlie. The granddaddy of them all. On the front page."

Then he said what he always said, that it had gotten blown out of proportion. Besides, he said, we were already separated. Then Grace would remind him that it had been the *mayor's wife*. At the Mets' Welcome Home Dinner to start the season. You're right, of course, Grace would say. Why would anybody make a big deal out of something as trivial as that?

She had left him the first time when she'd caught him on the road with one of the flight attendants working the Mets' team charter. She'd already been three months pregnant with Tom, just past her first trimester, okay with it now, excited about being a mother, even if this was the single most unplanned pregnancy in the entire history of birth control pills and every other contraceptive ever invented. She had decided to surprise him at the Westin in Chicago with a bottle of champagne; all of the games against the Cubs that weekend were in the afternoon, she thought they could have a weekend of romance in the suite he always booked for himself on the road. When she'd let herself in with the key that the kid at the front desk had given her, after she'd proved beyond a reasonable doubt that she was in fact Mrs. Charlie Stoddard, they were on the living-room floor.

The only thing that Charlie could cover himself with was the sports section of the *Chicago Tribune,* which had recently gone full-color.

Charlie had tried to act like the injured party, asking whether she was going to let him explain, or just believe her own lying eyes?

On her way out the door, after she'd narrowly missed the stewardess with the bottle of Moët, she'd told him that if he had finally turned into a country-western lyric, there were better ones to use than that.

"How about 'from the gutter to you is not up'?" she'd said.

They'd managed to get back together for the last couple of months of the pregnancy, Charlie even going to Lamaze classes with her, more interested in the stir he'd cause with the other couples than what he always referred to as the breathing crap, and things had seemed fine for the first year of Tom's life. But then it had become clear again that Charlie Stoddard, still the best pitcher in the whole world then, had no interest in being a father, and no talent for it.

"There's some course you ought to be able to take in being a father," Charlie had said. "Like, before."

"There is," Grace said. "It's just not a correspondence course."

She'd finally walked out for good in April of 1988, six months before he hurt his arm in that playoff game against the Dodgers, after his tryst with the First Lady of New York had ended up on the front page of the *New York Post,* the shot that Grace found out later had won the photographer first prize in the New York Headliners' Awards. It was sheer luck: the guy had just been taking a break from the Welcome Home dinner and had taken a walk to have a cigarette, when Charlie and the First Lady had come rolling out of the backseat of Charlie's limo, which he'd had the driver park safely away from the Lexington Avenue entrance to the Waldorf, on 50th between Lex and Third.

It wouldn't have been nearly as bad, Charlie always maintained, if he hadn't been holding her black mesh stockings in his pitching hand when the asshole began snapping away.

That's when she'd done the paperwork, had Tom's last name legally changed to MacKenzie.

It had never occurred to her at the time that he would ever grow up to be the same kind of pitching prodigy that his father had been with the Mets. Or, since she had just opened Grace Under Pressure at the time, that someday people, in what had become a *People* magazine world, would be as interested that the boy was her son as they were, at least outside of baseball, that he was Charlie's.

And what Grace MacKenzie *really* never saw coming was this:

The one who would hold the grudge about what had happened between Charlie and Grace was their son.

He was the one who had stayed mad forever.

She arrived in New York late Sunday afternoon; by the sheer luck of the draw, her monthly *Today* appearance with Katie was scheduled for the next morning. Labor Day was still a month away, but they wanted her to get the jump on it, tell viewers how they could turn that boring Labor Day barbecue into something more festive this year, the producer actually making suggestions about how they could make an end-of-summer ceremony like this both happy and sad at the same time.

"Maybe we could paint little smiley faces on the wieners," Grace had said to her new segment producer, a bald little twit with a twitty little beard named Jed Granger.

"That's why you're the diva!" he'd said, as if she were serious.

"Boy, I'll bet they don't get this kind of stuff from Martha Stewart over there at *The Morning Show*," Grace said, trying to sound as enthusiastic and queeny as Jed Granger.

"Her demographics, I swear," Jed said, "skew towards upscale *retirement* villages these days."

Grace was planning to stay at the Pierre, but they were booked with some kind of music awards show, and so she moved next door to the Sherry-Netherland, got a one-bedroom suite on the fifteenth floor with a downtown view of Fifth from one of the living room windows and another view, just as good, to the east, all the way to the river.

The Red Sox had flown to Arlington, Texas, that godforsaken place, after their Thursday afternoon game with the Yankees. Tom had pitched and won, preventing a Yankee sweep. He said he would call her from Texas but hadn't done it yet. She'd thought about trying to reach him on one of his multiple cell phones, but there was no point right now, he was still too hot about Charlie to pick up on any of them.

By now, she knew enough to give him space when he needed it. Besides, his new girlfriend, as close to a steady girlfriend as he could have, had just gotten back with her band from Europe and was supposed to hook up with him there after a brief stopover in New York. The charming Mia from the hot new group Naughty Catholic Girls. Their hit single, "Priests Who Turn," had just gone platinum the week before and, according to Tom, Mia had about a week before she went back into the studio in L.A. to begin work on a new CD, tentatively called *Other Cheeks*.

"We go to Anaheim after Texas," Tom had told his mother. "Mia and me are just going to lock down, order a bunch of room service and, like, catch up."

"She mention any new body art?" Grace said.

Tom sighed.

"Nothing you can see, Mom."

"Don't let this thing with your father make you nuts," Grace had said.

"Do me one favor, will you?" Tom said. "Give him a message?"

What, Grace said.

"Give him the old e-mail message, okay?"

Grace knew that one. It was the e-mail Tom had sent to his ex-agent, Todd Sarob, when he'd fired him the year before:

Dear Todd: Fuck you. Stronger message to follow.

Grace took a long bath once she was in the suite, talked to the writer for her segment, and the two of them worked on the spontaneous barbecue questions Katie was supposed to ask her during her prime 7:30 slot in the morning, when both of them were supposed to be perky about the advantages of turkey burgers over beef, and her new apple-chicken bratwurst over traditonal brat. Then she had one glass of the white wine the manager had left in the room for her before she went to meet Charlie at the Italian restaurant, Sistina, that he said his friend Mo Jiggy had recommended.

He'd started to explain who Mo was, but Grace said she'd read the long story about him in the most recent *GQ.*

"He wore that Shaft coat on the cover," Grace said. "The one where he posed with his dogs."

"Rottweilers," Charlie said. "Shaq and Kobe."

"Shaq and Kobe?"

"They were supposed to appear at this benefit concert he set up in South Central L.A.," Charlie said. "But they backed out at the last minute, and now he's got some general Laker issues."

"And he's who we look to now for tips on Italian food?" Grace said.

"He's opening a restaurant of his own in a few months," Charlie said. "Across the street from Rao's up in East Harlem."

"I know I shouldn't ask," Grace said. "But why there?"

"Mo says the maître d' at Rao's disrespected him one time. So he's got Rao's issues, too, even if he says they make the best spaghetti sauce."

"Sometimes," Grace said, "you can have too much information."

Charlie said, Hey, she was the one who wanted to know why they were going to Sistina this time instead of Il Cantinori.

"Mo also wanted me to tell you he liked your second book better than the first," Charlie said, "that he thought you were more confident and in command of your material, and he always liked your hair better short."

Grace wore a sleeveless pink cotton top and black slacks and pearls that Charlie had given her one time when he was trying to make up for something or other. He was waiting for her in the back of Sistina's one room, talking to a dark, pretty woman in a navy pants suit that Grace thought was a bit much for August. She stopped for a minute and watched her ex-husband focus all of his interest and energy on the woman, wondering if she was the manager or if Charlie was just killing time until Grace got here by hitting on the early diners.

The dark woman saw Grace before Charlie did and moved quickly to the front of the room, nearly side-swiping a waiter with what looked like the biggest helping of antipasto Grace had ever seen.

"Mees MacKenzie," the woman said. "*Ciao, bella!* Welcome! I am Maria, the manager."

"I'm just here to meet that poor deformed fellow you were just talking to in the back of the room," Grace said.

"Oh, Meester Charlie Stoddard," Maria said. "Our good friend for Sistina, he is in here all the time with . . ."

Grace put a hand on Maria's slender arm. "Sometimes you can have too much information," she said.

Maria smiled, embarrassed. "Of course," she said. "He is a popular man, our Meester Charlie."

"Isn't he, though?" Grace said.

Charlie started toward her, and Grace made a motion that he could stay where he was. She had been wondering all day how she would react to seeing him, now that his big secret was out in the open, telling herself to remain calm, not to overheat the way Tom had when he'd found out.

"You look beautiful, Gracie," Charlie said when she got to the table, kissing her cheek and pulling back her chair at the same time.

"The Red Sox, Charlie," was the first thing out of her mouth. "It has to be the goddamn Boston Red Sox?"

Charlie looked around the restaurant. "I think there was one couple up there at the front who didn't quite catch that."

"The Red Sox?" Grace said again. She motioned for the waiter and saw Maria get him started toward her with a good shove.

Grace noticed that Charlie had a Coke in front of him. Feeling bold, she ordered a Beefeater martini, dry, with extra olives. She saw Charlie raise his eyebrows. "Maybe it will help me work through the feelings I'm having."

"Okay," Charlie said, "I can understand why you're angry."

"Wine is for angry," she said. "Martini means I want to strangle you."

Charlie said, "Listen, I'm not as much of a schmuck as you think I am."

She said, "Really, Charlie. Who could be?"

The waiter, who seemed to have been gone about ten seconds, came back with her martini. Grace took it off his serving platter before he had time to hand it to her, reached over and clicked it against Charlie's glass before he could raise it off the table, and said, "Cheers, schmuck."

It had been one of those charming evenings out of the past, the ones he'd managed to erase from his memory when he still wanted Grace to be his love-at-first-sight girl, his dream girl, from Lexington High. He never wanted to remember this Grace MacKenzie, sitting there as she had all night with that dead-eyed bitch look he couldn't get off her face no matter how hard he tried.

It was why he'd started thinking about allowing himself just one drink about halfway through his entrée, some kind of pasta special Grace had talked him into after she and the waiter had talked about it in Italian, the guy probably telling her it had this much fucking pesto in it, Grace knowing how much he hated pesto. She had tricked him that way once in another patch-up dinner, at some Japanese restaurant in the East 50s, the first time Charlie had ever eaten Japanese in his life, telling him how much he'd like that little mound of green stuff on the side of his plate, it was the Japanese version of guacamole.

Which turned out to be that wasabi shit, which made him feel as if he'd swallowed a Roman candle. When he'd stopped choking, Grace had smiled and said, "Okay, I think I'm ready to make up now."

Tonight she got him with pesto, which at least gave him a reason to order the beer he was still nursing.

What could one beer hurt, anyway? Grace hadn't even reacted when he'd ordered it.

And what business was it of hers, anyway, she was just here to give him shit.

That would be the sequel to his first bestseller, he decided now at Sistina: *How to Take Shit from an Ex-Wife or Ex-Girlfriend and Act Like You Think It's Good for You.*

He had been selling the idea of him trying this with the Red Sox all during dinner, selling it harder than he had with Gabby, back to where he always ended up with her, desperately seeking her approval.

"The bottom line is that it's time the kid and I patched things up," Charlie said now. "He can't go on like this forever. I know I sure as hell can't."

Grace had her coffee cup to her lips. She stopped, looked at him, her eyes getting bigger, as if he'd said something surprising. "Patch? Like you would a small tear in something?"

Back to the bitch voice, the one that gave you frostbite.

I'm dead, Charlie thought.

If he couldn't get her to see, what chance did he have with the kid?

"I know what a total fuck-up I was as a father when I had a chance to be a father," he said. "I *know*, okay? But it's not like after that, I got much help from you."

Grace said, "I'm not playing this game tonight."

"I'm not saying this is your fault, Gracie. All I'm saying is, you could have made things a little easier, when he was little, but you were still too pissed off. You'll at least admit that, won't you? That maybe you helped set the tone here?"

She put the coffee cup down hard, rattling everything. "Even when you were there, you weren't," she said.

"And when I was there, he acted like he didn't give a shit whether I was or not."

"You'd ask what he wanted to do, and then tell him what you thought the two of you should do."

Charlie finished his beer. Fuck it, he waved the waiter over and ordered a weak Dewar's and water, Grace didn't have to know he'd promised Chang he was taking the pledge until he pitched in Norwich for the Trenton Thunder. When the waiter left, he said, smiling, "I don't want to play this game," willing to pay everything he had in his wallet for just one smile out of her, some sign of thawing on what had turned into one of her Ice Queen festivals.

The waiter brought him his drink. Charlie wrapped his right hand around it, took his first sip, and then toasted her, saying, "One for the road."

"He said on his way to The Last Good Year," Grace said.

"Not tonight."

"Dammit," Grace said, "you could have picked any team."

"We went over this," Charlie said. "I didn't think of the Sox as his team. I thought of them as Gabby's team. And Gabby was the only guy in baseball I thought I could bring this to without getting laughed out of the room. And you know he's always sort of felt responsible for '88. Even though it was my own damn fault."

"What about the Mets?" she said. "Wouldn't that be one of those heartwarming stories your legion of fans would love? Showtime Stoddard returning to the scene of his past glories, and his youth?"

Charlie said, "You used to call it the scene of the crime."

"The crime of wasted talent," Grace said.

"I got hurt."

"We all did," she said.

Goddamnit all to hell, he hated when she said that, as if she were saying, Game, set, match.

They were going nowhere and they both knew it. Charlie noticed her playing absently with the string of pearls she had around her neck, afraid to ask if he'd given them to her. Because even if he *had* given them to her, he still wasn't in the clear. Any guy could tell you that. Women loved to put that on you if they could, looking to trap you as soon as you raised the subject: You mean you don't *remember* when you got me these?

She sighed. "What can I do to talk you out of this? Because however you try to spin this, Charlie, they *are* his team. He's having his first big season, the way you had yours, and I want you to stay out of it."

"You can't talk me out of it," he said. He took another sip of Scotch and could feel the ice on his teeth, always a bad sign, it meant he was done with his drink almost as soon as he'd started. "It's too far along now. They're going to announce the thing tomorrow. The Red Sox, I mean. There'll be a little press conference before I pitch, giving the media from Boston and New York enough time to converge on Norwich. And I'll give everybody a bunch of jive about how, as crazy as this sounds, I've got to find out if there's anything left in my arm before I give it a real shot next spring."

"And they'll buy that?"

"Why not? Nobody is going to believe that *I* believe I could help out the Red Sox this year. Or ever, for that matter. Whatever I tell them about next spring. Something like this has only happened a few times in baseball history. Dave Stieb in Toronto. Jim Bouton—remember him, he used to do the sports in New York—came back throwing knuckleballs for the Braves. And a few years ago, Jose Rijo came back with the Reds after he'd been away six years, even though he already had five elbow operations in the books."

"But you do believe you can do this," Grace said.

"I believe. Yeah."

"And somehow you've gotten Ted and the Red Sox owner to believe."

"Believe is too strong. They're curious and they're scared to death by the Yankees, so I've got that working for me. Their lead is still six this morning, but it's gonna keep dropping if they keep pitching this way. So they're willing to take the whole thing this far."

"Too far."

"You say."

"They're not worried about what this does to Tom if you actually do make it to Boston?"

"If I make it to Boston, it's because I can still pitch. If I can still pitch, for just six weeks or so, I give the Red Sox a better chance to win. They want to win, Tom wants to win. If I give the team a better chance, the bottom line is that he'll have to stop feeling sorry for himself and suck it up and not act like some little boy who had his video-game privileges taken away."

"Ooh," Grace said now, in a fluttery little-girl voice. "Big manly jock talk."

"Maybe if we end up doing something together," Charlie said, ignoring the shot like it had missed him, "we might end up finding some common ground, understanding each other a little better, as corny as that sounds. As good as he's going, he really is still a kid, and he's never been through a pennant race, and maybe I can help him. You ever think of that?"

"You tried that one over the appetizer."

"There's only a handful of guys in the world who know anything about what it's like to have the kind of arm he does at his age," he said. "And I happen to be one of them. I wish I had somebody around to show me the ropes when I was his age."

Grace laughed now, loud enough so that people at the tables closest to them turned around.

"What's so funny?" Charlie said.

"You," she said. "You're funny. Only you could make this sound like a good thing for somebody else. This isn't about Tom, Charlie. This isn't about you helping him. Or you understanding him. Or him understanding you. It's about *you*. It's always about you. Your and your own stupid dreams."

He leaned forward now, hands gripping his knees under the table, knowing this would be a perfect time to call for the check, telling himself, just let it go, if he didn't this would be one more dinner to end up like all the others, which meant in a six-car pileup.

Except all he could hear now was his own voice. And the buzzing sound in his ears, like the hum of a big engine.

"It's not a stupid dream," he said. "It's not stupid and neither am I, Gracie. You be pissed off all you want, okay? The only time you're not pissed off is when you're looking for a change of pace. Or maybe you want to kid yourself into believing I've actually got some redeeming qualities, just so's you don't have to beat yourself up too much, you—the perfect Grace MacKenzie—for marrying such a complete asshole." He was a streak of light now, no stopping him. Tired of taking shit now. Even from her. "If you ever understood anything about me, or loved me the way you said you did, you should know better than anybody else that if there's even a chance for me to pitch the way I could, for his team or anybody else's, then it's anything *but* a stupid dream."

She didn't say anything, just stared at him, really acting surprised now, maybe at how hot she could still make him.

And he *was* hot.

She could still push all his buttons, he had to give her that.

He reached into his pocket, came out with his 1987 All-Star Game money clip, pulled out two hundreds, dropped them on the table, stood up.

"I gotta go," he said. "I'm pitching tomorrow, maybe you heard."

He knew he was putting himself back in jail with her, maybe for a long time. Only right now he didn't care. He walked past her and out the door without looking back—the way Tom MacKenzie had walked out of Shea—put his arm up for a cab, hesitated briefly when the driver said, Where to?

"Fiftieth and Second," he said finally.

He'd have one more drink with Healey and then turn in.

"Good luck tomorrow night, Charlie," he said to himself in the back of the cab, listening to a recording of Placido Domingo tell him to buckle up for safety.

"Why, thank you, Gracie," he said. "Your support means a lot to me, it really does."

"You say something?" the driver said, turning his head slightly.

"Something stupid," Charlie said.

12

"YOU DON'T EVEN know the name of a girl you slept with last night, is that what you're telling me?" Chang said.

They were in Charlie's BMW, but Chang was the one behind the wheel, driving them to Norwich. They had called the Norwich Navigators' office for directions, and the p.r. woman up there said that once they got over the Triboro, the trip shouldn't take them more than two and a half hours, depending on traffic.

"I want to know how you know I even went out last night, let's get back to that. Is there, like, some kind of scent I give off whether I've showered or not?"

"Stink," Chang said. "I prefer to think of it as stink."

"There's no way you could have known just by sitting down next to me in the car."

"But I did, didn't I?"

"We're moving into a very weird area here."

"You go party and stay out until God knows when before what is only the biggest start you've had in about three lifetimes, I'm the one who's weird." Chang nodded. "Gotcha. You're with the program now. Big time."

It was a few minutes after noon. Charlie actually felt better than he deserved after the four hours of sleep he'd managed after he finally got away from whoever she was at a suite she said wasn't even hers at The Mark, a Euro-trash hotel across Madison from the Carlyle.

It had started when he had run into his friend Bubba Royal, the old New York Hawks quarterback now working as a star analyst for CBS Sports, at The Last Good Year. They'd had one drink there and then Bubba had convinced him to take a run up to Elaine's for one more, saying it wasn't even midnight yet and Eileen's—which is what Bubba liked to call the place—was practically on his way home and when did he turn into such a pissant Boy Scout anyway?

Then at Elaine's, they'd run into the overflow from what Charlie found out were the brand-new, made-for-TV Dick Clark Music Awards at Radio City, Bubba explaining that this was New York's revenge on the ungrateful Grammy awards for bailing out to Los Angeles a few years before. Screw all them rap assholes with their Latrell Sprewell hair, is the way Bubba put it, at least Dick Clark used to run an American-type music show with American Damn Grandstand. Anyway, it turned out Bubba knew one of Dick Clark's publicists, Betsy Somebody, a redhead with some miles on her but a body that still looked pretty damn youthful to Charlie. Betsy then invited them to a party that took up an entire floor of The Mark.

Which is where he met the girl, Charlie explaining to Chang that he hadn't forgotten her name because she'd never officially told it to him.

"I was pissed off at my wife, is all," Charlie said.

"Ex."

"You ever been married?" he said to Chang.

"Not yet."

"Well, then, let me explain something to you: The twelve-rounders we still have don't know whether we're married or not."

"You're too old to be behaving like a horny teenager," Chang said. "Especially with some rock 'n' roll groupie."

"I don't think she was a groupie. She had something to do with the show." Charlie grinned, he couldn't help himself. "She just kept telling me she knew Dick."

He looked to see if he'd gotten any reaction from Chang, who merely squinted at one of the green signs on 95 North, looking for the one for 395 North he'd said had to be coming up soon a few miles back.

"I thought she meant Dick *Clark*," Charlie said.

"I get it, asshole," Chang said. "Even the night before this"—he gestured with one hand at the highway—"you can't control yourself."

"I didn't get drunk," he said.

"You told me you weren't going to drink at all."

"I wasn't," he said. "Until."

"Your mean ex-wife upset you the way she did."

"C'mon, lighten up, all I did was blow off a little steam." He put up one finger, fast, before Chang could say anything. "Which is the same way I blew off steam before one whole hell of a lot of games I won for the New York Mets."

"That was then."

"I'm telling you, I'm fine."

"It's your best feature, Charlie, I mean that sincerely," Chang said. "No matter what happens, you still think you've got a game plan here that's working for you."

"I guess that means you don't want to hear about *her* more interesting features," Charlie said. "Like the little tattoo that looked like a light switch right there on her inner thigh?"

Chang said, "You're bothering me now."

When he had called in the morning, Charlie had wanted to know why they had to leave so early. "Stretching," Chang said. Charlie had pointed out that before games he generally didn't feel the need to stretch for five fucking hours. Chang said, "I thought I pointed out that when I want your advice about your conditioning program, I'll ask for it."

Charlie said that was an answer he could live with, and would have the car out in front of his building at eleven-thirty.

Then Chang had gotten into the car with his alien powers and asked where Charlie had been and who he'd been with before they'd hit their first light heading north on Third Avenue. And didn't seem to care when Charlie told him he'd gone for a short run at nine o'clock sharp and even had time for a steam bath in the health club located on the second floor of his building.

"You have time to knock off a towel girl?" Chang asked.

They pulled off Route 32 and into the parking lot for Thomas J. Dodd Memorial Stadium at three in the afternoon. Inside the visitors' clubhouse, they met Doug Hughes, general manager for the Trenton Thunder, and Johnny Scanlon, the old Red Sox shortstop who managed the team. Hughes, who said he'd driven up special from Trenton that morning, handed Charlie a road uniform with No. 32 on the back and his name. He told Charlie that the Navigators, who were running tonight's show as home team, had arranged for him to hold his pregame press conference out in a little gazebo on top of the rightfield stands, at six o'-clock sharp. He said that Patrick Keenan was driving up from Boston and expected to be there for the press conference, but if he was late for that, he'd certainly be at Thomas Dodd in time for the first pitch.

Johnny Scanlon said, "I could go over the Norwich hitters with you, but you already know them all. They's young and they all swing from their cute rear ends."

Charlie said, "All pregame meetings should be this concise."

"Gonna leave you alone now," Scanlon said. He was short, round, bald except for a little white fringe around his ears, had a mashed-in nose, and generally reminded Charlie of a pug in a baseball uniform. He got halfway across the small clubhouse, turned, and came back to where Charlie was already seeing how well his No. 32 fit.

"I know you must get this all the time, and it must wear your ass out," Scanlon said in a slight Southern accent. He looked as embarrassed as if he were about to ask Charlie to sign something. "But I have to tell you, I faced you one time. Spring training, eighty-seven. They were still deciding at the time whether or not I should start the season on the bench in Boston or play every day in Pawtucket. We'd driven all the way to St. Pete to play you guys, over there at old Al Lang Field. Maybe it was the next year you guys moved to St. Lucie. Or the year after. No matter." He looked for somewhere to spit tobacco, decided on the floor of the locker next to Charlie's. "I was on the bubble at the time, everybody around the team knew it. But even though I'd made the trip from Winter Haven, they weren't going to start me, they's gonna wait until you were out of the game before they put me out there. Only I go to Johnny McNamara, the manager, I go, 'You've got to give me a chance to get one swing against Charlie *Stoddard*, for Chrissakes.' Mac goes, 'Okay,' crosses out whoever was going to start at short that day, put me in there instead. Lead off, I did. I end up getting three at-bats against you. Nine pitches. All but one a fastball I'm pretty sure. You mighta threw one splitter in there. But everything *hard*, man. Hard as I'd heard. Hard as I ever saw, before that day or since. Three times up, three times down. Same at-bat every damn time, just like they say: Good morning, good afternoon, good night."

He shook his head. "You were the best, and I'm just here to tell you I hope you got something left."

"I wouldn't be here—wasting my time or yours—if I didn't think I did."

"Check you later," Johnny Scanlon said.

Chang watched him go. Then, with that face of his that was like a blank computer screen, he said, "There's so much love in this room."

"Guy was just trying to give you a sense of who I used to be," Charlie said.

"I'm more entertained by who you are," Chang said.

Charlie was in just a gray pair of boxer briefs. He looked down and saw the flattest midsection he'd had since he was twenty, when all he thought he needed to stay trim were a start every fifth day and girls.

"Let's stretch," Chang said.

"On my back or my incredibly defined stomach?"

Chang made a snorting sound.

"Back," Chang said.

Charlie said, "You know, I can't believe I've never asked you this, but what's the rest of your name?"

"Oh, I get it," Chang said. "*My* name you want to know when you get horizontal."

He saw Ted Hartnett in the little sky box, sitting there with Chang and Patrick Keenan and Keenan's driver Booker, in the second inning, when he was trying to pitch out of bases loaded, one out, one in.

Charlie had been rubbing up a new ball, his back to the plate, staring into the outfield, noticing the signs out there for Arrow buses, Angela's Italian Ice, Connecticut Carting Corporation, a huge sign for the Foxwoods casino, one of those Indian deals they had up here, another one of those new casinos that looked like it belonged in the Magic Kingdom. He watched an Amtrak train go roaring past Thomas Dodd Stadium, close enough that Charlie could see faces pressed to the windows.

Then he looked up to the windows of the press-box level, way down at the end, and there was Hartnett's face.

Keenan must have flown him all the way in from the West Coast for this, Charlie figuring Hartnett wanted to see what there was to see tonight with his own eyes, not go by reports or what the numbers were, including the ones on the radar gun Charlie could see the guy holding behind home plate.

Charlie didn't need the gun. He hoped Hartnett didn't, either. It had taken him about thirty pitches into a first inning that was nearly a disaster for him to get really loose, find his release point, finish his pitches sometimes with the fingers of his pitching hand brushing the grass in front of him, his right knee so low as he was pushing through that it was already full of dirt.

Most of the pitches were too flat, he wasn't getting the late break he'd been getting the last time he pitched in Jersey. It was why the Norwich kids were getting such good hacks off him. He could have screwed around with more breaking balls once he got going. But not with Hartnett up there. He was playing to an audience of one now. And he knew Hartnett would know he was desperate if he started changing speeds, that he was more worried about getting outs than showing that his arm was strong again. Besides, Charlie knew you couldn't go a whole game trying to set up Double-A kids, even the real prospects, because they'd swing at any goddamn thing, they just wanted to hit the ball hard and kick his ass if they could.

Tonight was about throwing hard and throwing strikes, and once Charlie got into a rhythm, he was doing both.

He had his legs under him, thanks to Chang, keeping them loose the way Chang told him to by sneaking out every couple of innings and jogging in the parking lot. After an out sometimes, he'd go stand behind the mound and raise both hands over his head as if that were some sort of routine, when it was actually a way for him to stretch. And breathe, what felt like some of that Lamaze crap from Gracie's classes in the old days, if he started to feel anxious. Which he sure had in the first, trying not to give up four or five runs before the Norwich fans, all the ones in the area who'd come to see the forty-year-old pitcher like he was one of those Believe-It-or-Not freaks, had even settled into their comfortable seats.

He kept it to two runs and then got out of the second with fastballs. Norwich had three runs off him now, four hits. He'd walked a guy in the first and hit a guy, the Norwich shortstop, in the second with a fastball that shocked both of them, the ball tailing up and in like an updraft had caught it as the kid was getting ready to stride into it, hitting him square in the shoulder and laying him out like he'd walked into a glass door.

When the kid had gotten up and was walking slowly to first base, Charlie had walked over and said, "Sorry. I'm old."

The kid, who had HARTUNG on the back of his uniform, stopped. "No problem, man. And I'm keeping the ball." He started to reach up and rub his shoulder and then stopped, as if remembering the stupid ball-player thing about not rubbing.

"It hurts like a sonofabitch," Hartung said. "Even if I'll deny it later."

"Really?" Charlie said, knowing how hopeful he sounded.

Or just needy.

The kid grinned. "I'm gonna tell the guys in the dugout the pitch was softer than the inside of a Krispy Kreme."

"Hitters have no values," Charlie said.

He got the side in order in the third. Ten pitches, all fastballs, one strikeout, one ground ball, one fly ball. By now, the Norwich guys knew it was mostly going to be fastballs, and he didn't care. They got two more hits off him in the fourth, opposite field singles by the three and four hitters in the order, but no more runs.

When he got back to the dugout, Johnny Scanlon said, "How long you want to go with this?"

"Couple more."

"You feel good?"

"Great." He slipped his arm into his Thunder warmup jacket. "You know Hartnett was coming?"

"Not until he got here." Scanlon spit. "You're starting to look friskier out there than a guy just out of prison, looking to get his stick wet."

Charlie drank some water out of the bottle next to him. "You know what they say, Johnny. The worst I ever had was pretty damn good."

Charlie finally decided to throw some breaking balls in the fifth. He went to 1–2 on the leadoff hitter and then struck him out with an ordinary hook, not even close to the one he used to have, the one the sportswriters had nicknamed Lord Charles. The kid had guessed fastball and had no chance. He got the same count on the next guy, the Norwich first baseman, a black guy about six-five with an Afro spilling out of the cap with the cute little alligator on the front as if the cap were a size too small.

The big guy had seen the 1–2 curveball to the hitter before, so this time Charlie gunned a fastball, his Grade-A four-seam riser, the one that's supposed to say, Here I am, asshole, hit me if you can.

The first baseman swung right over it.

Charlie was playing with them now, playing with the whole thing, only knowing a few of their names, not even paying attention when he'd hear them over the p.a. system. Or forgetting them as soon as he did.

Like those girls' names.

He walked behind the mound and raised his arms, closed his eyes, telling himself to focus, if he was lucky he only had four more hitters to go and then he was done for the night and he could go talk to Hartnett about it over a beer, pitch by pitch.

He went 1–2 on the Norwich catcher, a fat kid with upper arms that looked as big as his thighs.

He knew the kid had to have been watching the sequence of pitches on the two batters ahead of him, because catchers always studied shit like that. He knew Hartnett had when they were playing, wearing him out in the dugout with a pitch-by-pitch analysis of what the other guy was doing, until Charlie would finally move away or say he'd forgotten something in the clubhouse so as not to hurt his feelings.

The catcher had to be deciding whether Charlie was going to come with a fastball now, or a curve, one more Lord Charles.

Curve, Charlie thought.

He didn't have to look for a signal from his own catcher, DiVeronica, because Charlie had been calling his own game from the start.

He went into his windup and threw the hardest fastball he'd thrown all night, one he'd find out later came in at 94 on the radar gun.

And the fat catcher with his high school face closed his eyes and hit the ball to Rhode Island, or Massachusetts, whichever New England state was closest in that direction. The kid hit it like Piazza had hit it that day at Shea. Hit the kind of home run they'd all be talking about afterward and showing on the news shows and wanting to hear all about from the fat catcher. The kind of monster home run everyone would now re-member better than anything that happened all night.

Fuck.

And piss and shit.

Charlie watched the ball go until his neck started to cramp. Then watched the fat catcher take his time getting around the bases and then watched him celebrate with his teammates as if he'd won the Little League World Series against Taiwan. Finally, Charlie called for another ball from the home-plate umpire and started rubbing that one up. When he thought he'd waited long enough, he looked up to where Hartnett was sitting with the rest of them.

Only his old roommate was already gone.

The Red Sox had an off day between the end of their series with the Texas Rangers and the beginning of the next one in Anaheim against the Angels. Patrick Keenan had sent the Gulfstream he leased from Net Jet to Dallas for Ted Hartnett. Booker and Keenan had picked him up at the airport between Springfield and Hartford. The plan was for them to drop Hartnett back there when the Trenton-Norwich game was over, then for the Gulfstream to fly him to Anaheim. No press. No interviews. No photo ops. Hartnett wanted to see the game with his own eyes. Keenan had made it happen.

"You know my motto," Keenan said. "Fuck shareholders."

Hartnett could already see that Keenan, the old producer, was getting more excited about Charlie's comeback than he used to be about a young actress on the couch.

Now Hartnett was shaking his head disgustedly as he watched Charlie start to jack around with breaking balls in the top of the fifth, wondering what the hell he was doing. Something he used to wonder about quite frequently when his boy would decide to get bored in the middle of a game.

He reached for the red-and-white pack of Marlboros that was permanently back in the inside pocket of his blazer.

Patrick Keenan poked him with an elbow. "I didn't know you were smoking again."

"I'm not."

"Well, that's good." He pointed to the field and asked the same question he'd been asking every few minutes all night. "How do you think he looks now?"

"He looked good *until* now."

"But he just struck out the last two hitters."

Hartnett said, "It's a real challenge for him, fooling twenty-year-old kids."

"Yeah," Chang said, "but he's doing it hung over, which I believe levels the playing field. Even if he denies that he actually is hung over."

"Yeah, this is the first time in his whole life he's done either."

"What?" Chang said.

"Misbehave, then lie about it."

"He is throwing good and loose. I don't know squat about pitching, but what I have noticed the last few weeks is there's this good way he has of finishing when he feels right."

Hartnett nodded, watching Charlie go to work on the Norwich catcher. He looked down at his program for the kid's name. Beau Doherty.

Charlie poured in strike one, and Hartnett heard Booker Impala Washington say, "Give it to me hard."

Curve for strike two.

Hartnett said to Chang, "What did you do to his shoulder?"

Chang said, "I *un*did. It wasn't just his shoulder. Upper back. Lower back. Even his neck. Back when he had his first surgery, they pretty much attacked every rotator cuff injury the same, even though every injury is different. And what they did was cause more harm than good, which is what most of these assholes do. You heard the old thing about the solution being worse than the problem? That's modern sports medicine in a nutshell. The way his arm was when he came to me, I'm not even sure the original trauma was the kind of injury he says it was. They probably took a picture, saw some kind of tear, started sharpening up the carving knives."

Hartnett looked at him. "You can tell all that without pictures of your own?"

Chang said, "When you're good, you're good."

The count was 1–2 on Doherty, and Charlie had stepped off the mound, was stretching again behind the mound. Hartnett noticed that every time he did, Chang straightened in his chair, nodding, as if he were somehow working with Charlie from up here.

"Now he's working out regularly?"

"When I can keep him out of the hen house," Chang said.

"Good luck," Hartnett said.

"It'll keep him young," Keenan said. Hartnett smiled, looking at Keenan in what looked like another one of his Palm Beach–sporty outfits: lemony-looking sports jacket, which Hartnett thought might be linen, rose-colored shirt, white slacks. "Look at me," Keenan said.

"Yeah," Hartnett said, still smiling at him. "Look at yourself."

Down on the field, Doherty swung at Charlie's next pitch and hit it so far over the Arrow Buses sign in rightfield that Hartnett finally lost sight of it, just assuming it was in the parking lot somewhere. Rolling all the way to that Foxwoods casino up the road.

Patrick Keenan said, "Sweet Mary, mother of God, protect us in our hour of need."

Chang said, "It's all right. I understand comets like that don't come back for another fifty years or so."

Hartnett stood up, calmly turned around, said to Booker, "Run me back to the airport?"

Keenan, still looking shocked, said, "You've seen enough? I think he might've just broken Booker's windshield."

"He threw the hell out of that ball," Hartnett said. "Ask the gun guy after. It was the hardest ball he threw all night. The kid just guessed."

Hartnett patted Keenan on the shoulder of a blazer so soft he was afraid it was going to start melting like lemon sherbet. "He's fine."

"He's fine," Patrick Keenan said. "I'm fine. We're all fine. What am I supposed to tell him after the game?"

"Tell him two things," Hartnett said. "One, tell him he still doesn't know shit about calling his own game. And two, tell him good luck next week in Pawtucket."

"We're moving him up?" Patrick Keenan said.

"You bet," Hartnett said.

He and Booker took an elevator down to the parking-lot level. Neither one of them spoke until they were in the car, Hartnett sitting up front with him.

"It's still crazy," Hartnett said.

"Good crazy or bad crazy?"

"Both."

"My favorite kind."

"It's like I used to say in the old days," Hartnett said. "It's a Charlie Stoddard world. Rest of us are just living in it."

They were about halfway to Hartford when Ted Hartnett punched out Grace's number on his cell, hoping to catch her at home, about six-thirty San Francisco time.

She picked up on the third ring.

"Hey," he said.

"I was going to call you later. How'd he do?"

"Unless he falls down a flight of steps, he'll be in Boston within two weeks."

"He threw hard."

"Hard as his goddamn head."

"You've just described all the men in my life," Grace said.

CHARLIE HAD FORGOTTEN how many parts of Fenway Park reminded him of the Bat Cave.

It was the same here as it was with Wrigley Field, Charlie knew, people confusing old and beat-down with quaint and charming. But then he had figured out early in his career that you were supposed to worship all old shit in baseball, all the stuff that had happened fifty or a hundred years ago along with any ballparks still standing from back then. It was like something spelled out for you in the Bible.

The real Bible, not *The Sporting News*.

The first time he'd ever been to Fenway as a kid, that first trip to the ballpark that was supposed to put stars in his eyes, he'd thought the outside, even the brick parts, looked like some old warehouse.

Charlie was there that day with his Uncle Sam, his mother's brother.

He would have been there with his father, a huge Red Sox fan, except for the fact that Frank Stoddard had gone out for a six-pack of Narragansett beer when Charlie was six and nobody had heard from him again until the veterans' hospital in Phoenix had called halfway through Charlie's rookie year with the Mets and told him a guy claiming to be his father was about to check out from liver failure.

Other things he remembered about Fenway, from when he finally made it there as a player: a bar, Who's on First, at the end of Yawkey Way; the big souvenir store on Yawkey Way, one that still needed a coat of paint; the small parking lot for the players at the intersection of Yawkey and Van Ness, where kids would stand at the fence and wait for ballplayers to show up in the afternoon. These were the Red Sox ball players who would eventually piss the kids off and make them crazy by always finding a way to lose to the Yankees or not make it to the World Series or lose the Series when they did make it. Which would make the kids grow up into pissed-off *adult* Red Sox fans, who would then raise pissed-off kids of their own.

These people, Charlie knew, just from being in the same sport, all assumed the same thing, from the time the Red Sox reported to spring training:

Anything that could go wrong for their team would.

It didn't matter whether it was Bill Lee serving up that fat pitch to Tony Perez in Game 7 of the '75 World Series or the ball going through Buckner's legs in '86 or Bucky Dent's home run in the 1978 playoff game or Roger Clemens ending up winning one goddamn World Series with the Yankees after another. Something would happen, and it would be another year and counting since the Red Sox had won their last World Series.

Charlie used to think that the dark, dungeonlike corridors that looked as if they'd been in place since Paul Revere just fit everybody's dark, pissed-off mood.

The field was always much better.

The fans loved the way the field looked, especially the high Green Monster wall that looked so close to home plate you thought you could hit it with spit, probably the most famous landmark in all of baseball outside of the place at Yankee Stadium where they honored all the dead Yankees. Fans loved the look of the place, and so did all the writers who got hard even thinking about what they liked to call the tiny little bandbox. Hitters, even lefthanded hitters, thought the place was just swell. Not pitchers. Pitchers, Charlie was explaining to Kevin Oslin, the Red Sox p.r. man, wanted the Green Monster chopped into kindling and sold on eBay.

"Wait a second," Oslin said. "You weren't drafted for this duty. I heard you volunteered."

He was all Irish, reddish-brown hair, a wide face and freckles, dressed in a white shirt and khaki slacks and wearing penny loafers, as if he'd just come from his eleven o'clock class at Holy Roller High School.

"I did volunteer."

"Which must mean you *wanted* the adventure of pitching here."

"I wanted to pitch for Ted. I wanted to pitch with my kid, even if no one seems to believe that."

They had been out on the field, and now Oslin was taking him down the creepy, narrow tunnel that took you from the Red Sox dugout all the way to the steps leading up to their clubhouse.

It reminded Charlie of the kind of underground place where you hoped to corner Omars and Yussefs and the rest of the bad guys with the diapers on their heads.

"You want to know how high the water gets in here when we get flooded after a good rain?" Oslin said.

"Not that much."

"Some of the rats are surprisingly good swimmers," Oslin said.

"Are we there yet?" Charlie said.

They came out of the tunnel and went up the stairs, Oslin showing him the side door into the manager's office at the top, around the corner from the main entrance to the Red Sox clubhouse, where the only thing that looked close to being new was the whorehouse red carpet.

"Nice lounge," Charlie said to Oslin. "Where's the main room?"

"What, you don't know a shrine when you see one?"

"A shrine to what?"

"You're gonna be our savior," Oslin said. "You tell me."

Charlie had pitched twice in Pawtucket, three innings of relief against the Norfolk Mets and then a start against Syracuse where he'd gone seven innings, thrown one hundred and three pitches, given up three runs and struck out seven, even shown off a fastball that had topped out three times at 94 mph.

Pooty Shaw, who'd briefly reinjured himself, had gone down to Pawtucket to catch him for that one, since old McCoy Stadium in Pawtucket was barely more than an hour from Boston. Pooty had jammed the knee on his good leg sliding into home against the Angels, and the team had sent him back to Boston to rehab the leg; when he was healthy enough, they'd decided to give him one game in Triple A, as much for him to see live pitching as to get officially acquainted, catcher-to-pitcher this time, with Charlie Stoddard.

When they came off the field after the top of the seventh that night, Pooty had said to him, "You can tell Pooty. The deal you cut with the devil—what you gonna owe on the ass end?"

"Meaning?"

"Meaning those last couple of fastballs had more hum than Alqueen."

"Alqueen?"

"My new fiancée."

"You're really fixing to get married again?"

"My agent is running the numbers right now."

Charlie mentioned that night that Pooty's lisp seemed to have disappeared almost completely.

Pooty leaned forward and opened his mouth wide and showed him the clear plastic covering the roof of his mouth.

"Pooty Junior's orthodontist hooked me up with this palate expander," he said. "I asked him to take a look-see one night and he said I had molar issues forcing my tongue up into a lisp issue. But he said he could fix it up and have me talking like one of the *Baseball Tonight* dudes in no time."

He nodded like, damn right, and said, "You see how I handled 'ortho-dontist' there?"

"Like you were throwing behind the runner," Charlie said.

"There you go."

Pooty left the next day to join the Sox at the end of their road trip, a four-game series in Chicago against the White Sox, before they came home to start a twelve-game homestand. The plan was for Charlie to re-main in Pawtucket, where the Pawtucket Red Sox had just started a homestand of their own, and then make one more start there before Patrick Keenan, Ted Hartnett, and Gary Goldberg—the Red Sox gen-eral manager who still hadn't found time to formally introduce himself to Charlie—decided whether or not to bring him up to the big club.

Chang, now on full scholarship with Patrick Keenan, had driven up to Rhode Island from New York the day before to work with him. The two of them had eaten at a Chinese restaurant not far from the Ramada where they were both staying. When Charlie got back to the room, the message light on his phone was blinking.

Ted Hartnett, calling from Chicago.

"Your kid came up with a blister on his throwing hand," Hartnett's voice said. "Yippy Cantreras has an ingrown toenail. Stroke victims re-cover faster than him. So I can't move him up. I'm taking Donnie Glynn out of the bullpen to start tomorrow afternoon. You're pitching Friday night at Fenway."

Just like that.

Now here he was.

The only other player in the clubhouse at noon was Pooty. He was com-ing out of the trainer's room when Charlie and Kevin Oslin showed up.

Pooty was wearing skimpy black briefs and Charlie noticed again that he wasn't built like a catcher at all. He was about six-three, probably not even two hundred pounds, no body fat on him anywhere, as lean as lead in a pencil. On his left arm, the one place on his body he said was re-served for tattoos—and, he explained, only for the woman who was his primary situation at the time—was ALQUEEN in big block letters, underneath the crossouts for Vonette and Sun, Pooty explaining to Charlie in Pawtucket that his agent had run some numbers and the crossouts were way cheaper than having them erased with some of that laser surgery.

"You're gonna hear about me putting 'elective' in front of 'surgery,'" he told Charlie, "the same day you hear me put 'minor' in front of 'surgery.'"

Charlie also noticed a couple of other crossouts down near Pooty's left wrist, but the names had begun to fade into the darkness of his skin, like they were old sunspots.

"Well, well, well," Pooty said now in the home clubhouse at Fenway. "If it ain't Cy Old."

Charlie had finally given up trying to reach Tom on the road, either at one of the team hotels (Ted Hartnett had given him the list of fake names Tom used, all of them belonging to rock stars like Jim Morrison and Jimi Hendrix who had died young) or on the various cell-phone numbers Grace had given him.

"These are all the numbers I have," Grace said.

"You mean there's more?"

"One more, as far as I know."

"Who gets that one?"

"Blondes, as far as I can tell," Grace said. "With a few rock singers who look like they slay vampires in their spare time thrown in."

Then she said: "What good is it going to do even if you reach him? He's just going to ask you what he asked me: What part of 'I don't want anything to do with him' isn't he hearing?"

"You used to tell me the exact same thing," Charlie said. "But I knew you didn't mean it."

"He means it, trust me."

This was after his start in Pawtucket, the day before he got the call from Hartnett.

"I'm gonna make it to Boston, Gracie. He's got to talk to me eventually."

"That's not what he says. He says that's the beauty of baseball, the catcher doesn't have to know the leftfielder's name."

Charlie said, "I've got news for you: If he pouts and acts like there's this big feud between us, the media is going to have a field day."

"Hul-*lo*?" Grace said. "There is a feud between you, in his mind, anyway. And by the way, you should have worried about the media long before this, this . . . what? What would they call it in baseball, Charlie? A wild pitch?"

And hung up on him.

Eddie Greene, the Red Sox equipment manager, an edgy little white dude with a skinhead haircut and matching diamond studs in each ear, gave him a locker down at the end of the lefthand wall as you came into the clubhouse. He saw he was between Jerry Janzen, the Red Sox' veteran centerfielder, and Ray J. Guerrero, the rightfielder, one of the rookie stars of baseball this season. Guerrero was the Puerto Rican kid who'd played with the Trenton Thunder last year and now was hitting .340, with thirty-eight home runs already, one hundred RBI exactly.

Guerrero came into the clubhouse about ten minutes after Charlie. He had a fair complexion and freckles and one of those hair situations going where you only bleached the top part white-blond. When he took off his t-shirt, Charlie saw an upper body that made him think Ray J. had come to America for the Nautilus equipment and free weights.

The first thing Guerrero did when his shirt was off was go stand in front of the full-length mirror near the entrance to the trainer's room and check himself out from all angles, as if he were thinking of giving himself a test drive later.

When he came back to his locker, Charlie introduced himself, saying, "How you doing there, Ray?"

"I jus' wanna have a good season," Ray J. said.

"Man, this ballpark is made for you," Charlie said.

"Jus' wanna have a good season."

"Well, nice meeting you," Charlie said.

Ray J. grabbed the sports section of the *Globe* off a stack on the long table in the middle of the room and headed for the bathroom.

"See you in about an hour there, Ray," Eddie Greene said, giving a little wave.

Charlie said, "Man of few words, huh?"

"You have no idea how few," Eddie said.

"He jus' wanna have a good season."

"I keep telling him," Eddie said. "He's already *had* a good season."

On the other side of Jerry Janzen's locker was the one belonging to Julio Paulino, the first baseman the Red Sox had signed out of the Mexican League in June after their regular first baseman, Ben Miller, had torn up his knee diving into the first-base stands for a foul ball. There was some dispute now about Julio's age, whether he was forty or forty-three, Charlie'd heard some sportswriters arguing about that on some Sunday morning talk show where four of them sat around and argued about everything. All Charlie knew was that when he came up with the Mets, Julio Paulino had already been in the big leagues for two years, with the Dodgers; even then, he'd looked a lot older than whatever age he said he was.

Pooty Shaw came over as Charlie got himself situated.

"See, this is a good thing for you," Pooty said. "No matter how old you are, you ain't still never gonna be older than Julio. We was in Texas the first time through this season, before this last? His whole family come into the clubhouse before the game, this sweet-looking wife and all these little Julios? I swear, I heard one of those little guys use the Mexican for 'grandpa.'"

"Maybe that's why Eddie had me locker down here."

Pooty said, "Yeah, he got you in here with people your own age, probably got some of your same interests and whatnot."

Charlie said, "You know that age is just a state of mind, right?"

"Yeah," Pooty said, "next to one of them other old states like Florida."

Charlie had planned just to take a room at the Westin in Copley Square for tonight, not knowing if he'd be on his way back to Pawtucket in the morning. But Pooty had insisted that he had plenty of room at his place way up on Commonwealth, a couple of blocks down from the Public Gardens. Charlie said, no no no, he couldn't put him out that way, and Pooty had said Charlie wouldn't be putting him out at all, this wasn't even in his townhouse, but a condo he rented on the top floor of the brownstone next door. That was where he put up Pooty Junior and his daughter, Swin, and their nanny, on account, he said, of his custody agreement with Vonette said the children couldn't live under the same roof with him and Alqueen.

Anyway, Pooty said, Pooty Junior and Swin were on their way back to Upper Saddle River, where their private school started up at the end of August.

"Havin' you next door will be a lot easier on me than having that nanny girl Uma over there walkin' around in no clothes all the time," Pooty said.

"Uma have a killer body on her?"

Pooty closed his eyes and shook his head, like he did at Shea when he was trying to clear his mind of negative Vonette images.

"Uma was a big girl," Pooty said.

He told Charlie they'd get together and fine-tune a game plan for the Tigers after Charlie had gone over their hitters with Hick Landon, the Red Sox pitching coach.

"Cy Old!" Pooty said again, smiling and showing off brilliant white teeth. "Got hisself back in the *big* time!"

Chang showed up in the Red Sox clubhouse at three o'clock. Charlie tried again to get some details about his financial arrangement with Patrick Keenan. Chang said, don't worry about it. All Charlie needed to know, he said, was that Keenan had made it well worth it for him to rearrange his schedule. Unless, of course, his start tonight turned out to be a one-shot flameout. If it didn't, and everything went well, Charlie pitching well enough to stay in Ted Hartnett's rotation, Chang would show up the day before his starts, either in Boston or on the road. Then he would stick around for the game, and be there the next morning to make sure Charlie's arm had recovered the way Chang thought it should. ("We're going to do something revolutionary," Chang said. "We're going to try to take care of your arm with more than ice and a jacket.")

"It can't just be Keenan's money," Charlie said. "You're doing this because you care."

"Don't flatter yourself. If I care about anybody, it's me."

"Wait a second," Charlie said, trying to act shocked. "This isn't all about me?"

"Maybe one of these days you'll actually figure out not everything is."

"Well," Charlie said, "that'll suck, won't it?"

"I'm serious," Chang said. "You're already famous, Charlie, even if it's not the way you want anymore, which is one of the reasons why you're doing all this. But if this all works out the way we both want it to, you're going to make me famous. Not only are you going to make me famous, you're going to answer a question for me one of these days."

"What's the question?"

"You'll hear it when you hear it."

They both got gray Red Sox sweat shorts and t-shirts from Eddie Greene and went for a short run that started on Yawkey Way and finally took them all the way over to Huntington Avenue, the two of them running easily, making up their route as they went along, making sure they didn't get too far away from the ballpark. When they came back, they went out to rightfield, Charlie explaining that they'd originally put the bullpen out there to shorten the field a little for Ted Williams. Wow, Chang said, looking bored as usual, that's a very interesting piece of trivia, he'd have to make sure to remember that one. They did some stretching out there, then some side-to-side sprints, as if Chang were training him to be a defensive specialist in the NBA. After that was a few minutes of long tossing. Then the two of them sat down on the warning track, backs against the bullpen wall, and did a few yoga exercises.

"The other boys are going to make fun of me," Charlie said.

"Just keep breathing and think happy thoughts."

"I've got just one happy thought for tonight," Charlie said. "Getting out of the top of the fucking first."

"You can't believe how many people use that at the ashrams," Chang said.

It was a few minutes past four when they came back into the clubhouse, almost all of the Red Sox players there by now. Charlie looked across the room to Tom's locker to see if he had arrived yet, but there was just a clean white home uniform hanging there, no street clothes.

He was on his way to take a shower when Ted Hartnett's head appeared in the doorway to the manager's office.

"Hey," he said. "Got a minute?"

Charlie grabbed a bottle of Poland Spring water out of the cooler in the middle of the room, walked into Hartnett's office, saw his son stretched out on a small leather sofa as Hartnett shut the door behind him.

"Yo," Tom MacKenzie said, in what Charlie always thought of as a *whatever* voice. "Pardon me if I don't, like, get up."

14

TED HARTNETT had seen a sixteen-game lead cut by ten games faster than you could cut into a pile of chips at the blackjack table when the cards went cold on you.

And it got better.

The team chasing his wasn't just any team, it was the goddamn Yankees, who had spent almost the last hundred years of American League baseball treating the Boston Red Sox like their cell-block bitch.

On top of that, Hartnett's starting pitching, which was the main reason his team had built that big lead in the first place, had turned into the emergency room on one of those television shows where all the doctors spent an hour running around like they were the ones who needed to be medicated.

Through it all, Hartnett had tried to put a calm face on all of it, talking a constant bunch of complete smack about what a long season it was even if we all forgot that sometimes, how he knew all along that his team had to come back to the field a little bit, how he knew the Yankees were too good to be playing the kind of ball they were playing in April and May and June.

Then he would go back to his office after telling the press all that and wash down another Zantac 75 stomach pill with another cup of black coffee, which he would then chase with another half-pack of Marlboros.

Now Hartnett had opened himself wide open, had done everything except stick a KICK ME sign on his own ass by signing a forty-year-old pitcher who happened to be his ex-roommate, and not just any old forty-year-old ex-roommate, but one who hadn't pitched in the big leagues in five years; one who said he had been miraculously cured by a trainer one Boston columnist was already calling Cato to Charlie Stoddard's Green Hornet. The columnist then explained he was only using Cato and the Green Hornet because he wanted to give Charlie a frame of reference from his own generation.

And wait, it got even better than that.

Because Charlie Stoddard's *son* pitched for Ted Hartnett. And Charlie Stoddard's son wasn't just any run-of-the-mill pitcher, he happened to be the twenty-year-old immortal-in-training phenom ace of Hartnett's ever-dwindling pitching staff.

The same phenom ace son who made no secret of the fact that he didn't want to be on the same planet with his father, much less the same baseball team.

So, Hartnett thought as he watched the two of them glare at each other, on top of every other swell thing that was going on in his life these days, he was about to become a fucking family therapist.

Tom MacKenzie had the headphones from his Discman around his neck. He was wearing some kind of baseball cap that looked as if it had been chewed by a forest animal, a yellow Speedo t-shirt about four sizes too big for him, baggy jeans, red leather basketball shoes. He had a day's growth of beard around the bunnytail of blond hair underneath his lower lip.

With all that, he looked like someone who belonged on the cover of one of those teen magazines.

As always, looking into his eyes—when he'd make eye contact, anyway—was the same as looking into his father's.

"If neither one of you is going to say anything, I will," Hartnett said. "And here's all I really want to say: The three of us in this room are going to find a way to make this thing work, for as long as the three of us happen to be together. What do you think about that, T-Mac?"

Tom said, "You don't care what I think, don't start acting now like you do."

He jerked his head in the direction of Charlie, who was standing against the white wall to the right of Hartnett's desk, thumbs hooked into the pockets of his jeans. Still a kid himself, Hartnett thought, in just about all the important ways.

"Neither one of you cares what I think about this shit," Tom said. "You were always gonna do what you were gonna do. So, like, whatever."

Hartnett noticed he had a pinch of smokeless tobacco in his cheek and a Gatorade cup in his hand, which he spit into now.

Hartnett had always thought that if you eliminated the spitting, you could shorten the ballpark day down to about three hours, including the game.

"I mean, you guys are supposed to know best, being the *adults* and all," Tom said to Hartnett. "That's if you count him."

Charlie straightened. "You really think Ted is just doing this to bust balls? Or do you think there's this chance he might be doing it because he thinks I might actually be able to help this team win?"

"Mom says you could get him to do anything you wanted in the old days. Run bare-assed through Times Square on a bet. Buy one of those broken-down nags they drive through Central Park and walk it into a bar. She says nothing has changed."

Ted could hear her saying that because she had said the same thing to him on the phone the night he called from the front seat of Booker Impala Washington's limo, on his way to the Hartford airport.

"You've been with me, what, a season and a half now?" Hartnett said. "You ever see me do anything except put the team first?"

"There's a first time for everything. Even putting something else first."

"You're wrong," Hartnett said to the kid in an even voice, knowing that if he lost it now, the room would turn into a lit fuse. "You don't have to accept you're wrong or admit you're wrong. But you are."

"Does he make you do his laundry?" Tom said.

Charlie said, "Shut up."

Tom looked at him with that sleepy-eyed look young guys thought made them look fierce. "I had to take shit from you when I was little. Not anymore."

"You were a nicer kid when all you did was feel sorry for yourself," Charlie said.

"Fuck you."

To Hartnett, Charlie said: "I'm wasting my time here. He knows everything. All guys his age know everything."

Tom said, "You sure as hell didn't."

"That's enough," Hartnett said.

He stood up, came around in front of his desk.

"Okay," he said. "If we have to do this once a day, we'll do it once a day. But we'll do it in here, not in front of the other players, not in front of the coaches, not in front of the press. Got it?"

They both nodded reluctantly.

"I'm not here to settle twenty years of bad blood, or whatever it is the two of you have got going," he said. "If Grace can't get the two of you to see eye-to-eye, I know I can't. But this shitstorm is not gonna get in the way of what we're supposed to be trying to do here. Which is win the goddamn game. T-Mac, you're the best I got. I know you're not going anywhere. Hell, you're gonna be here long after I'm gone. Your old man might only be here for tonight. But if he really does have something left in that arm, he's gonna be here for six weeks at least, and maybe more than that if we can hold on to this lead. And that's just the way it is."

Tom MacKenzie started to get up. "Sit your ass down," Hartnett said.

"I want to be clear on this, because the last thing in the world I want to do is ever talk this much to either one of you ever again," Hartnett said. "I don't want to read any garbage in the *Globe* or the *Herald* about why you two act the way you do around each other. I don't want to turn on that ESPN some night and see one of those *Up Close* touchy-feely deals where the guy leans in so close it looks like he wants to go down on you, wanting to know if Charlie called Tommy on his birthday or forgot to buy him a hobby horse one Christmas. Tom, you tell 'em you were never close and maybe this will bring you closer. Or maybe not. Charlie, come up with something about how you hope you can be a better spot starter than you were a father. And then, for Chrissakes go find something you just remembered you had to do."

Hartnett went over, opened his door.

"Just stay out of each other's way. Is that clear?"

"Crystal," Charlie said.

"Whatever," Tom said.

"I'm glad we could share this time together," Hartnett said. "Now both of you get out of my office."

Hick Landon, the Red Sox pitching coach, had played for eleven different teams during his own major league career in the '70s and '80s, his laundry list of stops even including the Mets right after Charlie left, where he hadn't pitched much in middle relief but had gotten to know Ted Hartnett. He came from a place he called One-Stoplight, Georgia, weighed in now at about two-seventy, Charlie was guessing, moved as slowly as a glacier and talked even slower. In an age where modern pitching coaches sat with stopwatches around their necks, used everything except Palm Pilots to chart games, and practically needed a briefcase to hold all their scouting reports and tendencies, Hick was a throwback who spoke in his own colorful shorthand and, at least according to Hartnett, had a better understanding of pitching and how to set up hitters than anyone he'd ever met.

Fastballs were oil in Hick's vocabulary.

His basic philosophy of pitching, he said, could be described in one damn word: humping.

When Charlie asked him to elaborate on that one, Hick moved a truly disgusting wad of chewing tobacco, the kind that was supposed to be more of a health hazard around baseball than a toxic waste dump, from one cheek to another, opening his mouth wide as he did, and said, "In and out."

"Oh," Charlie said.

Curveballs, he said, were nothing but ho's.

"Or hookers, I guessed you could call 'em," Hick said.

"Why don't you just call 'em hooks?" Charlie said.

Hick stared at him with eyes so droopy they seemed to disappear all the way into the amazing bags underneath them and said, "I ain't here to split hairs with you, son."

Changeups and off-speed pitches were "bools."

"Bools?"

Hick squinted and said, "As in *bool*shit."

Hick had started out as a pitching coach with the Cardinals when Joe Torre was still managing them. And he was still famous around the Cardinals for the Sunday afternoon game at Busch Stadium when Torre had sent him out to the mound to calm down Yippy Cantreras, an emotional righthander who had managed to escape from Havana, and the Cuban National Team, the previous winter, the same Yippy Cantreras now being used as Hartnett's fourth starter with the Red Sox.

Yippy usually became manic when he would pitch himself into some kind of jam, stalking around behind the mound, talking to himself in both English and Spanish, always looking up to the sky eventually, at least according to infielders who had played with him, and screaming at his Creator, "Why you always got to fock Yippy like this here?"

He was doing that against the Phillies when Hick finished his slow waddle to the mound, the same one Charlie would see on TV now, Hick looking like a big old turtle trying to make it across a road.

"What?" Yippy is supposed to have screamed as soon as Hick Landon got across the first baseline. "You tell me, Eek. What is Yippy doing wrong?"

According to legend, Hick had spit then, put his hands in his back pockets, and said, "Beats me, Pedro. But whatever it is, it sure is pissin' Joe off."

And began his slow journey back to the Cards dugout.

Now in the tiny coaches' room off the Red Sox clubhouse, Hick was going through the Tigers lineup that Charlie would be facing in a couple of hours.

"First four, in here," he said, dragging a meaty hand across the long-sleeved BASEBALL ASSISTANCE TEAM t-shirt he was wearing, one dotted with with tobacco stains that looked like dried blood.

"Next four," he said, "set 'em up with some kind of bool away, then come in on 'em with your red hot oil."

He squinted at Charlie. "Ted says you got a split goes like this on right-hand hitters. That right?"

He made a motion that was like a plane going down toward where his left hip used to be.

"I figured I better, pitching here," Charlie said.

"If'n you don't," Hick said, "they can just paste your sorry butt to that green wall out there like one of them little stick-it notes."

He dragged himself up, as if the meeting was over, and Charlie said, "We only talked about eight guys." He looked down at the lineup card Hick had given him and said, "What about the second baseman, Perry?"

Hick Landon said, "Ho ho ho."

"Nothing but hookers," Charlie said.

"No bool," Hick said.

Charlie's locker was as far away as possible from Tom's, as small as the Red Sox clubhouse was. He was sure that was Hartnett's doing, knowing from the old days that Hartnett would analyze everything on a team including where guys sat on the team plane. Charlie looked across the room and saw that Tom actually had two lockers; there was the one he used for his clothes and then another one on his right that was taken up by what looked like a miniature sound system, and several acoustic guitars. The locker to his left belonged to Snip Daggett, the Red Sox All-Star second baseman who Charlie noticed hadn't shown up until after five o'clock, a full hour after everybody else on the team.

Charlie decided that Snip Daggett had won all the day's fashion awards with a matching lime-green shirt and shorts outfit, black do-rag, and Jesus sandals.

When he did show up, Charlie immediately flipped through the media guide Kevin Oslin had given him and saw the Red Sox had Snip Daggett listed at five-seven. Charlie could see now that was a joke, Snip was really only about five-four. But he was leading the American League in walks and on-base percentage, so being a midget was clearly working for him.

Charlie turned to Ray J. Guerrero, just trying to make conversation, and said, "Snip reminds me of Lil' Bow Wow, you know? The little rapper? I met him after one of those music awards shows in New York."

"I have dogs," Guerrero said. "Big dogs." He went back to studying a page in *Baseball America* that listed all the players' salaries.

"That's the great thing about baseball, you know?" Charlie said. "A guy looks like your thumb can be as good as a guy six-five."

"I jus' wanna have a good year," Ray J. Guerrero said.

Tom MacKenzie came in from outside and flicked a switch on his stereo, and suddenly loud rap music filled the room. Charlie looked around and saw some of the young guys, including Snip, start shucking and jiving in front of their lockers.

All Charlie could pick up was the following refrain:

Took a meetin on that
Took a meetin on that
Then I shot the bitch cold
Called the meetin adjourned.

"That sounds like Mo Jiggy," Charlie said. "Does he have a new album?"

Guerrero smiled for the first time and said, "You like Mo?"

Finally, Charlie thought, common ground. "He's actually a friend of mine."

Ray J. said, "CD's called *Diddy This.*"

"I'll have to pick it up at Sam Goody's," Charlie said.

He reached into his duffel, took out Springsteen's *Greatest Hits,* turned his chair around so he was practically sitting inside his locker, put on his own headphones, skipped through songs on his Discman until he found the song he wanted, hearing the thump of Max Weinberg's drums that meant the beginning of "Better Days," let the song take him back to when he always used to get ready for games listening to music like this, listening to Springsteen growl now about being tired of waiting for to-morrow to come, for the train to come rolling around the tracks . . .

He closed his eyes and smiled, trying to picture himself, thinking about going through the Tiger order with the oil and the bool and the hooks Hick Landon had talked about. Springsteen was into "Blood Brothers" when Charlie felt a tap on his shoulder and turned around to see Pooty Shaw standing there.

"We got to get out to the pen soon," he said, when Charlie took off the headphones. He pointed at the Discman and said, "What you got goin' there?"

"The Boss."

"Say what?"

"The Boss. Bruce Springsteen."

Pooty gave him a look that was a mixture of sadness and disgust, one he got from Chang all the time.

"You into that thit?"

"Wait a second," Charlie said. "Your lisp is back?"

"Be all right, time the game starts," he said. "Got Alqueen bringing over a backup widget from the houth."

He said he was afraid he had done something bad to his palate expander last night when he and Alqueen were playing a game she called *The Undersea World of Pooty Cousteau*, and the thing had just busted completely a few minutes ago when he tried to bite into an apple.

"What are we talking about here?" Charlie asked. "Some kind of snorkeling deal with you and your thweetie?"

"Don't ath," Pooty said, wincing.

Behind home plate was what Patrick Keenan considered the only major improvement they'd made at Fenway Park since around the time Ted Williams, the Splinter himself, had called it quits. It was the huge area that began at the top of the screen behind the plate and rose several glass-encased stories toward the top of Fenway. Once the press box had been in there, giving the sportswriters one of the most wonderful views of baseball anywhere. Now the press box was way up at the top of Fenway, and underneath was where they had the luxury seating, in an area known as the 600 Club. The press hated the place, where they served gourmet everything and where you could only pay with a credit card. The common fans hated it, many of them saying it was as if they'd built a theater in the middle of a ballpark. Some of the Red Sox hitters said that the building of the 600 Club had changed the wind currents at Fenway and made it harder to hit home runs.

Patrick didn't care, because the 600 Club was a home run for *him*.

You didn't have to be around sports for very long to figure out that most teams and team owners looked at private suites the way oil guys looked at gushers.

Keenan had been to enough owners' meetings to know that no one had any idea what anybody else in baseball was really making—or losing—because the whole sport, as far as he could tell anyway, was being run by Hollywood accountants, the kind who wanted to tell you *Forrest Gump* was still in the red. But all owners did manage to agree on this one important thing: Private suites were pure profit, same as they were in pro football, where there just seemed to be more of them. The only problem with the ones at Fenway was that the park was older than Beacon Hill and not much bigger than a trolley car, and so the previous owners had only had enough room to build just so many of them when the project started in the early 1980s.

"Sometimes I look out there and it's as if my ballplayers are watching the people up in 600, when it should be the other way around," Ted Hartnett said to Keenan one time.

"Tell them to get over it," Keenan said.

Next to the 600 Club was what was known as the Yawkey Suite, named for old Tom Yawkey, the most famous Red Sox owner of them all, known for his good works, for the courtly manners of a gentleman farmer, and for having picnic lunches in the outfield during away games while he listened to Red Sox games on the radio with his wife, Jean.

If Keenan wasn't worried about hurting the feelings of some old fart Red Sox fan in the suite, he would occasionally refer to Yawkey as his Uncle Tom, pointing out that since Yawkey was such a gentleman, it was probably just an oversight that the Red Sox hadn't had a black player in their lineup until 1959.

It didn't take long after Keenan's group bought the team for the Yawkey Suite to become known as the best party in town, filled with the smartest people, and the prettiest. When the Red Sox had swept a four-game series from the Yankees in late June, moving what had been a six-game lead up to ten, the place had been wild every night, filled up with a mix of new friends from Boston and old ones from New York who'd made the trip up for the weekend. One night he'd have Fleet Bank fighting it out with old theater friends from the Nederlander Group in New York; the next night it would be the editorial board of the *Globe* sucking around their bosses from the *New York Times;* another was all the politicos, both U.S. senators from Massachusetts, one of whom Keenan still ran with sometimes, even if he was what his father would've called a fooking Republican; the mayor of New York City; the various restaurant owners and media types he had accumulated since he'd arrived in town; and, just to spice things up a little, about half of the modeling agency—

Very Big Babes—in which Patrick Keenan had recently bought a discreet half-interest.

"Nobody knows more phonies than you," Booker was saying to Keenan, as they watched the Red Sox–Tigers game.

Keenan said, "But they have to be interesting phonies."

"Yeah," Booker said, "that Harvard professor you had here the last homestand, the one whose eyes get all full up when he talks about old-time Red Sox teams? One urped on the California rolls? He probably gets real tired goin' through life with that lampshade on his head."

Tonight it was just Keenan and Booker in the cushy seats in the front row, watching Charlie Stoddard make the early innings against the Tigers look like he was working two jobs.

It was 4–1 Tigers, and Charlie had just walked the first two hitters in the top of the fourth.

"How many walks is that now, I've misplaced my calculator?" Keenan said.

"I don't know, but I think the number might have a comma in it," Booker said. He was leaning forward, hands on knees, studying every move Charlie made, sometimes even using binoculars.

Keenan sipped some Jack Daniel's from the tumbler he'd set on the rug next to him, the glass too big to fit inside the drink holder on the arm of his chair. "You think it's just nerves?"

Booker said, "Man looks like he fighting on hisself, trying to make every pitch perfect. Like a hitter squeezing on the bat so hard his hands like to start to bleed."

"He's bleeding," Keenan said, "I'm dying."

"Thing is," Booker said, "the damn velocity is there. It's his command that's for shit."

Charlie threw ball one to the Tiger third baseman, Joey Johnson.

"Forgot to tell you," Booker said. "A call come in for you while you was in the men's. That one you call Charlotte Ford? The head bitch from that Big Babes? She said she rearranged things and that she gonna be good to meet you about eleven or thereabouts. Said, and I'm quoting here, 'Tell him I've got the carrot, and I threw away the stick.'"

"She's got a clever way with words," Keenan said.

"Nice to see you bringing her out of her shell this way."

"Watch the game."

"Yes, Uncle Tom."

"Don't give me that shit," Keenan said.

They both watched as Hick Landon made his way up the dugout steps and began his trip to the mound, which always reminded Patrick Keenan of a luxury liner beginning an Atlantic crossing.

At the same time, Pooty Shaw took off his mask, called time with the home-plate umpire, seemed to adjust some kind of mouthpiece, and started toward the mound himself.

Hick Landon spoke first.

"Well, now, pitchin like a pussy, ain't we?"

Charlie said, "I can't put the fucking thing where I want."

Pooty Shaw grinned. "Boy, ain't that the story of Pooty's life."

Pooty took the ball out of Charlie's glove, rubbed it up hard. Then he said to Hick, "What's the deal, we on a short leash the rest of the way?"

Hick said, "More like a choke collar."

"Listen, we can get out of this," Pooty said to Charlie. "We got their number four coming up. Fat-ass white boy named Zach Stroud. See him there, droolin' in the on-deck? He told me before I come out that he can see the old man is ready to go."

Hick said, "Got a question."

Charlie looked past Hick and could see the home-plate umpire take off his mask and start the walk to the mound that always meant, Wrap it up.

"Fire away," Charlie said.

"If you put yourself in the hole against this asshole, do it on purpose. I mean, can you hump it up there three times after that?"

"Ooh ooh ooh," Pooty said. "In, out, in."

The ump was a square-jawed young guy who reminded Charlie of a cop. But he'd been doing a good job with balls and strikes all night, giving both starters one strike zone in the first inning and staying with it. Now he said what all umpires said:

"I hate to break this up, guys. But let's play."

Hick said, "Son, your old pal the skipper said I should tell you that if you're gonna make your move, now is the time."

Pooty said, "In, out, in. Your specialty."

Hick left them there. Pooty handed Charlie the ball and said, "You got to make your stand right here, baby. Start pitchin' up to your stuff. Get out of this, and we'll get you some runs this inning, I promise. Snip and Julio and me are the first three up. You just got to make sure this don't get out of control. Game gets to six, seven runs on you, and it's gonna look like a beat-down, even if we both know you pitched better than that."

Charlie went high and outside to Stroud for ball one, then acted frustrated on the mound, as if he'd completely lost it now. Then he threw one in the dirt and heard the sellout crowd at Fenway groan.

Two-oh.

He'd told Hick he could throw three hard strikes in a row to this guy. Of course he'd told him he could do it. Christ, he'd never told the truth to a pitching coach or manager in his life, even that night against the Dodgers when he knew his arm was hurt and he shouldn't even have been out there.

But could he really do it?

He came out of his stretch with a nice tight motion, short leg kick, and put strike one on the inside corner. Stroud took it, looking almost surprised, as if he didn't think Charlie had another strike in him.

Then Charlie did it again, working fast this time, trying to throw off the guy's rhythm after taking a lot of time before the first three pitches, and threw another strike, this one nicking the outside. Stroud thought it was ball three and stepped out so he could bitch to the ump about that.

Standing there and talking to the young guy without looking at him, screwing around with his batting gloves, helmet, cup, pounding dirt out of his spikes. Talking the whole time until the ump took his mask off and glared Stroud back into the box.

Charlie took a look at the runners.

Looked in at Hartnett, sitting there next to Hick Landon in the dugout.

Took a deep breath like he needed it. Like he was nervous. Except he wasn't nervous all of a sudden, he was in complete command.

Pooty set up inside and Charlie nodded and put strike three on the inside corner, and it was as if somebody had nailed Zach Stroud's bat to his shoulder.

Pooty stepped up in front of the plate and gunned the ball back almost as hard as Charlie had gunned it into his mitt. "Give 'em enough rope," Pooty yelled, "and see how they hang theirselves?"

Charlie looked over and saw that Stroud was staring at him as he made his way to the Tigers dugout.

"What're *you* looking at?" Charlie yelled at him.

He could see Stroud stop then, as if about to say something back. But Charlie had already turned away. He was looking all around Fenway now, feeling the full force of the place all of a sudden, hearing a better-days sound he remembered, the one he knew was the roar of the big time.

Hartnett watched Charlie throw three straight fastballs past Stroud, that dumb shit. The next Detroit hitter, Welles, then hit a perfect double play ball to Snip Daggett. Charlie was out of the top of the fourth, still trailing, 4–1. Snip walked to lead off the Red Sox fourth, Julio doubled him home, Pooty singled Julio home, and it was 4–3. Charlie retired the Tigers in order in the fifth, Hartnett actually thinking he was getting stronger. Ray J. Guerrero hit a solo home run in the bottom of the fifth, and the game was tied.

Charlie Stoddard finally ran out of gas with two outs in the sixth, walking two guys after he had two out, and Hartnett went out to get him.

"I can get one more out," Charlie said, when Hartnett arrived at the mound.

Hartnett's answer was taking the ball with his right hand, signaling with his left for Carlos Cinquanta in the bullpen.

"You might be right," Hartnett said. "But how about we don't take any chances in a tie game and you just take it to the house now?"

Pooty Shaw had joined them, as if he didn't want to be left out. He said to Hartnett, "See how we come on there at the end, boss?"

Charlie said, "I told you before. Bruce Springsteen is the boss."

Hartnett said, "Get out of here so all the people can give you your standing O."

Charlie started off the mound, and Hartnett put a hand on his right arm and said, "How'd it feel?"

"Great," Charlie Stoddard said to him, barely loud enough to be heard. "It felt fucking great."

Halfway to the first baseline, he took off his cap and waved it to the crowd, and then when he got a few feet away from the Red Sox dugout, Hartnett watched him stop and turn to all four corners of Fenway, blowing kisses to each one. Then, before he descended into the crowd of players waiting for him at the end of the dugout closest to home plate, Charlie pointed up to Patrick Keenan's suite.

He went into the dugout and high-fived everybody except Tom MacKenzie, whom Ted Hartnett couldn't see anywhere.

15

IT WAS a couple of hours after the Red Sox had beaten the Tigers, 7–4, on Ray J. Guerrero's second home run of the game, a three-run shot in the bottom of the eighth, one of those high Fenway jobs that carried all the way over the screen at the top of the Green Monster and out onto Lansdowne Street. Or maybe all the way to the Charles River.

It was after Charlie had stood on the field doing interviews with ESPN, Fox, all the local Boston stations, Channels 2, 4, and 7 from New York, the New England Sports Network, known as NESN, which televised most Red Sox games, then met with print guys out in front of the Red Sox dugout.

"I'm not all that different from Ray J., if you really think about it," Charlie finally said, after Kevin Oslin had announced he was taking his absolute last question. The question was from the NESN kid, and was about where Charlie thought he was going from here. "I jus' wanna have a good season."

"But are you thinking about your next start?" the kid said.

Charlie said, "Just my next stop. The bar."

Pooty's townhouse was at the corner of Commonwealth and Berkeley. Charlie's place, the one that had belonged to Uma the nanny and his kids, was right next door, as advertised. Pooty told Charlie just to leave his bags with the doorman, he had a good place where they could kick back and look at some fine women without Red Sox fans wanting to ask Charlie what he'd thrown to Zach Stroud, or just wanting to discuss what Pooty called Charlie's all-around situation.

Their destination was an area of Boston that Charlie remembered as the Combat Zone, where he and his buddies used to come looking for trouble when they were old enough to drink and drive, block after block of rough bars and even rougher women. But now it was undergoing one of those urban renewal gentrification deals like like they'd pulled in New York over the last ten years, the one that had turned Times Square into the Junior League.

Charlie saw they'd put a new Ritz-Carlton over here, at the corner of Avery and Tremont, overlooking a big chunk of the Commons they were trying to dress up along with everything else. Behind it was the place Pooty had described, with shiny SUVs out front, a rope line, a bouncer in a tuxedo, even a roving spotlight.

The place was called Pooty's.

"Yours?" Charlie said.

"My name," Pooty said.

"I can see that. If the sign were any bigger, it would look like the one for Citgo out behind Fenway."

"I put in a little of my own," Pooty said, nodding to the bouncer, "after my agent run the numbers on it. They woulda let me in for nothing, that's how hot they was to have me. But to get a profit stake, I had to break down and write the damn check."

Charlie noticed a few Red Sox players standing at the bar, which was up a few steps and to their right as they moved into the semidarkness. Down below was the restaurant area, which had a dozen or so tables, this area only slightly brighter than the bar. At the far end of that room was a small stage, big enough for a piano and a black girl singer in a beige cocktail dress so tight it made Charlie imagine too much chocolate ice cream stuffed into a waffle cone.

The singer had short hair and was pretty enough and fair enough to be Halle Berry's kid sister.

Pooty blew her a little kiss when he saw her notice him standing with the maître d'.

"Who's that?" Charlie asked.

"That right there is Sun."

"Sun, your former girlfriend? The one who did the bumper-car thing with your former wife at the Stadium that time?"

"The same," Pooty said, winking at Sun now. "Look at her there, and consider it an honor, Charlie Stoddard, on account of that being one *fine* piece of feminine womanhood."

"Don't tell me," Charlie said. "The kid's just trying to break into show business."

"Oh, don't worry," Pooty said, his voice almost a groan. "She already broken in."

"Alqueen?" Charlie said. "The one you describe as your primary situation? She's okay with Sun singing at your club?"

"She thinks Sun's with Snip now, and it was Snip came to me and asked if I could see my way clear to giving her the gig."

"But she's not with Snip."

"I got her living on the other side of Commonwealth, catty corner from where you're at."

"Let me get this straight," Charlie said. "You had the nanny next door and your ex-girlfriend across the street?"

"What is this," Pooty said, "fucking MapQuest?"

They sat down at a big table in the back of the restaurant, one they'd clearly been holding for Pooty. Yippy Cantreras was there waiting for them, sipping a beer. He had a shaved head and a pencil-thin mustache and was wearing one of those dark suits with an even darker collar, red tie against white shirt, red handkerchief matching the tie and set perfectly into the breast pocket of his jacket.

"You pitch like a man tonight," Yippy said, toasting him with his tall beer glass. "Even if you a very old man."

"Not so fast, Fidel," Pooty said. "People say you're really older than Julio, and we all know Julio older than mud."

Yippy shook his head. "The book say Yippy is thirty-four in *noviembre*," he said.

"Right," Pooty said. "And that boat you got out Havana *wasn't* as big and nice as one of them Love Boats."

"I risk my life on a dream," Yippy said, trying to look solemn.

Pooty whipped his head around, as if trying to see if someone was behind him. "Sorry, baby," he said to Yippy. "I thought for a minute you saw a sportswriter behind me, or somebody else who believes that I-reesk-my-ass-on-a-dream shit."

They sat listening to Sun work her way through some ballads, occasionally picking up the beat and turning something into hip-hop. Yippy said he was waiting for his wife, who'd had to run their children and babysitter back to Brookline.

"Man's talkin' about his American wife," Pooty said. "I don't want you should be confusin' Maureen with the Yipster's Cuban wife and all his Cuban children back there in the motherland."

Charlie said, "You've got a whole other family back home?"

Yippy shrugged. "I send the check."

"You couldn't get them out?" Charlie said.

Pooty laughed hard enough that he nearly choked on the champagne he'd just sipped. "Yeah, baby," he said. "Was that bad Castro man keepin' them back there in Havana, and not Maureen the big blonde insurance girl?"

When Sun finished her set, she came over to the table and sat down next to Pooty and immediately began rubbing his upper leg as if trying to get a troublesome knot out of it. Yippy left and came back with Maureen, who reminded Charlie of the *Brady Bunch* daughter who used to part her hair in the middle.

Was she a Maureen, too?

Or Marcia?

Jesus, who gave a rip?

Thinking: *The Brady Bunch,* Charlie?

You're the one who's older than mud.

The waitress, a redhead even taller than Maureen Cantreras, wearing a tiny halter top and tight jeans, came over now and asked Charlie if he was ready to move off Diet Cokes.

"I promised my trainer I'd be a good boy tonight," he said.

"You already look good to me," she said. "I'm Randy."

Charlie said, "Why don't you be good and get me a light Dewar's and water?"

He shook her hand, which she managed to wiggle around enough to give him a little jolt.

But then it never took much.

"I'm Charlie, Randy," he said. "Nice to meet you."

She walked away, swinging the jeans just enough, knowing he was watching her go. Pooty said, "Before you and the Big Red Machine go off and pick out furniture, why don't you go ahead and tell Pooty why your boy hates your ass this much."

Pooty wanted to know if Grace had done it.

Done what? Charlie said.

"You know what I'm saying," Pooty said. "She goes to him, he cheated on your sweet momma, whoo whoo whoo. Like women do, can't give their man a little room."

"It wasn't like that," Charlie said. "I try to pin some of it on her sometimes, but my heart isn't in it."

"Oh, I see, you one of them," Pooty said, nodding.

"One of what?"

"One of them was bad at marriage, wants to be good at divorce."

Sun had gone up for one more set. Yippy and Maureen had moved to their own table, which they immediately turned into the honeymoon suite, hands all over each other. Up at the bar, little Snip Daggett was surrounded by a lot of big girls, all different kinds, white and black and even a tall Asian so pretty she made Charlie want to go up there and buy Snip a drink, maybe suggest it was time they got to know each other a little better.

It was a move he would have tried to make if he weren't trying to catch Pooty Shaw up on why Tom MacKenzie acted as if he were the only victim of divorce in all recorded history.

Charlie checked his watch. Twelve-thirty. The night would have just been starting in the old days. But he was supposed to be meeting Chang in the Red Sox clubhouse at nine the next morning, Chang saying he had to be on the one o'clock shuttle at the latest, he had just started training the new Hitler in *The Producers.*

"The guy says he doesn't look sleek enough in drag," Chang said.

"In the show or real life?" Charlie said.

"Hey," Pooty said. "You listening to me? Or your mind starting to race with thoughts about Randy, who I got to be honest with you, knows more about our pitchers' strengths and weaknesses than Hick Landon."

Charlie said, "I was thinking of how early I had to get up in the morning. What'd you just ask me?"

"If you're sure your ex didn't brainwash the boy, even if she said she didn't."

"I really don't think she ever did," Charlie said. "By the time the kid was old enough, she'd stopped being as pissed at me as she was when we first split up."

"And you split up on account of she couldn't understand why you had to have some on the side."

"Basically," Charlie said, "yeah."

"It takes a special primary to get it," Pooty said. "That having your secondaries here and there doesn't necessarily have to affect your core relationship."

"I was young," Charlie said. "I honestly thought screwing around was just part of it."

"'Course it is," Pooty said. "If it ain't, what's the damn point? Nobody gets laid like this before they famous and into the big green."

Charlie told Pooty that he wondered all the time if it would be different if he were starting out now, him and Grace, both of them young, everything ahead of them.

Pooty said, "Nah, it'd be the same thing. You go into the store and they givin' stuff away, shit, you owe it to yourself to take a free sample."

"Anyway," Charlie said, "I think the stuff Tom found out about me, he did on his own. When he was older. And just got more and more pissed off that I didn't just cheat on his mother, but I cheated him out of a family."

"So there wasn't no one big thing."

"If there was, I swear, I don't know about it. This is all about me not being there. And he says that when I was there, I acted like I didn't want to be. You can also throw in that he was growing up in the same house with basically the world's most perfect woman, the beautiful and successful Grace, driving him to all his practices and games, all the rest of it. Nothing could possibly have been her fault, everything had to be my fault."

Pooty was still sipping champagne. Charlie waved at Randy for one more drink. She put up a finger of her own, then slowly licked it.

Pooty said, "Then he started to get good in baseball and Daddy wasn't there to watch."

"Nope."

"Now he's the one going, Whoo whoo whoo, telling you you don't care."

Charlie nodded.

"And you was afraid to tell him the truth on that, am I right?"

Randy brought the drink in record time, saying, "Don't get too drunk now," in a husky voice. On the stage, Sun was doing a passable job with "Someone to Watch Over Me."

Charlie was exhausted all of a sudden, as if all the adrenaline that had carried him all night was spilling out of him.

"What truth is that?" Charlie asked Pooty Shaw.

"The truth that you didn't care all that much. The truth that the only career you ever really care about or had it in you to care about was your own damn career. That truth right there. Not that made-up shit you get from all the phony-asses tryin' to pass theirselves off as one of them Jell-O-sucking Cosby dads."

Charlie smiled, because he couldn't help himself. "You know something? You're right."

"Damn right I'm right. And it don't make you a bad person, even if you was a bad daddy. But there it is. The only ones who throw theirselves into their kids' careers are the ones who didn't never have what you had. Then when you lost what you had, from what I gather, you was tryin' so hard to get it back somehow or some ways, you didn't have no time to worry about was your boy gonna turn out to be everybody's All-America or not."

Charlie clicked his glass against Pooty's and drank some Scotch. "An old friend of mine once told me the key to life was hanging around with people smarter than you," he said. "I think I'm gonna stick with you, baby. At least until your primary finds out about all your secondaries and kills you in your sleep."

"Ask you something?"

"Anything."

Pooty said, "You want Randy?"

"Not tonight, dear."

"All right then. I'll go on up there, create a little divergence, and you get out of here and go get some sleep, 'fore you lose your head."

"You're a good man, Poot."

"Have my moments," he said.

He headed for the bar, Charlie headed toward the door. He was about halfway there when he heard, "Hey!"

He turned around and saw Pooty smiling at him.

"Welcome back," he said to Charlie Stoddard.

NAMES, CHARLIE was telling Pooty, *goddamn* he loved baseball names.

They were sitting in the dugout watching Tom MacKenzie toy with the Tampa Bay Devil Rays, and what got them started on names was Dre' Hadley. Hadley was Pooty's backup except when Tom was pitching; then he was the kid's personal catcher, the way Ted Hartnett had been Charlie's. Charlie was saying to Pooty that the first time he ever saw Hadley's name in the papers, he just assumed the guy was black, because of the apostrophe at the end of his name, and because he always took that to be some sort of black thing. And how shocked he was to find out that not only was Hadley white, he was Canadian white.

"It's like in the old days, the Red Sox had this guy pitching for them named Reggie Cleveland," Charlie said. "Guy has to be black, right? Uh uh. *He* turns out to be a fat white Canadian, too."

"Dre' used to have one of those hockey goalie names, like Drejean or something," Pooty said, pronouncing it Dray-*john*. "Then he got with some brothers when he got to the minors and it was like they did some sort of oral surgery on him. After that he was Dre', like you see."

They wouldn't have been talking like this if the Red Sox were in the field, because it had taken Charlie about two batters to understand you didn't do anything except shut up and pay attention when Tom had the ball in his hand. But the Red Sox were still batting in a long bottom of the second, three runs in, two on still. So Charlie was telling Pooty about this teammate he'd had with the Orioles, his last year in the bigs before this, a middle reliever named Je'Rod Anderson, and how one time he'd asked Je'Rod what was up with his name.

Je'Rod Anderson had told him he'd just thrown an apostrophe in there one day when he was filling out a Blockbuster application, tired of what he called "that boring Jerod shit."

Jerod, he said, being his birth-certificate name.

"But my lady, Rita?" he explained to Charlie. "She just said it was lacking something. The way my hair was lacking something 'fore she put the rows down? Anyway, there I was filling out the Blockbuster thing, and I just let it happen. Then I come home and show her the squiggy in there between the 'e' and the 'r' and Rita says, 'Now you stylin, baby!' Been that way ever since."

"Je'*Rod*," Charlie said to him that day in the bullpen.

"Got some weight to it now," Je'Rod Anderson said.

Snip Daggett struck out to end the Red Sox third, and Tom MacKenzie ran back out to the mound like he was running the anchor leg on a relay team. Charlie asked Pooty if it bothered him, not catching Tom, and Pooty shook his head.

"I found out a long time ago," he said, "pitchers got their ways and like that, the way a woman does. So you just do whatever you can to stay on their good side, stay away from unnecessary eye contact if you find yourself on their bad side, and it's pretty much all blue sky after that."

Charlie had thought about watching the game from the bullpen; he was trying to stay out of Tom's way, and it was hard to do in the Red Sox dugout, which felt as cramped to Charlie as everything else at Fenway. But Pooty told him it would be fine, Tom was superstitious as hell and always sat between Hartnett and Hick Landon between innings. So Charlie and Pooty were at the opposite end of the dugout, down at the first-base end, watching the kid work for the first time since the blister on the tip of his middle finger had healed.

"This ain't something you want to watch from the cheap seats, anyway," Pooty said. Charlie saw he had another cup of coffee going, and another Nutrageous candy bar on the bench next to him. From the time Pooty arrived at the park, he alternated coffee and candy bars, even if he wasn't playing; by the middle innings, he usually had enough of a buzz going to charge a machine-gun nest.

On the field, Tom MacKenzie threw a fastball past the Devil Rays centerfielder, RaShawn Duffy, for strike two. The crowd made a big noise for that, then another as the scoreboard flashed the radar-gun count on the pitch, which was 99 mph.

Pooty said, "You ever see anybody throw like this boy in your whole damn *life?*"

"Yeah," Charlie said. "As a matter of fact, I have."

The kid pitched with his hat so low you could barely see his eyes. He wore his red stockings high, what Charlie once would have called the old-fashioned way, except now it seemed like half the kids in the big leagues were doing it. He wore his uniform baggy, jersey and pants, like he'd bought the whole thing at the baggy section of the Gap, and was constantly fluffing out the short-sleeved jersey, as if it were still as tight as a straitjacket on him. Between pitches he was a bundle of nerves, even more than Charlie had been. But when it was time for business, when the ball was in the glove and he was ready to rock and roll, Tom Mac-

Kenzie was in complete control of everything: the place, the crowd, the moment, the Devil Rays.

Himself and his amazing stuff.

He struck out Duffy, then struck out Marcus King, the Tampa Bay shortstop, and when he got King he made this flashy whirling motion with his right arm, like he was throwing a big uppercut.

"Take me now, Jesus, I can die happy!" Pooty shouted, then said he was going for more coffee, he thought maybe Eddie Greene had tried to run some of that half-caf on him the last couple of choca-chinos he'd made up for him.

Tom sprinted off the mound, and Charlie watched him wedge himself in between his manager and his pitching coach. Wally Garner, the bench coach, offered Tom a jacket. Tom shook his head, no. He took his cap off, ran a hand through his spiky blond hair, bounced his feet up and down, pulled a tin of tobacco out of his back pocket, and stuffed a little more Skoal into his cheek. It figured that he'd thrown that little punch after the third out, Charlie thought. He was like a boxer now between rounds, barely able to sit down, wanting to get right back out there.

Charlie stared at him, fascinated, ready to turn away if the kid looked his way, trying to stay away from that eye contact Pooty had talked about, thinking:

I was the exact same way.

Gimme the ball.

He wouldn't admit to anybody, even Pooty, but being this close to it all was ridiculously exciting.

Dre' Hadley came walking down to the ancient water fountain next to where Charlie was sitting. Hadley was still a pretty young guy, despite the way he'd already bounced around in baseball, he just looked older because of his bald head.

Charlie said, "Having any fun yet?"

"Dre' 'adley is loving life, eh?" he said in a thick French-Canadian accent. "Put down the one finger, give him a nice target, strike one. Do again. Strike two. Then strike three, you out, *au revoir,* sucker. I marry him, he not a boy."

"How come he likes you better than Pooty?"

"He never explain," Dre' said. "He T-Mac, eh? He don't have to explain nothing to nobody. He just say one day I catch and I catch."

"You two do seem to have a nice rapport going."

"Strike one, strike two, strike three," Dre' said.

Julio Paulino flied out to Duffy of the Devil Rays in deep center for the Red Sox' third out. Tom grabbed his glove, slapped his hat crookedly back on his head. He was back on the mound before all the Devil Rays were off the field. Gimme the ball. It was the last week of August. The Red Sox lead was down to four games, lowest it had been since the last week of April. The scoreboard on the Green Monster, the one that looked as if it had been there since the beginning of time, showed the Yankees leading the Orioles 6–0 in the fourth at Camden Yards. Charlie had been in Boston less than a week, and it hadn't even taken that long for him to get a sense of the general hysteria about the Red Sox, in the papers and on the talk shows, the latter sounding more and more like a psycho ward in which some of the crazies got to play host and some got to play caller, and somebody had hidden all the Prozac. Because they were all sure it was happening to them again.

But Fenway was just fine tonight.

T-Mac had the ball, eh?

He pitched eight-plus, gave up just two dink hits, struck out thirteen, didn't walk anybody until King, the shortstop, was leading off the ninth. It was then that Tom started fussing with his pitching hand, obviously feeling some tenderness where the blister had been. Tom gave Hartnett a look, and Hartnett was already on his way up the dugout steps. It was 6–0 Red Sox and they were in the clear, so he wasn't taking any chances. Not with this kid. Ever. Hartnett took the ball from him, and the kid sprinted off the mound one last time, stopping just long enough at the top of the dugout steps to throw one more trademark uppercut. There were 34,000 and something at Fenway, whatever a sellout was supposed to be. It sounded like more than that now. A lot more.

Tom grinned and did a dead fall into his teammates, like a rock star flinging himself into the crowd. He slapped hard high-fives all around, chest-bumped some of the guys. Outside, the crowd was chanting "T-Mac" now, wanting him to come out for a curtain call. So he went back up the steps and leaned out and waved his cap at Fenway. Came back down and started walking down the dugout to where Charlie and Pooty sat, head bopping from side to side, as if he were still feeling the beat.

He walked right up to Charlie, Charlie briefly wondering if there was a television camera on them and what the idiots might be saying about this heartwarming little scene.

"At least you stayed around for the whole game for once," Tom said. "I should give you the game ball."

Charlie pitched once more on the homestand, the last game of the Devil Rays series, getting bounced around again in the first inning, three runs this time, settling down after that, walking away with another no-decision. The Red Sox finally won in the twelfth. He lost his next start, at Jacobs Field in Cleveland, even though he felt like he'd pitched his best so far: six innings, one earned run, five strikeouts, two walks, a fast-ball that was still in the 90s in the sixth. On the flight home in the night, Pooty sat with him in the back of the plane and said, "Well, at least you got yourself one of them quality starts."

It was one of those stats the seamhead nerds had come up with to make mediocre pitchers look better than they really were. If you gave up three runs or less over six innings, they called it a quality start. Charlie knew better. He knew that if you gave up three runs for every six innings you pitched, that was an earned run average of 4.50. Even in a designated-hitter league, more hitting in the American than the National, Charlie thought the number sucked, no matter how much the seamheads tried to dress it up.

"Yeah," Charlie said to Pooty, "I got a real nice personality, too."

He was settling back into the life, after all this time away from it. Not because he felt secure enough to do that, not because he had any assurances from Patrick Keenan or Ted Hartnett or anybody that he was a sure thing to stay in the rotation and last the season. Just because he had pitched and then pitched again five days later and done it again after that. It was enough of a routine for now.

He was a part of something, for as long as it lasted.

He just wanted to get a fucking win.

He stretched with the other pitchers in the late afternoon, ran with them, shagged balls in the outfield with them, somehow managed to do it and stay out of Tom's way. The last time they'd spoken was after the kid's start against the Devil Rays. At least you stuck around this time. Sounding this way to Charlie: At least you stayed around, *asshole*.

Charlie mostly hung with Pooty, at home and on the road. He liked being with him, liked the way he didn't treat the whole Charlie-Tom situation as life and death. Liked the way he kept things loose from the time he showed up at the ballpark. On top of all that, all the baseball stuff, Charlie was totally fascinated by the constant complications of Pooty's love life, with Alqueen and Sun; with the bitchy calls he'd get from Vonette, always on the clubhouse phone; with the women he had waiting for him on the road, Pooty somehow able to convince all of them that they were in his regular rotation.

One night, Charlie was home in the condo, having a pace night, when Pooty called him from one of the local sports-talk stations, WAIL, telling him to put the radio on, the next hour was All-Pooty, all the time. Somehow, Vonette found out about it in New Jersey and called about halfway through and started yelling at him about late child-support payments.

"Well, there," the host, a guy who called himself Moose, said when he finally cut Vonette off. "I wish we could share that last comment with you, gang, but that's why they invented the seven-second delay."

"And maximum security woman prisons, where hard-case bitches like Vonette Shaw got no chance of parole," Pooty said.

He told Charlie that Alqueen would sometimes get her urges, and he'd have to fly her in on the road, as he'd done in Cleveland, at the Ritz-Carlton down the block from the ballpark. This, he said, required more planning than he liked, especially since he had an old friend in Cleveland, a tour guide at the Rock and Roll Hall of Fame, which happened to be right across the street from the hotel. So he had to explain to the guide—Nykesha, her name was—why she had to move out of his junior suite and back into her own apartment even though the Red Sox–Indians series still had two games left in it.

"I was watching this show on the History Channel the other night," Charlie said. "Eisenhower had simpler logistics for Normandy."

Pooty said, "You just got to have a game plan and stick with it."

Another reason Charlie felt so comfortable with Pooty was because he felt so detached from most of the young guys on the Red Sox. And with the exception of Charlie, Julio, Yippy Cantreras, and a couple of guys in the bullpen, the Red Sox were basically a very young team, most of the players not looking much older than the kids Charlie had played with over in Jersey. Young guys full of muscles, non-smilers, looking as if they'd rather pump iron and drink their muscle shakes instead of fuck around the way he had when he was young.

"It's like they want to play forever," Charlie said to Chang.

"Duh," Chang said, dragging the word out so he sounded like a mall girl.

Charlie was pitching the next afternoon against the Tigers at Fenway, a makeup of a rainout on the last day of the last Red Sox–Tigers series; the two teams had finished their season series, but both happened to have an open date, so it was either play the game now or wait until the day after the regular season ended. The Sox would finish their series against the Twins tonight, play the Tigers, then go on a short road trip to Toronto and then New York to play the Yankees. Chang had arrived on the noon shuttle; they had just come back, from a run all the way down Commonwealth to Boston University and back, and now they were in the clubhouse, standing at the door to the trainer's room. It was only two in the afternoon, but every exercise machine was being used, and there were three or four guys waiting to use the free weights.

"I know I don't hit any of the clubs Pooty says these guys hit," Charlie said. "But I never see any of them acting as if they're having any fun."

"Maybe working out, feeling good about themselves and their bodies, is fun for them. You ever think of that?"

"You know what they really get off on doing? Showing off their muscles, no shit. They all walk through the clubhouse like they're runway models, and keep giving each other rips."

"It's called showing off the fruits of your labors."

"They act like fruits sometimes, you ask me," Charlie said. "And please don't give me one of your wellness speeches."

"Wellness is gonna get you your first win tomorrow night," Chang said. "First in five years. I promise." He slapped Charlie on the ass and said, "Let's go frolic in the outfield grass."

"Speaking of fruits," Charlie said.

"Hi ho," Chang said.

Chang went out and worked him in the outfield until Charlie was ready to drop, then they went inside and used one of the massage tables, and he gave Charlie as rough a going-over as he'd had in weeks, back and shoulder and neck, the backs of his legs, even the balls of his feet.

It was Yippy's turn to start, but he had nothing against the Twins and didn't make it out of the third inning, having such a meltdown after serving up a grand-slam home run to his former Cuban National teammate, Fernando Ferrera, that Charlie was afraid he might burst into tears when Hartnett came to get him. Minnesota ended up winning 9–3, and it looked like the lead might drop to three over the Yankees, only the Blue Jays, in last place in the American League East, somehow scored four in the top of the ninth to beat the Yankees in New York.

The Sox still four up.

Twenty-eight games to play now.

First of September two days away.

If Charlie stayed in the rotation, that meant at least five starts for him the rest of the way, including tomorrow night's.

Plus playoffs.

If they made the playoffs. And the Sox were probably going to have to win the division to do it, because the two best records in the league suddenly belonged to the Mariners and the A's in the American League West; whoever didn't win the West was going to get the wild card, unless somebody completely collapsed out there.

It meant the Sox had to hold off the Yankees somehow, something they managed to do, at least when it was just the two of them, about every half-century or so.

Charlie told Pooty he might see him at Pooty's for one drink. He'd asked Chang if he wanted to have a late dinner, but Chang said he had plans. Charlie said, What kind of plans? Chang said, The kind that if I wanted you to know what they were, I would have told you.

Charlie showered after the game, signed autographs for about twenty minutes on Yawkey Way, and took a cab back to his apartment, which had turned out to be more elegantly furnished than he would have anticipated. He'd asked Pooty who his decorator was and he'd said, "Kara." He'd sighed then. Charlie said, "Don't tell me you had something going with your decorator, too." And Pooty said, "'Til Uma run her off."

Charlie cranked up an old Stones CD, *Steel Wheels*, fixed himself a Scotch, lit a cigarette, went and stood on the front terrace, looking down on Commonwealth, light traffic on both sides of the grass median down there, with all the cute benches.

Thought about doing what he always thought about doing at this time of night, which meant call Grace.

They'd spoken just the one time on the phone since he'd turned Sistina into the Holocaust Café. He wasn't sure what the hell he'd even say to her now if he heard her voice at the other end of the phone. And what could he tell her, anyway, that she hadn't heard from Tom? Or Ted Hartnett?

Back in the big time, wish you were here?

He did wish she were here. Maybe he'd call her after he got a win. After he was on the board again. Maybe he'd even ask her to come watch him pitch, just for old times' sake.

He finished his drink and thought about having another one. He decided he'd have it at Pooty's instead. He'd tried wellness now for one loss and two no-decisions. Wellness could stay home tonight. He was going out. He flicked his cigarette butt over the railing and went to get the new summer blazer he'd bought around the corner at Brooks Brothers the other afternoon, wondering as he did if Randy might be working.

POOTy WAS WiTH Sun at his usual table when Charlie walked
in, a couple of minutes past midnight, surprised to find the place as
crowded as it was in prime time. Maybe everything had started late because the game between the Red Sox and Twins had ended late, another
one of those baseball games that felt as if it had lasted longer than his
marriage to Grace. Charlie gave Pooty a wave that said he'd see him in a
minute, he was going to the bar.

Snip Daggett was at the corner of the bar closest to the front door,
talking with a short, dark-haired woman in a sleek, expensive-looking
black pantsuit. Charlie gave him a nod and Snip nodded back; since
Charlie had joined the team, their only conversations had occurred at
the pitcher's mound, all the infielders convening for group therapy
when Charlie would find himself in another tough spot. The rest of it

had just been Hey and Yo and S'up? and How *You* Doin'? All clubhouse shorthand, nothing more.

By now Charlie had started to get a read on the various clubhouse relationships around the Sox, where everybody fit in the room. There were twenty-five guys on a baseball team, and all teams had cliques and alliances and the kinds of friendships that began when pitchers and catchers reported to spring training and ended on the last day of the season, the players breaking into groups based on age, race, ethnic deals, God. Sometimes it was as simple as pitchers hanging with pitchers and infielders hanging with other infielders. Snip Daggett was twenty-three, one of the younger members of the team, and he was with Tom. Snip was black and Tom wasn't, but one thing Charlie knew about sports by now was that it was the greatest lab experiment for good race relations in history. Snip was young, Tom was young, and they were buds, even if one of them came from the roughest part of West Palm Beach and Tom came from a rich white-boy section of San Francisco. Charlie didn't know how much they ran together on the road, but they lockered next to each other, seemed to like the same loud rap music, sat together on the bus, played cards together on the team plane.

So Charlie gave Snip the same kind of room he gave his son; let them have their turf. He wondered sometimes what it would have been like if Pooty was Tom's catcher instead of Dre', if Pooty would have been forced to declare himself somehow, having to choose between father and son. But Dre' caught Tom, so it wasn't an issue. Maybe it wouldn't have been an issue with Pooty anyway, and he was always going to take Charlie in like a stray, he had that kind of heart to him, even if he tried to hide it behind all his jive talk.

Charlie couldn't remember analyzing stuff this much when he was young. Or maybe he was really older and wiser, even if he could never convince the shit-givers in his life of that.

They were four deep around the bar, but a seat opened up as Charlie was trying to figure out where to set up headquarters. He sat down and, as soon as he did, saw that he was wedged in next to Ashe Grissom, now the number-two man in the Sox rotation with both Tyler Haas and Lew Gentry out for the season.

"Buy an old-timer a drink?" Charlie said to Grissom.

"Isn't this crowd a little young for you?" Grissom said, when he saw who it was next to him. "You get lost on your way to the bar at the Four Seasons?"

"It's like I heard this actor say one time," Charlie said. "I can play younger."

Charlie had already picked up on the fact that Ashe Grissom was the most popular player on the team. He was Denzel Washington–handsome, had been both an academic and baseball All-America at Stanford, where both his parents were professors, the father in English, the mother in political science. They had named him after Arthur Ashe and basically raised him to be the first African-American president of the United States. Just from the bullshitting they'd done while shagging balls together in the outfield, Charlie liked him a lot.

Pooty also pointed out that Ashe Grissom, who was still single, had a black book that included movie stars, pop singers, Miss Universe types from countries as far away as Thailand, network-news babes, and a bunch of models who Pooty said made even the other supermodels look like the ass-end of a dog-sled team.

The bartender's name tag said she was Aimee. She had light brown hair streaked with gold, green eyes, a lot of freckles, and wore a white shirt whose front just sort of exploded on you, the way Charlie imagined a twelve-gauge shotgun would.

"Aimee," Charlie said, "how about you get me a Dewar's and water about the same color of your pretty hair?"

She looked at Grissom and said, "Teammate of yours?"

"Guilty," Grissom said.

"You remind me of another one I know," she said to Charlie.

"Just older?" he said, trying to be helpful.

"Oops. Is that what it sounded like?"

"Can I ask which ballplayer?"

"Tom MacKenzie," she said.

Grissom said to Charlie, "Uh, before you fall in love with her, you ought to know that Tom and Aimee are friends."

"He's just telling me that because I'm his father," Charlie said to Aimee.

She laughed and said, "Right," and went to get his drink.

Ashe Grissom said, "She seemed to like you before you decided to make a full confession."

"She acted like she still didn't believe me."

Grissom said, "Well, you have kept yourself up."

"Does Tom really date her?"

"'Date' is kind of strong," Grissom said. He turned on his stool so he was half-facing Charlie and half-facing the restaurant. "Let's just say she has made herself available to him for the occasional late-night rendezvous and gropefest in Pooty's office."

"Would it be a problem if he came in here and saw us talking to her?"

Grissom smiled. "For me, no."

Aimee came back with Charlie's Scotch. Grissom said she should put it on his tab, and he'd have another Sam Adams when she got the chance. Before she went away again, she asked Charlie if he were really Tom's father.

Charlie said, "I can't believe Tom hasn't mentioned it to you."

She blushed slightly and said, "We don't talk about baseball a lot when we're together. And I *never* read the sports section if I can help it." Well, Charlie said, he was really Tom's father. Aimee said, "Wow, I was thinking you were kind of cute when you sat down, but now this is like some creepy Shakespeare thing we'd, like, do in my acting class."

Charlie and Grissom sat there for a few minutes in silence, listening to Sun work through "All of Me" despite the loud buzz of the place. When she finished, Charlie said, "Do you get the idea Tom is getting more cool with this? Me being around, I mean?"

"Nah," Grissom said. "He's only cool with it in the sense that it just gives him another thing to be pissed off about."

"He really that pissed off all the time?"

Grissom said, "About everything except pitching. I actually think it pisses him off that pitching *doesn't* piss him off the way everything else does, so he can't spend all his time playing the angry young man. But now you're around, so who knows, it might be a clean sweep."

"He didn't look like too much was bothering him tonight," Charlie said.

"When he gets going like that," Grissom said, "they could blow up the Green Monster during his windup and he wouldn't notice. He gets that zone thing going. And then it doesn't matter how late he stayed up, whether he was screwing around until dawn with an Aimee or just drinking and shooting the shit with the guys. When it's time to hump it up there, in the immortal words of our Hick, that is exactly what he does."

Charlie said, "I was the same way."

"So he told me."

"He said that?" Charlie said. "About me?"

"Charlie," Grissom said, "I don't want this to come as breaking news, but when you get a few drinks in old T-Mac—which is not that hard to do, frankly—he can tell about starts you made against the Cubbies in July of '87, before the rest of the Mets rotation crashed and burned that year."

"You're kidding, right?"

"Nope. Of course, that's usually right before he goes into one of his riffs about what a worthless no-account sonofabitch turd excuse for a father you were."

Ashe Grissom motioned to Aimee for two more. "Most of us have it memorized by now. But it can still be a very lively presentation."

Just not nearly as lively as Pooty's turned out to be.

Alqueen, who was supposed to be spending two more days at the Canyon Ranch in western Massachusetts, showed up first. Ashe Grissom spotted her as soon as she came in.

"You know those logistics Pooty is always talking about?" he said. "With his primaries and secondaries?"

Charlie said, "I think of them as a reason to live."

Grissom said, "I think they're about to be severely challenged."

"How come?"

"Because his primary just showed up unannounced."

Charlie had always liked old movies, from all his years on the road, hanging around in the hotel waiting to go to the ballpark, and by now knew most of the great performances: Spencer Tracy in anything, Brando, the pre-slob Brando of *On the Waterfront,* the early DeNiro, Tom Hanks, Russell Crowe lately. But sitting at the bar at Pooty's, he decided there had never been an acting performance like they saw now from Pooty Shaw.

Who acted happy to see Alqueen Carville.

As Pooty was greeting her with hugs and kisses, with Sun watching them from the stage, Charlie stood up.

"Tell me you're not going down there," Ashe Grissom said.

"Got to."

"Can I ask why?"

Charlie laughed and said, "Because I've been there, that's why."

He walked to the end of the bar, where Snip was still chatting up the doll-like brunette.

"Snip," he said.

"S'up?" Snip said, looking at him through eyes that always seemed to be half-closed, as if he were about to nod off.

Charlie said to the brunette, "Can I borrow your date for a few minutes?"

Snip said, "Yo? In the *middle* of somethin' here."

"Alqueen just showed up," Charlie said to him. "Pooty's the one in the middle of something."

Snip bounced off his stool as if coming hard out of the batter's box after pushing a drag bunt past the mound.

"Check you later," Snip said to the woman, who narrowed her own eyes down to slits of her own and said to him, "It *is* later."

Snip said, "Or I can lose your number, you want to put some of your lip and attitude on me."

As he and Charlie made their way down the steps to the restaurant, Snip said, "Bitches," as if that summed up everything.

When they arrived at the table, Pooty was saying to Alqueen, "Honey baby, you said you'd give Pooty a heads-up call when it was time to leave the spa ranch."

Up on the stage, Sun said to the audience, "We're gonna take a short break now," and started to make her way across the floor at a very good clip.

Alqueen said, "I missed my big hunky man, is all."

Pooty, eyeballing Sun as she closed in on the table, trying to act cool about everything, as if he were still in control of the sitiuation, said, "Not as much as I missed you, my sweet Hostess cakes."

Alqueen turned out to be a knockout, with shiny black hair cut into some kind of bob, wearing a pink dress that showed off her long legs. Charlie also noticed a diamond ring on her left hand as big as a backyard floodlight.

"Well, well, well," Charlie said, trying to act jolly, "I meet the lovely Alqueen at last. I'm Charlie Stoddard, the charity case Pooty took in."

"Oh, looky here," Alqueen said, ignoring him so she could give Sun a mean look. "If it isn't Britney Speared."

Snip moved around the table to greet Sun, saying to her, "Girl, you got them good pipes goin' tonight, why don't you go up to the bar and let Snip get you one of those Cosmopolitans you say eases your parchment?"

Sun, putting a mean look of her own on Alqueen, said, "I'm fine right here."

Charlie clapped his hands and said, "Well, the gang's certainly all here!"

He did all the talking now as he pulled out chairs, saying Snip and Sun, why don't you sit over here, and Alqueen and Pooty, you go over there on the other side, would that be all right? "I'll sit in the middle," Charlie said.

"Neutral like," he said under his breath to Pooty.

"Yeah," Pooty said, his voice just as low, "like fucking Switzerland."

＊   ＊   ＊

Sun really didn't seem interested in blowing Pooty's cover, just in torturing him a little bit, and directing mean-spirited comments at Alqueen any time she saw an opening.

It occurred to Charlie once again that women could engage in a full-scale land war without ever raising their voices.

Ashe Grissom, a team player all the way, gave Charlie a thumbs-up sign from up above as he walked Snip's date to the door. Grissom would explain to Charlie later that the brunette, an advertising executive named Carole, was a secondary of Snip's trying to move up in the standings, so she had grudgingly decided to be a good sport after Grissom described what he said was the gritty family drama being played out at Pooty's table.

Charlie drank Scotch and tried to make himself the life of the party, always bringing the conversation back to Sun and her singing and how, man, he just couldn't wait to see what she had in store for them in her last set.

"Set is what I plan to do here for a while," she said, and took a dainty sip of a drink that was the color of Alqueen's dress.

Alqueen said to Snip, "How long you been going with her?"

As if Sun wasn't even there.

Snip said, "I'm not sure about the exact dates and all, just that we still in our honeymoon period. Isn't that right, baby girl?"

Sun said to Alqueen, "Pooty said you've been off at one of those fat farms?"

"It's a *spa*," Alqueen said. "Though probably not the kind you're used to, the ones where they do all that *work* on the various parts of yourself."

Charlie said, "Alqueen, I have to say, you're even prettier than Pooty said you were."

"What's that supposed to mean, *work?*" Sun said.

Alqueen shrugged and made a motion like she was trying to push her breasts up underneath her chin.

"You're saying I had my boobs done?" Sun said. "I just want to understand how far we all want to *go* with this?"

Looking at Pooty when she got to the last part.

"All I'm saying," Alqueen said, "is that you look a lot healthier than when they did that piece on you and Vonette in *People* a few years ago after that little fender-bender you all had over to the Yankee Stadium."

Sun made a motion for one of Charlie's cigarettes, and he got busy shaking one out of his pack and then lighting it for her. Sun took a drag, blew out a stream of smoke, and said, "Least I don't need my *eyes* done."

"Nothing wrong with my eyes," Alqueen said, lightly touching the area underneath them with the tip of her middle finger.

"'Cept you can't *see* nothing with them," Sun said.

Pooty looked up, happy all of a sudden. Charlie saw that Sun's piano player was back up on the stage.

"Well, there you go," Pooty said, "Artie looks like he all rested up and ready to play more of that sweet music you make even sweeter."

"I'm fine," Sun said again.

Pooty gave her a fake laugh and said, "Well, yeah, baby, but I am the boss around here, last time I checked, anyways."

Now Sun gave Pooty a look.

"Ex*cuse* me?" she said.

"Sun, do you take requests, by any chance?" Charlie said. "Because I am an absolute sucker for Judy Garland."

"Ain't all she takes, what I hear," Alqueen said, looking off, as if Sun's entire existence had begun to bore her.

Charlie heard Artie work his way into what sounded like the first few bars of "Blue Skies." Sun had her arms crossed and kept her gaze on Pooty. Snip was putting his tiny cell phone near the candles in the middle of the table, as if desperately searching for any kind of callback number.

Charlie had been so focused on the action at the table that he hadn't noticed until now that Tom MacKenzie was standing at the corner of the bar where Snip had been, and that some Detroit Tigers, including Zach Stroud and Chris Connelly, were down at the opposite end, making a lot of loud, drunken noise.

"You're telling me I *have* to sing now?" Sun said to Pooty finally. "Like that there is some kind of *order?*"

"Look at the crowd here," Pooty said. "I'm just askin' you to go back up there and give people some more happiness."

Alqueen said, "She could do the same thing by going over to the bar."

Sun said, "You know something, Pooty? I can't believe you haven't married her already, she seems to have enough bitch in her to suit your ass."

"Ladies, ladies, ladies," Pooty said, giving Charlie a pleading, do-something look as he did. "Can't we just all of us get along?"

"Ladies?" Alqueen said. "All I see here is ho's."

"That's it," Sun said, leaning forward, fire in her eyes. "It's time for me to tell this bitch who's who and what's what around here."

Charlie believed she would have done just that if Zach Stroud had not picked that particular moment to come walking over to the table.

Pooty would describe everything that happened after that as his man, Charlie Stoddard, taking one for the team.

Stroud was one of those guys who looked even bigger out of his baseball uniform than he did in it. He had long black hair brushed straight back, almost down to his shoulders, tattoos up and down both arms, most of it snake stuff. Charlie didn't know much about him other than his power numbers for the season and what he'd seen when he pitched against him, but Pooty said Stroud had put on about thirty pounds of muscle between last season and this, which usually meant steroids.

"Wonder juice 'stead of Wonder Bread," Pooty said. "Builds strong bodies in all *kinds* of unhealthy ways."

Stroud poked Charlie on the right shoulder now, too hard, and said, "Hey. Hey you. Old man."

"What's the bouncer doing here?" Alqueen said.

Sun got up, announcing to the table that *she'd* decided it was time to sing, saying to Alqueen before she left, "We got some unfinished business here when I come back, Miss Miss."

"Just stay away from my man's business," Alqueen said, busying herself looking for something in her big, heavy purse.

Charlie looked up at Zach Stroud, grinning, and said, "You're probably not going to believe this, but I'm happy you showed up, big guy."

"You're the one showed me up," Stroud said. He was weaving a bit from side to side. "After you struck me out. It was even on *SportsCenter*." He turned to Chris Connelly, standing there with him, and said, "Wasn't it?"

Connelly was a head shorter than Stroud, but had the same long hair, tattoos of his own, huge forearms, and seemed to be even drunker than his teammate.

"Showed you up on national TV," Connelly said, and burped.

"Open bar on the team plane, fellas?" Charlie said. He turned to Pooty and said, "The night just gets better and better, doesn't it?"

Pooty said, "I don't mean to sound selfish or whatnot, but it's pickin' up for me all of a sudden."

Stroud poked Charlie again, even harder than before, and said, "I'm talking to you, asshole."

Sun began to sing "Somewhere over the Rainbow."

Snip Daggett, who had stayed out of it until now, stood up and said, "I see *you* talkin'. And I see a couple of assholes here for sure. What I *don't* see is nobody here wants to talk to you."

Zach Stroud looked down at Snip, as if looking at him from a high floor, and said, "Stay out of this, squirt." He turned back to Connelly and said, "I heard they call the boy Snip because they snipped off all the good parts of him."

"Boy?" Snip said, but they didn't hear him because they were laughing so hard, and probably because they didn't expect Snip, laughing himself, like he was in on the joke, to jump back up on his chair like a gymnast hopping up on a balance beam and throw a neat punch that hit Zach Stroud square on the nose.

"The *fuck!*" Stroud yelled, putting a beefy hand to his face and coming away with blood all over it, and all over his white muscle-boy t-shirt.

He started to grab for Snip, who was still on the chair as a way to take away Stroud's decided advantage in both height and reach, but Connelly piled into Snip first, the two of them ending up in a pile on the floor.

The Tigers centerfielder, Kenny DeLuca, came running from the bar then, but Pooty stepped in and hit DeLuca with a forearm to the chest, knocking him back.

Pooty said, "You sure you want some of this?"

Pooty turned to Alqueen then and said, "Baby doll, why don't you go and powder your nose?"

"I'm fine," she said, sitting back down. "Knock his dick off, sweetums!"

There was a lot of yelling and commotion now at Pooty's, but over it all, Charlie could hear Sun, a trooper, pressing on with her song, moving into the part now about birds flying over the rainbow and why, then, oh why, can't I?

Charlie was trying to set himself at the same time he tried to create some spacing between him and Zach Stroud without tripping over Snip and Chris Connelly, who were trying to throw punches at each other and grunting out curses at each other as they rolled underneath the table.

Ashe Grissom, who later said he made his move from the bar when he saw DeLuca make his, was trying to wrap up Stroud from behind. But Stroud, acting like some kind of wounded bear, roared and threw his arms up in the air, and Grissom went flying backward, landing on a nearby table filled with Japanese tourists who were all frantically snapping pictures with cameras the size of shot glasses.

"You want some of *me?*" Stroud said to Charlie.

"Not that much."

Stroud threw a big roundhouse right at Charlie and missed badly. But he was moving in now, and Charlie knew that when he got inside, he didn't plan to miss with his next punch.

Charlie flashed on another fight a long time ago, that one outside the bar, remembering how that one had ended for him, just as Tom MacKenzie showed up to his right.

"Jesus," Charlie yelled at him, "stay out of this."

"You're not the boss of me," the kid said.

"Your *arm!*" Charlie said, as Zach Stroud, seeing that Charlie wasn't giving him his full attention, hit Charlie an open-handed shot to the side of his head.

"Stay the fuck out of this!" Charlie said to Tom.

"You say," Tom said.

"You're gonna get hurt!"

"Nah," the kid said, grinning. "I don't do that."

As Stroud went for Charlie again, Tom said, "Hey, big boy," and threw a ferocious left hook that caught Stroud in the midsection, caught him good, forcing a sound out of Stroud like he was about to be sick.

When he doubled over, hair covering the whole front of his face, the kid, smart enough to use his left, smarter than Charlie had ever been, backhanded him, and Stroud went down as if one of the railroad ties Pooty had decorating the ceiling had fallen on him.

Tom stood over Stroud, snarling at him to get up, when DeLuca started to come from the kid's blind side. Charlie shouted for the kid to duck and stepped in himself, about to throw a right hand, because that was the only angle he had. Only, Pooty stepped in front of Charlie now, saying, "Your instrument, baby."

So it was DeLuca, another bear, and Pooty now, squared off, hands up, no one in between them.

"Oh shit," Pooty said. "Here come another ten thousand worth of goddamn mouth work."

It never came to that. Pooty didn't have to do anything to defend himself, because Alqueen and Sun did it for him.

Alqueen came around the table in a flash and blindsided DeLuca with a shoulder bag even bigger than Charlie had noticed before, hitting him a clear shot that snapped DeLuca's head back as if the bag were filled with bricks. It was about the same time that Sun, running from the stage area when she thought her man was in peril, slammed DeLuca on the top of his head with the handheld microphone she'd been using.

DeLuca went down the way Zach Stroud had. He would have hit the back of his head on the floor, except that Snip and Connelly had rolled back out from under the table and broken his fall.

Charlie, his head throbbing from where Stroud had hit him, looked up and saw Tom back up at the bar, already having a beer, shaking his head at Charlie like, you dumb shit.

Or maybe, act your age.

Tom drank the rest of his beer down in one shot, gave Charlie a longer look this time, one he couldn't read, and walked out the door.

Pooty said to Charlie, "That last part there, with my girls, that make you as hot as it did Pooty?"

18

GARY GOLDBERG, the Red Sox' rodent-like general manager, was doing most of the talking—yelling, really—in the Yawkey Suite. Patrick Keenan sat back and kept blowing on the frothy part of his latte and let him. Ted Harnett knew why. Goldberg's fury about what had happened at Pooty's, and on the front pages of the Boston papers, was genuine. Hartnett knew Keenan was mostly amused by it once he'd found out nobody on his team had gotten hurt; Keenan had established that when he'd called Hartnett's apartment first thing in the morning. But he had told his manager at the same time that Goldberg was going to want to play bad cop later and they were going to play along with him.

"It's a small price to pay for being in play this way," he said to Hartnett.

"Do you mean Gary wants to play bad cop or bad witch?" Hartnett said.

He knew the showman in Patrick Keenan was always thrilled with any kind of good play, the buzz it created, the way it put him in the spotlight, even indirectly.

"When I've finally left this world and moved on to the next," Keenan told Hartnett once, "I want the cause of death to be that they stopped talking about me."

And today they were talking about Charlie Stoddard and Tom MacKenzie and what the more precious locals called the Olde Towne Team all over the old town.

The *Herald,* the one tabloid in town, went with this headline:

STODDARD AND SON SOX IT TO STROUD!

Inside the paper, splashed across pages 2 and 3, were all the pictures the *Herald* had purchased from the Japanese tourists, remarkably good ones, Ted thought, from Instamatic-wielding amateur photographers, especially since he was familiar with the strip-club lighting at Pooty's. The *Globe,* the more staid of the two Boston papers, played it relatively straight, even if they did run the story and one picture on page 1.

Their headline read:

RED SOX FATHER AND SON TURN OUT
TO BE REAL 1–2 PUNCH

The *Globe* had also purchased photographs from the tourists, including the one of Tom MacKenzie on the front page, Tom looking as happy as Hartnett had ever seen him without a baseball in his hand, throwing his vicious left hook to Zach Stroud's midsection, Stroud's long hair flying out in all directions as if he were being electrocuted instead of punched in the gut.

It was ten the next morning. When Hartnett had showed up in the clubhouse about an hour and a half earlier, Eddie Greene had told him that Charlie and Chang were already in the outfield, doing their stretching and agility drills and long tossing.

"So he's in one piece," Hartnett said.

"I was here when he come walking in about eight," Greene said. "He looked to me like he had all his parts working."

"The only person who ever did as much as he did with as little sleep was Mantle."

"He mostly seemed worried about you," Greene said. "His head would whip around every time the door would open, even if I told him you usually go straight into your office. No shit, he was like a kid waiting to find out if he was gonna get detention 'cause he got caught smoking in the men's."

"He could've burned down the Old North Church and still started today," Hartnett said.

He told Eddie Greene to send Charlie into the office when he and Chang came back in from outside. But when they finally did, a few minutes before ten, Keenan called from upstairs and said he'd appreciate it if Hartnett would escort today's starting pitcher up to the suite for coffee and a good reaming by his general manager.

"You'll be a good lad and do that for me, won't you?" Keenan said.

"It's a game day," Hartnett said.

"Humor me," Keenan said, and hung up.

So here they were: Keenan, Booker Impala Washington, Goldberg, Hartnett, Charlie. Gary Goldberg was in his early thirties but was almost completely bald, wore wire-rimmed glasses, favored sleeveless v-neck sweaters, buttoned-down shirts, and khaki slacks, and had a voice that made you think life was constantly squeezing his balls. As far as Hartnett knew, the last time he had played competitive baseball was in the Darien, Connecticut, Rec League when he'd been twelve years old. But somehow he had become one more seamhead running the sport. Goldberg had started out as a summer intern for the Red Sox about ten years before, and somehow began to move quietly through the system, studying the smallest details in the Red Sox organization chart as if he were trying to break some kind of World War II code, never passing up an opportunity to show his bosses how much he knew about the flashy Cuban shortstop in A ball, or the wild lefthander who'd cut his walks in half at Pawtucket. Somehow he'd moved from there to scouting, and gotten the reputation in the baseball trade papers as a crackerjack judge of personnel. From there he'd become assistant to the scouting director, then an assistant general manager, and when the previous general manager had gotten fired by the previous owners for spending more time in topless bars than he had in his office at Fenway, Gary Goldberg had suddenly been the man in charge. The mouse had finally become king rat at Fenway. Patrick Keenan had kept him on when he bought the team, and ever since, the little dweeb had made enough good, safe moves, with trades and with free agents, to keep the Sox in contention. But this season Keenan was making no state secret of the fact that he was tired of just being in contention, that he wanted to win, which is why everybody who followed the Red Sox knew that Goldberg's skinny ass was on the line this season if the team didn't hold off the Yankees, win the two play-off rounds you needed to win the pennant, make it to the World Series even if they didn't win it.

The same as Harnett's own ass was on the line, no matter how many times Keenan told him he'd loved him like the son he'd never had.

Goldberg had immediately gone red-faced on them and started sputtering about all the fun at Pooty's as soon as Hartnett and Charlie walked into the Yawkey Suite. He had kept it up for about ten minutes straight now, his voice sounding more and more like screeching tires all the time, the way it did when he went on the radio and some host started second-guessing one of his trades. He was also spitting so much that Booker, the one closest to him, would mimic using the Living section of the *Globe* as an umbrella when Goldberg wasn't looking.

"I suppose you know that if it had been up to me," Goldberg was saying to Charlie, "you never would have pitched here in the first place."

Charlie said, "There's a bombshell. Let's call the radio."

Hartnett thought he might have heard Keenan giggle, but the owner quickly covered it with what sounded like an asthmatic coughing fit.

"That's right," Goldberg said. "I forgot I was talking to Showtime Charlie, the guy who makes a joke out of everything."

Hartnett was hoping Charlie would just shut up, not make things worse. But he was who he was, even when he was caught in the crosshairs by an uptight little prick like Gary Goldberg.

"Okay, have it your way, Gary," Charlie said. "Three Detroit Tigers walk into a bar . . ."

"I know you think you're a riot," Goldberg said, his voice going up another octave, on his way to dog whistle now. "I know you think this is a big laugh, holding the whole organization up to ridicule this way. But you know what the real laugh around baseball is? That *we* signed *you*.

"And how to do you repay us?" Goldberg continued, pointing a shaking finger at the papers spread out on the coffee table. "With crap like this." He looked over at Keenan and said, "And with no disrespect meant to Mr. Keenan, this is what happens when you lead with your great heart and allow sticky sentimentalism to get in the way of good baseball sense."

"His problem is, he ain't got no sticky in him," Booker said to Hartnett in a whisper.

Goldberg wheeled on Booker and said, "What did you say?"

"Said, damn right, Gary, show the boy some stick," Booker said.

Goldberg turned to Hartnett. "What do you have to say about the spectacle he and his son created last night, and the way he put his son in harm's way?"

Hartnett decided there was only one thing to do now.

Lie through his fancy, newly-capped teeth.

He said, "As a matter of fact, I read him the riot act on our way up here, Gary. Told him I had half a mind to cut him on the spot, except that we need him so much to give us innings right now. If he didn't know where I stood on all this before, he sure knows now, I can tell you that. We will not tolerate this sort of behavior around the Boston Red Sox, and we certainly don't want our dirty laundry spread all across the newspaper this way, like it was the clothesline hanging between a couple of double-wides at the trailer park." He turned to Charlie and said, "Isn't that right?"

Charlie looked down at his sneakers and said, "Yes." Schoolboy voice.

Hartnett, just going with it now, feeling like he was on a roll, said, "I told him that I didn't care who started it last night, or who threw the first punch, any of that. I told him that if he didn't walk away the next time something like this happened, he could damn well go back to pitching for the New Jersey Jackoffs and making a living at those pathetic card shows of his."

Charlie, doing his best to look sheepish, said, "I want to apologize for acting like a wiseass before, Gary. I know you don't care what happens to me, and you shouldn't. But Tom could have gotten seriously injured last night, and that's why you have my word it won't happen again."

Patrick Keenan, Harnett could see, seemed completely entertained by the total bullshit of the moment, and the way it had disarmed his general manager.

"Well," Gary Goldberg said to Charlie, just because he had to say something tough, "you better goddamn well see that it doesn't." And left.

Booker Impala Washington was the first to speak once Gary Goldberg had slammed the door behind him.

"Tell you what he really wanted to do, Showtime," Booker said. "Bend you over and spank your bottom."

"Right before he let me spank his," Charlie said.

"Hey, Charlie," Hartnett said. "Why don't you shut the fuck up for once?"

He put enough behind it that he got the attention of everybody in the room.

"I just got you out of this, and Mr. Keenan let me because neither one of us wanted to listen to Gary's shit for another minute." Hartnett looked over to Keenan. "Am I right?"

"It's too early in the day for dick-swinging," Keenan said. "Even if it is a little bitty one like Gary's."

He waved a hand at Hartnett that was like telling him, it's your show now.

Hartnett said, "Now you might be just enough of a self-destructive bastard to throw away the lottery ticket we've handed you here. But what you don't get to do is take us down with you." He gave Charlie a long look before saying, "I thought you learned your lesson a long time ago about asshole behavior like this. Apparently, you didn't."

"You know that's not true."

"Do I?"

Charlie said, "I wasn't looking for a fight. I was trying to break one up, first between Pooty's version of the Supremes, and then with Stroud and his buddies. They were the ones looking to tangle. I didn't even know Tom was in the joint until he showed up next to me and started swinging. Ask anyone who was there."

"I did. They told me neither one of you could back down." Harnett blew some air out of his mouth like he was blowing out steam. "Talk about dick-swinging."

"It wasn't like that," Charlie said.

"It never is."

They were eyeballing each other good now. A moment from out of the past when both of them would be too drunk and they'd go too far on something. Or go all the way. One of those scenes they managed to forget when they got going about how great everything was in the old days, how much they laughed. How they were closer than brothers.

"I need you right now, Charlie," Hartnett said. "But not nearly as much as you need me."

"You think I don't know that?"

"It's just like the old days, isn't it?" Hartnett said. "Like they always said. You still don't miss a party or a start."

Booker Impala Washington walked over and picked the front page of the *Globe* off the coffee table in front of Patrick Keenan, his way of easing all the tension in the room. It was, Hartnett knew, just another part of his job description. Thinking of Booker as just another limo driver was like thinking of the Beatles as just another band.

"You see the color quality those little Jap guys get?" he said. "Man, they're startin to get the technology jump on us all over again."

Patrick Keenan, already dressed for the day in a beige suit and open-necked pink shirt, stood up.

"Charlie," he said, "why don't you go downstairs now and get ready to win one for our Townies."

On their way down in the elevator, Hartnett said, "Grace is going to be here for the game."

"From the coast? What, the bartender from Pooty's called her and she took the redeye?"

Hartnett said, "She was in New York to do *Today*. She's probably on the shuttle up right now."

Charlie said, "You're certainly up to date with her schedule all of a sudden, aren't you?"

The elevator doors opened, and Hartnett got out first without answering him.

Life was already fucking complicated enough today.

Tom MacKenzie came wandering into the clubhouse about noon, not even looking Charlie's way, acting as if nothing out of the ordinary had happened the night before, as if it had just been another night out with the boys, even if his old man had been one of the boys this time. When Tom got over to his corner of the clubhouse, Snip Daggett popped up off his locker stool, assumed a boxing position, threw some air punches, pow pow pow, before the two of them high-fived each other. Yippy Cantreras tried to sound like that boxing announcer, making his voice deep and shouting, "Les' get ready to rummel!"

As usual, there was a lot of healthy food laid out on the long table in the middle of the room: fresh fruit, big plates filled with celery stalks and carrot sticks, a bowl of cottage cheese with Saran Wrap still over it, another bowl filled with ice and yogurt containers. Charlie knew Tom was as likely to go near any of it as he would a bath house. By now, Charlie knew the kid's pregame meal, whether he was pitching or not, whether the game was in the afternoon, like today, or at night. Fifteen minutes after he showed up, one of the clubhouse kids would bring him two Big Macs from the McDonald's down the street, two large orders of fries, and a couple of chocolate milk shakes.

He must have called from his car today, because this time the food was waiting for him, the Big Macs on one paper plate, the fries on the other. He sat down and attacked it like a homeless person getting a free meal on Thanksgiving.

"That shit will kill him," Chang said, sitting in front of Charlie's locker.

"Yeah," Charlie said, "junk food is obviously ruining his whole season."

"It'll catch up with him eventually, is all I'm saying."

"I'm not up for one of your wellness lectures today."

"I'm just trying to make polite conversation," Chang said. He'd gone with a white t-shirt today, white Knicks basketball shorts down to his knees, high-topped white basketball shoes. "Though I know it's probably not as exciting as the kind you get in the bar before the fights start."

"Why don't you go over and talk to Tom? Tell him how concerned you are about his diet."

"You think he'll say anything to you about last night? Tom, I mean. Or just continue to look at you like an empty locker?"

Charlie said, "You know, he might've been watching my back last night, even if he'd never admit that."

"More likely, he just likes Snip and Pooty better than you," Chang said. "Then again, he seems to like everybody better than you."

"Is this the beginning of the shit-giving about what happened last night?"

"I'll talk to you about it after the game. Don't you have to go meet with Hick now to see if you're supposed to do anything different with your friend Zach and the rest of those phlegmwads?"

Charlie said that's exactly what he had to do right now. Chang told him to keep drinking water, it was still the best way to deal with a hang-over. Charlie said he wasn't hung over. Chang said he was full of it. Charlie said, So what else is new?

He went into the coaches' room with his copy of the Tigers' batting order. Hick said it was basically the same plan they had before, he'd be happy to go over it again if Charlie had one of those short-term forget-ful things going for him, the kind where you could remember who sat next to you in fifth grade but not what you had at Denny's for breakfast. Charlie said his memory was fine, thank you. Hick said, "The only thing you might want to think on changing is maybe buzzing a couple of them lardasses you and your boy was sparring with last night at the fights." Charlie said he'd be happy to do that, depending on how the game was going, he certainly didn't want to get himself back into another situation where anybody would want to accuse him of pitching like a pussy.

"That there was just one of those colorful figure of speeches has made me such a lovable character," Hick said. "I didn't mean nothin' by it."

"I knew it had to be something like that."

"Well, then," Hick said, "if we's done here, I think it's about time for my morning constitutional."

It turned out the Tigers were giving Zach Stroud the day off, saying it was because of bruised ribs suffered in what their pregame press re-lease said was "a non-baseball accident." But Kenny DeLuca and Chris Connelly were both in there, Connelly batting second in the order. Charlie threw ball one to him in the top of the first, a nothing curveball off the outside corner. Connelly stepped out of the box and called out to Charlie, "You had nothing last night 'til your kid saved your sorry ass and you got nothing now." When he stepped back in, Charlie threw a fastball behind his head that just missed hitting him in the helmet as Connelly dove back, trying to get out of the way.

As soon as Connelly picked himself up, he started for Charlie. But Pooty was too quick for him, grabbing him from behind, pinning his arms, trying to act calm about it, smiling the whole time like it was no big thing. Charlie stood his ground in front of the mound and watched it happen the way it always happened when somebody got buzzed like this in baseball and wanted to start something. He saw players from both teams start out of their dugouts, all of them moving in slow motion, seeing how it was all going to play out, mostly waiting to see what the home-plate umpire, Al Halsey, would do. Halsey was a rookie, Charlie knew, but carried himself like a veteran, a cool black guy who had been behind the plate when Charlie had pitched in Cleveland. He called a good game, didn't take any lip, told hitters to get back in there and hit and pitchers to get on the damn rubber and pitch, this wasn't one of those marathons that was going to last until Christmas. Now Halsey was as quick getting out from behind the plate as Pooty had been grabbing Connelly, getting out between home plate and the mound, and throwing his arms out at both dugouts like he was a school crossing guard.

"This all stops right now!" Halsey said to Charlie, then waved at both managers and told them to get their asses out there now, and leave the reinforcements behind. Connelly acted as if he were still trying to get loose from Pooty, but he really wasn't; whatever Pooty was saying even had him smiling now, and they were just going through the motions. Halsey gave both managers an official warning, which meant that the next pitch close to anybody, whether the batter got hit or not, meant the pitcher who threw it was out of the game. Charlie moved down close enough to hear Ted Hartnett say that you couldn't start the whole stupid warning process over something that had happened in a bar, and Halsey said, "Watch me."

Halsey seemed to have everything under control until Tom MacKenzie came to the top step of the Red Sox dugout and yelled over at Connelly, "Dude? How many times you guys plan to get your dicks handed to you on a one-day trip?"

Connelly broke loose from Pooty now and took a few steps toward the Sox dugout. This time, Halsey got in his way, told him to go pick up his bat or he was gone. Halsey had just put his mask back on, but now he took it off again, walked over to the Sox dugout himself, pointed at Tom, then made the you're-out motion that meant Tom had been ejected.

"For what?" Tom said.

"For being the kind of snotnose who doesn't know when to cut the shit after I specifically tell everybody to cut the shit."

"I wasn't even talking to you," Tom said.

"But now I'm talking to you, junior. Hit the showers."

Hartnett had stayed near the mound, just to make sure Charlie wouldn't say or do anything stupid, ignoring what was going on with Halsey and Tom. They both knew that throwing a starting pitcher out of the game on his day off was like ejecting a beer vendor.

To Charlie now, Hartnett said, "The floor show is officially over. Understand? I need innings from you today. Lots of them. So give them to me and cut the crap."

Charlie said, "Used to be, if somebody had run his mouth at me the way Connelly just did, you would have dropped him before I ever got the chance to stick one in his ear."

"Get this through your thick head once and for all," Hartnett said. "I'm not that guy anymore. You're not that guy anymore. This isn't then."

He took the ball out of Charlie's glove, slammed it back in there hard, started walking.

"Just pitch," he said over his shoulder.

For the next five innings, Charlie pitched.

On a day when he thought he might have nothing, it turned out he had everything. Not the stuff he used to have. Just as much as he still had left. Location, velocity, late movement on everything he threw. The whole deal. He came back in the first to strike out Connelly, then DeLuca after him. He gave up two singles to start the second, pitched out of that, got the next eight hitters in all before he gave up a double to start the Tigers' fifth, a ball that skipped under Julio Paulino's glove and went all the way to the rightfield corner. Stranded Frazier, the guy who'd hit it into the corner, at second. The last Detroit hitter in the fifth was Angel Broussard, their rightfielder. Struck him out swinging.

Pooty was waiting for Charlie near the first base coach's box.

"That's it, baby," Pooty said. "Don't rush nothin'. Set them up and then just fall back."

"Fall back?"

"It's a good thing, don't worry," Pooty said. "I can't teach all the brother talk your first month on the job."

"You sure you wouldn't be happier in the NBA?" Charlie said.

Before Charlie walked down the dugout steps, he looked up toward the Yawkey Suite, where Gary Goldberg had officially joined the parade of shit-givers in his life that morning. And despite the sun reflecting off the glass, he was pretty sure he saw Grace up there, sitting in the front row between Patrick Keenan and Booker.

By the sixth, he felt even better than he had in the first, throwing strikes wherever he wanted and whenever he wanted, telling himself he was just playing catch with Pooty, daring the Tigers to hit him, now that Ray J. had hit a grand slam in the fourth to go with Pooty's solo shot over the rightfield wall and made it 5–0, Red Sox. DeLuca got a bloop single with one out, but then Charlie got Zach Stroud's replacement, Arnie Korval, to hit into a 3-6-1 double play, Julio to Snip and back to Charlie covering first.

He kept running after he made the play, looked up at the Yawkey Suite again, sure that it was Grace now, Charlie feeling full of the day now, pointing up at her the way he used to point to where she was sitting behind the plate with the other wives at Shea, in that brief period when she actually sat with the other wives. Pooty was running with him, squinting into the sun to see where Charlie was pointing.

"That her?" Pooty said.

"You bet," Charlie said.

Only they both watched then, as Grace stood up, stared down at Charlie, then walked away, into the back of the suite.

When they got to the dugout, Pooty said, "God awmighty, man, you got family ties goin' even that bald doctor on *Oprah* couldn't untangle."

AFTER A COUPLE of innings in Patrick Keenan's suite, Grace could tell that Booker Impala Washington was more than the street-cool character he wanted you to believe he was, as if that were just a part he was playing, with his red beret turned around on his head the way he turned the language around; the way he gently played with Keenan. He reminded her of that old television show, *Soap,* one of her all-time favorites, the one where the black butler, Benson, was the coolest and sharpest person in the room. It was the same way with Booker today, though it wasn't much of a challenge for him, especially when you put him up against the people in the row right behind them: the bleached-blonde anchorwoman from Channel 7 right behind, the boy publisher of the *Herald,* the city councilman who kept leaning over and wearing her out with conversation about the "gas" Charlie was throwing.

One thing was certain: Booker was way ahead of everybody, Patrick Keenan included, in noticing how well Charlie was pitching against the Tigers, at least after both teams had their little boys-will-be-boys scene in the first inning.

"Your boy seems to have forgot what year it is," he said, after Charlie struck out the Tiger shortstop in the second.

"He's not my boy anymore," Grace said. "He's Patrick's. And Ted's. Maybe even yours. But not mine."

She turned and saw Booker smiling at her, as if they had a private joke going. "That so," he said, not quite making it into a question, letting her know in his laid-back way that he wasn't buying it for a second.

Grace said, "He always did some of his best work with no sleep, I'll give him that."

"It's a guy thing," Booker said. "Like not askin' for directions in the car, even though you're lost."

"Tell me about it," she said.

"Ted must have told him you were coming," Keenan said. "He seems to keep looking up here."

"Maybe there's too much of a reflection off the glass," Grace said, "and he's just trying to figure out who the babe is between you and Booker."

She had planned on spending the next week or so in New York, maybe even going out to visit some friends in East Hampton for Labor Day. She loved being in the east in September, especially in the Hamptons once the summer crowd left. There was also the meeting she'd had in New York with some television people the Tuesday after Labor Day, a couple of biggies-on-the go who wanted to talk to her about doing a syndicated, half-hour version of the *Grace Under Pressure* segments she did with Katie Couric. She had gotten offers like this before, but this time was interested enough to have a lunch meeting with them, even though they'd made it clear that they wanted to do the show out of New York.

Then Ted had called her at seven-thirty that morning to tell her about what had happened at Pooty Shaw's bar, and how father and son had at least been united on the front pages of the Boston papers and all over the local morning news shows. And, just like that, without really thinking about it, she'd said she was coming up.

"Why?" Ted said.

"I can help you referee," she said. "Or maybe I just want to hang around a little bit and see how this all turns out."

As usual, Ted had put the best possible face on Charlie's role in what had happened. He told her he'd already awakened both Pooty and Snip, wanting to get their side of it before he listened to Charlie's spin, and they'd made it pretty clear that Charlie had told Tom to stay out of it.

"You're as forgiving with him as ever," she said.

"I got it from you."

Grace said, "I've built up my immune system. There's these new vitamins you can take, and everything."

"I don't think he started this one, Grace," he said. "He's pitching this afternoon, by the way."

"Father or son?"

"Father."

"Maybe I'll come watch," she said. "See his great drama in person. Maybe we could have dinner, unless you're leaving right after."

"We're out of town over the weekend," he said. "Toronto. But we don't leave until tomorrow. So if that's a real invitation, I would love to take you to dinner."

He said he would arrange for her to sit with Patrick Keenan. She said she'd try to get there for the start of the game. Then she got herself organized more quickly than she usually did leaving a hotel, told the front desk at the Sherry she'd be back on Tuesday, got out to LaGuardia for the ten-thirty shuttle with plenty of time to spare, dropped off her bags at the Four Seasons, and took a cab over to Fenway Park, which still reminded her of a ballpark that should have been part of the tour on *Antiques Roadshow.*

The pregame conversation in the suite was about the bar fight. Then it was about the near fight in the first inning after Charlie nearly hit the second batter in the head, Booker explaining that Connelly had been in the bar fight. She told Booker that sometimes you could have too much information. Booker said, "Yo? You can't tell the idiots without no scorecard."

More and more, she tuned out Booker and everyone else in Keenan's suite and focused in on what Charlie was doing on the mound. As if she was the one who'd lost some kind of fight.

With herself.

She still knew how complicated everything was, even more than Charlie himself knew. And yet: There it was, right in front of her in the colorful little ballpark, the one she knew had even made John Updike go weak at the knees, the high green wall in the outfield, the green grass, the bright red seats off to her right when the green finally stopped over there. There Charlie was, on the mound live and on the television sets scattered around the suite, the ones that kept showing closeups of him every few pitches. Charlie taking deep breaths before he'd start his windup. Charlie grinning at something Pooty Shaw would say when Pooty came out to the mound. Charlie even running off the mound a few times the way Tom did, when Tom was on top of his game the way Charlie was today.

She wasn't sure about the real reason she had come up here.

Right in front of her, though, in front of her and all around her at Fenway Park, was why Charlie had come back.

She felt herself smiling after the fifth, when she could see him staring up at Patrick Keenan's suite now, knowing this was one of those baseball afternoons that made them all into little boys, made them all believe they would never grow old and could keep playing like this forever; knowing that, more than all the girls, this had always been her real competition for him.

Maybe that's why she gave him a look and then walked away to get herself another iced tea.

She could see him starting to labor in the fifth, even if he did end the inning with a strikeout. She saw him taking more time than he used to between pitches. One time, they showed him in the dugout, sitting next to Pooty, nodding as Pooty kept talking to him, as if Pooty were giving him some kind of pep talk, and Charlie finally just put his head back and closed his eyes. And in that moment, there and gone, he looked his age, Grace knew, every minute of it. Every low-class girl and late night of it.

Then he was back out there, the sixth inning now, the Red Sox ahead, 5–0, and when he beat the runner over to first base to complete the double play the first baseman had started, they did another closeup of him as he and Pooty made their way to the dugout, and Grace saw him looking up again, in that moment looking happier than he had been in ten years. Or more.

Looking whole, even though she knew she'd never say that out loud to him, or anyone else.

She didn't walk away this time. Instead, she turned to Booker and said quietly, "He would have paid any amount of money to have this."

"If my math's correct, he's working on thirteen out of the last sixteen," Booker said. "Pardon my Spanish, Miz MacKenzie, but you believe this shit? This is what the young ones called pitchin' at a holla."

"Call me Grace."

"*Amazin'* Grace," Booker said. "How sweet it is!"

Patrick Keenan came back from the bar, where he'd spent the last couple of innings chatting up the anchorwoman, sat back down to Grace's right. He said, "Listen to this crowd, will you?" Grace noticed the Irish in his voice seemed to come and go. "Thirty-three thousand and change making a sound like that," he said. "You can hear it even through the windows." He leaned over to Grace and said, "Have you ever heard anything like this?"

"Actually," she said, "I have."

The few times they had met before, Patrick Keenan had always reminded Grace of her father. They had the same good looks, the taste in clothes, the same style and charm and need to flirt with every woman in sight.

"May I ask you a personal question?" he said, still leaning in.

"Please don't make it the one about why good girls like bad boys."

He said, "I've never wanted to question that one, I've just thanked the Good Lord for it every day since I decided not to enter the seminary."

"What would you like to know?" Grace said.

Keenan said, "If your ex-husband knows that you are seeing my manager from time to time."

"Did Ted tell you that?" Grace said.

"I make it my business to know my business," Keenan said.

"Even when it's none of your business, Mr. Keenan?"

"Especially then!"

"The answer is no," Grace said, the words coming out sharper than she meant, and louder. "Because there is really nothing to tell. We have dinner occasionally if we happen to be in New York at the same time, or if I've snuck into town to watch my son pitch. Sometimes I have dinner with Tom one night and stay around the next to get caught up with Ted."

Keenan started to say something else, and Grace cut him off.

"Ted Hartnett and I are what we have been for almost twenty years," she said. "Friends."

"Is that his choice, or yours?" Keenan said. "The friends part?"

"And I think we will go back to watching the game now," Grace said, with that sincere perkiness she faked so well on television.

The Red Sox were out in the bottom of the sixth. Charlie was walking slowly back to the mound. The sellout crowd—why, Grace had always wondered, were they constantly referred to as the "Fenway faithful"? Was that some sort of rule somebody had passed for sportswriters and broadcasters?—was giving him another standing ovation.

Booker stood up suddenly and couldn't contain himself, he started pounding a fist on the window in front of him. He smiled at Grace when he sat back down.

"Amazin' Grace," he said again.

She said, "Which one of us are you talking about?"

"Him," Booker said. "But just for today."

"Was lost," Keenan said. "And now he's found."

Grace looked at the two of them standing there, two more who'd been turned into little boys by baseball, and thought:

Grace and the boys.

It was the story of her life, wasn't it?

Charlie knew the seventh inning was going to be his last. He knew he was fading in the sixth, and Pooty knew it. So did Ted Hartnett and Hick Landon. When he got back to the dugout, Hartnett said he wanted to get Bobby Cassidy, the Red Sox closer, a couple of innings of work today, just because Cassidy hadn't pitched in three days.

"You good with that?" Hartnett said.

"Good like Nedick's," Charlie said, an ancient New York line they used to hear from one of the old clubhouse guys around the Mets.

Hartnett smiled for the first time all day. "We are old."

"But young at heart," Charlie said. "I'm leaving here today with seven shutout innings."

"Do it."

And he would have done it if the wall hadn't gotten him for the first time.

The fucking wall. Charlie had decided to read up on it since he'd been in Boston. The Green Monster: Looking over the shoulder of everyone who'd ever pitched here, tempting every hitter, even more famous than the goddamn ivy on the outfield walls at Wrigley Field, another place that was too goddamn small and where the home team never won the World Series. The wall: Three hundred and ten feet from home plate, even though it looked closer than that. Thirty-seven feet and two inches high, then a twenty-three foot screen on top of that. Charlie knew it all now, the way he knew about the scoreboard at the bottom and what was behind it. Behind it was one more Bat Cave place at Fenway, a crawl space where the scoreboard guys sat, still putting the numbers up by hand, watching the game through the slats in the board, occasionally chatting with the leftfielder who was always just a few feet away. Charlie had gone out to the crawl space the first week he'd been in town, just because he'd heard about it so long and never actually seen it, wanting to see if it was true that ballplayers really scratched their names into the concrete walls. And there they were, names out of the past and present, the most famous graffiti in baseball, a part of the permanent record of the place; he wondered if pitchers, especially, came out here after they were retired to see if their names were still there, like part of some kind of war memorial, on the side of the wall only the scoreboard guys could see.

The fucking wall. Which is the way all pitchers thought of it, no matter how much they tried to blow smoke up your ass and say it really was an advantage for them, it made them a better pitcher, and smarter, it was the hitters who got all messed up trying to pull everything, like they were only here to pick up cheap home runs. The wall: Made out of green fiberglass sheets now, full of dents from all the balls hitting it, half of those balls outs in other ballparks, even if the new ballparks—the retro ones that wanted to be instant Fenways and instant Wrigleys— kept getting smaller by the year, another way to screw pitchers. The Green Monster: with a Staples sign as a bookend in foul territory to the left as you looked from home plate, across the facing of the upper deck; that famous Citgo sign in the distance, like some old satellite hovering in the sky; the Fleet sign another bookend, over toward center, set halfway up one of the light towers.

The Tigers' designated hitter, Ev Callaway, hit one off the wall with two outs in the seventh, maybe ten feet above the scoreboard, the ball clipping the wall on its way down, a chickenshit nothing Fenway double, what should have been a routine fly ball for Dahntay Gentile, the Red Sox leftfielder, who just had to stand with hands on hips and wait for the stupid thing to come down.

Pooty called time and came out to the mound as Chris Connelly came walking toward the plate from the on-deck circle.

"We are one damn out away from the seven shutout," Pooty said, no smiles now, all business. "Let's not step in nothin' now, track it all the way to the damn showers."

"I hear you."

"I can get you outta here this minute, you got nothin' left," Pooty said. "If Cassidy can get six outs, he can sure as hell get seven."

"I'm all right. It's not like the bastard hit it out to Lansdowne."

Pooty nodded at Connelly. "Once assface there picked hisself up, he got some pretty good hacks on you."

"In, out, in," Charlie said.

Pooty said, "You been waitin' a long time to get a W, is all I'm sayin'. Don't let them start to think they're in the game. Trust me, my brother, leads bigger'n this go faster here than shit through a goose."

"I've got one more out in me," Charlie said.

He got behind Connelly 2–0 with fastballs. Pooty gave him the sign for a curve away. Charlie shook him off. Pooty stubbornly put down the sign for a curve again. Charlie shook him off again. It almost made Charlie laugh, as tired as he was, the kind of lovers' quarrel he'd been having with catchers his whole life. Even smart catchers like Ted Hartnett and Pooty Shaw. Pooty shrugged now and went through a series of signals because Callaway was watching from second and they didn't want him to figure out what was coming and tip off Connelly.

In the middle of the sequence was the sign that meant fastball.

Pooty moved the glove inside.

Charlie tried to come inside but gave the bastard too much of the plate, way too much, and as soon as Connelly hit it, Charlie knew it was in the screen. He remembered Bill Lee, the whacked-out lefthander who'd pitched pretty damn well for the Red Sox back in the '70s—even though Fenway was supposed to be death for lefties—telling him at a card show one time that the wall was so close he sometimes imagined himself scraping his knuckles on it when he went into his windup.

Charlie turned in time to see the ball catch the screen just above the top of the wall, and now it was 5–2, Red Sox. Still two out in the seventh.

Shit.

Pooty didn't show any emotion, just calmly reached behind him for another ball from the umpire. He threw the ball hard back to Charlie, pointed at him with his mitt, then held up his index finger, which meant one more out. Still. Charlie nodded. Goddamn, he felt beat.

He looked over at the dugout and saw Hartnett on the top step.

Charlie rubbed up the new ball, eyeballing Hartnett now the way they had in the Yawkey Suite earlier, then slowly shaking his head.

No.

His eyes saying: Don't even think about it.

DeLuca was supposed to be up next, but he'd pulled a leg muscle going into the alley for a ball Snip had hit, and been replaced by a kid Pooty said was a Triple-A call-up, one who was supposed to be next year's sensation, somebody named Nick Tuths. So it was Tuths up now.

Another one half my age, Charlie thought.

Maybe he'll want my autograph if he gets me the way Connelly just did.

He walked Tuths on four pitches.

Pooty called time again, took two steps toward the mound. Charlie said, "Get back in there." The way Bob Gibson used to tell his catchers to get out of his face and go catch.

Pooty grinned, put his mask back on, got back into his crouch. Charlie looked over, and now Hick Landon was with Hartnett on the top step. Goddamn, he'd always hated it when they started that top-step bullshit, as if he couldn't figure out for himself that he better get the next guy or else.

He asked for a new ball, just to buy himself a little more time, got it from the ump, turned and started rubbing it, turned back around when he heard the crowd react to something, saw that Zach Stroud had come out of the Tigers' dugout to pinch-hit. Stroud: with a small bandage over his right eye where he'd clipped a chair going down at Pooty's, trying to do a big stare-down on Charlie as he walked real slow toward the plate.

Charlie ignored him, just stared in at Pooty's sign, focused on the glove. He threw strike one to Stroud, then two balls, both fastballs inside, the second one just missing the inside corner. It had either gotten quiet now at Fenway, for the first time all day, or he was back in that zone, all the way back there, the quiet place he used to find in moments like this, as if he'd pressed the mute button, making the ballpark—in his mind, anyway—as empty as Shea had been the day Pooty was batting against him.

Pooty called for a breaking ball outside. Again. Charlie shook him off, motioning with his glove for Pooty to go through all the signs again, just waiting for him to go back to the first sign; trying to make Stroud guess where they were going.

He threw this one a foot outside, saw Stroud reach for it and tap the ball weakly past the mound, between Julio at first and Snip at second.

Charlie realized about two beats too late that he should have been busting it over to first base, that Julio had strayed too far from first base trying to backhand the ball, and that Charlie had to cover. Like it was that first night over in Jersey when he'd vapor-locked on a play just like this.

He started running now, the whole play in front of him, then to his left, Snip coming hard for the ball, barehanding it, Stroud coming hard down the line, Charlie giving a quick look down to see where first base was.

He got there maybe a step ahead of Stroud, reaching down as he did for Snip's low throw, thinking of all the days in the outfield with Chang where he'd gotten low out there, low as he could go, and spent what felt like an hour moving from side to side, back and forth, what he called the monkey drill, his fingertips down in the grass as he went. He caught the ball and touched the corner of the bag ahead of Stroud. As he did, he managed to stop himself and throw his hip out just enough that Stroud, who he knew would have loved to have run right through him, went flying fat-ass-over-teakettle past him, doing a face plant behind first base at Fenway.

"Goddamn, Zach," he said, standing over him. "We made *SportsCenter* again. Call all your friends."

Stroud tried to say something back, but started choking on a mouthful of dirt.

Charlie flipped the ball to the first base ump then, slapped Snip on the back, walked slowly toward where the Red Sox were waiting for him, all of them on the top step now, and looked up one last time at the Yawkey Suite.

Thinking: Goddamn, Gracie.

Unless these assholes rough up the best closer in baseball, I'm back on the board.

CHARLIE'S LAST VICTORY in the big leagues had come five years and three months and two days before. It hadn't seemed like a big deal at the time, had only gotten that way after he'd retired, when he realized he couldn't remember his last W. So he'd called his friend Seymour Siwoff at the Elias Sports Bureau, where they knew everything that had ever happened in baseball, and found out he had pitched two innings for the Expos against the Phillies, the fifth and the sixth, given up five hits and three runs on a day when the Expos had scored eight runs in the sixth and come from 6–0 down to win. By doing that, they had gotten Charlie the 131st win of his career. He had gotten eighty-three of them in his first four seasons with the Mets, before he'd hurt his shoulder, which meant he had so little to show for the next decade he always imagined those later years as some kind of grease spot in the *Baseball Encyclopedia*.

But whatever happened from here, if he got hit by a bus tomorrow, he had one more now. He had the one Stieb had gotten when he'd come back from the dead with the Blue Jays, the one Charlie had told Chang about, the one he said Stieb would have given anything to get.

Charlie had pitched seven goddamn good innings, and if they weren't the seven shutout innings he wanted, they were good enough. He had his win and the Yankees, playing a makeup game of their own at the Stadium against the Royals, from a rainout they'd had in either April or May, had lost. The Red Sox lead was back to five games, at least for now, with one calendar month left in the regular season.

Rob Kendall had come up from Jersey for the game, telling Charlie afterward about this book idea he'd been pitching to a couple of small publishers in New York, a down-and-dirty book he'd start writing now, hoping for a happy ending.

"A happy ending for the Yankees or the Sox?" Charlie said. "Or just me?"

"Even though it wouldn't do me any good in New York, I'd say for you and the Sox," Kendall said. "I have to spend most of my time with the Yankees, because that's still the day job. But if I plan things out right, I can still sneak off and watch you pitch every five days, build everything around you and your heartwarming comeback and the last month of the season, then the playoffs. I thought about starting with that game when you hurt your arm in '88, go into more detail than I ever saw anybody do about that, make that the prologue and then cut to the present."

Charlie adjusted the ice on his shoulder. "There aren't any big details," he said, knowing he sounded hot all of a sudden. "I shouldn't have pitched that day and I did and it cost me."

"Well, yeah," Kendall said. "It's just an outline."

"Sorry," Charlie said. "I guess I'm still a little wired."

"Anyway," Kendall said. "I think if I do it right, the book might not suck, actually."

"You know I'm not a big reader," Charlie said, trying to make things light again. "But is that what guys like Hemingway were shooting for, not sucking?"

Kendall said, "I ever tell you my favorite Hemingway story? Yogi met him one time at Toots Shor's in the old days, when that was the place to be for everybody. Toots was introducing everybody around and told Yogi that Hemingway was a writer. And Yogi, trying to be polite, just to make conversation, said, 'What paper do you write for, Ernie?'"

It was just the two of them now at Charlie's locker, the clubhouse just about empty, most of the guys blowing out of there the way they usually did after a day game, especially knowing they didn't have to fly to Toronto until late the next morning. Charlie had done his big group interview, then so many individual TV interviews he was waiting to see a microphone that had C-SPAN on it. Kevin Oslin had finally hooked him up with a couple of afternoon drive-time radio shows in Boston, then reminded him afterward that he had to do *Imus in the Morning* at 7:30 the next morning, followed by *The Today Show*.

"Katie says she can't wait to talk to her friend Grace's hunky ex-husband," Oslin said.

Kendall finally said he was going back to his hotel to write his column. Kevin Oslin said he had some work to do upstairs. His cell phone chirped then. "Oslin," he said, pulling out one of those new phones that were the size of matchbooks. Next he did about a minute of vigorous head nods before he folded the toy phone back up and stuck it back in his pocket.

"That was the owner of the baseball team," Oslin said. "He would like you to come upstairs to have a bit of the bubbly and celebrate today's triumph." Oslin grinned. "That's an exact quote, by the way."

"He really say a bit of the bubbly?" Charlie said.

"He did."

"The guy goes through life as if he's being quoted," Charlie said. "He say who's up there with him?"

"No," Oslin said. "I was asked to pass the message along. I've done my job. Now I'm out of here, I've got a date with an Emerson College girl."

"You're still dating college girls?" Charlie said.

"Despite what some of the gloomier Jesuits told me," Oslin said, "God is good."

Charlie finished getting dressed, thought about taking the elevator up to Keenan's suite, decided to walk up the ramps instead, just to be alone for a few more minutes. But when he opened the clubhouse door to leave, Chang was on his way in, his leather traveling bag over his shoulder.

"I'm on my way up to Keenan's," Charlie said. "You want to come with me and make sure I don't drink too much champagne?"

"I'm on my way to the airport."

Charlie said, "You said before the game you had something you wanted to talk to me about after? You got time now?"

Chang said, "Sure. I quit."

Charlie barked out a laugh. "Yeah, right, now that the two of us have conquered baseball, we should probably move on to another sport."

Chang said, "I'm not kidding, Charlie. I quit."

Charlie was still holding the door open. He stepped outside, and now the two of them were on the landing at the top of the stairs.

"You can't quit," he said. "I'm gonna pitch like this the rest of the way. And, who the fuck knows, we might actually *go* all the way."

"If it doesn't interfere with your very busy social life," Chang said.

"Oh, come on, man. Is this still about last night? I'll tell you again what I told Ted, what I just told the writers. Again. It wasn't my fault."

Chang set his bag down, acting weary, as if he were the one who'd just pitched seven innings.

"Nothing that's ever happened to you is your fault."

Charlie said, "Here we go again."

"No," Chang said. "Here *I* go. You want to pretend you're fully committed to doing this right this time, go ahead. You think you can convince the writers and everybody of the same thing? Well, have at it. But we both know that as much as you go through the motions, you're still half-assed Charlie. Smoke when you feel the urge. Have a few pops with the boys. You're the man, Charlie. Just leave me out of it."

"You can't do this."

"You still don't get it," Chang said. "Even now."

Charlie said, "I thought you told me you were going to hang around so I could make you famous."

Then: "C'mon, man, you can't do this to me, not today."

Knowing how whiny that sounded, the same way he had sounded when Chang had first started working on his back.

"I don't mean to rain on today's parade, Charlie, I really don't. But you're going to find a way to fuck this up, I'm more convinced of that than ever. Same as you did with your wife and your kid and your first career. They can all stand by and watch you do it again and then say 'Poor Charlie, he still can't catch a break.' I don't have the time, no matter how much Keenan is paying me to hold your hand."

He picked up his bag now and said, "Good luck. You're going to need it."

Charlie watched him walk down the steps, as if he wanted to leave through the dugout. At the bottom, Chang looked up and said, "Oh, yeah, I almost forgot. Enjoy the party."

The headliners at the party were Patrick Keenan, Ted Hartnett, Pooty Shaw and Alqueen, Booker Washington, Grace MacKenzie.

And Tom MacKenzie.

There were other guests in the room, but the whole thing seemed to be running out of gas now that ninety minutes had passed since the end of the game. There was an eyeshadow junkie Charlie recognized from one of the local stations, he was pretty sure her first name was Sharon and he was almost as sure that she was the eleven o'clock news and not the six, but he couldn't swear to it. After Keenan had boomed out an introduction—"Ladies and gentlemen, please welcome today's winning pitcher for the Boston Red Sox baseball team"—and then led the applause, Sharon managed to make a nifty broken-field move across the room and get to Charlie first.

She didn't introduce herself, as if she just assumed he knew who she was.

"Congratulations," she said. "It's fun to watch an actual grownup show the boys how to do it."

She leaned a little bit more on "do it" than Charlie thought was necessary.

"You have no idea how wrong you are about the grownup part," he said, starting to worry that he might need the Jaws of Life to pry his hand away from hers. "If you don't believe me, ask my ex-wife over there."

"Her loss is my gain," Sharon said. "I've been thinking we should get to know each other better since you hit town."

"I've been thinking I need a drink," Charlie said.

Sharon said, "I get off at 11:31."

Pooty appeared at this point, having left Alqueen standing by the wet bar. He grabbed Charlie's arm in a jolly way and said, "C'mon, baby, we get you movin so's you can mingle a little bit here, be the people person I know you are."

When they were clear of Sharon, Charlie said, "Yo, Tonto: What took you so goddamn long?"

Pooty said, "I know you were there quicker for me last night, but I can't lie to you, my brother. It was nice to see somebody else besides myself suffering for a change."

Charlie asked the bartender for one of those small bottles of seltzer water, still hearing Chang's voice in his head, telling him to enjoy the party. Wondering if Chang was really serious about quitting, even if he'd looked serious as an arresting officer. Maybe he'd cool down when he got back to New York.

Alqueen was talking to Patrick Keenan, Charlie saw. Pooty was with Grace and Tom now. When they weren't looking at him, Pooty made a motion to Charlie. Like: Get your ass over here.

Charlie walked across the room, smiling at Grace, kissed her on the cheek when he got close enough. "Hey you," he said. "I thought the only thing you hated more than night baseball was day baseball."

She said, "Congratulations, old-timer."

"Thanks, Gracie."

Pooty said, "I'll leave you two old married folk alone, to talk on whatever it is old married folk still talk about in a civilized fashion. All Vonette does is yell these days, she gets on the phone, wants to know why I haven't sent the check to her voice coach." He picked up Grace's hand, kissed it, said to Charlie, "I'll be taking my leave now, me and Alqueen are booked for an early dinner at that restaurant over to the new Ritz."

Charlie said, "You old romantic."

Pooty said, "You pay and you pay and you pay."

Charlie looked at his son, who had actually cleaned up for the occasion. He must have had the light-green suit he was wearing over a black t-shirt stashed in one of his lockers, because Charlie remembered him showing up in a Red Sox sweatshirt with the sleeves cut off and blue jeans. Maybe it was the presence of his mother, or because he was a guest of the owner of the team. "What'd you think?" Charlie said to him.

Tom said, "You shouldn't've shook off Pooty on Connelly there, that's what I think." He drank beer out of a bottle. "Like, you didn't notice that after you buzzed him in the first, he'd been sitting on the inside pitch all day?"

Charlie laughed. "You're right."

Tom said, "Other than that you, like, righteously shocked the shit out of me."

"Beautifully put, Tom," Grace said. "The private-school tuition finally paid off."

He gave a little slump to his shoulders and looked even younger than he was. "Mom, he shocked the shit out of me, okay?" To Charlie he said, "I never thought you'd pitch this good."

"You want the truth?" Charlie said. "Neither did I."

Tom said, "I'll be right back, Mom. Sharon Carr over there? From Channel 7? She said she wanted to ask me something."

They both watched him walk across the room in the suit that looked a little too big for him. Grace said, "I'll bet I know what she wants to ask him, too."

Charlie said, "She gets off every night at 11:31."

Grace said, "I would have guessed a lot earlier in the day."

Grace had black jeans on, a silky-looking white blouse, and a sports jacket that looked as white as a new baseball. No jewelry around her neck.

None on her hands.

He always checked her hands.

They made small talk for a few minutes, Grace telling him about her television meeting in New York the next week. Charlie told her she was too smart to do television full-time, become another talking head. She said she didn't know if a show was her dream job, but maybe it was time for a change, maybe even to make the big move back east.

He smiled. "I'll help you pack."

She smiled back. "You might not believe this," she said. "But I'm happy for you, I really am."

"I do believe it."

She smiled again. "Did the earth move?"

"Relative to what?"

"Still a pretty big day for you, fella."

"It was until the game ended," he said. "Then that trainer I told you about—Chang?—up and quit on me."

"The trainer with the Lazarus powers?" she said. "The one who can bring geezer pitchers like you back from the dead?"

"Him."

"You're not kidding, are you?"

"Wish I was," Charlie said. "I don't know, maybe it was inevitable. Maybe I run off everybody who really gets to know me eventually."

"Did he tell you why?"

"You want to know the truth, Gracie? He sounded like you. Said I was a career screw-up, he just didn't use those exact words. Said I could explain away last night all I wanted, but if I hadn't been in the bar at that time of night, nothing would've happened. Basically told me I was still a self-absorbed jackass and that he was outta here."

"I don't want to make a joke out of this, because I can see you're really upset," she said. "But I have to say, he made some very valid points."

He looked past her now, watching Tom lean down to hear something Sharon Carr was saying, Sharon Carr somehow managing to lean into him as he did. Behind them, down in the seat area where people actually watched the games from up here, he saw Ted Hartnett talking to Keenan and Booker.

"I told him I'd keep working at it," Charlie said. "I told him I had been working harder than I ever had in my life. Which happens to be the truth. But I don't see why that has to mean that I can't go out and have a few laughs." He sighed. "Not that anybody was laughing very much at Pooty's last night."

He took another deep breath, let it out slowly, said, "I know you don't care about what I'm going to tell you. But I've been as celibate as a priest since I started this."

He wasn't counting the girl after the Dick Clark Music Awards, on the grounds that he just wasn't.

"I think you need a better example than priest," she said. "But then you never did spend much time reading the front of the paper."

"You know what I meant. You can ask Pooty."

"I love Pooty," Grace said. "He was telling me how the action really got started last night, after some brief introductory remarks about his primaries and secondaries. It all sounds more complicated than Agatha Christie."

Charlie said, "Bottom line? I haven't gotten drunk one time since the Red Sox signed me. Maybe I've smoked a couple of packs of cigarettes. That's it, the whole laundry list. I end up taking the heat last night, and all I was trying to do was be a bud to Pooty."

"He told me."

"And you believed him?"

"As a matter of fact, I did."

"I *want* this, Gracie. I'm not gonna do anything to jeopardize it, not this time around."

"I can see how much you want it," she said. "Maybe I had to see it all again with my own eyes to understand." She turned slightly, so Tom and Sharon were now in her field of vision. "By the way, do you think Anchor Slut over there has any issues about going for the son once she couldn't have Daddy?"

"Maybe we're all just looking for a mature woman."

"Watch it, buster. She's fifty if she's a day."

He said, "Hey? I'm glad you were here today. I'm glad you saw. Even if I don't win another game, at least I got one."

"You don't believe that."

"What?"

"That part about getting just one."

"No," he said. "I don't."

He said, "You want to have dinner?"

She hesitated for a moment, and then said, "Actually, I've got plans."

"You just got here. Who do you have plans with?"

"Ted," she said.

Charlie looked over to where Hartnett was still standing with Keenan and Booker, drinking beer out of a bottle himself, smoking a cigarette. "You have a date with Ted?"

"I would hardly call dinner with one of *our* oldest friends in the world a date," Grace said.

She sipped her wine. Charlie didn't say anything, and neither did she. But there was something between them now that hadn't been there about two minutes ago. Not one of their storm fronts. But the weather, he knew, had suddenly changed.

Even a self-absorbed jackass could figure that out.

He didn't know what to do about it, so he just said, "I gotta go."

Then: "Enjoy the party."

He knew it had been a while since he'd put a W in the books, but he knew this, too:

You weren't supposed to feel like this much of a loser on the day when you finally won a game.

SKYDOME, WHERE THE Blue Jays played, had always looked to Charlie as if it had been built with Legos. It was supposed to have been the new Space Age ballpark when they built it back in the '80s, with a retractable roof and its own hotel out there in the outfield, where people who were willing to pay extra on that side got a ballpark view. Except there was a famous time, not long after SkyDome opened, when it had been the other way around, and alert players and spectators— and one enterprising cameraman from the Jays' TV broadcast—had gotten a memorable view of the hotel. A couple had forgotten to put the shades down, or maybe left them up on purpose so they could flash everybody, and so there in the middle of the game was the sight of a babe going down on the guy. Big time, as Charlie recalled. The two of them gave a much better show than the Blue Jays were giving that day, and after that, people had to sign an affidavit or something when they registered at the hotel that they promised to behave themselves.

It turned out to be a lousy weekend for the Red Sox, one of those weird series that started on Saturday instead of Friday. Tom won his start, but then the Sox lost the other two games, including a sixteen-inning mess on Labor Day afternoon. This all happened while the Yankees were sweeping the Tigers three straight in Detroit, even if their Labor Day game was finally rained out after they'd waited nearly five hours to play it.

Now the Sox lead was down to three.

Ashe Grissom, who'd gotten hot at the end of August after a bad month for him that started at the All-Star break, his record up to 15–10, would pitch the opener of the Red Sox–Yankees series at Yankee Stadium, which was the last time the two teams would meet until the last weekend of the regular season at Fenway Park.

Charlie would go Wednesday night.

Pooty was constantly doing his rap about the big time on Charlie now, before games, during games, after games, in the bar, on the team plane. This here is the big time you laid it all on the line for, he'd say. You understand what I'm sayin'? Pooty would come out to the mound sometimes for no particular reason, like he was lonely back there behind the plate, and it was like he was picking up the conversation they'd had in the clubhouse, saying: How many times you see yourself in a situation like this here when you were out the game, Charlie Stoddard? This guy up to the plate ain't no problem with you. Know why? On account of you *got* no problems, that's why, on account of this here's your damn dream.

On the flight from Toronto, which didn't take off until about ten o'clock because the game had gone so long and then they had to sit on the runway for a couple of hours because the airport was fogged in, he and Pooty sat in the back, the way they always did.

"You ever hear the old joke about Adam and Eve?" Pooty said. "Boy gets his first hard-on and says to her, 'Stand back, baby, I don't know how big this thing gets.' Well, there ain't nothin' gets no bigger than you pitchin' in a game like this at the Yankee Stadium, in the middle of a race like this. You understand what I'm sayin'?"

"I try to keep up."

"Well," Pooty said, "there you go."

Charlie hadn't been back to the apartment on 66th since he'd packed his bag after the Norwich start and headed for Pawtucket. He and Pooty shared a cab into Manhattan, Pooty finally dropping him off in front of his building about 12:30. Charlie asked if he was going straight to the team's hotel, the Grand Hyatt next to Grand Central Station. Pooty said no, he had a stop to make downtown, he was meeting someone.

Charlie said that's all he needed to know, that way he wouldn't have to perjure himself later.

Charlie thought the refrigerator would be completely empty, but found one Corona still in there. He opened that, put on *Baseball Tonight* on ESPN to watch the highlights of the Red Sox–Blue Jays game and everything else that had happened in baseball since they'd gotten to the Toronto airport.

They ran a clip of Ted Hartnett being interviewed at SkyDome, the guy with the microphone trying not to smirk—Charlie noticed it was getting harder and harder for sports announcers to even give the final score without smirking—as he asked about the Sox lead shrinking this much. Hartnett wouldn't give him anything, just said that if somebody had told him coming out of spring training that he'd be three games ahead of the Yankees with three weeks to go, he would have said, "Book it."

When Hartnett walked away, the reporter, a girl, smirking now, said, "But does this book have an ending Red Sox fans know all too well? Corky Colter . . . ESPN."

Charlie hadn't spoken to Hartnett since he'd found out Grace was having dinner with him that night in Boston. He had thought about it a couple of times, thought about just going into Hartnett's office and closing the door and asking what the hell was going on, just how cozy the two of them had gotten over the last few years. But he knew that if he did that and then didn't like the answer he got, or thought his old room-mate was lying to him or holding something back, he'd say something.

And maybe, after all the years when they'd both held more back than either one of them wanted to admit, they'd have to put it all on the table.

Charlie knew that, for all the reasons Hartnett had given for his own marriage breaking up, the real reason he had never wanted to be mar-ried to Kate was because he had wanted to be married to Grace. Even when Charlie was still married to Grace. And he knew that as much of a friend as his man Gabby Hartnett had been—hell, as much of a friend as he was being *now*—that when it came right down to it, nut-crunching time, he had always been on Grace's side, had always thought Charlie was a total dick for the way he had treated her and finally blown the whole marriage sky-high.

Charlie knew Hartnett never thought he was worthy of Grace, even if he never came right out and said it when they were with the Mets, at least not until the end . . .

Christ Almighty, history could just wear your ass out.

Fuck history, Charlie thought now, watching the replay of the ball go-ing right through Snip's legs in the sixteenth so the Blue Jays could score the winning run. He didn't want to fight with his manager right now, he didn't want to fight with Grace or his kid or fight in any more bars, he didn't want to take another trip down memory lane, especially one that took him back to October of 1988.

He just wanted to pitch.

The next night, Ashe Grissom had a three-hit shutout going into the bottom of the eighth. He was trying to make a 1–0 lead stand up, the run coming on Dahntay Gentile's seventh-inning home run off the rightfield foul pole. Then Tim Kelly, the Yankee third baseman, singled off Gris-som's glove, and their designated hitter, Aurelio Arguello, a big guy with a perfect uppercut stroke for the Stadium, hit one off the facing of the upper deck in right, and just like that it was 2–1, Yankees, which is the way it ended.

Now the Yankees were two games behind the Sox.

What had been a sixteen-game lead was down to that.

Afterward, Charlie drew the biggest crowd of media to his locker. Like old times. He noticed Rob Kendall, hanging at the back, taking it all in, as if he were more interested in the scene than in what Charlie had to say.

"Are you the guy who can stop the bleeding?" some little dork with a radio microphone asked.

Charlie made himself look frantic, and then started patting himself all over the place.

"Jesus," he said, "am I hit already?"

The dork stayed with it.

"If you lose tomorrow," he said, "the lead is down to one."

"You're *shitting* me?" Charlie said, and got a laugh.

From the back, Rob Kendall said, "How many times over the last five years did you think about pitching a game like this, in a setting like this, in a race like this?"

Charlie said, "Only every day." Then he grinned and said, "Am I going too fast for anybody?"

Kendall said, "No, you're still speaking at perfect notebook speed. And in real short sentences, like always."

A woman Charlie thought he remembered from one of the cable channels, a snappy dish with long black hair and lips just pouty enough that you didn't worry she'd injected them with puffy juice, said, "You were always the one with the good lines, Charlie, and not just at the ballpark, from what I hear. Why don't *you* give us the headline for tomorrow night?"

He leaned back, closed his eyes as if thinking really hard, then nodded as if to say, Okay, got it.

"Here it is," he said. "'Charlie to Yanks: I'm Back.'"

He had one of the clubhouse kids call him a cab. He knew Grace was probably still in town after her television meeting, and thought briefly about giving her a call at the Sherry-Netherland. He could call and ask if she wanted to have a late drink and tell him all about it, give her a chance to make fun of the suits.

Except that wasn't why he'd be calling, he'd be calling to see if she was even in her room, or maybe out with Ted again.

He got into the cab outside the Press entrance and told the guy 66th and Second. The guy pulled around and got on the Deegan heading south, asking if Charlie wanted him to go over the Third Avenue Bridge or take the Triboro. Charlie told him to take the Triboro, so he could get his favorite view of the big town.

What goes around comes around, he was thinking. All those years when Ted had wanted to be him, so he could be the one with Gracie, and now maybe it had all turned around, and Charlie was the one on the outside, eating his heart out, watching them.

Or maybe he was making it out to be more than it really was, the whole thing was nothing more than two old friends getting together and shooting the shit about old times, when everything had been a lot simpler, even when it had felt complicated as hell, when the only decision after the game had been which bar you wanted to go to.

He told the guy to take him to The Last Good Year.

"Does that year have a cross street, by any chance?" the driver said.

Charlie told him 50th and Second, left-hand side.

The bar was every bit as crowded as Charlie knew it would be, the way it always was when it was Red Sox vs. Yankees, whether the game was in New York or Boston. People would come to watch the game and stay. Or they'd go to the game and then come back here, just because over time Healey had positioned The Last Good Year as the saloon capital of the New York Yankees. The Mets, Charlie knew from listening to WFAN in the taxi, had beaten the Braves and gone back into first place in the National League East. So after so much of the summer when even the truest of Yankees true believers—Healey being a vocal exception every time he'd get over-served in his own establishment—had resigned themselves to the Red Sox running away with the AL East for once, the city was suddenly insane with the idea that there might be another Subway Series between the Yankees and Mets.

Charlie had grabbed an old Knicks cap out of his locker before he left the clubhouse, the one he wore sometimes when he ran in the outfield, but even with it pulled down close to his eyes, there were shouts at him from the barflies who recognized him as he made his way quickly, head down, through the front room. He looked up just long enough to make eye contact with Terry, the bartender, who pointed toward the back room, which meant Healey was back there.

He was sitting with a girl Charlie knew he was supposed to know, one of the stable of what Healey actually still called fillies, every last one of them thinking they were the only woman in Joe Healey's life.

He was, Charlie realized now, the white Pooty.

Healey jumped up when Charlie arrived at the table, said, "Evelyn, dear, you remember my scummy turncoat friend Charlie Stoddard, don't you?"

Evelyn was a redhead with a lot of freckles and a lethal-looking overbite. "Hey, good-looking," she said to Charlie.

He leaned over and kissed her on the cheek. When he straightened back up, he threw out his arms and said to Healey, "How about you give us a kiss, too, you big lug?"

Healey said, "Kiss my ass." He waved at the closest waiter, a tiny Scot named Little John Henderson. "I'll have another Canadian Club and ginger ale," he said to Little John. "And whatever the Boston guy is having."

Charlie said a Bud Lite would be just fine. Little John asked if he was sick. Charlie said no, he just wasn't in the mood for a Scotch, he wanted a beer instead. John wanted to know what had happened to him in Boston that had him drinking like a woman.

When Little John was gone, Healey said, "I never thought I'd be able to root against you, but I'm actually doing fine with it."

"I'm happy for you."

"When my Bombers finish with you tomorrow night, they'll need dental records to identify you."

"Evelyn," Charlie said, "why do you put up with a lowlife like him?"

Evelyn said, "He has a job."

"I'd think about trying to get you drunk," Healey said when Little John brought their drinks, "but as I recall, there were times when that improved your control in the old days."

"One beer," Charlie said, clicking glasses with him, and then Evelyn. "Then I am going home and going to bed. Alone."

He thought he might have felt Evelyn rub her leg against him, but couldn't be sure.

"Ellie Bauer's out there at the bar," Healey said. "I'll bet she'd walk you home."

Charlie's head whipped around.

"Relax," Healey said, "I'm just busting balls."

They had been at the table less than ten minutes when Terry poked his head into the back room and yelled to Healey that there was a call for him at the bar. He excused himself, telling Evelyn to behave.

"I'm as devoted to you as you are to me, honey," Evelyn said with a blank face, then extended her cigarette for Charlie to light it.

"It really wasn't for me," Healey said, when he came back. "They were looking for you."

"Who's looking for me at this time of night?"

"One of Mo Jiggy's guys, calling from Beef."

Charlie knew Beef. It was the half-restaurant, half-topless joint downtown that Mo owned now, free and clear. Charlie remembered reading in the paper that he had bought out the other partners, most of whom were New York Hawks football players told to sell their shares by NFL commissioner Wick Sanderson after the Hawks had won the Super Bowl a few years before. Charlie had been down there a few times when he and Healey got drunk enough, just for laughs, and also because the dancers were like the Rockettes, just naked.

Healey said, "The guy, Jamal his name was, got one of those Barry White voices, said he'd tried your apartment and when you weren't there, Mo told him to call here."

Charlie said, "Is there some sort of new floor show he wants me to see?"

"Kind of," Joe Healey said. "But only because your son is in it."

Beef was downtown in the West Village. Charlie knew from past experience that even if you gave cab drivers the exact address, they'd still get lost sometimes trying to find their way around in the meat-packing district, where all the warehouses tended to look alike, in pretty much the same way the boy prostitutes down there did. The driver got lost now, made a couple of U-turns, finally pulled up in front of a small neon sign that had "Beef" written out in script, and a lasso underneath that was supposed to be a G-string.

The black kid at the door said, "Help you, Gee? This here is members only." Charlie told him in a nice way that he was a friend of Mo's, and that Jamal had called and told him Mo wanted him down here fast.

Beef, he could see, was exactly as he remembered it. There was a horseshoe-shaped bar, huge, dominating the middle of the room. Off to one side were two dance floors, brightly lit. On the other side of the bar was the restaurant, where you really could get some of the best beef in town, just not the kind they were really advertising with the name of the place.

Charlie had never referred to women as "beef" in his whole life, but somehow it had caught on with the younger guys, especially the ones in sports.

On the dance floor closest to the front door were two tall dancers, both of them nearly six feet tall in their spiked heels. They both had blonde hair tied into pigtails and were dressed the way girls used to dress for '50s sock hops: saddle shoes, low white socks, plaid dress.

Everything except tops.

The song playing was a slow version of "Runaround Sue," and they were doing a version of what Charlie knew was the old dance known as the Stroll, the one the teachers sometimes did at a school dance after they got into their own punch. You formed two lines, and then everybody had to take a turn, by themselves, trying to do some kind of funky stroll, usually looking whiter than Utah in the process.

The blondes were the only ones in the line right now. The stroller was about to be a very drunk Tom MacKenzie, being cheered on by them and just about all the people in Beef who had crowded up close to the dance floor. The ones cheering the loudest, Charlie could see, were Dahntay Gentile, Ray J. Guerrero, and Snip Daggett, all of whom looked as drunk as Tom MacKenzie.

Tom was wearing an old Joe Montana No. 16 white jersey from the 49ers, baggy jeans, high-topped work boots untied, one of the paisley do-rags the dudes wore under their football helmets.

Tom bowed to the crowd, backed up a little, then tried to make a few Pharoah moves, arms stretched straight out from his shoulders, that Charlie could have sworn he remembered from *Soul Train,* snapping his fingers, bopping his head from side to side. But as soon as he got between the dancers, he went into this pratfall, and made it seem as if the only way he could keep himself from hitting the floor was by grabbing on to the dancer to his right and sticking his head between what Charlie had to admit, even from a distance, were world-class breasts.

It only made the crowd cheer and clap louder than before. Some of the guys started to chant, "Tee-*Mac,* Tee-*Mac.*"

A voice behind Charlie said, "And to think they put this shit together with no rehearsal time *at* all."

Charlie turned to see that it was Mo Jiggy himself standing next to him, Mo's bald head as smooth as a black marble, one of the floating spotlights reflecting off the diamond in his ear so that the stud looked as if it were giving off a beam of light of its own. He wore a starched white shirt with no collar, a pair of tight leather slacks.

"Maurice," Charlie said, "I wish we were meeting up again under circumstances a lot less fucking weird."

They gave each other one of those fast embraces, the guy version of women air-kissing each other. Mo said, "He been goin' like this a good hour now. Seems to have developed a real nice rapport with Tonya and Nancy."

"Tonya and Nancy?" Charlie said.

"Got their big *Holiday on Ice* number comin' up right after this," Mo said.

"Couldn't you get Tonya and Nancy to take him upstairs to one of the Do-It Rooms without calling me?"

"They willin', don't you worry," Mo said. "They both think old T-Mac as cute as a junebug. But the boy keeps sayin' he was born to dance."

There was a groan from the crowd as Tom tripped over his laces and went down. But Charlie and Mo watched as he bounced back up at the count of three.

"I don't suppose you asked his teammates to get him out of here," Charlie said.

"They say they ain't leavin' until after they see *Holiday on Ice*," Mo said. "They said some guys on the Devil Rays practically gave them a damn commercial like you see on TV for Broadway? Told them if they only saw one show while's they was in New York, it had to be Tonya and Nancy."

"How would you describe it?" Charlie said.

"I think you got to start with slippery," Mo said.

The next song was "Earth Angel."

Charlie said, "I never figured Beef for oldies night."

Mo said, "Been checkin' you out in the papers since you come back, and I'm frankly not sure what you got goin' with your boy. Truth be told, if he *weren't* your boy, my whole position on him would be, Fuck him, go Yankees. You understand? But he is your boy. And if he don't watch himself the rest of the night, he gonna end up on the front page again, only in New *Yawk* this time." Mo put his arm around Charlie and said, "I figured you might be able to take some of the heat off me when I tell him to get him outta here."

On the dance floor, Tom was trying to incorporate pitching from the stretch into a new dance number.

"He's been here an hour, you said?"

"Went over and greeted him myself, got him all excited, meeting one of his musical heroes. Said he was just gonna warm up here and then him and his buddies was gonna take it up to No Fly Zone after this. You know No Fly Zone?"

"As I recall," Charlie said, "it's this place without what you always say is that am-bi-ence you've got going here."

"The girls ain't nearly as nice to look at," Mo said. "The bouncers definitely ain't so nice. And I know for a fact they got a photographer works for Page Six of the *Post* on speed dial."

Charlie said, "So how do we get Michael Jackson out of here?"

"I'll put a wrap on the oldies. Then I'll send Tonya and Nancy over to the Red Sox table, same's I would a round of drinks on the house."

"And then I just go over and say, 'Okay, Beav, time to go'?"

Mo said, "Wait a few minutes 'til he goes takes a piss. Boy's got to turn it loose soon, 'less he's some kind of camel. Then I'll send a couple of my boys, Shaheen and Jamal, one that called you, to wait for him outside the men's, and the three of you can throw him into my Suburban and go tuck him in."

"What if he doesn't want to go home?"

Mo said, "People say no to Shaheen sometimes, on account of he's no bigger than a munchkin. But ain't nobody I ever heard about's said no to Jamal."

"Sounds like a plan."

"How *you* doin', by the way?" Mo said. "You seem to got your shit together lately."

"I still talk the talk," Charlie said. "But every time out, I feel like I'm hanging on by my fingernails."

"I'm thinkin' of going to the Stadium tomorrow night, sit up there in my big suite and check you out with my own eyes."

Charlie said, "I know you're a big sports agent and all-around entrepreneur now, but I want you to know that even with my retarded musical tastes, I loved *Diddy This.*"

"Dissin' on Diddy is a reason to live, for some," he said. "By the way, how come you didn't call me to negotiate with that old dandy owns the Sox?"

"I'm only making chump change," Charlie said. "Maybe next year, if I live."

"I would've got you more," Mo said.

"Even you would've had a problem," Charlie said. "They knew I would have paid them."

Mo poked Charlie now, and pointed toward Tom. "It's showtime, Showtime. There goes your boy to take a leak."

They could see Tom making his way toward the place in the back where the men's room was. As he did, he saw a short guy in a black Raiders jacket follow him. The short guy was followed by someone in a dark suit and a bowler hat, about six-eight and maybe three hundred pounds.

"Jamal?" Charlie said to Mo.

"Won Employee of the Month here four straight months," Mo Jiggy said.

22

TOM WAS ABOUT as happy at leaving Beef as he was leaving ballgames when he still wanted to pitch. But Jamal said in his deep voice, "Be nice, y'all," as he finally scooped him up and carried him out the door to the Suburban.

"I can *walk!*" Tom said.

"Just be thankful you don't got to," Jamal said.

Shaheen drove. Charlie sat in the front with him. Jamal was in the back with Tom, who was slumped against the door on Shaheen's side.

Shaheen, who was about the same size as Snip Daggett, wasn't much of a talker. He said "Where to?" and Charlie gave him the address of the apartment on 66th and that was the last thing Shaheen said all the way uptown.

Charlie would turn every few blocks to see how Tom was doing. He looked over and kept saying "fuck" and "shit" a lot, until Jamal got tired of that and gave a hard Three Stooges twist to his nose.

"Hey!"

"Be nice, y'all," Jamal said again, then checked Shaheen's mirror to make sure his bowler was still on straight.

When they got to Charlie's building, Jamal said to Tom, "You want to do this easy or not easy?" Tom said he'd behave. Shaheen and Jamal still walked him across the lobby and toward the elevator, Charlie right behind them, saying to his doorman, "It's all right, Odd Job's with me."

When they got to Charlie's apartment, Jamal said, "Mo said we just wait a while."

"We're fine now," Charlie said.

Jamal said, "Y'all are fine when Mo says y'all are fine." He reached into his pocket, and Charlie was wondering if he was going to show him a gun. Jamal handed him a business card that had "Jamal" written on it and an 888 phone number underneath. "I'm just a phone call away," he said.

When they were inside, Tom said, "This, like, way sucks." He did a little backward flop on the couch and said, "You got any beer?"

"Don't you think you've had enough?"

"Dude, how many times do I have to tell you you're not the boss a me?"

"I'll cop to that," Charlie said. "But in return, you've got to do me a favor."

"What?" The kid tried to put on a face that was sullen, but just looked sleepy instead.

Charlie said, "Lose the 'dude,' okay? It makes me want to call my man Jamal."

"Jamal can eat me, okay?"

It made Charlie smile. "*Now* you say that."

Charlie heard what sounded exactly like a wolf whistle, and realized it was Tom's cell phone. The kid ignored it until it stopped. "Just a girl," he said.

"Oh, that's the famous girl phone."

"Mom tell you?"

"Mom know you're drunk this much?"

Tom made a snorting sound. "Mom thinks I'm just high-spirited and occasionally have to blow off steam the way all young guys like me do. That's what she told the *Boston Globe* in spring training, anyway."

"She's not stupid, you know."

"Stupid about me the way you were," the kid said, "or just stupid?"

He tried to focus his eyes enough to give Charlie another sullen look, his hard-guy look, the one he seemed to have been practicing his whole life.

Charlie said, "You sure you don't want a Coke or coffee or something?"

"I want a beer."

"If I get you a beer," Charlie said, "can we talk a little bit?"

"What are you, a bartender? I just want a beer, not conversation." Charlie noticed he struggled a bit negotiating his way through "conversation," as if the word had a couple of hairpin turns in it.

"I just want the conversation. Jump ball."

"Whatever," Tom said.

"Don't go anywhere," Charlie said.

"Too tired."

"Jamal really is downstairs in the car."

"Classic."

There was a wall separating the living room and the kitchen, with one of those openings in between. On the living-room side there was a counter about as high as a bar, where Charlie usually ate breakfast. He leaned through the opening now and said, "You think this shit between us is ever gonna stop?"

"Why should it?" Tom MacKenzie said.

"Corona okay?"

Tom nodded. "Jesus, I was just trying to have a little fun, you know?"

Charlie said, "Aren't we all."

Charlie looked at his watch. Two-thirty in the morning now. The kid was on the carpet in front of the couch, leaning back against the cushions, long legs stretched out in front of him. Instead of making him more tired, the Corona seemed to have jacked him right back up to where he was on the dance floor. The girl cell phone was making so much noise, every ten minutes or so, he finally said he was putting it on buzzer. He had taken off his Montana jersey and the do-rag; underneath the jersey was a navy t-shirt that read PEPPERDINE BASKETBALL, the words in bright orange. The work boots had come off, too, and he was barefoot, Charlie noticing some kind of small tattoo on one of his ankles. Tom said they at least had to have some music, it was too quiet in here. He braced himself on the couch and got himself up and went over to the wall unit with Charlie's sound system built into it, went through a stack of CD's, announced that most of them sucked, but that *maybe* he could force himself to listen to the Stones' *Let It Bleed* without, like, wanting to throw himself out the window. He said he'd hipped himself to the Stones after he and Mick had met one night at a party in Los Angeles.

"'Midnight Rambler,'" Charlie said. "It's the third song."

Tom said, "I'm cool with that," found the song, sat back down on the couch.

They were both smoking. Charlie had decided to have a Corona himself. Two-thirty in the morning, he was pitching tonight, and here he was smoking and drinking. He briefly thought about Chang, how this was a scene that would make *him* want to throw himself out a window.

At least the two of them were here.

Tom did most of the talking. Charlie listened. He wasn't sure how much the kid would remember in the morning. Maybe none of it. It was all right. Charlie would remember. At one point Tom said that Charlie could call downstairs, tell Mo's guys they could leave, he was too tired to try to escape. Charlie called Beef, and the bartender said she'd tell Mo he could bring Shaheen and Jamal on home. Tom said, "You know, I thought it was jive that Mo Jiggy was really a friend of yours." Charlie said, "It's like Pooty says, I'm a people person." Tom started to say something, and Charlie held up a hand. "I know," he said. "Whatever."

Tom went back to his ramble about things Charlie had done in his life that pissed him off, all the way back to the Stuart Hall School for Boys.

"I'll tell you another thing," Tom said, as if suddenly picking up with a conversation he was having inside his own head. "You not being around meant I had to deal with those rich assholes she dated."

"You're blaming me for guys your mother was seeing?" Charlie said, laughing. "I object."

Tom waved his beer bottle at him. "Overruled," he said. "There weren't that many of them, believe me. I always thought it was easier getting elected Pope than it was getting a date with Mom. Christ, when I was old enough and we'd be somewhere and I'd see guys think about making a run at her and then just know they shouldn't even try, you know? Like: Grace MacKenzie? I got *no* shot. But some managed to make the grade." He looked around on the coffee table, squinted and found where he'd put the ashtray, picked up his cigarette. "Maybe anybody else would've thought they were good enough guys, but all I could see were these yupped-out *dicks,* like Doctor Bob coming to these games at Washington High, sucking around *me* as a way of winning brownie points or whatever with *her.* And I swear to God, it was even worse when you'd show up once a year and I'd look over to the bleachers in, like the third inning, and catch you already looking at your watch."

Staring at Charlie now with Charlie's own eyes.

"I was watching," Charlie said.

"Yeah," the kid said, "but you know you weren't *really* watching."

"Guilty," Charlie said.

"That's it? Your whole answer? Guilty? I mean, that right there is *epically* classic." He drank some beer, wiped his mouth with the back of his hand. "This is your idea of conversation? Shit. I remember you told me one time, guys are no good at talking to each other. Maybe we just should have stayed with that."

"You want the long answer?" Charlie said. "Okay, here it is: By then I didn't even want to watch the games I was in. I couldn't even fake that I was into somebody else's. Not even yours."

"Dear old Dad."

"I didn't know how to be a dad." He held up a hand. "That's not true. I didn't *want* to be a dad when your mother got pregnant. *Then* I didn't know how to be a dad. And after your mother and I split, I never spent enough time doing it to learn how to do it right."

"You never fucking *tried!*" It came out big, the force of the words even surprising Tom. He stood up now, no easy job for him, swaying a little bit like they had sailed into some kind of rough water. Which, Charlie had to admit, they probably had. "Don't try to run that bullshit on me you always did on her, like we're supposed to feel sorry for you, all right? Don't even think about going there."

Charlie started to say something, but Tom cut him off. "Why are we even doing this? Mom says you can't change."

Charlie said, "I used to think the same way, but I'm not so sure."

"You should've seen some of those fuckin' guys," he said.

"Which guys?"

"The boyfriends."

They were back there.

"Thinking I was the best way for them to get in good with her. Showing up all over the place for my games, Washington against anybody, they didn't care. One of them was this Brit publisher who kept trying to tell me how much the whole thing reminded him of cricket, for Chrissakes. Another guy trying to act like he was part of it, you know? Like what I was doing had anything to do with them." He sat back down, on the couch this time, arms outstretched behind him. "Know why I liked baseball the best of all the sports? Because you could be part of it, the team or whatever, when you wanted to be, and the rest of the time, 'specially if you were a pitcher, they had to leave you the fuck *alone.*"

"I know," Charlie said. "I know." He wanted another beer but knew that if he got up, Tom would want one, too. He stayed in the beat-up leather easy chair, the one thing in here that he felt really belonged to him, the thing that had somehow survived all the time it had spent in storage, all the years since Grace had given it to him as a joke the first year they were married, telling him that even though it wasn't a couch, maybe it could turn him into a couch potato someday, one who didn't think it was breaking the law to stay in at night.

"You *know*," Tom said. "You don't know anything about me."

"Maybe," Charlie said, "but I know about that. What you just said. Because I always liked the exact same goddamn thing about pitching. You only had to be a team player every five days. And you want to know something? You didn't have to be much of a team player then."

"You got anything to eat?"

Charlie told him he'd called the deli before he'd gone to the ballpark, there was some bread and peanut butter, chips and cookies, a gallon of milk, and some of those small cereal boxes. "The basics," he said.

Tom went into the kitchen, came back with a bag of Oreo cookies, and started eating them the way Charlie did, separating them, eating one side and then the other. Sat there and ate cookies and really looked like a kid and kept talking, rambling now: About how when he was twelve he looked up all this *stuff* on Charlie's career, that's what he called it, *stuff*, like he was researching a term paper, like he knew somehow that it went with the *stuff* in Charlie's closet, all the baseball possessions he couldn't throw away. Thinking that if he impressed Charlie with how much he knew, on one of those afternoons or even weekends they'd get together, one of those times when Charlie was in the area to play either the A's or the Giants, that maybe they could really talk, even if it was just about the *stuff*, even though he knew Charlie's out was always that guys didn't talk. Maybe he'd even see, without Tom having to talk about it, how much he wanted him to be a fucking dad. So he learned everything he could about Charlie's great years with the Mets. Only every time he brought up one of those games he had down cold, asking questions about things that had happened during the game even though he already knew the answers, Charlie would blow him off.

"You gotta understand," Charlie said, "going back to those years, which is all *anybody* ever wanted to do, just made me feel worse about how I was just hanging on. I just didn't want to play that game where I sat around and talked about the good old days. It turned out I'd do enough of that shit later at card shows."

"But I wanted to play that game," Tom said. "Only it didn't matter what I wanted, right?"

"No," Charlie said. "It didn't."

Tom said, "You want to know the really *really* best part? You didn't want to talk about my career, either. Even after I started to get *really* good, in high school, you didn't even pretend to care. I used to think that it was because you wanted to be with her instead of me, which was probably part of it. But then I started to think, maybe I was *too* good."

Charlie didn't say anything. He had never thought of it that way. But then he'd never tried to see things the kid's way. At least not until now, anyway. Over time, he'd just gotten used to Tom being angry all the time, making Charlie out to be the bad guy for screwing over his mother the way he had, and screwing over him in the process, and Charlie'd accepted that's the way things were, the way he'd accepted the way his career had gotten monumentally screwed over after he got hurt.

All those years when he'd gotten so comfortable being a victim.

"It just got to the point where I figured you were better off without me, since I just pissed you off more and more by showing up," Charlie said now. "I'd made a mess of everything else in my life, now I'd made a mess out of whatever deal I had going with you."

"You never asked me," Tom said in a quiet voice, staring at Charlie, looking as if he'd gotten sober all of a sudden. "Nobody ever gave me a vote."

"I was too wrapped up in my own shit," Charlie said. "But you know that already, don't you?"

"Goddamn, I hated you!" he said. "When it didn't seem to bother you, that just made me hate your guts even more. And when she didn't hate you, it made me hate her sometimes."

Somewhere in Charlie's memory, he remembered Grace telling him once that sometimes one member of the family tried to be mad enough for everybody else.

The music had stopped. Tom rolled himself over so he was laid out on the couch now, finally starting to fade.

Still talking, though.

"The thing you never got is that I didn't want you to be some kind of Super Dad," he said. "I already had Super Mom."

"Tell me about it."

"I could never understand why she wasn't more pissed at you."

"She did all right, kid, believe me."

"How could you dick around on her that way?"

"I'm gonna tell you something that sounds weak," Charlie said. "But I didn't know any better."

"You're right, it is weak." He nodded at Charlie's CD. "Like your taste in music. I mean, like, earth to Charlie." Sounding like Grace. "It's over for Sting, okay?"

Then Tom said, "You really popped the mayor's wife at a Welcome Home dinner?"

"You know about that one, huh?"

"Everybody in baseball knows that one. Everybody except me thinks it was, like, the coolest thing ever."

Charlie was out of cigarettes. He knew there was an emergency pack somewhere, but he was too whipped to go on a room-to-room search. He wanted to get some sleep, is what he wanted to do.

But he knew this might be his one shot.

Charlie said, "You want to know the God's honest truth? I didn't know how good I had it with your mother any more than I knew how good I had it when I could pitch like . . ." He smiled. "Like you," Charlie said. "And I've spent the last half of my life fucking paying for it."

Tom said, "And what? Now you think you can make things right, with everybody? More classic Charlie."

"You have no idea how good I am at kidding myself."

"Mom says she's spent half her life waiting for you to grow up."

"I know. Says she still is. Waiting, I mean."

Tom said, "All you ever cared about was you. Now I'm suddenly supposed to believe you care about me. Why, because we're supposed to be on the same team? Give me a fucking break."

"That isn't my entire plan," he said. "But it's a pretty big part of it."

"Well, good luck," Tom said. He reached behind him and propped up the pillows underneath his head, closed his eyes.

Charlie told him he'd be surprised how many people were wishing him luck lately without really having their hearts in it. But Tom Mac-Kenzie was already asleep, mouth open, snoring slightly. Looking like the twelve-year-old who'd looked up all the stuff. Charlie dragged himself off the chair, went into the bedroom, grabbed the quilt from his bed, came back and covered Tom with it. He turned off the lights, just the lights of Manhattan coming through the big picture window, and watched the kid sleep.

He couldn't remember the last time he'd done that.

Maybe I should have stayed in more often, he thought, right here in Gracie's leather chair.

Maybe, Charlie thought, he'd gotten the same thing here he got from the Sox:

A start.

23

BY THE TIME Charlie woke up, a few minutes after ten o'clock, Tom was already gone. The couch was a mess, as if he'd tossed off the back cushions in the night to give himself more room to move around. Or just flailed around—fighting with the bed is the way Grace always put it—the way he had when he was little. Now the cushions were underneath the coffee table, and the quilt was covering the mess of ashtrays and beer bottles on top of the table. The Montana jersey was rolled up underneath some pillows, at the corner of the couch where his head had been. All in all, Charlie thought, the living room looked as if it had been searched.

The kid had left a single piece of white fax paper on the carpet near the front door, with this heartfelt message written on it in big block letters:

LATER

T

Charlie wasn't hung over, it was practically impossible for him to get drunk on beer, he knew he'd just come out of the gate feeling sluggish and slow because of lack of sleep. So he got into his old Mets sweatpants, dark blue once but now faded to the color of a hazy sky, a gray hooded sweatshirt that miraculously had nothing written on it, and went for a run, the one he liked the best, all the way up to the entrance to the Central Park reservoir at 91st and Fifth, once around the rez, back to 66th, mostly keeping it to a light jog, only opening it up every ten or fifteen minutes. He figured the distance to be four miles, maybe a little more. He realized he could make that easy now. A four-mile run on a day when he was pitching. If somebody had seen him running around Manhattan in the old days before he was pitching a big game for the Mets, they would have thought Charlie Stoddard had lost a bet. Or his wallet, to the guy he had to be chasing.

He showered when he got back, ate a bowl of Shredded Wheat, had one cup of black coffee. He'd bought a *Daily News* at the Hudson News at 72nd and Third, and opened it now to the page that had the box scores on it. He used the back of Tom's note to copy the Yankee batting order in big red Magic Marker letters, starting with Jahidi Gleason at leadoff, then Tim Kelly, then Arguello and the rest of them, picturing the sequence of pitches he wanted to use on every one of the bastards, before drawing a red line through their names, bang, they were dead.

When he was done, when he'd pitched three perfect innings in his head, nine up and nine down, he saw that it was already noon. He decided he might as well go up to the Bronx now, get there as early as Hartnett, he'd just drive himself crazy trying to kill time here. He noticed the back page of the *News* now on the coffee table, a picture of Ashe Grissom bent over, back to home plate, Aurelio Arguello in the background, running between first and second after his home run, his right fist pumping the air. The headline read:

2 GOOD
Yanks win, 2–1.
Sox lead down to 2

Stripped across the top of the back page, over where it said *Daily News,* was this headline, almost as big as the one next to Ashe Grissom:

CHARLIE TO YANKS: I'M BACK

In a cute touch, the "B" looked the same as it did on the front of Charlie's Red Sox cap.

There it was. It was like he'd told Mo Jiggy: He could still talk the talk. But could he still back it up in a game like this, against a team like the Yankees? He thought about that while he read the story they'd done on him, drank one more cup of coffee, and went downstairs to get a cab.

Pooty always said it wasn't the games that killed you, hell no, it was the waiting, the goddamn waiting in baseball was worse than one of those sexually transplanted diseases.

"**Y**ou're either in or you're out," Chang said to Patrick Keenan and Booker Impala Washington. "And I'm out."

Booker was wearing his blood-red beret today. The rest of him was in black even though it was eighty degrees outside. He said, "C'mon, dog. In or out. You sound like George Clooney in *Ocean's Eleven,* tryin' to be as cool as Frank was in the original. Which I might add was a piece of shit, the original, I mean, even with Dean and Sammy and the rest of them in it." Booker whistled. "And that young Angie Dickinson. Oh, man. Like a big bowl of 'nilla ice cream."

"I think you've got to cut our Charlie a bit more slack," Patrick Keenan said to Chang. "Just because our cause is just, no matter how much he rubs you the wrong way."

"Slack isn't the word you're looking for," Chang said, continuing to impress Keenan with the way he was dug in on this. "I believe slacker is the word you're looking for. And by the way, he's not my Charlie anymore."

"Amazin' how much you sound like the man's wife," Booker said.

They were in Chang's office at the Millennium. Booker had called the day before from Keenan's suite at the Four Seasons to set up the appointment. Chang had asked if something was wrong with Mr. Keenan. Booker had said, "I could tell you his back went out or he can't stand it no more waitin' to have his other hip replaced, but that would be jive and we'd both know it. He just wants a few minutes of your time, which he's willin' to pay for." Keenan had watched Booker as he carried on his end of the conversation, smiling the whole time. Booker had said, Uh huh uh huh uh huh for a minute before finally saying, "I know you *say* your mind's made up on Charlie Stoddard, but why don't you at least give my man and his wallet a chance to change your mind."

So here they were in the late afternoon, a few hours before the Red Sox would play the Yankees at Yankee Stadium. Patrick Keenan kept talking to Chang like the door was still open for him to come back and work with Charlie again, saying he understood it was too late for him to get out to the ballpark and work with Charlie *today*, of course he had other clients and other obligations, he was a businessman, his whole life didn't revolve around one baseball pitcher. But Keenan said he was sure that, when he had a chance to take a step back, Chang didn't want to sit out a pennant race like the one the Sox and the Yankees were having.

And pass up a chance to reflect in a client's glory, the way he would if Charlie actually did help the Red Sox win.

And, Keenan told him, if that meant changing their financial arrangement to Chang's benefit, well, let the games begin.

"This isn't about money with me," Chang said.

"Never is," Booker said. He was in the corner, doing lateral raises with Chang's dumbbells.

"You know," Keenan said, "I truly don't believe it is about the money with you."

"Don't patronize me."

"I'm not, son, believe me. But the more I listen to you, the more I realize we're not talking about money, and we're not talking about medicine, or healing, or physical therapy. We're talking about art with this ART therapy of yours, no pun intended."

"I'm better at what I do than anybody," Chang said. "Anybody. I don't know if it's so much art as a gift I believe I have. I wouldn't tell that to Charlie, because he'd laugh, or he just wouldn't get it, the only gift that's ever interested him is the one he used to have for throwing fastballs past anybody with a bat in his hand. But I know what I can do. There's so many athletes I watch, just on television, playing through some injury or coming back from some injury, and I know I could help them. I know I could *save* them before some twitchy orthopedic surgeon gets his hands on them, performs another surgery they really don't need and not address the guy's real problem. But I can't help them. Why? Because I'm not in the club." He used his fingers to put quote marks around *club*. "Even the people who end up in this room, at first they think I'm some kind of homeopathic nut, waiting for me to start sticking my little acupuncture needles between their toes. So I'm still flying underneath the radar. And I know Charlie could go a long way towards changing that for me. I told him he was going to make me famous and maybe he could have. So it's not like I don't have my own agenda here. But more than anything, I know my way is the right way. But not just when you've got a few hours to kill before you go out again to show everybody you're still the king of the keg parties."

In a gentle voice, Keenan said, "But the punishment on this one doesn't fit the crime."

"It wasn't just one crime," Chang said. "This is about the whole rap sheet. Shit adds up, and then you just finally have to pay for all of it."

"Tell me about it," Booker said.

"I would very much like you to reconsider your decision," Keenan said. "And, as I said before, I would be willing to make it more than worth your while."

He had been leaning against Chang's massage table. Now he went over and sat down at the empty chair next to Chang's desk. Patrick Keenan hated to admit it, but sometimes he felt his age. Especially when he was doing what he was doing now, what he'd done, in some form or fashion, from the time he'd gotten out of college.

Selling himself, as hard as he could.

"I had Booker do an Internet search on ART," Keenan said, "and print me up some of what he found. And having read through it, I am willing to build our training methods around yours, starting next season. With you overseeing it all."

In the corner, Booker whistled again. "Give the dog room," he said.

Chang said to Keenan, "You're serious about this."

"As serious as I am about beating the Yankees."

"What you just said—you'd be willing to put that in writing?"

"I'd be more than willing," Keenan said. "But once we shake on it, that wouldn't be necessary." He smiled. "You want to be remembered as a great healer. I just want to be the owner who ends all the suffering for the Boston Red Sox. Which can only start by beating the Yankees." He smiled. "We might not be as different as you think, son."

"You really read up on this?" Chang said to Keenan.

"You mean about how that chiropractor out there in Colorado—Dr. Leahy, was it?—was working on patients with carpal tunnel syndrome? And started finding scar tissue in places where conventional medical thinking said it shouldn't belong?"

"Most of these quacks think the only scar tissue they have to worry about is at the point of the injury."

"Fewer bad places for them to worry about," Keenan said.

"I wouldn't just be doing this for Charlie. If I did come back. Which I'm not saying I'm doing."

"But if you do come back, and it makes him happy to think you did do it for him, well, what's the harm?"

"You're not just doing this for him," Chang said.

"You want to know why I'm doing this?" Keenan said. He stood back up. "I'm doing it because the Red Sox sold Babe Ruth to the Yankees. I'm doing it because Johnny Pesky held the ball in Game Seven of the '46 Series while Enos 'Country' Slaughter came all the way around to score the run that took another Series away from the Boston Red Sox. And because poor old Joe McCarthy decided to pitch Denny Galehouse in the playoff game against the Indians in '48." Now Keenan put his hands out, palms up, as if saying, You asked for it. "I'm doing it because Lonborg had to go on two days' rest in Game Seven in 1967 and because the venerable Spaceman Lee threw that fat eephus pitch to Tony Perez when the Reds were ready to go in Game Seven eight years later. And because Tony Conigliaro got hit in the eye and because Luis Aparicio slipped going around third on Opening Day in 1972 against the Tigers and then did the same thing the last weekend of the season, in a year when the Tigers ended up beating us by half a game. And because of Bucky Dent and Bill Buckner."

"Amen," Booker said.

Keenan said, "I'm sorry if I'm glazing your eyes, Mr. Chang, but I know where you're coming from now and you need to know where I'm coming from. This race we're having with the New York Yankees might come down to one silly game, and maybe Charlie Stoddard will be the one pitching it for me. If somebody else on my team needed somebody like you, I'd be selling myself to them today. I don't need Charlie next year. But I need him now. Which means I need you."

"Do I at least get to think this over?"

"I think you already have," Keenan said.

"This is that important to you."

"You want to leave your mark, I want to leave mine. It's as simple as that," Keenan said.

Chang said he couldn't come back right away even if he wanted to, he'd made a commitment to go out to San Francisco and work with Johnny Alderman, the 49ers quarterback, before the team doctors tried to cut on his hurt shoulder and cost him a chance at two Super Bowls in a row. He said that if everything went well out there, he might make it back for the last week of the regular season. Keenan said to do the best he could, reminding him one more time that he would certainly make it worth his while.

Then Patrick Keenan went in for the kill, giving Chang what he said was the most important reason of all why this had to be the season for him, and for the Red Sox.

Some of it fact, some fiction.

Somewhat like his whole wonderful life.

Charlie sat with Pooty in the corner of the Red Sox dugout closest to the runway that led back down to their clubhouse, watching the Sox stake him to a 2–0 lead in the top of the first. Snip Daggett singled to start the game. Jerry Janzen, a soft-spoken Pensacola white guy who'd been fast enough to play wide receiver for Steve Spurrier at the University of Florida, the one his teammates called White Lightning, tripled Snip home, then Ray J. hit a sacrifice fly deep enough to dead-center for Janzen to walk home.

Pooty said, "I wasn't this excited with Aleesha last night when she went to work with her lotions and fragrances and whatnot."

Charlie didn't even turn his head. "Don't take this the wrong way," he said. "But I'm not interested in your love life today."

"You would, you knew Aleesha."

"I mean it, Poots."

"I'll catch you up later," Pooty said. "You say *now* you don't want to know, but I know you do, deep down in your heart."

"Okay," Charlie said, "just answer one question for me: Is she single?"

"Not technically, no," Pooty said.

Charlie turned back to the game, and just as he did, he heard Pooty say, "God*damn!*"

Now Charlie looked over and saw that Pooty had his head tilted back as far as it could go, like one of Charlie's yoga positions, two fingers pushing up hard on the roof of his mouth. "God*damn*," he said, "I told the girl be careful."

Charlie leaned over and said, "Please don't lisp tonight, I'm begging you."

Pooty said, "Think I want to?"

"Maybe you should just talk a little less."

"That's it," Pooty said. "Lash out at the ones love you the most."

Julio Paulino made the last out of the inning. Charlie grabbed his glove, stuck his game cap on his head, the one that already had so much dirt and sweat stain on it that it looked as if he'd been wearing it since Opening Day. Pooty made a fist with his right hand and Charlie did the same, and they lightly went knuckle to knuckle. Charlie was on the top step of the dugout when he heard someone say, "Hey."

Ted Hartnett.

Hartnett said, "Go knock the living shit out of them."

Charlie grinned and said, "I'm pretty sure you've used that pep talk before."

Hick Landon was behind Hartnett. Hick didn't say anything, just tried to make a humping motion with his hips that only succeeded in making the front of his road uniform jiggle like a bowl of Jell-O.

Charlie stepped onto the dirt in front of the dugout, and as soon as he did, the sellout crowd got up and gave him a standing ovation. A New York crowd doing that for a Boston pitcher. Except Charlie knew they didn't care what uniform he was wearing, not right now. This was because they remembered. Even Charlie knew the cheer was for what he used to be, not what he was now. It was always that way in baseball, even when it was the Yankees against the Red Sox. Baseball always had a better memory than all the other sports combined. He was an ex-Met, the team Yankee fans hated almost as much as the Red Sox and maybe more. But he had belonged to New York once, and that was all that mattered tonight. When he got out to the mound, he finally took off his cap and waved it around over his head. The cheer built one more time, the crest of one last wave, then stopped. Charlie threw his eight warmup pitches, and Pooty threw the ball down to second base. The Red Sox infielders threw the ball around. Pooty came out to the mound, the way he always did. It was time for them to concentrate on Jahidi Gleason, who wasn't a name on Charlie's little Magic Marker list now, he was digging in at home plate. Gleason: the Yankee rightfielder, hitting a tidy .358 for the season.

"How's your mouth?" Charlie said.

"Ready to take a big bite out the New *Yawk* Yankees," Pooty said. He rubbed up the baseball hard and then handed it to Charlie. "Just hit the glove, dog," he said.

Charlie growled.

Gleason, a lefthand hitter who looked fat but could run, went through the same ritual he always did, before every pitch, ending it by pointing his bat directly at Charlie.

What are you looking at, Fat Boy?

Gleason took strike one down the middle, fouled off a curve he should have clobbered, then Charlie broke off a splitter that fat Tony Gwynn couldn't have touched when he was winning all the batting championships. Gleason missed it by a mile for strike three. Then Charlie got Tim Kelly to ground to Miguel Estrada at short. And struck out Aurelio Arguello on three pitches. He gave one of those little fist pumps like Tom did after he struck somebody out, sprinted like Tom to the third base dugout. What the hell, Charlie thought.

Like father, like son.

Charlie hadn't seen Tom all day, not even in the clubhouse, but saw the kid now, sitting in the middle of the bench, a few feet from Hartnett and Hick Landon and Wally Garner.

Charlie high-fived the guys waiting for him on the top step when he came off, then walked over to Tom, who looked as bored as if he were in physics class.

Tom said, "That feel pretty good?"

"Epic," Charlie said.

■   ■   ■

Grace still couldn't believe she was here, sitting with Patrick Keenan and Booker behind the Red Sox dugout. When Charlie had come running off the mound after he'd gotten the last out in the first, she suddenly found it necessary to reach down for the bottle of water at her feet.

"It's okay," Booker said, once Charlie had disappeared down the dugout steps, "you can come out now."

Grace straightened up, trying to look indignant. "I wasn't hiding, Booker."

"Who said you were?"

Keenan, the old man looking like a happy boy, said, "Let's not argue, children. We all know that Grace is just here because I convinced her she's Charlie's good luck charm."

"Aren't I, though?" Grace said.

Booker said, "Admit it, Grace MacKenzie. You're happy you came."

"When it's three up and three down, I'm happy I came," Grace said. "And what just happened to your brother accent, if you don't mind me asking?"

"I'm not really a homey," Booker said, affecting a proper British accent now. "I just play one on TV."

She had planned to be landing in San Francisco by now. She and Ted had eaten dinner the night before at Daniel, her favorite restaurant in New York and maybe the whole world. And she had told him she was going to sit out the rest of the season—the regular season, anyway—because she didn't want to be a distraction.

For who? he said.

And Grace had said: For anybody.

Restaurant Daniel was on 65th Street, near Park Avenue. After she had insisted on paying the check, Ted had walked her back to the Sherry-Netherland. Then came a long and awkward silence as they stood under the clock in front of the hotel. Ted the big talker finally said, "Nightcap?"

Meaning in her suite.

"Not a great idea," she said.

He said, "Because of us. Or because of Charlie?"

"Maybe a little bit of both."

"It always comes back to him," Hartnett said. "For both of us."

"I've stopped feeling sorry for him, at least the way I used to. You should try it."

Hartnett stared at her and said, "You're not the one who hurt his arm."

He took her arm then and said, "Walk with me."

And told her, even though he said he'd promised Charlie he never would tell her, or anybody else.

This was it:

Game Three against the Dodgers had been in the afternoon. Charlie had moved into the Gramercy Park Hotel in the spring after Grace had moved out, not wanting to be in their apartment if she wasn't. Charlie and Ted Hartnett had taken a cab back there. Hartnett had changed at the ballpark and Charlie had changed at the apartment, and then, Hartnett told her, they did what you were supposed to do after you'd won a big game, what they'd always done.

"Got stewed, as my father used to say," Grace said, as they kept walking down Fifth.

"Royally."

They'd started at Rusty Staub's old place on 74th and Third, knowing there'd be a big Mets crowd there, then moved down to T.J. Tucker, then over to The Last Good Year. For some reason, they'd decided to stop at P.J. Clarke's before they went uptown to Elaine's.

It was one of those nights, Ted Hartnett told her, when her ex-husband was a happy drunk until he wasn't.

"Like when he'd be strong right up until he was weak," she said.

Hartnett said they had a fast cheeseburger in the back room and then moved up to the bar. They thought the cheeseburgers would help, but they didn't, they were already too shitfaced by then. And it was here, he told Grace, that they finally went straight at something they'd only ever talked around in the past. Without looking at her, passing the NBA Store now, Hartnett said, "How I was in love with you.

"I told him it was a bunch of crap," Hartnett said. "And that he was my best friend, all that. He said *that* was a bunch of crap, he was dumb but he wasn't stupid, anybody could see it. And I just lost it, right there in front of old Phil the bartender, let it all out, told him to shut the fuck up, that he didn't know what he was talking about, that he never knew what he was talking about when it came to you, that he'd never deserved you, he wasn't in your league and never would be, not if he lived to be a hundred. And then he said he knew I'd had dinner with you when we were out to play the Giants, and I said, what if I did?"

"It all sounds very mature," Grace said.

They were walking east now, past St. Patrick's.

"Oh, yeah," Hartnett said. "High-class dialogue all the way. You would've been proud of both of us."

Anyway, he said, they finally took it outside, just so they could stop being the floor show inside. Out the side door, around the corner to their left, to the front of that office building on 55th, he said. The fresh air hit him hard, he said, and he knew it hit Charlie hard, because when they started up again out there, Charlie took a swing at him.

Hartnett said he ducked it. As soon as he did, he grabbed Charlie by the front of his sports jacket and threw him hard into the wall.

Too hard.

"Way too hard," he said. "I spun him a little when I grabbed him, so he hit the wall with his right shoulder, and then he tripped and landed even harder on it when he fell, he was too drunk to break his fall."

Hartnett said he knew Charlie was hurt right away and said they should call somebody. Charlie said get the hell away from him, he was fine. Hartnett said, Have it the way you want it, and said he was going home. Charlie said, Suit yourself, I'm going back to the bar.

"I apologized the next day, and he apologized," he said. "I asked how his shoulder was, and he said what he'd said outside Clarke's, that it was fine, leave him alone."

Then they played all night and into the morning against the Dodgers after Dwight Gooden gave up that two-run homer to Mike Scioscia in the ninth, tying the game at 3–3. And when Davey Johnson, the Mets' manager, started to run out of pitchers, he asked Hartnett if he thought Charlie could pitch the eleventh—Davey said they had their big sticks coming up in the bottom of the eleventh, and he knew in his gut the Mets were going to score—and Hartnett said that the only way to find out was to ask Charlie himself. Not knowing what he'd tell Davey if Charlie said he was hurt.

He went back into the clubhouse and said, "Davey wants to know if you've got three outs left, even if you did pitch yesterday."

Charlie said, damn right he had three outs in him. Or as many as Davey fucking needed.

You're sure? Hartnett said.

Sure, I'm sure, Charlie said. Tell him to call out to the bullpen in about ten minutes, I'll be warm by then.

"He was hurt and wouldn't say so," Hartnett said. "There was a part of me knew he was hurt. I let him go out there. So, in a way, I did it to him twice. And we ended up losing the game, anyway."

They had made it all the way back up Madison, walked west on 60th and then around the corner and were back at the clock in front of the Sherry.

"Neither one of you ever told me," she said.

"I think it made it a little easier for him, his version," Hartnett said. "Leaving out how it all started for him with a stupid drunk fight."

"He didn't have to pitch," she said.

"Yeah," Hartnett said. "He did. He was Charlie. He had to pitch."

"Why are you telling me this now?"

"I don't know," he said. "Maybe so you'll know why I had to do this. Even knowing the mess it would make for everybody. All because a long time ago I messed up one of the greatest arms in baseball history."

"It's better that I know," she said.

"You just can't tell him you know."

She said she wouldn't. He didn't ask for a nightcap this time around. She told him maybe she'd see him in October, gave him the kind of kiss on the cheek his favorite aunt would, and then she was gone through the revolving doors faster than Charlie had just come off the pitcher's mound at Yankee Stadium.

She sat there in the living room of the suite for a long time, drinking wine, thinking about something that had happened a few blocks away a long time ago. She fell asleep on the couch and was still there when her phone started ringing in the morning, her son first, then Patrick Keenan, who wouldn't take no for an answer.

Now here she was, at night baseball, watching Charlie not only get them one, two, three in the first, but in the second and third as well.

Nine up, nine down.

CHARLIE WALKED Jahidi Gleason to start the fourth, pitching around the fat shit when he should have gone right after him. But Kelly hit a honey of a double-play ball, Estrada to Snip to Julio Paulino, and Charlie struck out Arguello, hero of last night's game, again. By now it was 4–0 for the Red Sox, Pooty having hit a two-run homer right down the line in left that dove over the wall like a seagull diving into the ocean.

The Yankees still didn't have a hit off Charlie Stoddard.

Hick Landon said to Hartnett, just loud enough for the manger to hear, "He threw that last one ninety-five to old Rodriguez there."

It was Hick Speak, Hartnett knew. There had once been a pretty good third baseman for the Texas Rangers named Aurelio Rodriguez, and Hick had apparently decided he could only handle one Aurelio in baseball. So Aurelio Arguello had been "Rodriguez" from the day he'd showed up in the big leagues, and would be until the day he retired.

"I can read the numbers on the scoreboard," Hartnett said.

"Four no-hit in the books," Landon said.

"Hick," Hartnett said, "don't take this the wrong way, but please shut up."

"You still got that superstitious goin', where you can't talk about a no-hitter?" he said. "Even them bullshitters on the TV don't do that no more."

Hartnett said, "If you're just gonna keep yapping like you've turned into one of the TV bullshitters, I'm gonna go have a smoke. And hope you've shut up by the time I get back."

"Don't let the camera catch you," Landon said. "You know how that gets the commissioner's panties in a wad."

"What are you, my mother?"

"There ain't no need to snap at me about none of this."

Hartnett walked toward the runway, not even looking at Charlie, reaching for his cigarettes, same as he would in the old days when Charlie would go through a batting order like this. Like he was knocking back drinks and they were all going to be young forever, and the world was never going to lay a glove on him.

The Yankees got their first hit in the sixth.

It was no cheapie when it finally came, a clean line drive up the middle by the Yankees' designated hitter, Dennard Toussant, Jr. It was the same Dennard Toussant, Jr., who had ended Tyler Haas's season with a line drive up the middle off Haas's pitching hand. The Yankees had decided at the trading deadline that they needed more stick, so they had done what they had done since the beginning of time, which was to make the kind of trade for a big stick that had always made the rest of baseball scream, giving the Angels three top minor-league prospects for Dump Truck Toussant, Jr., and a bunch of cash.

Charlie shook the hit off, getting out of the inning without the Yankees doing any further damage. But he gave up a double to Gleason in the seventh, then walked Tim Kelly on four pitches. Two runners on, for the first time in the game. He had been hearing it from the Red Sox fans in the place, a good number of them—a brave fucking minority, Charlie thought—all night. Yankees fans, on the other hand, had mostly been quiet, only making real noise when Toussant singled to break up the no-hitter. They were making some real good noise now, though. There was a chance for their team to get back into it, and suddenly the Stadium began to shake as if one of the subway trains passing outside were running right under the infield.

Out of the bleachers, the maniacs out there known as the Bleacher Creatures began a sing-song chant of "Charrrrrrrr-lie . . . Charrrrrrrr-lie."

Suddenly, they didn't love him at Yankee Stadium nearly as much as they had in the top of the first.

Pooty called time. Charlie knew by now that Pooty led the league in trips out to the mound. Sometimes it was about strategy, sometimes about where he was supposed to throw if the ball was hit right back to him. Sometimes he was bored and wanted to talk.

Pooty wasn't big on down time.

"Now you got to tell me the truth," Pooty said. "Even though you're a pitcher, and y'all lie like the bitches y'all are."

Charlie took off his cap, used the back of his long-sleeved pullover, the kind he wore even when it was hot and muggy like tonight, to wipe the sweat out of his eyes.

"Is this a social call?" he said.

Pooty said, "We got guys up, righty and lefty, Donnie and Carlos, you feel like you might be losin' it."

"I'm good."

"Good ain't good enough," Pooty said. "We win this one here tonight or they gonna be tied up with us in first place by tomorrow night, you can take *that* shit to the bank."

"I said I'm good, goddamnit," Charlie said, knowing he sounded hot. "Now shut your big mouth and get your skinny ass back behind the plate."

Pooty smiled. "That's it, baby. Talk bad to me." He turned and walked away, but Charlie could still hear him as he was putting his mask back on. "Oooh, I'm so bad."

Pooty went back behind the plate and signalled for a splitter and Charlie snapped it off and Aurelio Arguello, who hadn't been able to read Charlie all night, just clipped the top of the ball and gift-wrapped a pitcher's dream, especially in a spot like this: a comebacker to the mound that even included a charity hop that put a bow around the whole thing. Charlie turned and threw to Estrada, and Estrada jumped over Kelly's take-out slide and bounced a throw to first that Julio Paulino scooped up like a champ.

Charlie walked slowly toward the Sox dugout, the place quiet for just an instant before the Red Sox noise came again. For some reason, he looked up into the crowd behind the dugout when he got close, and saw Patrick Keenan and Booker, both of whom shook their fists at him.

He sat down next to Pooty, toweled himself off good, drank almost a whole bottle of water, and started to wonder if he might just have nine innings in him.

"Okay," he said to Pooty, "now you can tell me about Aleesha."

"Aleesha who?" Pooty said, unwrapping a Nutrageous bar.

Hartnett came over then and said he was pulling him after the eighth. Charlie tried to talk him out of it. "You get three outs," Hartnett said, "then we'll let Cassidy get three."

It happened exactly that way, and then Charlie was leading the charge out of the dugout to congratulate Bobby Cassidy when it was over.

Booker waited until Charlie was finished with all his press after the game, and then he gave him Grace's note.

"She was here?" Charlie said.

"Only 'til she got fraidy scared in the seventh," Booker said. "She went up to the top of the ramp, and peeked around the corner 'til you got out the jam."

"Girls have no stomach for sports sometimes," Charlie said.

"Grace under pressure, my ass," Booker said.

25

"**TOM CALLED** me this morning," Grace said to Charlie.

They were sitting in her suite at the Sherry-Netherland. She was wearing a white t-shirt and blue jeans and had her bare feet tucked underneath her on the couch. The glass of wine she had just poured for herself was on the end table closest to her. Charlie was across from her, a long glass table between them, sitting in an uncomfortable antique chair. Grace had told him she'd ordered some Dewar's for him, and a bucket of ice, it was in the kitchen. He said he didn't want anything right now. "Okay," Grace said, "who are you and what have you done with my ex-husband?"

He said, "When I ordered a beer instead of Scotch at Healey's the other night, Little John—the little waiter you used to think was so funny, before you didn't think anything at Healey's was funny?—said I'd started to drink like a woman."

"I must have missed the memo," Grace said. "Beer doesn't count now?"

"I just set the bar too high," he said. "In bars, I mean."

She smiled. "Stop, you're confusing me."

Her note had said, *Stop by the Sherry later if you don't have plans. Gracious living, good drinks. Me.*

When she'd answered the door, he'd been holding the note in his hand, telling her that his plans would have had to involve becoming the first pitcher into space for him to pass up a drink with her.

Even if he wasn't drinking at this exact moment.

"He told you about last night?" Charlie said.

"He did."

"I wasn't sure how much he'd remember."

"There did seem to be a few holes here and there. And a certain lack of detail when he explained how the two of you hooked up in the first place."

"What did he say?"

"He said you just happened to run into each other at some restaurant Mo Jiggy owns downtown."

"It's more of a club, actually."

Grace raised an eyebrow. "Is it the kind of club where everybody has their clothes on?"

"Like, ninety-nine percent."

"I'm sure it's a lot like the old Rainbow Room."

"The important thing," Charlie said, "is that one of us finally made the first move."

"I'll drink to that," she said, raising her wine glass. "For both of us."

"I felt like maybe I got my foot in the door, anyway."

"How drunk was he, by the way?"

"He'd had a few," Charlie said. "But I probably would've had no shot getting him to talk if he didn't have some kind of major buzz going."

"Boys will be boys."

Charlie shrugged. "We have no choice. There's nothing else for us to fall back on, remember?"

It was quiet in the suite, except for the faint noise from the Fifth Avenue traffic nine floors below them.

Grace finally said, "Thank you for doing it. Making the effort with Tom."

"I didn't do it for you, Gracie," he said. "I could tell you I did, but I'd just be lying. I'm not sure I did it for him. Who the hell knows? The bottom line is that it's the first time the two of us talked in, I can't remember how long it's been since the two of us talked."

"See," she said, "it wasn't the torture you probably thought it would be." She gave him a long look and said, "Maybe you won't wait five years next time, or however long it's been."

He wanted a cigarette. And a Dewar's and water. Followed by another Dewar's and water.

And then, nine more after that.

"Next time we might even try it sober."

"You were drunk, too?"

"Nope."

"Tom drinks too much, doesn't he?"

"He says you don't think he does. Says you just think he's just sowing some wild oats."

"That's my cover story," Grace said. "In my heart of hearts, I just keep hoping he'll grow out of it."

He smiled now. "Like I did."

"You did?" she said.

"We're having such a nice, civilized conversation," Charlie said, "maybe I'll join you in a nice, civilized glass of wine."

"Bottle and glasses in the kitchen, next to the little set-up I had for your Scotch. I promise not to tell any of the bar boys you went sissy-pants white wine on them."

He went into the kitchen and poured himself a glass. Tasted it. He usually only had a glass of wine when he was out to dinner, and usually not even then. But this wasn't bad. The bottle said Kendall-Jackson. That meant California, he knew that much. When he came back into the living room, he thought about sitting down at the other end of the couch, but went right back to the antique chair instead, thinking: You're going good, don't do something stupid and blow it. Worrying about every word he said and every move he made. They'd been together, in some form or fashion, for more than half their lives, all the way back to when he fell for her like a ton of bricks in high school, and sometimes it felt as if they'd gone all the way back to first date.

If this was a date at all.

"I have to ask you something," he said now, even with the voice inside his head telling him to shut the fuck up. "And if you don't want to answer," he said, "and want to call it a night right here, I just want you to know I'm cool with that."

She just watched him, both hands on her glass, waiting.

"But if you do answer it," he said, babbling on, "I promise to be cool with the answer, even if it doesn't happen to be the one I'm looking for. I just want to be clear on that." He made a big *whew* sound, like the air going out of a balloon. "Goddamn, Gracie, maybe this is too much talking for me in one week."

"You are getting somewhere near your actual question, right?" she said.

He slapped his hands hard on his knees.

"Are you and Ted, like, really *seeing* each other?"

There it was.

There was another ugly antique chair right next to his, same color, just as small as the one he was in. Grace got off the couch and came over and sat in it, turning it slightly so she was facing him.

"I was doing much better when you were over there," he said.

"Shhhh."

He sat there, not sure he wanted to hear whatever was coming next.

"No," she said. "If you mean it the way I think you mean it—and knowing you, there's only one way you *could* mean it—the answer is, no. We're not seeing each other."

"You can tell me the truth."

"No," she said.

"No, you can't tell me the truth, or no, you're not dating him in the way I don't want you to be dating him."

"I'm not sleeping with him, Charlie. I never slept with him, though I will admit I thought about it a few times when you were playing the field. *More* than a few times. I'm not sleeping with him now, I didn't sleep with him when we were breaking up, I frankly can't ever see that happening between us, even though I know he keeps holding out hope."

"It's a long time to hold out hope."

"We are friends," she said. "That's all we've ever been."

Eyes big and wide and serious and locked in on him.

"Okay?" she said.

"Okay."

"I'm actually surprised you asked," she said. "The way you work, it could have taken years to get the question out."

"Can I make an observation?" he said.

He reached down and took a sip of wine and then leaned back down to put the glass on the carpet next to his chair, and when he came up this time he had managed to move into her space.

"Shoot."

"I want to throw you down on that couch."

She sighed. "It was that kind of smooth love talk that helped you win my heart in the first place."

"I'm just trying to be as honest with you as you were with me."

"And don't think I don't appreciate it."

She got off her chair, made a motion with her hand that he should stay right where he is, and went back to the couch by herself.

"Now listen," she said, "and listen good." Lowering her voice and doing her bad John Wayne impression. "This is important. Okay?"

"Okay."

"You've always got me. Maybe not in the way you want. Maybe not even in the way *I* want sometimes. But you don't have time for me right now."

"Right here right now?" he said. "My schedule's wide-open."

"You know what I mean. Right now there's only room for baseball, and maybe the little area you started to carve out last night with Tom. And that's it. You need to stick with the basics. Keep your eye on the old ball. That's what they say, right?"

Something like that, he said.

"You know I'm right about this," Grace said.

"So what you're telling me," he said, smiling at her again, "is that the kind of quickie where we only get about half our clothes off is out of the question?"

"It is sooo tempting," she said, "when you put it that way."

She walked over with her wine glass as if she were on her way to the kitchen for the refill, leaned over quickly and kissed him on the mouth, then straightened up before he could try to make it into something more.

"Beat it," she said. Then pulled on his arm and said, "Now."

At the door, she said, "I know you want nice, fast solutions to everything. But you can't square the books with your son in one drunken conversation. I'm frankly not sure you can ever square the books, that's going to be up to Tom. But I do believe there's a chance to make things . . . decent between the two of you. And if that's going to happen, it's all on you. Which means you've got to stay with it, buster."

Charlie said, "I'll keep that in mind." He leaned against the door-frame as if it was all that was holding him up, feeling all of a sudden as if he'd pitched two games tonight instead of just one. "There's a lot of people I have to make things right with," he said.

"I told you," Grace said. "Don't worry about me right now."

"I didn't mean you," Charlie said.

"That sounds mysterious."

"It's all the time I spent hanging around with the mysterious Chang."

"Is there something else on your mind?"

"Just sleep," he said. "Say good night, Gracie."

She did.

They all watched it happen after that, the way it had happened to other Red Sox teams when everything would turn to sludge.

They started losing, and couldn't stop the bleeding for more than a game. So it was that people in Boston started to believe it was 1978 all over again, even though that Red Sox team had played like champs the last two weeks of September after they'd blown their big lead on the Yankees that year and Red Sox fans already had them dead in the water. And because this was Boston, Charlie knew, they didn't just think it was '78, they thought it was every goddamn heartbreak season the Red Sox had ever had, against the Yankees and everybody else.

Charlie beat the Orioles 2–1 in Baltimore. But Tom jammed his toe covering first base the next night, and even though he was only supposed to end up missing his next start, it ended up being two. The kid kept telling Ted Hartnett the whole time he could pitch through it, just give him the ball, stop treating him like some kind of baby. Finally, in the clubhouse at Camden Yards after Tom had been bitching at him in front of the whole team, Hartnett said, "Dizzy Dean thought he could pitch through a bad toe once."

"Who's Dizzy Dean?" Tom said.

"I'll take that one," Charlie said, raising his hand as he did. "Ol' Diz was another hardhead hothead kid who wouldn't listen and wrecked his career."

Tom turned around. "Like you, you mean." The look on his face said he wasn't saying it to be smart, or nasty, he was just stating a fact.

"Like me," Charlie said to him. "Forget about Dizzy Dean, the manager was just being polite by using him. He's really telling you not to be like me." Charlie looked straight at Hartnett and said, "Isn't that right?"

Hartnett said, "Your father and me are both smarter than we used to be."

So the Red Sox lost two of three in Baltimore while the Yankees were sweeping Tampa Bay. The Yankees were one game out, nine games to play for both of them. The second-to-last weekend of the season, one week before they would finish the regular season with those three games against the Yankees at Fenway, the Sox lost two of three to Detroit; they also lost Yippy Cantreras for the last week of the season when he sprained his left ankle halfway through his start on Sunday.

"Love Boat might not pitch 'til spring training," Pooty said, using the nickname he'd given Yippy. "Boy's got the pain threshold of some old woman in a nursing home."

The Yankees swept the Blue Jays at Yankee Stadium.

Now the Yankees were a game ahead.

One more series before Fenway. Tom still wasn't ready to pitch, Hartnett deciding to hold him back until the opener of the Yankees series on Friday night. The goddamn Devil Rays, a joke team from the time baseball had made one of its classic asshole moves and put them in that ugly dome in St. Petersburg, were supposed to be the kind of pushover the Red Sox needed. But they gave Charlie all he wanted on Monday night, the game 2–2 in the seventh before Jerry Janzen hit one into the screen to give Charlie and the Sox a win that they only needed the way sick people need transfusions. He had a 4–1 record now, with an earned run average of just under three runs a game. It looked like the Sox might win 3–2 for Ashe Grissom the next night, until Pooty picked up a sacrifice bunt with runners on first and second in the eighth and threw it so far over Julio's head at first that Charlie was afraid it was going to end up in the Charles River. By the time Ray J. Guerrero ran the ball down in the rightfield corner, two runs had scored, the guy who had bunted was on third, and the Devil Rays were ahead to stay. And the only thing that didn't make the evening an entire fucking disaster was that the Indians came back to beat the Yankees in Cleveland.

The next night at Fenway, Hartnett had to start his lefthanded setup man, Carlos Cinquanta, in place of Yippy (Love Boat) Cantreras, who'd had the doctors put him into a walking cast so he could look more wounded. The Devil Rays scored five off Cinquanta before he got anybody out. It ended up 11–0 for the Devil Rays on a night when the Yankees' No. 4 starter, a rookie from Jamaica named Bob Marley Rojas, came within two outs of a no-hitter, finally settling for a two-hit shutout.

On the last day of September, in a season when they had taken first place on the third Sunday in April and kept it until the Yankees passed them, the Red Sox were two out with three to play and had to sweep the Yankees to win the American League East.

The front page of Thursday's *Herald* read this way:

BOSTON RED SUCKS

The Indians had locked up the American League Central a long time ago. In the West, the Oakland A's hadn't been able to catch the Mariners, but they had finished by winning nine of their last ten; even if the Angels swept them the last weekend, they had still locked up the wildcard in the American League. Because of the way the Red Sox had played the last couple of months, the Mariners and A's officially had the two best records in the league. It meant that if the Yankees got one game at Fenway, one out of three, the Red Sox were out of the playoffs, gone, screwed, as impossible as that would have seemed in July.

At least, Charlie thought, this is the way it was in the old days, when the American League was just one league, when there weren't two divisions, or three, when there were no wildcards, when baseball wasn't trying to copy all those other sports in which it seemed like half the teams in the league made the playoffs. This was old-time knockout baseball. Win the pennant or get the fuck out.

Tom MacKenzie went out on Friday night, his first start in two weeks, and gave the Yankees two hits, struck out sixteeen, just absolutely snuffed the bastards. The Red Sox still weren't hitting, but they hit enough to win, 2–0. Now they were one out with two to play.

Charlie would pitch Saturday afternoon. Ashe Grissom would pitch Sunday. But Grissom's start wouldn't mean one whole hell of a lot if Charlie got beat on Saturday, because if he got beat on Saturday, the Red Sox were gone.

Mo Jiggy was right at Beef, he told himself.

It's showtime, Showtime.

He sat in the apartment that had belonged to Uma the nanny and Pooty's kids, sipping one of those nonalcoholic beers all the beer companies made now, this one called O'Douls. He hadn't had a real drink since he'd had that glass of wine with Grace in New York. He'd thought about it a few times when the Sox hit the skids after leaving Yankee Stadium. Then it was the last week of the season and he knew he was going to pitch against the Yankees on Saturday with all the money on the table, so he'd told himself he'd celebrate with a glass of Scotch after he beat the Yankees. That was the deal he made with himself, and he'd stayed with it, right up until now, one o'clock Saturday morning, two hours after the kid had beaten the Yankees himself.

Hadn't just beaten them, Charlie thought.

Thrown them in front of a bus.

Charlie had watched it all, loving it all, knowing he had pitched this way once, but wondering if he was as good as this cocky kid, his cap turned a little to the side, so it was low over his right eye, working fast, giving the Yankees hitters looks after he struck them out. Charlie had seen Pedro Martinez when he'd first come to Boston, he had seen Clemens in his prime, but he wondered how they could have ever looked better than Tom MacKenzie had looked tonight, when he would have shoved even Babe Ruth's bat right up his fat ass.

After Tom finished doing his press, he found Charlie in the trainer's room and asked what he was doing after the game.

"You asking me to have a drink?" Charlie said.

"Don't make a big deal out of it," he said. "I'm just asking."

Charlie said, "Thanks, but I'm in a complete lockdown mode."

Tom was dressed in a blazer, Hawaiian shirt, regulation jeans. "I got a date, anyway."

"Who with?"

"That Sharon from Channel 7."

"She a little old for you?"

"She says I'm wise beyond my years." Tom grinned. "And that we can both teach each other things."

Charlie said, "Let her go first." Then: "Hey, didn't your mother say you had some kind of rock star girlfriend? Whatever happened to her?"

"She ran into Indiana Jones one night in Beverly Hills when he was lonely."

"You know what old Sharon says. Her loss."

"You gotta win tomorrow," Tom said.

"I keep telling myself I've done this sort of work before."

"Whatever works." The kid cocked his head to one side and said, "You're okay?"

"Humming," Charlie said.

He was lying.

He had felt something behind his shoulder against the Orioles in Baltimore, the last inning he had pitched. He'd told himself it was nothing to worry about, telling himself it was normal and would be gone by the morning. But when he'd done the pitcher's checklist in his hotel room at the Cross Keys Inn the next morning, the pain had been even worse than the night before when all the ice he'd put on it hadn't helped at all.

All pitchers, righthanders and lefthanders, fastball pitchers and junkball artists, old guys and young guys, knew about the checklist if you'd pitched the day before. As soon as you were vertical in the morning, and sometimes before that, you waited to see what would happen the first time you tried to move your arm. Waiting to see if something hurt, shoulder or elbow or wrist. Even giving a little wiggle to your fingers, making sure the circulation was all right; all pitchers started worrying about that after David Cone's fingers had gone numb one time, and it'd turned out he didn't have a rotator cuff problem behind his shoulder, he had a goddamn aneurysm.

For as long as he'd pitched, Charlie had had the same routine, whether he was alone in bed or not, whether it was Grace with him or some Ellie Bauer of the night. As soon as he was awake, before he even went to take a piss, he would stand up next to his bed, standing there in his underwear usually, and slowly bring his arm forward, never rushing, not wanting to make any sudden moves, then reverse the motion, taking it all the way back. If he didn't feel anything there, he'd slowly bend his right arm from the elbow, like some old-fashioned pump, a few times, making sure everything was all right there.

The shoulder hurt like hell that morning in the Cross Keys Inn, enough that he had to stop doing the rotation exercises Chang had given him. Of course he didn't tell anybody about it. Not Hartnett. Not Grace. Not even Pooty, though he thought Pooty suspected something, the way he'd been struggling his last inning against the Devil Rays.

Maybe Tom had seen something, too, maybe that's what he'd meant when he asked if everything was okay tonight.

It wasn't the killer pain from the old days, the one that could drop him to his knees the first time he tried to rotate his arm the next morning. But it was bad enough against the Devil Rays that he was shaking off Pooty at the end almost every time he'd call for a breaking ball.

He might have told Chang if he was still around. Only Chang wasn't around. So Charlie wasn't going to tell shit to anybody, because he was afraid if he did they'd pull him, even if it meant pitching Ashe Grissom on short rest for Saturday's game. If Hartnett did that, it would mean all hands on deck, starters and relievers, on Sunday, unless Yippy decided to suck it up, throw down his crutches like some holy roller on TV and walk. Nobody had to draw Charlie a picture. He was forty years old and a hell of a lot more than that in dog years, and everybody had been waiting for him to fall apart from the beginning, get old in front of everybody like he was poor old Joe Hardy from *Damn Yankees,* which he really hadn't known anything about until Grace had dragged him kicking and screaming once to see it on Broadway, Jerry Lewis playing the Devil.

Charlie thought: I'd sell *my* soul just to get through today.

He turned off the television, which had been showing highlights of Tom's performance, sat there in the dark now, thinking about arms. Even knowing from experience that you had a better chance understanding women than understanding why some guys had the arm and some didn't. You could line a bunch of the best guys up on some kind of split-screen deal, and watch them all go through their motions, and the motions would pretty much look the same, and so would their release points, and then you'd find out the guy at one end was throwing ninety-five and the guy at the other end was throwing eighty-five. Some power pitchers—Clemens, Ryan, Randy Johnson—those fuckers went forever, like they were freaks of nature, bringing their arms forward in what all the doctors said was a motion all wrong for the human arm, pitching every five days, throwing more than a hundred pitches every time they did, still throwing in the mid-nineties when they were past forty years old. There was no logic to it. Some lasted, some didn't, end of story. Some made one wrong move or pitched on one cold day—or hit themselves the way Charlie had—and their arms blew, and that was that. It was the same goddamn mystery now as it had been when Walter (Big Train) Johnson was the power pitcher who went forever, not Randy (Big Unit) Johnson. In the old days guys like Walter Johnson went on three days' rest, or even two. Now when a pitcher went on less than four days' rest, the fans and the sportswriters and the shouters on the radio acted like he should get the Purple Heart. In the whole history of baseball, how many guys—really—had been able to throw a ball the way Tom had tonight? The way Charlie himself could once. Twenty, tops? It was all talent and luck. And maybe Chang was right, maybe it was the way you took care of yourself, too. Except sometimes you could take care of yourself and it still didn't matter for shit. Herb Score was young and strong and had a strikeout left arm, and then one day Score took a line drive to the eye and was never the same pitcher in another game for the rest of his life. Sandy Koufax had arthritis so bad he quit when he was thirty, at the top of his game. Booze got Sam McDowell, and drugs got Doc Gooden even before a bum shoulder did. And one day a lefthanded strikeout kid from the Cardinals, Rick Ankiel, went out in a playoff game and started throwing balls to the screen and into guys' backs and over their heads, like the kid was having a pitching breakdown, and didn't stop for years. Roger Angell, the baseball writer from *The New Yorker,* a serious guy about baseball but a good guy, told Charlie one time at Shea that in the end, the talent to throw the way he could was a gift from the gods. Just that. A gift from the baseball gods, handed out to a chosen few.

"I wish the gods'd send along a hangover cure, too," Charlie told Angell.

He was always such a riot.

Now somehow he'd gotten it back for these six weeks, or whatever it was, and he wasn't going to let anybody take the ball away from him now.

He reached over and turned one lamp on and walked over to the yellow legal pad on Pooty's desk, wrote out the batting order the Yankees had used that night: Gleason, Kelly, Arguello, Dennard Toussant, Jr., Jimmy Dwyer, the shortstop, Chuck Krummenacher, the second baseman. All the way through Kenyon Desmond, the Yankees catcher who hit ninth.

When he'd been a kid, Charlie knew in his bones, he would have gone through them the way Tom had, doing whatever he wanted, right up in their faces from the first pitch of the game. Because the gods had gifted him with one of those arms.

Until, of course, he'd elected to piss all over them.

THE GAME WASN'T until four, because of television. When Ted Hartnett walked into his office at ten in the morning, feeling as if he were somehow already late, Charlie was in on his couch.

"What are you doing here?" he said.

"Good morning to you, too, skip."

Hartnett threw his old leather satchel, the one with all his notes and index cards stuffed inside, on his desk, went over and fixed himself a cup of coffee from the pot Eddie Greene always made sure was full and hot when the manager showed up in the manager's office. Whenever he showed up.

Harnett sipped some black coffee, lit a cigarette. "Why are you here?" he said again.

"Truth?" Charlie said. "Even this early—for me, anyway—there was no place else *to* be."

Hartnett looked at him, trying to detect any signs of a hangover. But Charlie actually looked fresh. Chipper, even. "You ready?"

"Been ready since I woke up at four. And five. And then six."

"Better waking up then than just coming in. At any of those hours."

"Those days are over."

Hartnett watched Charlie get up now, fix himself a cup of coffee with a lot of extra sugar. Maybe it was from hanging around with a sugar junkie like Pooty. He sat back down on the couch and said, "I need to tell you something."

Hartnett said, "If this is the one where you thank me for believing in you and giving you this chance when nobody else would have, why don't we save that? Let's just concentrate on beating those shitweasels in the other clubhouse so we can live to play another day."

"It's not that," Charlie said. He looked around the office, as if trying to find the right words, which Hartnett knew could be a challenge, especially when he was trying to say something deep or serious. Charlie said, "I need to square the books with you once and for all."

That was one of Grace's expressions, Hartnett knew. In her world, somebody was always squaring the books with somebody else.

"They're squared?" Hartnett said. "Okay? You're here. You think I did you some big favor? Maybe it's the other way around. Maybe we could've got another pitcher who gave us the innings you did, pitched the way you have. And maybe not. I don't think we're here if you didn't give me the five wins you're gonna have given me after you win today. Case closed. We're square."

"No," Charlie said, "we're not."

Charlie got up now, shook a cigarette out of Hartnett's pack, lit it. Plopped himself down in the chair closest to the desk. The two of them smoked in silence. Charlie had his head back, staring up at the ceiling, finally blew a perfect smoke ring, a beauty, that floated up there.

"You didn't hurt me," he said.

"Excuse me?"

Charlie leaned forward, butted his cigarette out in the ashtray closest to him, one that said TWINS ENTERPRISES around the outside.

"That night. After Game Three. When you threw me up against the wall outside Clarke's instead of doing what you wanted to do, which was punch my lights out."

Hartnett thought: We're back there again. And again. And again.

In a soft voice, he said, "I saw you hit your shoulder. I saw the way you went down. I knew you were hurt and I didn't tell anybody and I let you pitch the next night in relief even though you started on Saturday. We've gone over this a hundred times, usually in a bar someplace."

Charlie said, "I just let you think it was you."

Hartnett didn't say anything now.

Charlie said, "I was as pissed at you as you were at me that night. I thought there was something going on between you and Grace, and I was so shitfaced there was nothing you were going to say that was going to talk me out of it. No matter how much you denied it."

"I was there. Remember?"

"Not for the whole night," Charlie said.

"It was two in the morning by then," Ted Hartnett said, "And why are we doing this now?"

"Because," Charlie said. "Okay? Just because. Because you've got to own up sooner or later. I'm doing it later. I thought Chang had gone all hokey on me when he said that the only way you make the most of a second chance is by cleaning up the shit you left the first time around. I finally came around to figuring out the Chinese prick was right."

"You're telling me I didn't hurt your shoulder."

He saw Charlie manage a smile. "Yeah, you hurt my shoulder. It hurt like hell. For about twenty minutes. You were already gone by then, and I was back in there holding court at the bar."

Hartnett said, "I had to go cool off or I was afraid I was going to kill you."

"You went home, and I went to Elaine's after Clarke's. And made a whole bunch of new friends and went to an after-hours club after that." Charlie paused. "Where I was screwing around with a couple of babes, showing them how I pitched from a full windup, when I slipped and fell down some stairs and landed on my shoulder." He stood up again. "Chang always said he wanted to ask me a question before this was all over, like he was Mr. Mysterious Oriental. But I knew what the question was. He wanted to know how I really messed up my shoulder. I let everybody else think it was because I threw all those pitches before Davey got me out of that Saturday game and then came back too soon." He paused again and said, "And I let you think you did it, because that way I didn't have to own up myself."

Charlie said, "But I did it to myself." He smiled again. "Chang was right about one other thing. He said I'd always blamed everything that happened to me in my life on everybody except me."

Hartnett leaned back, hands clasped together down near his belt buckle, looking down as he squeezed his ruined fingers so hard he made them hurt. Foul-tip hurt. Still not saying anything. Sometimes he did it just because he knew long silences could make Charlie Stoddard nuts.

But he was only doing it now because he wasn't sure what he wanted to say.

Charlie said, "I'm sorry, for what it's worth. I'm not sure it's the lousiest thing I've ever done, just on account of everything I put Grace through. But it's up there."

He was looking down at the floor. He looked up at Hartnett now. All the years, everything that had happened, all the shit between them, right here in this small room. Hartnett knew he should feel something. Pissed off that Charlie had let him carry it around this long. Betrayed, maybe. It seemed like it should matter more to him, get more of a rise out of him.

Only it didn't.

Because the only thing he really cared about was winning the game.

What did his ex-wife, Kate, say when she was doing some big magazine piece? When it's hard, write it soft.

"Get out," he said. Softly.

"I thought you might say that."

"Get out," Hartnett said. "Then go for the run you always go for. Then do the work you'd do with Chang if he were here. Then get with Hick and Pooty and come up with a way to beat the fucking Yankees."

Hartnett came around the desk so he was standing over Charlie. "I always knew you were a selfish prick," he said. "In those days, I mean. I'm not sure you're all so different now, even now that you've had this attack of honor, or whatever it is."

He put out his hand. Charlie grabbed it like it was a lifeline and shook it, probably thinking he got off easy.

"You want to square the books?" Hartnett said. "Beat the Yankees."

Charlie said it was a deal.

Hartnett said, "I talked to Grace a few days ago. She told me you were getting chatty all of a sudden."

Charlie said, that's what happens when you stop getting laid.

Pooty showed up around noon, way into his sugar and chocolate and caffeine game-day high already.

"Never shoulda come down to this," he said, taking the stool next to Charlie, in front of Jerry Janzen's locker. Janzen was doing what he usually did to get ready for a game, watching replays of Nascar races in the Sox video room.

"Look around this place," Pooty said, agitated. "Shit, we got more tight assholes in this room than . . ." He stopped, frowning, as if he'd stumped himself. "Help me out here," he said to Charlie.

"You're the guy with the words."

"We got a lot of tight assholes, all I'm sayin'."

"How's *your* ass, since we're sort of on the subject?"

"Aw, me and Alqueen got into a thing."

It came out "thang" with him.

"She said, then I said, and before long, the girl was doin' what she does on occasion." Pooty reached into a Dunkin' Donuts bag that was about the size of a tall kitchen bag and took a big bite out of a powdered donut, the white covering the whole bottom half of his face before he even started to chew. "Finally dumped a bunch of my clothes on the stoop."

"I don't think they call them stoops at your end of Commonwealth, Poots."

"Woman needs to get herself into one of those anger manager deals." The first donut was gone in two bites, so he reached back into the bag, coming out this time with one of those huge cinammon rolls. "Maybe it's just my destiny, God's plan for me, havin' a weakness for these high-strung bitches."

"And big tits," Charlie said.

"Them, too."

Pooty said he needed one of his choca-chinos to wash down these donuts. Charlie put an old Phil Collins CD, his greatest hits, into the Disc-man, leaned back in the rocking chair that had just shown up in front of his locker one day, a gift from the team. He'd turned the rocker around, so his back was to the rest of the room. Now he closed his eyes, listening to little Phil ease into "Another Day in Paradise," the very first cut.

He didn't open his eyes until he felt someone poking him, turned around and saw that it was Chang, motioning for him to take the head-phones off.

He was dressed all in white, down to white chinos, except for a red 49ers cap. He had the same leather bag he'd left with a few weeks ago slung across his shoulder.

Charlie turned the rocker around, took off his headphones. "Is there any point in asking what you're doing here?"

"I happened to be in the neighborhood."

"Oh, right," Charlie said. "I forgot how inscrutable you are."

"C'mon," Chang said. "We've got work to do."

"That's it? We've got work to do?"

"We'll bond later."

When they changed into shorts and t-shirts and were stretching in the outfield, Charlie said, "My shoulder's been a little sore."

"I know," Chang said.

"No one knows."

"I watched you pitch the last couple of times, the guy I was staying with on the coast had a dish. *I* know, okay?"

"You could tell just by watching television?"

Chang said, "I'm like one of those horse whisperers, just with horses' asses."

Ted Hartnett came out of his office shirtless, wearing only his uniform slacks, looking for Hick Landon and Wally Garner, just in time to see Charlie and Chang walk out the clubhouse door.

Pooty came out of the trainer's room at the same time, carrying one of his industrial-sized coffee shakes.

Hartnett said to Pooty, "Did you know he was coming back?"

"Who? Bruce Lee? No way. He just shows up ten minutes ago at the man's locker, says, let's get down to it, like he's been here all along."

Hartnett went back into his office and tried to call up to Patrick Keenan's suite; sometimes the old man and some of the swells he watched the games with showed up early, like they were having a football tailgate party. When there was no answer, Hartnett called the apartment Keenan had bought in the residential part of the old Ritz-Carlton, up on Arlington.

This time Keenan picked up on the first ring.

"Guess who showed up just in time for our big game against State?"

"Mr. Chang," Keenan said.

"You had something to do with this."

"Of course I had something to do with it. And if I'd moved faster when he was still pouting, he wouldn't have spent the last ten days doing his laying-on-of-hands thing with that slow healer who quarterbacks the 49ers and never quite manages to cover."

"How much money did it take?"

"I had a friend once, a dear friend, named Big Tim Molloy. Owned the New York Hawks football team before his untimely passing, a face-down into the old veggie tray before an exhibition game. Big Tim used to say that there wasn't a single problem he'd ever encountered in business that couldn't be solved with a suitcase full of money."

"He gets Charlie through today, it was worth it," Hartnett said. "God-damn, I hate the Yankees."

Keenan said, "In the interest of full disclosure, I might also have mentioned my history of various heart procedures, up to and including my recent bypass."

"You said you had a bypass two winters ago, when you didn't want me to quit."

"So my timeline is a little off," Keenan said. "What is this, the O.J. trial?"

Hartnett said, "You told him you were going to die, didn't you?"

"Technically," Keenan said, "we're *all* dying, aren't we, Ted?"

"You're a piece of work, you know that?"

"So I am. I just told Mr. Chang that before I die, I wanted to win a World Series in Boston. But not any more then I wanted to beat the Yankees."

Pooty saw Charlie looking up toward Keenan's suite right before the Red Sox took the field for the top of the first.

"She up there?" Pooty said.

"San Francisco," Charlie said. "Said she'd watch the last chapter from a nice, safe distance. Said this wasn't about her, anyway, it was always about Tom and me, win or lose."

"We don't need her cloudin' up your mind," Pooty said. "Which, let's face it, is fair to partly cloudy on your best day." He turned around on the bench and said, "How's your arm?"

"Perfect."

"Like I said, y'all lie like bitches."

"I'm fine," Charlie said.

"Better be," Pooty said. "Because I'm gonna tell you somethin' straight out: We beat the damn Yankees and we're goin' all the way. Mark my words. Besides us, they're the best out there, have been all along, even if they took their sweet time getting theirselves in gear."

"I hear you."

Pooty leaned over and said to Charlie, all business now, "You just go 'til you can't go no more today. Then I'll tell the man to come get you."

W hen Chang came out of the Red Sox clubhouse about 3:30, Hartnett was waiting for him at the top of the steps.

"How is he?" Hartnett asked.

"You want me to bullshit you the way your starting pitcher would, or do you want the truth?"

"What do you think?"

"He's hurting, that's what I think."

"How much?"

"Something's going on back there. He wouldn't let me feel around too much, he just says something's barking at him. Then, of course, he tells me it's nothing major. As if he'd know." Hartnett noticed he was wearing the old Mets jacket Charlie kept hanging in his locker, no matter how much grief his teammates gave him about it. "I did the best I could," Chang said.

"He can pitch today," Hartnett said, not even bothering to make it a question.

"Yeah, he can."

Chang leaned against the wall. "He finally told me what happened to him. Back then."

"He's telling everybody, isn't he?"

Chang said, "You gotta watch him close. I'll do the same. I was gonna watch upstairs in Mr. Keenan's suite, but I can stay down in the clubhouse if you want."

"Stay," Hartnett said.

"He'll win this game," Chang said.

"How can you be so sure?"

"Because," Chang said, "he can't not win the game."

The Yankees got their first run in the second. They had runners on first and third and two out when Julio Paulino let a weak ground ball from Dennard Toussant, Jr., roll right between his legs. Rascual Ortega, the runner on third, could have scored using a walker. Paulino came running over to the mound when the play was over, getting there about the same time Pooty Shaw did, and began apologizing in both English and Spanish, alternating between waving his arms and hitting the side of his head with his first baseman's mitt, as if that gesture would let the crowd know that *he* knew he didn't deserve to live.

Charlie would find out much later that even the announcers wondered what Paulino was saying that finally made Charlie put his head back and laugh.

It wasn't anything Julio Paulino said. It was something Pooty said.

He took off his mask, spit, and said to the Red Sox first baseman, "See, this actually's a good thing, Grandpa."

"How you say that to Julio?" Julio said, pointing to the scoreboard, where the "E" for error was blinking like the hazard lights on your car. "How you say E-3 a good thing?"

"On account of at least we got that Buckner shit out the way early," Pooty said.

That was when Charlie laughed.

Charlie told Paulino to relax, he'd keep them to just one run, which he did. Then watched from the dugout as the Red Sox went right after the Yankees in the bottom of the first. Dre' Hadley, who had caught Tom the night before, was back in the lineup, as a designated hitter this time; Hadley had gotten three hits off Joe Cowen, the Yankee starter, the last time he'd faced him, back in May, and that was good enough for Hartnett, who surprised everybody by batting him cleanup. Hadley rewarded his manager's confidence his very first time up, hitting the first pitch he saw from Cowen into the screen. Jerry Janzen, whom Hartnett had moved up to number three in the order—batting Ray J. behind Hadley— had doubled to right before Hadley hit his Fenway shot. It was 2–1, Red Sox, in the big game.

The Yankees got the lead back in the fourth. Their shortstop Jimmy Dwyer, who'd hit six home runs all year, reached out on what Charlie thought was a honey of a one-two waste pitch away and got better wood on the ball than Charlie thought he could. The wind—probably blowing out of some other fucked-up Red Sox season, Charlie figured—picked that particular moment to turn around and start blowing out to left. So what looked like a routine fly ball coming off Dwyer's bat, what *should* have been a routine fly ball, ended up landing nice and soft in the bottom of the screen. Charlie had walked Toussant, Jr., to start the inning, and Chuck Krummenacher, the Yankee second baseman, had dragged a perfect bunt past the mound right after that.

Three-run homer.

It was 4–2, Yankees.

Charlie felt as if somebody had kicked a hole in him the way you kick a hole through a plate-glass window.

"There you go," Pooty said, when the inning was over. "Now we got Bucky Dent out of the way, too."

Charlie said, "You certainly are an optimistic bastard today, I'll give you that."

Pooty sipped on a tall choca-chino Eddie Greene had brought him from the clubhouse, then pointed out toward the field at Fenway. "Only the bottom of the fourth, baby," Pooty said, good and hopped up now, knees banging together, all his nerve endings right there for you, like exposed wires. "Only the bottom of the fourth. Look out there. 'Cause there's still a whole lot of green between us and the bottom of nine."

Hartnett had walked down from the other end of the dugout. He reached over as if patting Charlie on the back, but as he leaned down, he said, "No more runs."

Charlie nodded.

"You hear what I'm saying to you?" Hartnett said.

"I'm good," Charlie said.

Which was not technically true, since even though he was hiding it pretty well, and the Yankees were hardly getting great swings off him, his shoulder felt as if someone had shanked him from behind.

It had really started, what had been a normal ache for a couple of weeks just exploding on him, when he tried to put something extra on the fastball he used to strike out Jahidi Gleason. He wasn't sure if Hartnett and Hick Landon saw him wince, but Pooty sure did. He came walking out casually, no big deal, and, when he got to the mound, asked if Charlie wanted the trainer.

"Wasn't even my arm," Charlie said. "I just landed funny." He looked over at the dugout, caught Hartnett's eye, and tapped his foot hard down near his landing area. Then he put up a hand like he was fine.

"No do that hip-hop, be-bop stroll of yours back to home plate," Charlie said. "Like you don't have a care in the world."

"Which be-bop stroll is that?" Pooty said.

"I don't know," Charlie said. "One of your black things."

Pooty Shaw minced back like a runway boy instead.

Cowen walked Pooty on four pitches to start the bottom of the fourth. The Yankees pitching coach, Harry Schofield, must not have liked what he saw. Charlie saw him motion to Kenyon Desmond, the Yankees catcher, who called time while Schofield made his way to the mound. Charlie got up then and made his way down the dugout. Hartnett had told him that Chang was in the clubhouse if he needed him. Charlie walked through the runway and up the stairs and through the clubhouse door and found Chang and Tom MacKenzie in the middle of the room, watching the game on television.

Charlie knew that Tom would sneak back here and hang out when he wasn't pitching—and even when he was—sneaking a smoke sometimes, or bullshitting with the Red Sox designated hitter if the guy was riding the stationary bike between innings to stay loose. Sometimes he'd play a few hands of his season-long gin-rummy game with Eddie Greene.

"S'up?" Tom said, trying to sound casual. "You looked like you stepped on a nail after you struck out the fat guy."

"I'm just having a little trouble getting loose."

Chang said to Charlie, "Let's go into the trainer's room."

On the television screen, Janzen walked.

Tom said, "Mind if I watch?"

"Only if you can keep your mouth shut," Chang said to him. "Which I know is a constant challenge in your family."

Charlie climbed right up on the table. He kept his mouth shut now, except to say, "Stomach or back?" Chang told him stomach and went right for the place where it hurt before Charlie even told him, no screwing around now. Charlie bit down on the towel he'd brought in with him.

Now Chang dug his fingers into the back of Charlie's neck.

Through clenched teeth, Charlie said, "Can I ask you what you're looking for?"

"About three more innings," Chang said.

27

THE TELEVISION SET in the trainer's room wasn't working, so Tom was standing in the doorway, so he could keep an eye on the set closest to him in the clubhouse. Chang had told him he wanted to know when the Red Sox had two outs.

"One out," Tom said. "Bases loaded. Dre' singled to center, then Ray J. dunked out in front of the leftfielder and scored Lightning. Pooty nearly hit one out to right, but the guy reached into the bullpen and caught it. It's still 4–3, them."

Pooty came walking in, saying, "Wind shifts while my damn hero shot's in the air. Meaty-ology can kiss my ass."

From the table, Charlie turned his head. "Oh goody," he said. "Let's have a party right here in the hospital room. I sure hope the nurses don't catch us."

Chang had hopped up behind Charlie on the table, and was working on his back now from a crouch.

"There you go," Pooty said, nodding. "Doggy style."

Chang talked now as he worked, explaining to Charlie that he obviously hadn't been doing enough of his external rotation exercises, and how as a result his levator scapula muscle was clearly in spasm. The kind of stuff Charlie had heard before while Chang was lecturing him, letting him know how smart he was.

"Say what?" Pooty said.

"His elevator is in spasm," Tom said.

Chang looked back at them, then said to Charlie, "It's not just you, then. The whole sport is filled with comedians."

Chang said the levator scapula was creating the tension in the neck, and so Charlie's nerves weren't firing properly into the rotator cuff. So he was working on that, and on his infraspinator muscle and another one called the terses minor, which were really the key muscles for the rotator cuff.

Tom, serious now, said, "Throwing a baseball can mess all that up?"

"Only on every pitch," Chang said.

He stepped back into the clubhouse and said, "Yes!"

"What?" Charlie said.

"Miguel just walled one. He only got a single out of it, since he hit it so hard, but Dre' scored. Tie game."

"Still one out?"

"Yeah . . . no. Snip just lined the first pitch to Kelly. Two now."

Chang said to Charlie, "Roll over on your back real fast." He clapped his hands together. "C'mon, move it, this last is important."

He said he needed to work on Charlie's cervical spine.

"Finally," Charlie said. "My cervical spine."

"You feel better?"

"Actually, I do."

Chang worked on his neck from the front now, then said it was time for Charlie's favorite.

"Aw, man," he said. "Not the thumb in the armpit."

Chang said, "Just a quick hit on your subscapular."

He didn't waste any time, went in deep, started twisting. Charlie screamed.

"Okay," Chang said. "We're done."

Charlie got off the table, saying he'd sweated so much he needed to change the red pullover he was wearing under the brand-new white No. 32 Eddie had given him that morning. But first he moved his arm in a big circle, forward, then backward. The morning checklist now, just in the middle of the game. "Better," he said to Chang. "*Lots* better."

From the middle of the clubhouse, Tom yelled, "Out number three! Red Sox 4, Yankees 4."

Charlie looked at Chang. "You get me those three innings?"

"Why not?"

"You're the best," Charlie said, and Chang said, "Tell me something I don't know."

The shoulder didn't hurt so much when he threw his fastball, which somehow was still clocking out in the low 90s. But breaking balls, Jesus, they made him feel like it was ten years ago, and all that could get him through even some shit mop-up appearance in a blowout game was half a bottle of Advil.

He gave up a walk and a single in the fifth, pitched out of it. The game was still 4–4. The Sox didn't get the ball out of the infield in the bottom of the fifth. Somehow, going on mostly fastballs now, shaking Pooty off on almost anything except changeups, he pitched a one-two-three sixth, including a strikeout of poor Aurelio Arguello, the fifth time he'd struck him out the last two games he'd faced him.

He watched Arguello walk slowly back to the Yankee dugout, staring out at Charlie, like he couldn't believe this kept happening to him. And Charlie thought: I'm the one who should be confused, you dumb bastard.

Because I got nothin'.

In the bottom of the sixth, Pooty Shaw put one in the screen, and took about an hour and a half as he Cadillac-ed his way around the bases, doing all his hip-hop and be-bop now.

It was 5–4, Red Sox.

Charlie sat there smiling, watching Pooty milk the moment, and didn't notice that Hartnett had sat down next to him.

"You told me the truth before today," he said. "My office, I mean."

"I did."

"Do it again. Because I can bring Carlos in right here, have him get me through their lefthand hitters, then turn the fucking season over to Bobby."

Charlie could see Hartnett had his cigarette hand behind him, the smoke coming up from behind him like exhaust fumes.

Ted Hartnett said, "A whole hell of a long time ago, I told you you had three more outs in that arm, and you didn't."

"Got three now, though."

"Your wife says you could always talk me into anything."

Charlie said, "Let me earn the W."

"You already have."

"Three more outs," Charlie said.

He went out in the top of the seventh and struck out Dennard Toussant, Jr., on a splitter he knew he shouldn't throw but did, one that made him scream on his follow-through, it came out of him before he could even try to hold it back. Pooty whipped off his mask right away, took two steps out from home plate. Charlie screamed at him now. "What are *you* looking at?"

"You sounded like you just got your rocks off," Pooty said.

"Maybe I did."

He walked Dwyer. The little fucker wasn't going to do it to him twice in the same day, even if the wind had turned around now and was blowing in. Thank God. While Dwyer trotted down to first, Charlie walked down behind the mound, between the mound and second, and casually dug his own left thumb into his right armpit, like he was just scratching there instead of scratching his balls. Maybe he could make some of it go away by doing that the way Chang had.

Krummenacher hit a slow roller to Snip, who closed fast on the ball and made this neat backhand flip to Estrada, who was covering second. But Krummenacher beat the throw. Two out. Kenyon Desmond at the plate. Desmond was the biggest goddamn catcher Charlie had ever seen, about six-seven and two hundred and sixty pounds, muscle on muscle, a great big goober out of Gooberville, Arkansas. Or maybe it was Gooberville, Alabama.

Charlie threw him a first-pitch fastball, and Desmond hit it high and deep to left.

Charlie was sure it was out.

So was the ballpark and probably all of New England.

Charlie turned and watched. Aware that it was quiet as church at Fenway all of a sudden, even with all the Yankee fans in the joint. Carl Yastrzemski had been hanging around the clubhouse a couple of weeks before, and had told Charlie that it got so quiet at Fenway when Bucky Dent hit his home run in '78 that Yaz still swears he could hear the ball hit the screen, right before his leg buckled underneath him, as if somebody had hit him from behind with a two-by-four.

Charlie watched the flight of the ball and felt the wind on his face, the wind that had held up Pooty's hero-shot to right, more wind than he'd noticed before, and could see it starting to hold the ball up. Unless he was just seeing what he wanted to see.

Dahntay Gentile, their leftfielder, had turned his back to home plate, wanting to be ready if the ball didn't end up in the screen at the top of the Green Monster and he had a carom to play.

Only the ball wasn't going to make it out, Charlie could see that for sure now. Pretty much everybody at Fenway could see except Gentile, who was still facing the leftfield wall, looking small outlined against all that big green.

Out of the corner of his eye, Charlie saw Jerry Janzen then.

He saw White Lightning Janzen flying from centerfield, going at full speed on his great wheels, watching the flight of the ball, watching it start to come down now, Charlie sure it was going to hit Dahntay Gentile on top of his 8¾ Red Sox cap, the biggest head Charlie had ever seen in baseball.

The shit you thought about.

It was still quiet enough at Fenway that Charlie could hear Janzen yelling, but he couldn't tell if he was yelling for Gentile to look up, or just get the hell out of his way. Gentile did turn at the last second, just in time to see Janzen make his dive, cap flying off his head behind him, the huge outfielder's glove on his right hand stretched out as far as it would go.

Then Janzen was sliding across the outfield grass right behind Dahntay Gentile, the glove flat on the grass, Janzen catching a break being lefthanded, which meant he didn't have to try to backhand the ball in front of the Green Monster.

Charlie watched as Jerry Janzen caught the ball, then went sliding into Gentile, who fell in a heap on top of him.

For what Charlie thought was an extremely long, shitty moment, he couldn't see Janzen or his glove, as the ump came running down the line from third base, wanting to see if the ball had stayed in Janzen's glove.

Janzen rolled out from underneath Dahntay Gentile and showed everybody at Fenway Park that it sure had.

The ump stopped, planted, kept pumping his arm as he made the out sign, a few feet from the seats down the leftfield line that were practically part of the action at Fenway.

Now the place got loud.

Somehow during the proceedings, without even knowing he was doing it, Charlie had dropped to his knees behind the pitcher's mound, same as he had that day Piazza had cut his heart out at Shea Stadium.

Pooty helped him up.

"Can of fuckin' corn," Pooty said.

It was still 5–4, Red Sox.

Which happened to be the way the sucker ended.

28

PATRICK KEENAN, calling on Kevin Oslin's cell, said he was having some people over to his place at the Ritz, and did Charlie want to stop by? Charlie told him he was too tired and reminded him there was nothing to celebrate yet, anyway. Charlie said there was still a game to play and they were still the Red Sox, so there could still be a bad moon rising. A line from another one of his old songs. Patrick Keenan said it wasn't a celebration of anything other than Charlie's performance, and if he changed his mind, they'd all be there a while.

Charlie went back to his locker and finished his press, doing some individual television interviews now, and about fifteen minutes with Jeremy Schaap of ESPN, for what he said was going to be their Sunday Night Conversation. Then Charlie went across the clubhouse to the manager's office and closed the door and sat there with Hartnett and

Rob Kendall, all of them sipping on beers. Pooty came in after about fifteen minutes, telling Charlie he was on his way over to Pooty's and he'd catch him there later if an old man like him hadn't lapsed into some kind of coma.

"There's a new show I want you to see," Pooty said.

"I've already seen Sun."

Pooty looked off. "Sun doesn't sing there no more."

"You fired your—what?—primary secondary?"

"Her call. Girl just up and quit. Said she was movin' to L.A. to chase her dream."

"Which is?"

"She says it's to be a hip-hop star," Pooty said. "I think she just wants to marry a rich label. One of them with 'death' in the name."

When he was gone, Hartnett said, "Pooty should've been catching you back in '88, you would probably have been better off. He's smarter than me."

Charlie said, "He doesn't like to let on, but he's smarter than all of us."

There were still kids waiting on Yawkey Way when Charlie came out at nine o'clock. The security guys still out there tried to clear the way for Charlie so he could get to one of the cabs lined up across the street. But he stayed and signed autographs. For free. A long way from that last card show at the Meadowlands Hilton.

Finally he said one more, and a kid in an old Red Sox cap, one Charlie knew they'd used back in 1975, red with a white *B* and a dark-blue bill, handed Charlie his game program and a Sharpie, saying, "My dad thought they were, like, whacked when they signed you, dude."

"They were," Charlie said, signing the cover of the program. "And, kid?"

"Yeah?"

"Don't call me dude."

He got into the cab and gave the driver the address on Commonwealth. But when they got to Kenmore Square, Charlie told him to stop.

The driver said, you just got in. Charlie handed him a ten and told him to keep the change, saying it was a nice night, he'd decided to walk the rest of the way home.

Boston was the biggest college town in America, and now it was Saturday night for them in full swing, everybody out on the streets younger than Charlie. It was as if a block party had started as soon as Bobby Cassidy had popped up Tim Kelly to end the game and might go all night. People recognized Charlie as he went along, calling his name, dodging through traffic sometimes to shake his hand, asking him to sign caps and balls they were still carrying, and t-shirts and even a couple of halter tops, worn by girls who looked as if they had to have just come from high school cheerleading practice. Charlie took his time, took it all in, thinking: This is why nobody gives it up until they have to. Until they're too old or too hurt or both.

And sometimes they kept going after that.

This was the drug, the narcotic you heard retired guys saying they still hadn't been able to shake, the stroke from the people on the street, the old buzz he'd felt as soon as he'd opened his eyes in the morning and one that hadn't left him yet, probably wouldn't leave him until he finally went to sleep tonight. Jordan came back for it. Lemieux came back from cancer. They told Sugar Ray Leonard he might go blind if he kept fighting, and he kept fighting and would fight tomorrow if somebody would give him a license. He was a boxer and he wanted to box. What was the line Rob Kendall had used on him? Singers gotta sing.

Pitchers gotta pitch.

Even when people think they're whacked for even trying.

Chang had worked on him after the game and somehow, even after one hundred and twenty-one pitches, his arm felt better than it had before the game. Better than it had in a week. When he was on the table, Charlie said to Chang, "You never know, they might need me to get them an out tomorrow." Chang stopped what he was doing with his hands and said, "You're kidding, right?" Charlie said, of course, he was kidding. But before he left the clubhouse for good, he poked his head into Hartnett's office one last time and told him Chang had worked one of his miracle cures—again—whatever bullshit talk he tried to talk about Charlie being hurt.

He got to the apartment and told himself he was just going to rest for an hour or so and then head over to Pooty's for one drink. Before he did anything, he tried Grace in San Francisco, got her answering machine instead. He left a message saying he loved the Boston Red Sox, and her, and Jesus, not necessarily in that order.

Then, just for the hell of it, he left a message on Gary Goldberg's voice mail at the Red Sox offices. Goldberg had steered clear of him and everybody else around the team lately, not spending any time in the clubhouse at all once the Sox had gone into the goddamn tailspin that had made everything come down to tomorrow. Maybe Goldberg, the little rodent, was thinking that if he stayed out of sight while the Sox officially blew the last of their lead and the whole season in the process, Patrick Keenan would forget to fire him when it was all over.

"Hey, Gary," Charlie said to the tape. "Charlie Stoddard here, about nine-thirty Saturday night. My new representative, Mr. Jiggy, will be calling you next week about a contract for next year. Right before our first fucking playoff game."

Now he drew the drapes, poured himself a small glass of Dewar's, neat, took one sip, said "Cheers" to himself, then put his head back on the couch and closed his eyes, and the next thing he heard was the phone.

As he fumbled in the dark for the talk button, he checked his watch. The luminous dial said it was five minutes after one, which meant he'd been asleep for nearly three hours.

"Talk to the conquering hero!" a voice shouted, over the shout behind him and the music.

"Who is this?" Charlie said. Thinking it was a crank call. Or some beery Sox fan who'd somehow gotten his number.

"Finally showed them, huh? Showed everydamnbody. Even me!"

Tom.

"Hey, kid," Charlie said, talking loudly himself, giving the kid a chance to hear him over the New Year's Eve celebration obviously going on behind him. "What are you doin'?"

"What am I *doing?* I'm drinking to you. 'Cause tonight it's all you, man. Star of the day." He giggled. "Or night. Or morning. Whatever the fuck it is."

A husky female voice said, "Hi, Charlie," and then Tom must have taken the phone back. "That was Sharon. She wanted to say hi."

"Where are you?"

"Pooty's! Everybody's at Pooty's except you. The guess of honor."

Charlie told him to stay where he was, he'd be right over.

Pooty's was packed, and the people were still coming at one-thirty, the rope line out front snaking all the way around the block. They all cheered when Charlie got out of his cab. He waved. The kid working the door opened it for him with a bow.

Inside, Charlie checked the bar first, but there was no sign of Tom. Same thing in the restaurant area. The tables were all full in there, including the one where Pooty and Booker Impala Washington sat. They were both watching the new singer, a tall black woman with short hair, one who actually reminded Charlie a little bit of Sun, just with more heft to her, more hips for sure, more breasts showing at the top of the V in her red sequined dress, the bottom of the V nearly going all the way to paydirt.

"Okay, where's my kid?" Charlie said, taking the seat to Pooty's right.

"Still upstairs in my office with the news ho' a few minutes ago."

"Jesus, Poots, he sounds drunker than shit. How come you haven't gotten his ass out of here?"

"I'm his teammate," Pooty said. "Not his daddy."

Booker said, "He finally call you, like he kept threatening to?"

Charlie said, yeah, a few minutes ago.

"Kept saying when he was sittin' here he wanted to see you. Buy you a big-assed drink."

"Should I go get him?"

Booker grinned. "Not 'less you're lookin' to get yourself in a weird three."

Pooty said, "The shape he was in, he won't be in there long."

"I'll wait," Charlie said. To Pooty, he said, "Who's the new singer, by the way?"

"Vonette."

Charlie tilted his head. "Vonette your ex-wife? Vonette the alimony ho' from hell?"

Pooty shrugged. "It started with her sayin' she had some nice talk at a couple of those karaoke nights back over there to Jersey. That made her dial up the voice lessons I mentioned? Finally she tells me if I just give her a chance, she might start bein' nicer to me." He waved his hand at the stage. Vonette smiled and waved back. "Here it is, right here on my stage, one night only."

"She looks a little bit like Sun," Charlie said.

Pooty sighed and said, "Don't she, though."

She was singing some kind of medley that included a song Charlie didn't recognize and "Makin' Whoopee." Charlie kept looking over at the bar. After about ten minutes, he saw Tom come walking around from the far side, his arm around Sharon Carr, who looked even drunker than he was.

"Go get 'em, tiger," Booker said. "You need backup, just holla at me."

Tom stopped to get drinks for them at the bar, from his old friend Aimee, as if he couldn't wait for a waiter. Sharon sat down three tables over. Charlie walked over, smiling, and sat down next to Sharon. "I don't mean to be a pushy dad," he said to her, "but this *is* a school night."

Her eyes were red, puffy underneath. She looked her age all of a sudden, Charlie thought. Grace might have been right about her being fifty. "Funny," she said.

"And Sharon? Not for nothin'? Your top is on inside out."

She looked down and saw he was telling the truth. She got up just as Tom arrived with the drinks and told him not to fall in love while she was gone, she had to go fix her face in the ladies' room.

Tom set a wine glass down where Sharon had been sitting. He was holding what looked suspiciously like tequila. He raised it now to Charlie and said, "It's all you, man," and drained the tequila in one shot. He had a slice of lemon in his left hand, stared down at it, then chucked it toward the bar area.

"What're you drinking, pop?" He made a motion like he was shooting Charlie with a pistol. "Pop!" he said.

"I've had enough," Charlie said, trying to keep it casual. "You seem to have been a little over-served, though."

Tom leaned over and wagged a finger close to Charlie's nose. "Don't worry about me," he said. Then he brightened and said, "But when did you?"

"I sort of thought we were handling that."

"'Course we are! 'Course we are. But be honest, Pops. Only because you sort of got backed into it."

"I don't know," Charlie said. "Maybe you're right. But I do know this: We've got a game in about twelve hours."

"Showtime Charlie!" he said, toasting him with his empty glass. "A team guy to the end!"

Tom frowned now, looking toward the bar, then at the other tables. He leaned over and whispered to Charlie, "I seem to have lost my date."

"Not necessarily a bad thing," Charlie said. "Why don't I write a note to her, the way I would to a teacher, and put you in a cab?"

Tom wagged the finger in his face again, even closer than before, making Charlie want to grab it. "No, no, no," the kid said.

"Well, okay then. Maybe I will have a drink."

"How come you didn't want to have one last night?"

"I was pitching today. And I'm old."

"Pitching the next day never stopped you in the old days, what I heard."

"Wasn't old then," Charlie said. "And I had an arm like yours."

Only on loan from the gods, he knew now. The kid didn't know that, at least not yet. If he was lucky, he never had to know.

"Coulda had one drink with your son," Tom said. "But you fuckin' blew me off. Again."

"I don't remember it happening exactly like that," Charlie said, even knowing there was no point in debating him. "I just couldn't last night."

"Always your way," Tom said. "You ever pick up on shit like that?"

He was looking less and less like the happy drunk now. Charlie knew from experience: There was always the moment, drunker you got, when it went the other way. Then you weren't happy. He remembered being in Clarke's one night with Billy Martin after the Baseball Writers Dinner, back when Charlie was with the Mets and Billy was on another tour with the Yankees. There was some fan who'd somehow wormed his way into the conversation, and every couple of minutes the guy would raise his glass and say, "Billy, you're the greatest." They kept drinking to that until one time the guy told Billy he was the greatest, and Billy dropped him with a right hand.

Tom wasn't going to want to fight him. But he was getting less happy by the minute. Maybe this was what Charlie would have gotten if the kid had gotten drunker at Mo Jiggy's. And they'd still be nowhere.

Or maybe they were still nowhere, and Charlie, the great kidder, had just been kidding himself.

"Let me get you out of here," Charlie said. He put his hand gently on the kid's arm, which immediately got yanked away.

"Don't touch me!" he said, then told Charlie he had to go find his date.

"Will you let her take you home?"

"Tired of this place now."

Charlie told him to stay where he was, he'd go find her.

He walked through the tables and then down the stairs to where the men's and ladies' rooms were. When he got to the bottom, a blonde girl in a tight Red Sox t-shirt and even tighter jeans came out of the ladies' room, popping gum and somehow managing to tuck the t-shirt into the jeans.

"Hey!" she said to Charlie. "You're . . . you!"

"So I am!" he said.

"No shit. It's . . . you!"

"I . . . know," he said. "Listen. You know Sharon Carr? From Channel 7? Does she happen to be in there?"

"The babe with the facelift? She's tossing her cookies." The girl smiled at Charlie, trying to look seductive, took his hand. "But she's only using one stall."

Charlie said, "That's very generous of you . . . what's your name?"

"Jade."

"Well, that is extremely generous of you, Jade. But I've got to get Sharon back to the assisted-living home, she's already missed curfew."

Jade left. Charlie knocked on the door, called out Sharon's name. She said in a shaky voice she'd be right out. The door opened a couple of minutes later. Charlie told her he thought Tom was ready to leave, and still wanted to leave with her. He noticed she was now the color of an old dollar bill.

"Grownups," she said, "should not drink tequila."

"I don't know," Charlie said, "it always made me whoop."

She went up the stairs ahead of him. When she was halfway up, she saw the same thing Charlie did, which was Tom MacKenzie making out like crazy with Aimee the actress/bartender.

It seemed to give Sharon Carr, even in her weakened state, a second wind.

She went up the stairs two at a time, as if she'd suddenly found her finishing kick at Pooty's.

Tom and Aimee didn't notice Sharon at first, mostly because they were in the midst of giving each other a full body massage, oblivious to everything except each other, including the two women who had just stumbled past them, nearly knocking Sharon over as they made their way past her on the stairs.

As they passed Charlie next, he heard them say they were going to use the pay phone at the bottom of the stairs and find out where that lying witch Marcia was.

Sharon steadied herself and kept going. When she got to the top, where Aimee had mashed Tom into the doorframe, she put down her shoulder and pushed her way in between them, as if she were trying to break a flying wedge on a kickoff return.

Charlie stopped halfway up, wanting to see how his son was going to get out of this, curious to see if the kid was any better at busting out of this kind of Turkish prison than he had been.

He thought about Alqueen and Sun's catfight and also wondered if there was something in the water at Pooty's that made women start acting as if they had all the testosterone.

Aimee fell back a little after Sharon's initial charge, and then saw who it was that had clipped her.

"Oh, look," she said. "It's the woman you said reminded you of your mom."

"Back off, drink girl," Sharon said. "He's with me."

Aimee gave her hair a little toss and said, "You sure?"

Charlie moved up a couple of more steps, so he didn't miss anything.

Tom was still rocking slowly from side to side, but grinned now and showed he was another member of the family who didn't know when to keep his mouth shut. "Maybe the three of us could work this out?" he said. "Back at my place?"

Somehow both women, at almost the same time, said, "Dream on."

Aimee moved over so she was next to Tom, and tried to put her arm around him. Sharon grabbed it and pulled it off. Aimee looked down at herself, shocked, and then gave Sharon Carr a good shove.

Sharon swung her expensive purse—Charlie found himself thinking Grace could tell him what brand—and clipped Aimee on the side of her head.

For some reason, Aimee noticed Charlie then. "The old bag's out of her weight class," she said. "*Way* out."

Sharon said, "You're calling me fat."

"Mooooo," Aimee said.

Whatever effects Sharon had been feeling from her tequila flu seemed long gone. Or maybe she was feeling the tequila more than ever. Because she threw herself into Aimee now, trying to pull her hair, both women in this fierce, clumsy wrestling match.

Tom watched it for a couple of minutes, laughing intermittently, before deciding he ought to break it up.

Charlie watched as he tried to insert himself in between them, but as he did, he stepped on Sharon Carr's ankle, which made her yelp in pain. Then Charlie saw it all happen at once, Aimee trying to slap her as Sharon reached down for her injured ankle, Aimee spinning herself nearly out of the picture when she missed, Tom falling over the hunched-over Sharon, turning around himself, back to Charlie, his balance completely gone.

He reached behind with his right hand, arm flailing in the air, trying to find the bannister.

Money hand, money arm.

All he found was air, though, and now Tom MacKenzie started to go over backward. Both Aimee and Sharon reached for for him. Too late. Charlie heard one of them scream, not able to tell which one, not really caring, because he was more focused on diving for his son the way Jerry Janzen had for Kenyon Desmond's fly ball at Fenway.

He dove up the stairs with his arms stretched out so that when Tom fell into him, Charlie was able to cradle his right shoulder, taking the full force of him, even as the two of them went crashing into the wall.

Then Charlie held on for dear life, Tom still on top, as the two of them came bumping and sliding down the rest of the stairs until they landed underneath the pay phone in a heap.

Pitcher as catcher.

At least this time, Charlie thought, there was a catcher.

When he could breathe again, he said to Tom, "You all right? Your arm, I mean?"

Tom reached up with his left hand, gave his shoulder a good squeeze, then moved his hand slowly down the arm. "Arm's fine," he said. "My ass is another story." He nodded at Charlie. "How about you? You seemed to take most of it."

"I'm fine. You're grounded. But I'm fine."

Charlie got up into a sitting position. They both leaned against the cigarette machine next to the phone, both of them still breathing hard, oblivious to the crowd staring at them from up above.

Finally, Tom said, "Thanks, dad."

"You're welcome," Charlie said. "But you're still grounded."

He helped his son to his feet, told him to forget his two mud wrestlers, he was taking him home. On the way, he said, he had a story to tell about arms.

From the top of the stairs, he heard Pooty talking in a loud voice.

"Oh, look, Vonette," he said. "It's the cute tumble boys from Gymboree."

ASHE GRISSOM, who looked as tired as Charlie felt from the start, lasted the first three innings, giving up just two runs. But Hartnett had seen enough of the way he was laboring with every pitch. He brought in Yippy Cantreras after that, Yippy having informed him before the game that he could pitch, that Chang had worked on his ankle and, madre dios, it was the same kind of miracle that'd happened in his life when the little boat bring him to America. Yippy survived the fourth, barely, after loading the bases, and Carlos Cinquanta managed a one-two-three fifth. The Red Sox tied it then when Ray J. Guerrero hit his forty-ninth home run with Janzen on first, Ray J.'s ball actually deep enough and high enough to dead center that it clipped the flagpole out there.

When Ray J. got to the dugout, Charlie said, "Don't tell me. You just wanna have a good year."

would pitch himself out and it would still be tied and Hartnett would have to finish the game with one of his middle relievers instead of his star closer. Or that Cassidy wouldn't have his fastball and Hartnett would have to bring in one of his middle relievers to pitch out of a jam in the ninth.

It happened that way, because in the 162nd game of the season, Bobby Cassidy didn't have his fastball, or anything else.

The Yankees started the ninth at the top of the order, and five batters later they had two runs in off Cassidy and two guys on for Chuck Krummenacher. Krummenacher was a lefthanded hitter. Hartnett didn't hesitate. He was on the field before anybody knew it, signaling to the bullpen with his left hand, which meant he wanted Michael Prosser, the lefthanded kid the Sox had brought up from Pawtucket at the end of July.

Charlie knew enough about Red Sox history by now to know that a lefthanded kid named Jim Burton had given up the winning run to Cincinnati in Game 7 of the '75 World Series.

Not this time at Fenway.

Michael Prosser struck out Krummenacher.

Two outs.

Hartnett came out of the dugout again. Took the ball from Prosser and signalled for a righthander, Dicky McManus, the veteran they'd picked up off waivers after Lew Gentry went down. McManus was two years younger than Charlie. Everyone knew this was his tenth and last stop in the big leagues, he'd moved around almost as much as Hick Landon had.

McManus went to 3–2 on Jimmy Dwyer, and then Dwyer went the other way with a line drive that seemed a sure thing for rightfield when Julio Paulino dove to his right and backhanded it for the third out.

Yankees, 6–4, going to the bottom of the ninth.

Hartnett came down to the water cooler, his cigarette on his hip.

"Even if we tie this thing up, we seem to be running out of pitchers here," Charlie said.

Hartnett stared right through him. "Ya think?" he said.

"Or," Pooty Shaw said, "we could win the motherfucker right here."

The Red Sox nearly did. With two outs, Julio doubled off the Yankees closer, Kris LeFebvre, and Pooty singled him home. Dahntay Gentile singled to right, Pooty didn't stop running until he got to third. So it was first and third, two outs, and Fenway was insanely loud. The Yankees stayed with LeFebvre. The Sox needed one to tie, two to win. Dre' Hadley, back in there at DH, blooped a single to right that landed behind Krummenacher's dive and kept rolling into short right. Pooty walked home with the run that tied it, and now here came Dahntay Gentile, running all the way with two outs, Wally Garner jumping up and down in the third base coach's box and waving like a sonofabitch.

Gentile stumbled making too wide a turn at third.

He didn't go down, but he had to put a hand out to keep that from happening, which broke his stride just enough. Jahidi Gleason made a perfect throw to the plate and Kenyon Desmond put the tag on Gentile, and it was 6–6 going to extra innings.

It stayed that way through the tenth. And eleventh. The Red Sox threatened in the bottom of the tenth, the Yankees did the same in the top of the eleventh. Both managers kept going through pitchers the way they would beer nuts watching a game at home on the couch.

Tim Kelly singled to start the Yankees' twelfth. Arguello singled him to second. Danny Reid, a righthander, was pitching now for the Sox. All they had behind him in the bullpen was Cal Calabrese. He was the thirty-five-year-old lefthander who'd been a star for the Sox when he was a kid, setting some kind of record for elbow operations after that, the kind where they transplanted stuff from everywhere except your butt. Now he was being allowed to finish up with the Sox in mop-up roles.

Charlie looked down the dugout and saw Hartnett pick up the bullpen phone, wondering if he'd called out to find if Calabrese was ready, or if he was just dialing 911.

Hartnett nodded. He turned his head as he did, staring right at Charlie, then hung up the phone behind him.

Charlie got up and walked down there.

"S'up," he said. Sounding like Tom.

"Guess who wandered down to the bullpen a few minutes ago? Your kid."

"And?"

"I told him to warm the fuck up."

"You can't do that," Charlie said. "You of all people should know that. You can't mess with an arm like that."

He didn't say "again."

Hartnett said, "He says I can."

"You talked to him?"

Hartnett waved at Pooty and told him to go out to the mound. "He told me he could get me three outs."

"He threw a hundred fucking pitches Friday night," Charlie said.

"Hundred and one, to be exact."

"Whatever," Charlie said. "Don't do this."

"Oh, I'm gonna do it," Hartnett said. "In about one minute."

"He says he can pitch," Charlie said.

"Says he's good to go," Hartnett said. "And you want to know what else he said? He said you were the reason. Maybe you can explain that to me later."

Pooty stayed out at the mound until the home-plate umpire shooed him. Then Hartnett walked up the steps again, for what seemed like the tenth time in the hour. He signaled with his right hand, and not long after that, the roar you heard at Fenway was for Tom MacKenzie, walking in from the bullpen.

It wasn't Tom's regular guy, Dre' Hadley, catching him now. It was Pooty. Charlie could see Pooty doing all the talking on the mound. Tom listened, rubbing up a new ball, looking all around Fenway, everybody in the place on their feet, cheering and stomping and waving banners, believing after all the nightmare things that had ever happened to them in this place that this kid could get them out of it.

The kid nodded, and smiled. Piece of cake.

He was trying to pitch the inning in relief that Hershiser had pitched for the Dodgers back in '88, in Game 4, after Charlie blew out his arm in the eleventh. This was Randy Johnson coming in against the Yankees in Game 7 of the World Series in 2001, even though Johnson had started Game 6 the night before.

Tom slapped Pooty on the ass and then looked over into the dugout, maybe at Charlie, maybe not, and Charlie read his kid's lips.

Fucking epic.

Charlie watched him strike out Toussant, Jr., on three fastballs. Good morning, good afternoon, goodnight. But then he walked Rascual Ortega, the centerfielder, loading the bases, still one out. Another walk got the go-ahead run home. Or a fly ball to anywhere, probably, except left, where Dahntay Gentile seemed to be playing deep shortstop now.

Kenyon Desmond had moved up in the batting order. Tom went to 2–2 on him and threw a fastball to him, about shoulder high, that Desmond didn't come close to. The crowd at Fenway exploded for that, and then did the same about fifteen seconds later when they saw the place across the facing of the upper deck where they put the count from the radar gun.

Which said the fastball Tom MacKenzie had just thrown came in there at exactly 100 mph.

Everybody was up now. Charlie and everybody else in the dugout could feel them pounding on top of the dugout roof; as old as everything was at Fenway, he was afraid they might bust it. He got off the bench and went to the top step, all the way at the end, and sat there.

Not just watching now.

Doing what the kid had always asked.

Really watching.

Bases still loaded. Two outs now. Unless there was some kind of Buckner mistake in the field, Jimmy Dwyer had to get a hit off Tom MacKenzie to get a run off him. Or work him for a walk.

Fat chance, Charlie thought.

Tom went to 0–2 on Dwyer, and the little shit who'd turned into a slugger lately must have thought he'd waste one here rather than come right after him. Except the little shit was wrong. Because the kid threw one 98 on the outside corner that Ted Williams himself couldn't have hit in his prime. Dwyer took it, and Tom was running off the mound, into this wall of noise as big as the Green Monster, before the home plate ump had his arm in the air.

Dahntay Gentile hit one over the Green Monster about five minutes later.

Red Sox 7, Yankees 6.

The game had started at one-thirty in the afternoon and hadn't ended until the lights were on at Fenway and it was nearly seven o'clock. Charlie would hear later there were still fans in the place, the ones who wouldn't leave—or couldn't let go of the game—until after nine.

Patrick Keenan was down in the clubhouse when the Sox finally came in after a couple of victory laps around the field, led by Tom MacKenzie. Keenan said he only showed up for special occasions like Opening Day or the last day of the season. Or, he said, holding a champagne bottle in triumph over his head, when his Red Sox beat the New York Yankees in a game they would be talking about long after his poor, scarred heart had finally given out on him.

Booker Impala Washington said to Charlie, "He gonna outlive us all, you know that, right?"

"I figure."

"Your boy's gonna take us all the way now. It's in the air, and you can't stop nothin' that's in the air like this. Even in Boston, Mass. Gonna put us on his back the way Hershiser did the Dodgers that time."

"I figure," Charlie said again, and smiled. "And he's not mine, by the way."

"You sure?"

"He's better than I was," Charlie said.

Booker collected Keenan then, saying they had about ten parties stacked up like planes over Logan Airport. When he was gone from the stool in front of Jerry Janzen's locker, Chang sat down in it, carrying one of those tall paper cups Pooty used for his choca-chinos. Charlie raised his head up a little, as if to see inside. "What you got there?"

"A bit of what Mr. Keenan Himself calls the bubbly."

"You slut," Charlie said.

"It takes one to know one," he said, and drank some champagne. "How's your arm? I heard you took a little tumble last night."

"Who ratted me out?"

"Your kid."

"I thought his mother raised him better than that." He took Chang's cup, took a sip of champagne. "When did he tell you?"

Chang said, "When I had him up on the table. Now he says he's gonna stay on that table for the next ten years."

Charlie put out his right hand. Chang put the cup down and shook it. "Thank you," Charlie said. "For everything."

"Ten o'clock tomorrow. I'm gonna be looking for something."

"What?"

"Three more weeks."

Tom was back on the field doing interviews. Charlie walked across the clubhouse, emptying out fast now, and knocked on the door to the manager's office. The door was open. Hartnett was at his desk, the little reading glasses he'd been wearing that day at Yankee Stadium at the end of his nose, scouting reports for what Charlie knew were the Oakland A's—who the Red Sox would play in the first round of the playoffs—scattered in front of him, Marlboro going in his ashtray, cup of coffee, still steaming, near his right hand.

"You doing anything when you're done?" Charlie said.

Hartnett looked up. "I'm not gonna be done for a while."

"Well," Charlie said, "I just thanked Chang. And I didn't want to leave without thanking you."

Hartnett said, "If we don't score when we did, you were pitching next, I was only giving the kid one inning."

Charlie grinned. "I coulda got you three."

"I'm kind of glad you didn't have to."

"Not as much as I am."

There was one more silence between them, and then Hartnett said, "Anyway, I got work to do."

Charlie stood there in the doorway.

"What?" Hartnett said.

"Nothing."

"You heading home?"

"Yeah?"

Gabby Hartnett didn't look up. "Got girls there?"

"Not tonight."

Charlie left him sitting there, went back across the room to his locker, realizing he hadn't showered yet. Pooty had left him a note on the rocking chair, saying Charlie could meet him at Pooty's, or he'd call the apartment in about an hour.

He went in and took a long shower, came back, got dressed into his white shirt, jeans, blazer. He'd put his wallet on the top shelf of his locker along with his watch. When he reached up for them, he saw the baseball, with this note underneath.

Here's the game ball I promised you one time.
T

The phone rang as soon as he walked into the apartment.

Pooty, calling from Pooty's.

"Get your ass over here, even if you don't want to stay long," he said. "We got half the team here, 'ceptin' your boy, who just left. Said he was gonna go home, lock the door, get hisself some rest."

"He drinking?"

"Uh uh. Said he's with that Chang now, got a whole new approach on his all-around situation. I just give him some takeout and send him on his way."

"Takeout?"

"Aimee," Pooty said.

Charlie said, "I'm thinking about packing it in myself, Poots. I'm whipped."

"One drink," Pooty said, his voice not much more than a whisper now. "I'm up in my office. Thought I might have myself a private party. But I got one of them primary situations going here . . . You got to help me out, baby. Just this last time. Come in that side door I showed you. In the alley? Come up the stairs."

"I'm gonna level with you," Charlie said. "The thrill of watching women fight with each other is sort of gone for me."

"Hurry," Pooty said, and hung up.

Charlie had only been up in Pooty's office one time, when they wanted to get away from the riffraff and watch the end of a Yankees game in peace. You came in from behind, walked down an alley, there was a door you'd miss if you weren't looking for it, a long flight of stairs.

Charlie went up the stairs now, knocked gently on the door.

"Hey, man," he said. "It's me. Charlie."

"Come on in."

Pooty, all spiffed up, was behind his desk wearing a dark gray suit, dark gray shirt, dark gray tie. He called it his "mono" look. For that monochromatic thang, he said. The ice bucket with the champagne was next to the desk.

On the other side of the desk sat Grace MacKenzie, in a pale blue summer dress.

"You know me," she said. "I never miss a Charlie Stoddard start. Or a party."

Charlie smiled. "I asked around, thinking you might have snuck into town without telling me. But Booker said he hadn't seen you in the suite all weekend."

Grace said, "I am here to tell you that the wives' section has as much big hair as ever." She nodded at Pooty. "My friend here handled the tickets. I got to know both Alqueen and Vonette a lot better, at least before Vonette had to get back to the children. Once I explained how you handled bad boys, I think they found some common ground."

"Maybe your next book could be about that."

To Pooty, he said, "You got me here under false pretenses."

"No, sir," he said. "Told you I had a primary situation goin'. It just happened to be with your primary."

He stood up, looked at his watch. "Oh my, looky here," he said. "I don't want to miss Marissa's second set."

"Marissa?" Charlie said.

"Marissa's the new girl," Pooty said, avoiding eye contact.

He'd left an empty champagne flute for Charlie on the desk. Charlie took the bottle out, poured some for himself, sat on the edge of the desk, and clicked his glass off Grace's.

"Tom just left," she said. "And he sure did have a lot to tell me about before he did."

"Boys will be boys," Charlie said.

"Maybe not forever," she said. "He told me about the game ball."

"I just stayed 'til the end of the game."

"Good boy."

He took another sip of champagne.

"You know that one night in my life I told you I always wanted back, Gracie? I finally got it back."

"The one when you shouldn't have pitched?"

"Actually," he said, "the one right before it."

"I don't understand."

Charlie said, "I'll explain it to you sometime."

She held out her glass, and Charlie poured more champagne for her. He hadn't noticed the music before. He smiled and listened to Springsteen sing "Human Touch."

"You were here the whole time," Charlie said, shaking his head.

"Didn't we already go over that?"

Charlie put his glass down, leaned over, and kissed her. She let him, much more kiss from her than he'd gotten at the Sherry-Netherland that night, more than he had gotten in a long time.

After what felt like about twenty minutes, he pulled back, just a little, and said, "How long you plan on hanging around?"

She said, "At least until the Red Sox win another World Series."

"Could take three weeks," he said. "Or it could take another ninety years."

"Either way," Grace said. "I can wait."